Praise for

The Paris Lawyer

Winner of the Grand Prix Sang d'Encre

"Sylvie Granotier's *The Paris Lawyer* is a beautifully written and elegantly structured novel of a woman's attempt to solve the central mystery of her life, along with several other mysteries along the way. It captures the reader from the first page, and never lets go."
—*Thomas H. Cook, winner of the Martin Beck Award, Barry Award for Best Novel, Edgar Award for Best Novel*

"Everything in this book—the plot, the atmosphere, the characters, and the style—is perfectly mastered from beginning to end."
—*L'Echo*

"Full of surprises and twists that will keep you reading late into the night."
—*Cosmopolitan*

"The author has a distinctive style and an unsurpassed talent for delving deep into her characters' minds. It is a disturbing read."
—*Madame Figaro*

"Reading this is like having a fever. The author takes the reader from dark humor to cold anxiety at a diabolic pace."
—*Notre temps*

"Sylvie Granotier interweaves the past and present with a sure hand, and her characters have a psychological depth that is rare in crime fiction today. This is a complex tale, skillfully told, that will keep you in suspense to the very end."
—*Patricia MacDonald, Edgar-award nominee*

"*The Paris Lawyer* is a powerful, well-written thriller, but also a meditation on the nature of love and marriage, and whether we can ever escape the past and reinvent ourselves."
—*Crime Fiction Lover*

More praise for

The Paris Lawyer

"A solid and interesting read, and I would certainly consider reading more by this author."
—*Rachel Cotterill Book Reviews*

"*The Paris Lawyer* is a credible double mystery told in a way that brings both story threads together. It's got a distinctive French setting, a strong protagonist, some well-developed and likeable other characters and a haunting link of past to present."
—*Confessions of a Mystery Novelist*

"*The Paris Lawyer* has a particular French sensibility, combined with a clever take on lawyer-based crime fiction… a slightly meandering, low key sort of a story builds into something that becomes extremely involving. It's almost sneaky how the combination of an isolated location, a man with a secret and a central character with a confronting past, all combine as Monsigny's investigation into her own background and the defense of the murder accused, twist and turn together. The story deftly balances the idea of a lawyer, trial-based book; with many of the aspects of a psychological thriller."
—*AustCrime*

"Granotier's strength is portraying the minds of her main characters."
—*Ms. Wordopolis*

"Well developed characters, good dialogue, and two solid mysteries kept me turning the pages. …Ms. Granotier does an excellent job developing her characters; it was easy to identify with the Catherine and her youthful ambitions."
—*Queen of All She Reads*

"The writing is subtle, racy, controlled. It is written with great art!"
—*RTL.be*

The Paris Lawyer

Sylvie Granotier

Translated from French by Anne Trager

LE FRENCH BOOK ▌

M

First published in France as *La Rigole du Diable* by Albin Michel
©Albin Michel, January 2011

English translation ©2012 Anne Trager
First published in English
by Le French Book, Inc., New York
www.lefrenchbook.com

Translated by Anne Trager
Copyediting by Amy Richards
Cover designed by Ink Slinger Designs
eBook designed by Le French Book

ISBNs
Trade paperback: 978-1-939474-01-8
Hardcover: 978-1-939474-68-1
Kindle: 978-0-985320-64-5
Epub: 978-0-985320-61-4

1

One early afternoon, in all other ways like any other afternoon, her mother takes her out in her stroller, soothing her with a lilting mother's voice. She tells her about the wind that sings and then softens in the branches and the swallows that skillfully skim the pond for a few refreshing drops of water before flying into the clouds in perfect circles.

The little girl does not understand every word, but she follows her mother's fingers as they imitate playful birds gliding down to her face.

Then her mother and she will go home for snack followed by a nap.

It is a reassuring life, where nothing unexpected happens.

They stop at the edge of the woods, in the shade of the trees. The little girl toys with the light, squinting to change the intensity of the rays.

Before the screaming starts, before her mother's distant terror horrifies her in turn, before the panicked shrill pierces her ears, and the little girl takes refuge in sleep to bury an anxiety far too great for her to bear, her mother gives her a generous and warm hug, leaving her with the sight of the entire sky, and says, "I'll be right back." A final broken promise. Sitting as she is, the child cannot see the body, or what is left of it, sprawled on the ground, beaten to a pulp. Yet that moment of abandonment remains forever engraved in her adult memory.

The sky is calm and clear above the Seine River in Paris, where traffic is nervous and gray along the banks. Catherine Monsigny cannot figure out what links this fleeting moment with that fixed point in her past, that fuzzy, probably reconstructed memory that usually is tactful enough to leave her alone. She has even tried to convince herself that it has stopped broadcasting from that faraway land of her childhood.

She crosses the Pont Neuf, parking her scooter at the Place Dauphine. She mindlessly yanks off her helmet, banging her ears in the process, then stows it in her top box. Catherine shakes her head to free her hair, and grabs her briefcase and large bag.

She walks quickly toward the courthouse, cursing her short legs. She slips into her court robe as she climbs the steps, and by habit she automatically replaces those old uninvited images with a quick summary of the case she is about to defend.

Her client—what's his name again? Ah yes, Cedric Devers—is accused of assault and battery. He admits using force and justifies it by pointing out the harassment that preceded it. According to him, he met a woman—Monique Lemaire, fifty-six years old—in a bar, took her back to his place for a short session between consenting adults. Ciao, no see you next time, because there won't be one.

Monique did not see things the same way, harassed him by phone, and one night too many, she took to ringing her seducer's doorbell until he reacted. He opened the door. That was a fatal error. Stubborn with drink, she wouldn't take no for an answer and tried to force her way in. He had to stop the noise and ended up pushing her. She fell, which resulted in a few bruises and three days' disability leave.

Catherine has not yet met her client. They have spoken on the phone. She glances around to find him. He's not anywhere in sight. She pokes her head into the courtroom to check the proceedings.

The pending case is not yet over.

Just as well. Her client will have the time he needs to arrive.

Too bad for him. She does not like waiting.

She paces.

"Maître Monsigny?"

She senses fingers lightly brushing her shoulder, spins around, and looks into the deepest gray—or perhaps green—eyes she has ever seen. She feels as though she's falling into them. She grasps for something to catch her balance, and her professional composure kicks in, as it does every time. She throws him a sharp look and spits out, "Cedric Devers? You're late."

The thirtyish teenager, classy despite the jeans and sweatshirt he has tossed on, stares right into her eyes, unbothered, like a child, without blinking.

Would he never stop looking at her?

The lawyer turns away and walks toward the courtroom, because it is high time to do so and because she wants to escape his embarrassing look.

She sharpens the professional tone in her voice now that Cedric Devers has thrown her off. What an uncharacteristic sensation.

"I asked you to wear a suit. You are performing here. The first thing the judge will see is your attitude and your clothing, and the judge's impression counts."

"So you're a woman?" He bites his lip to crush a smug ladies' man smile. Too late. The very tone of his question says he's taking up the challenge. Women are his preferred prey.

Male crudeness can become a woman's weapon. Even as she says to herself that he really does have beautiful eyes, Catherine's reflex is to lash out. "Studs don't turn me on. All I'm interested in is supporting women's causes. Yep, I'm a feminist bitch. Come on."

"We've got a little time, don't we?"

"There's no way to know, and arriving late always plays against a defendant. That's not so hard to understand."

"There was a huge line to get in."

"You should have read your summons."

"Reassure me. You're my lawyer, right? I mean, you are here to defend me?"

"That's right. And I won't wear kid gloves. Nobody will. You might as well get used to that."

For an instant, a crack appears in Cedric Devers's display of self-assurance. He's just another poser. He opens his arms and in an uncertain voice says, "Should I, uh, explain?"

She taps the case file under her arm, letting him know that it is all in there and that she does not need any additional explanations.

He stops at the door. "Is Monsigny your maiden name?"

"It's my name. Period." She tightens her lips as she hisses her counter-attack. She has no intention of doing him the favor of explaining that she is single and fossilizing. He would take that as an invitation.

He gets the message, aware that he has just skillfully cut off the branch he had yet to sit on: she thinks he's an idiot.

The truth is, Catherine is working. She has gotten a quick portrait of Cedric Devers: forty years old despite looking younger, a graphic artist who manages his own agency, a good income, clean cut. Now she has to discover the other Cedric, the victim, because appearances have a huge impact, despite the professional neutrality members of the legal system display.

"Once we are in the courtroom, point out Mrs. Lemaire."

He nods and says nothing.

She will defend him as best she can. That is her job.

They are still in the entryway when she stops him with her hand and gives him an approving look.

"Stay in this state of mind: a little worried, a little fragile, not so sure of yourself. It will help you more than posing as a small-time ladies' man."

She does not wait for an answer and enters the courtroom.

The ordinary trial clientele—the scared, the disconcerted, the regulars—are on the public benches. On the defense benches, people in black robes, some with ermine trim and some without, are preparing to represent their clients. Some indifferent colleagues have the bored look of professionals who have more important things to do elsewhere. Others are reading the paper or whispering among themselves.

Devers sits down at the end of a row and with his chin points out a stocky woman.

Monique Lemaire works in a bar, a job that doesn't play in her favor, implying that she has certain life experience. She won't be able to act like an innocent maiden. Yet she is smart enough to be careful about her looks. No jewelry, no makeup, dark pants, an impeccable white shirt buttoned up high under a modest jacket. Still, she's built like an old kettle. Catherine can't help wondering what he saw in her.

Lemaire turns to her attorney, and Catherine notices that the shirt, as plain as it is, looks like it is going to burst from the pressure of her heavy, plump breasts.

Okay, the lady exudes sex. Some women are just like that. Their bodies speak for them. In this case, it speaks for the defense.

Catherine greets the colleague she is facing. He's nicknamed Tsetse because he has a genius for annoying never-ending sentences.

He is the good news of the day.

The bad news lies in the prosecutor-judge duo, a twosome fed up with seeing couples who stay together only because they are poor and who hit each other because they don't have enough space. So separate! But where would they go?

This scenario is being played out once again in the case before Catherine's. The couple live together; they are repeat offenders and

have three kids and problems with alcohol. The two of them together earn only fifteen hundred euros a month, which is not enough to
pay two rents.

For a change, Cedric Devers offers the court someone who is
well off, which could lean the balance to the wrong side.

Catherine, forgetting that she herself was late, throws a vengeful
look at her client before pushing him to the front of the court. They
had been five minutes away from missing the hearing.

As was foreseeable, an attentive court questions the plaintiff and
goes easy on her.

Mrs. Lemaire is upset. Her story is reasonably confused. She is
determined to accuse her passing fling and vehemently emphasizes
that he went to bed with her on the first date, which was also the last,
something she neglects to mention. Everything indicates that she
was perfectly consenting. She had thought he was nice. He threw
her out early in the morning with the excuse that he had to go to
work, even though she needed to sleep because she worked at night.
He just as well could have called her a thief while he was at it.

Devers proves to be a quick learner. He listens attentively and
respectfully and answers questions directly, without any flourishes.
Humbly.

The barmaid plays up the emotions, and her act rings more of
loneliness and being ready to grab onto the first ship that passes. He
states the facts and says with dignity that he too was distraught that
night. He is sorry about how this misunderstanding, for which he is
most certainly responsible, has turned out. One lonely night he felt
for a woman in distress. She hoped for more than he could give. He
is annoyed with himself for this mistake, for which he is clearly the
only person responsible.

The barmaid's lawyer gesticulates. He gets excited, cannot
imagine an excuse for the unjustifiable behavior of a man guilty of
taking advantage of the naïve trust of a worthy woman. He em-
bellishes his clichés. His words flow one after the other without any
meaningful conclusion.

The prosecutor stares at the woodwork, looking like she's men-
tally writing down her shopping list. The presiding judge wearily
fiddles with the case file.

For Catherine, it is time to wake everyone up.

She stands, and from the top of her five-foot-five and a quar-
ter-inch frame, she raises a soft yet clear voice, using short, sharp
sentences to describe a well-established man with no history of

violence, as demonstrated by his attempt to reason with an out-of-control woman who was banging on his door in the middle of the night. Out of compassion and fearing a public scandal, he had opened that door. There was no actual act of violence, but rather a clumsy movement resulting from his exasperation with the stubbornness of a woman who was under the influence of alcohol, an idiotic gesture that was understandable and whose consequences he regrets, as he himself had said.

She asks that he be acquitted and sits down, whispering to him that they would have the decision at the end of the session.

When the judge leaves with her mountain of case files under her arm, they also leave, and Catherine abandons her client to call her office.

She goes out to the courtyard for a smoke, where she watches Devers's agitation from the corner of her eye. He isn't acting like a smartass anymore. He even comes and asks her what she thinks, like a worried child whose mischief has proven worse than expected. He has a certain charm when he stops playing the tough guy, and Catherine experiences some pleasure in stripping him of the vestiges of his protective armor.

She doesn't really know. With a court like that anything is possible, and it is impossible to tell what side it will come down on.

He congratulates her on her closing argument. He notes that she was brief, showing regard for the number of cases that followed; that could have appeased the court. No, he's not dumb.

From time to time, the look in his eyes changes. He no longer appears to be grasping the information that the person in front of him is sending him silently, absorbed as he is in a contemplation that glazes over his eyes and makes them bigger.

It is disconcerting.

She says, "It's true that your girlfriend did not start out with a good deal. Life is unfair."

Cedric Devers closes his eyes. "Can you say that again?"

"Life is unfair. It's a platitude."

She frowns slightly. He's strange.

After being so clearly worried, he doesn't pay particular attention to the verdict.

She expected a week of public service. He is acquitted.

She holds out her hand to her client. She is expected elsewhere. She is in a hurry; she lets him know.

He opens his mouth to speak, changes his mind, and closes it again, which is just as well, as she has no intention of raising a glass to their victory with him.

She puts her robe back in her bag, intending to drop it off at the dry cleaner. His eyes take in the thin figure that her tight skirt and fitted jacket highlight. He can't resist devouring her in his mind's eye, where he lifts her blond hair into a chignon, revealing her graceful neck. He exaggerates her thin waist with a red leather belt, imagines a flowered dress swirling around her thighs. When she has disappeared, he still sees her going up a step, her dress opening, showing her frail legs. The summer-colored fabric falls to the floor, and her breasts appear, small and round.

He turns around. He should get to work.

Catherine finds her scooter, checks the time and decides she can make a detour to the Goutte d'Or.

2

The building is run-down. Poverty and time have left deep scars in its façade. The structure looks like it will collapse at any minute, and like the grassroots association it houses, it remains standing more out of steadfastness than soundness.

Catherine climbs the shaky staircase, trying to ignore the leprous walls, the rancid odors, and the broken glass that mark the way to a door that announces "Rights for All."

She has already tried to get the distressed building's owner to renovate, but he is skilled at making regulations work in his favor. Her efforts have been in vain. The deterioration continues, as unyielding as the despair of the undocumented immigrants the lawyer volunteers her time to defend.

She has not yet said her last word. In either area.

The door to the two-room apartment that serves as an office stays shut only when it is locked, so it is open practically all of the time, a powerful symbol for the association's chairman, Daniel, who persists in seeing half-full glasses, even when they are empty.

Inside, all the furniture has come from the neighborhood streets, where each step made in economic advancement rejects the preceding one. It is the IKEA syndrome: a three-seat sofa comes in, and a two-seater goes out; an ergonomic office chair replaces the basic model. Daniel has had to stop the association's volunteers in their enthusiastic retrieval of treasures brought to the office at all hours.

A toilet flushes.

It has been fixed, Catherine notes with satisfaction.

Daniel exits the bathroom, buttoning up. He's wearing his bad-day look, his eyebrows knotted up, like his hair, and his eyes outlined with dark circles, like his nails.

"If you have bad news, just forget about telling me, please. Souad got pulled in after jumping a subway turnstile at La Chapelle, where it's crawling with ticket inspectors. Mimi is back on the streets, and Ali is in solitary again. He thinks he's clever, but in all likelihood, he'll be deported. For three grams of hash. But how are *you*?"

"I'll let you know in two hours, after I see my boss."

"And after, I'll invite you to dinner to celebrate."

"It's not a good day for that."

"Yesterday wasn't good, and tomorrow won't be any better, right? Let me guess. You came to pick up Myriam's file."

She smiles. Yes. He turns, looking sullen, and runs his fingers through his hair without any notable effect. It's still the same tousled, uncontrollable mop. He reaches for the drawer, opens it, and removes a folder. He holds it out to Catherine and goes to his computer to sulk.

He is hypersensitive, as weak people tend to be, and his activism protects him from life, two bad points in Catherine's mind.

For her, the association is a stepping-stone, and her volunteer work a learning process. She is sure that she is ten times more useful and efficient than Daniel, who is burdened by his kindness. And today, she has won the jackpot. That is, if her boss will allow her to take on the case of Myriam Villetreix, née N'Bissi, who wants Catherine to defend her in criminal court next spring. Just in time for her birthday, an eminently favorable sign, Catherine has decided.

"Old goat seeks young chick for rural ecstasy."

This faux personal ad, written with Daniel's typical humor and stuck on the folder she is holding, accompanies the photo of a sixty-some man in a wool polo shirt buttoned all the way up. He has smooth gray hair, clear and gentle eyes, and a soft frozen smile. Gaston Villetreix, the victim. Catherine opens the file and finds Myriam's letter.

> Gaston was a kind husband. He had happiness to catch up on, and I helped him with that. Why shouldn't I enjoy what he had now? I thought the people here liked me, but they're all spitting at me. And prison is horrible. Especially when you haven't done anything. I cry all the time now. He liked my cooking. It never made him sick. If someone put poison in it, it wasn't me, that's all. My cousin said Daniel never left anyone in trouble and that's where I am. Thanks for what you can do. Myriam

Catherine still can't differentiate the sincerity from the cunning in Myriam's letter. She looks at her comrade's stoic, straight back and says, "Sorry to disturb you, Daniel. Is there an address for the cousin?"

"Where do you live? Cousin, that's like brother or buddy. It's not her second cousin. In this case, it's the girl who gave her our address. 'On that infamous September 11, 2001. You should have seen it, the ten of us staring at the television. Then, knock, knock.'"

"You already told me the story a hundred times, Daniel."

"Excuse me for still finding it crazy. She's a really nice girl. She works in a hair salon on the boulevard near Barbès, next to the Barracuda shoe store. Do you know where that is? Her name is, um, Tania. Tania, uh, Tania. Just say Tania. Everyone knows her."

When Catherine pokes his shoulder to say good-bye, Daniel nods without getting up, totally absorbed in his screen.

Actually, Catherine is attracted to older men, and Daniel does not realize that his teenage behavior is counterproductive. Damning, in fact. Perhaps Myriam also needed the maturity of an older partner to reassure her.

Provided that Renaud accepts. "Accept, Renaud," she says to herself.

It's her first real case, her first major felony. And an unusual case. The press could run with it if she were to handle it with some skill.

She pulls the door shut, but it veers open again, and then she presses the time switch, which provides exactly two seconds of light before the bulb goes out. Total darkness. Better not think about what is crawling under her feet.

Not scared! Her father measured the degree of her childhood terrors by the frenetic intensity with which she repeated, "Not scared."

She starts singing. "Stand by me. No, I won't be afraid..."

Her father had been a poor orphan who had worked hard to finish medical school. He was thirty in the 1970s, and Catherine has no idea what kind of music he listened to.

Is life ever anything like a John Lennon song? Certainly not her father's life, admirable man that he is, a man whom she is incapable of admiring.

At the Barbès intersection, a market of poverty and destitution is in full, meaningless swing. Old clothes are being exchanged, illicit cigarette sellers block the subway turnstiles, and the sidewalks are littered with uninviting business cards for local witch doctors.

Catherine adjusts her earpiece under her helmet, keeping an eye on four-wheeled enemies, and calls her office.

"Sophie, it's Catherine. I'll be right there. Is Maître Renaud there? Did I get any calls?"

Then she listens to her messages.

Cedric Devers: "I did not have an opportunity to thank you, but you were very good. Thank you very much."

She raises an eyebrow just long enough to make a face at the ambiguity of the "you were very good." It is rare that a client ever takes the time for a thank you, so it's worth accepting, particularly when he has such green eyes. Or were they gray? Changing. Right there, the graphic artist is listed in the "imaginable" column among those worth keeping an eye on.

Stephanie would like to know if the flabby lawyer intended to let her soft fleshy padding win the war or if they would meet at the gym.

"In my dreams," Catherine says to herself.

She'll text her, because with Stephanie you know when a conversation begins—sometimes even before you lift the phone to call—but when it ends is quite another story.

Felix: "We're starting to prep for the New Year's party with karaoke and all. The whole class will be there. Would you, oh great star of the courts and the tortes, deign to join our humble troupe of organizers?"

What an asshole! They had all been jealous when Renaud, her first choice of potential employers, hired her after a single interview.

She calls back and leaves a message: "Dear answering machine, kindly transmit to the ordinary legal galley slave that a genetic miracle has allowed me to remain simple and that, despite joint invitations from the chancellery and the presidency, it will be my pleasure and my preference to come mingle with the court proletariat, if only to measure the distance that now separates us. I heard about a rental that's not too expensive and has a basement for dancing. I'll find out more. Hugs."

Catherine thinks they are planning really early before she realizes that it is almost December. She drives down the Avenue de l'Opéra, which is so familiar to her, she hasn't really looked at it in a long time, and parks in her usual spot, under the windows of Renaud's law firm, where she can check regularly to make sure some zit-faced delinquent is not sawing through her lock.

In the lift, she checks her hair, brushes it so it falls smoothly onto her shoulders and then puffs it up a bit. Maître Renaud does not appreciate carelessness or casualness.

She tosses her things into the wilds of her office, making no notable change in the scenery. Experience has proven that once disorder reaches a certain level, it gets no worse.

She says a quick hello to Sophie, who holds up crossed fingers.

She knocks.

"Come in."

She loves Maître Renaud's rugged bass voice, with its barely perceptible accent that stresses incongruous syllables. He doesn't have the sharp phrasing of Parisians. Neither does she. But Maître Renaud's powerful and sensual voice emanates from deep in his diaphragm, while her thin voice tends to dissipate all over the place.

She is always awed by her boss's office, with its chalk-white walls, wide armchairs covered in soft olive-colored leather, and the arrogant sheen of a 1920s desk. The whole is gently impressive. A huge photo fills the left wall, perfectly lit by the French window on the other side of the room. Your eye has to settle on it for a long, calm moment in order to discern that the monochrome black vibrates with the barely perceptible movement of the sea, which extends into a deep night sky.

There are never any papers on the boss's desk, because the mind of a great man contains all the information it needs. And Maître Renaud never pretends to be busy with some other task you would be interrupting, because a great man has nothing to prove.

His beauty is equal to his IQ, and he has the charm of someone who has never thought to be bothered by his appearance: He is stout without being soft and has intense, indecipherable black eyes and well-defined lips.

Despite his reputation for being an old lion who likes young flesh, he has never tried anything with Catherine. He would only have to open his arms for her to fall right into them, which would be a perfectly huge catastrophe. For her. Be that as it may, she thinks about it every time they meet one on one.

She uses a neutral tone to announce the acquittal. There is no need to show off. Renaud says that in his firm excellence is the minimum sentence.

He takes note without any comment and says without any transition, "You will be facing the most repressive felony court in France."

Catherine forces herself to remain impassive while a two-drummer rock band rips through her chest.

"You have a lot to lose and quite a bit to gain, which generally go hand in hand. The case will not exempt you from your duties here at the firm. You can work on the train. The firm will pay your expenses until, as we hope, your client becomes creditworthy again."

"Thank you, sir."

"It will be a tough fight. I trust you will prevail. One word of advice: Double check the marriage story. Otherwise, no investigating. We are not in the United States here. The inquiry is over, the facts are in the file. Do not give in to your storybook imagination."

She shows appropriate restraint and thanks him one time only, simply.

Renaud hates emotional effusion, which he likens to water on the knee, with its invisible and pernicious effects.

She leaves, remaining calm and dignified, but immediately outside the door, she leaps over to Sophie's desk, lifts her arms, and sways.

Sophie does not react. Catherine follows her eyes to the boss's door, which has not been fully closed and has swung open again, giving the elder attorney a perfect view of the young employee's enthusiastic display.

Catherine stammers her excuses and goes back to close the door while Sophie covers up a smile with a heavy file that must have seen quite a few more.

3

You can dream of a minimalist apartment with elegant simplicity, where having only what's essential inevitably results in something beautiful, and meanwhile you can enthusiastically collect cheap memorabilia, wobbly furniture, and castaway clothes with no future, which inevitably produces something ugly. Similarly, you can dream of having your boss's ideal office while wallowing in a dark cubbyhole with a table cluttered with disorderly notes.

Catherine reviews her resolutions for the year every January and puts "order and simplicity" at the top of the list, only to acknowledge as December comes around that her good intentions have gone unheeded.

She scans the telephone numbers jotted down on sticky notes. She unsticks some of them, balls them up, and tosses the ball toward the garbage. It misses. She reaches down to pick it up.

The cloth had been sucked on, nursed, and kneaded so much that only a few threads are holding it together. It lies on the green grass, so near but inaccessible. Buckled into her stroller at the beginning of the never-ending abandonment, she screams. Her small, too-short arm can't reach it. Her mother is not there; her mother is not running up to her; the bridge that has connected her to the entire world has disappeared.

Catherine sighs, opens her hand above the wastebasket, straightens, and piles up three files. One that is not securely closed slips, and papers scatter. She picks them up, readjusts them, and closes the files.

Wealth and power are the only escape from disorder and accumulation. One day her successful career, like Prince Charming's kiss, will transform her into that rare creature, elegant, impeccable, with solid taste and exemplary organizational skills.

She grabs her smartphone. "Dad?"

"Oh, it's you!"

Three words that say much. "You never call; I miss you, but I don't want to burden you or interfere with your life, even though I sacrificed everything for you, and I am alone, and my daughter's life is the only reason I have to live."

Catherine takes a familiar leap to get beyond the parental knack of inspiring guilt, a skill her father has raised to the level of fine art.

"I'm getting ready to leave Renaud's office. It's done. I'm going to defend a client on a felony in the *Cour d'Assises*. I'll be leaving next week."

"You're leaving Paris?"

"I'll be going back and forth."

"Can you tell me what it's about? If your superstition allows it, that is."

"A murder in the Creuse."

The phone goes so silent that Catherine checks to see if her father is still on the line.

"Yes. Yes, I'm still here. Did you say in Creuse?"

"Don't you say in *the* Creuse? I know, I know, it's not very glamorous, and you can find better, but at my age, this is a terrific opportunity. A great rural story."

"A murder?"

"Dad! It's the *Cour d'Assises*! It's a felony trial. A black woman accused of killing her farmer husband. Not bad, huh?"

"Is it the Limoges or the Guéret court?"

"That's the best one yet! You actually know the region?"

A silence could have settled in, but Catherine fills in right away, too impatient to notice. "I'm going to be really busy, and that's an understatement. But I'm happy. That's why I wanted to tell you..."

"I was hoping you would come to Gaillac. When is it?"

"March 6th to 8th."

"But the eighth is your birthday!"

"That's what I was saying. We've got time. And we'll see each other at Christmas."

"Okay. I won't keep you any longer."

"But Dad, I was the one who called you!"

"No, I appreciate it. Really. You'll tell me how it goes? How long will you stay?"

"I'm going to the detention center to see my client. I'll come right back. It's a first meeting."

"I'd be surprised if you wanted to hang out there. It's not such a great place."

"Just as well. I'm not a tourist. Isn't there a slogan, 'Creuse, where kids run free and happy'?"

"Rivers. Where rivers run free and happy."

Yes. An old ad has popped out of who-knows-where.

Catherine laughs at her mistake. He doesn't, the gloomy one whose face is frozen with sorrow, the career widower with his lost happiness and broken life, tied down with a huge, unique, impossible love. Will the Monsigny daughter please rise! The one who paid in full for a paternal decision. The father whose life had been interrupted once and for all. But, *he* was the one who built that dam, brick by brick. *He* was the one who chose to raise his child in the stagnant water of a present without a past and to horde the four years of running water, of happy idyllic memories. If you believe what he says. There is nothing but his word to go on, because there is absolutely no evidence of that paradise. He eliminated it all. Pictures, clothing, objects—anything connected to the dead woman was written off following the decree issued by him alone that this was best for the orphan child.

There is no point in turning it over and over. Catherine has learned to get by without memories or any sign thereof. She opens her eyes, which she closed in exasperation as she hung up.

She has asked him to move to Paris a hundred times. He's the one who is retired. She doesn't have seven hours to take the train and then endure his concerned looks overflowing with expectation.

Let him keep his secrets. She has her own. A photo, surrounded by an old-fashioned cardboard frame, a single picture, her sustenance, found in a book of Rimbaud's poems. She knows that it is her mother, because she has the same blond hair, the same smile. The young woman advances, conquering, radiant, all of twenty years, without any fears, with a hand—a hand wearing a wedding ring— forever extended toward the future and her spellbound husband, dazzled by his shining wife, Violet. On the sly, Catherine talks to this unknown woman, asks for her advice, and draws strength from the sparkle in her eyes.

It's a strange picture. Perhaps it was taken on their honeymoon, in front a sign with the name of a town, whose letters are partially masked: "vave le." She'll never know the full name.

Catherine is sixteen years old. She has just finished lycée, with honors. It is the day of her most intense feeling of hatred.

She waits like an ordinary patient in an ugly modern waiting room with light-colored wood and glass, the walls a sad beige covered with dull reproductions. She is anxious to join her friends to celebrate graduation, an outing her father has authorized. He is solemn and determined, monopolizing the time, saturating it with silence until he makes his preliminary declaration. "As you know, your mother died."

A stupid, clumsy introduction.

If, at least, he showed some emotion, broke down in tears. But no, he represses everything and talks like a bad teacher reciting to his class. "We were living in the countryside. She took you for a walk, as she did every day."

"I know."

"No, you don't know. You think you remember, but those are invented memories. You were too little. And you were sleeping. It was nap time. She left the stroller in the shade near a clearing, where she wandered off. When you woke up, you started to cry, and someone who was walking by heard you. He is the one who found Violet's body. Beaten to death. But you could not have heard her. She was too far away."

She holds back an insolent question: How can you be so sure? Were you there? She represses a desire to jump up from her chair, go home, and lock herself in her room to get ready. This is supposed to be a happy day. Thanks, Dad.

Then he does a horrible thing. He announces that today she has the right to ask questions, any questions she wants, but afterward they won't ever talk about it again. At sixteen, only the future counts. That is why he will not tell her where it took place. He does not want her to fret over searching and knowing. Everything was done to find the murderer. Everything. She can believe that.

And there are no relatives to find either.

Her mother was English, rerouted, lost, without a family. Apparently they were quite happy to start a life that would begin with them and satisfied to send down their own roots. Does refusing the past destroy the future?

"Did she have an accent?"

"A slight one. It was smooth, pretty."

Of course.

The teenager is ashamed of her reedy, worried voice when she asks the only question that comes to mind, "Did she love me?"

"More than anything else. She breastfed you for eight months."

A bitter taste of nausea invades her mouth. This is not what she expected.

She has no more questions. He would not know how to answer them. "It was the worst possible disaster. I would have died of sorrow, had you not been there," he adds, silencing her even further.

He is only interested in his own pain, in fact. It's a fool's bargain. She can't even look at him. He should have chosen some more intimate place, not his office. She should be in his arms, protected, coddled, reassured without this desk between them.

If she opens her mouth she'll scream; if she moves she'll break everything.

He concludes in a professorial tone. "You don't build a life on a past defined by the irreversible. You don't deny it; you set it aside, so that you don't keep tripping over the remains."

Except he does the opposite, letting death hinder him, leaving him incapable of overcoming a sorrow that is too great for him to bear. For the first time, Catherine comes face to face with the inconsistencies of the adult world. She decides that she will be coherent. She promises herself that she will sacrifice nothing for him. She is ready to be condemned to hell rather than break that promise. She loves her father. He is her only family. But she will not sacrifice for him. He is responsible for his own choices. She will be responsible for hers.

She will leave Bordeaux. She will go to Paris to study. She will study law.

She erases herself from her father's past by leaving him, just as his silence erased his daughter's past. Now they are equal.

She takes out the notebook where she writes down everything and starts a new page. Now that she has the felony case, she puts her notes in the official notebook.

She reviews the key elements in Daniel's story from memory.

Myriam N'Bissi, thirty-three years old, stumbles into the association on September 11, 2001. This is not a coincidence. The family, whose name she says she doesn't remember, who had brought her back from Gabon, housed her and reduced her to slavery, is glued to the television like the rest of the planet. Myriam takes advantage of the situation. She gets lost in the city before someone gives her the address of Rights for All.

She sees Gaston's picture in Daniel's office: old goat looking for young chick. Daniel gives her Gaston Villetreix's letter. He's sixty-one years old and looking for a wife, even an undocumented immigrant. He would be able to take care of her. He owns his own home.

Catherine notes that Myriam knows how to read.

They meet and hit it off. They get married.

Check the marriage? Why did Renaud say that?

Myriam settles down in the village of Saint-Jean-les-Bois.

"I love it," Catherine says.

He's some old man, in any case, going to get an illegal African immigrant and bringing her back to his small town.

She tries to imagine the tsunami that hit the old man's life and the village, but because she has no experience with either small towns or old people, she doesn't get any further than folkloric representations of a black woman in traditional garb and clogs dancing in the farmyard with a grandfather wearing a beret.

The marriage lasts six years, until Gaston dies. The doctor signs the death certificate. Officially, the cause of death is cardiac arrest. He had just eaten dinner with his wife, spicy chicken she had prepared.

Myriam inherits and decides to sell the family estate that Gaston's new lifestyle had already begun to work through.

The Villetreix cousins are outraged. Not only is that just not done, but also, they have been counting on inheriting from the old bachelor.

All of a sudden, they recall a jar of cyanide from an abandoned gold mine. It was kept in the barn to get rid of pests. It disappeared, they say, and then they found it in Myriam's kitchen cupboard. They request an autopsy, which is granted, and it reveals that Gaston did, indeed, die of cyanide poisoning.

Catherine gets this information from Daniel, who gets it from Myriam, which means that it all needs to be checked.

Catherine reserves a train ticket online for the morning of November 4th. She has to get off at a stop called La Souterraine and then take a bus or rent a car to get to Guéret.

She looks at a map.

She'll have to see. The advantage of the train is that she can work, but there are a limited number of trains, and, above all, she won't have any way to get around when she is there if she doesn't rent a car. Despite what Renaud says, she counts on driving around a bit to size up the place and get a feel for the atmosphere.

Just in case, she plans to come back on the last train in the evening, but logically she should be back earlier.

Gaston was poisoned. That is a fact.

Why would Myriam have waited all these years? What happened that would have pushed her to commit this crime? Assuming she wanted to get out of the marriage. Preferably flush with cash.

She was finally comfortable after experiencing a tough life. Would she really have taken the incredible risk of falling into the hands of the justice system and losing everything, gambling that she would prevail, free and rich? That would be a risky bet.

And what about the cousins? If they were guilty, would they take the risk of revealing the murder?

And they didn't have anything to gain from killing Gaston.

Unless they succeeded in getting Myriam convicted.

But then, they would have accused her immediately after Gaston died. In any case, no victim is innocent.

Why does she think about women when she says the word victim? Then Catherine puts an end to the stream of questions for which she has no answers. She'll have to go over all of this with her client.

Catherine is anxious to meet her. She's like a character from a novel, a modern-day heroine. What a story she's had!

The little Gabonese orphan manages to escape from her torturers in an unknown country, seduces an old cynical farmer, turns his dismal day-to-day existence upside down, and introduces him to the pleasures of life. But envied by diehard racist misers, she finds herself accused of murdering a man she has come to love tenderly and ends up in criminal court, where the young upstart attorney Catherine Monsigny, in the brilliant beginnings of her career, has her cleared of all suspicion and returns her to freedom.

"Catherine!"

Sophie then comes out with an overused and not-at-all funny pun that harpoons her back to planet Renaud.

"Do I have to petition you for the petition?"

"I'm nearly done."

"How much time does nearly amount to? Give me a rough figure."

"Half an hour?"

She writes "GREED" in capital letters in her notebook. She underlines it four times for good measure.

Renaud can say what he likes, but she'll do things her way. Only the results count, and she intends to impress her boss. He respects her, but she would like him to admire her. As soon as the thought takes form in her mind, she regrets it like blasphemy.

Her morning client's eyes ricochet back in her mind. Cedric Devers's green eyes. Why are they so striking? As if they remind her of others she has seen. Her mother's eyes are emeralds.

She shakes herself.

She glances at the text message she has just received. Stephanie!

She responds hastily, "Cnt mk it. Running 18. Preparing criminal case in Guéret +++. Cu."

An answer comes just seconds after her message. "Where's that?"

She responds, "Nvr mnd."

She turns off her cell phone, ready to return to boring paperwork.

But first, she goes for a smoke in the storage room whose window opens onto a gloomy sky.

4

A food peddler tries to tempt the train travelers with his plastic-wrapped sandwiches and various snacks and candies but finds few takers. No one is talking on the cell phone either, even though the passengers have their ringtones on loud. The train is too noisy. And the announcements coming over the scratchy PA system at every stop are deafening. All intellectual activity is doomed from the start.

"Buy earplugs for the next trip," Catherine says to herself.

Better yet, she puts on her brand-new noise-canceling headphones, plugs them into her telephone, and starts her music in random mode.

Bowie, "Absolute Beginners." That's perfect.

She returns to her computer screen and opens the press file with all the articles about the case that Renaud is defending in court at the end of the week. He is representing a pedophile who wreaked havoc in an upscale fundamentalist Catholic boarding school where many cabinet members send their children.

"Hard lines," Bowie sings. Right on target, David.

Catherine had not dared to ask her boss why he had been so annoyed by the media coverage. What does it matter if you are blamed or praised, as long as people are talking about you? Could the great attorney be afraid of losing?

The idea barely has time to cross her mind before she chases it away.

Maître Renaud afraid? Unthinkable. Is God afraid? And if God were afraid, his creatures would surely be condemned to lives of sackcloth and ashes.

The train slows and comes to a stop. It's only Orléans. Guéret is the city you never reach.

Catherine dives back into her work. The landscape flashes by, begging for attention on the other side of the windows, rolling out its seasonal garb of reds, rusts, and golds that vary each time a waterway encounters the smallest ray of an indecisive sun. Meanwhile, Catherine is absorbed, busy with her case files, blind to nature.

Going over the articles, she notes the names of the journalists covering Renaud's hearing, which she plans to attend. All she'll have to do is chat with them and mention her fascinating case on trial in the spring. It's a riveting true-crime story.

In her mind, she sees the reporters on their bench. Renaud, dressed in his court robes, has just whispered in her ear. She leaves him to introduce herself to the journalists, with the pretext of slipping them some confidential information.

Or perhaps she'll use a simpler approach and ask them a banal question. "Will you be here for the three days?"

There will be one reporter, of course, who will invite her for coffee during a break. Then the ball will be in her court. If the national press covers her case in Guéret, it will be the start of her renown.

The modesty of the city where she ends up brings her back to reality. Catherine thought that a regional administrative capital—a *préfecture*—would necessarily be big. How can she possibly attract Parisian reporters to this faraway dead-end town? They have trouble crossing the capital's beltway.

The bus she has taken from La Souterraine to Guéret lets passengers off at another train station, this one no longer in service, something Catherine notes as the first local quirk.

It's time to get her bearings. She stands still, her back to the station.

She can walk to the jail, according to the map she unfolds and turns until the drawn street is in line with the real street in front of her. With her finger, she follows the line that veers to the, um, right.

She hopes that no one sees her hand, the one she writes with, shake like the idiot she becomes when she's trying to find her way. She is totally thrown off by space, another handicap stemming from the primal scene.

That day, asleep at the edge of the inextricable woods, awakening terrorized without the reassuring maternal point of reference, confronting a stranger's face before taking in those of the crowd, which multiply her childhood confusion. That day, she lost her sense of direction forever. Big causes, small effects.

She reaches the traffic circle, checks the map, and walks around it. The small street must be the right one. Then there is a left turn. Victory.

It is a ten-minute walk at most to reach the tree-lined square that harbors the massive opaque city hall, with the courthouse at a right angle. The square seems to be reserved exclusively for parking. Damned cars.

Then, right up the sidewalk in front of the courthouse, she'll come to the jail, which, with its stone masonry and small caged windows, looks like a child's drawing.

Catherine is aware of being terribly young. Her small size doesn't help. Her classic suits are supposed to make her look older, but instead, she looks like a teenager dressed up like a woman. She is wearing her best clothes for this important day, a pants suit with heels and a black Burberry raincoat, gifts she extracted from her father to celebrate the start of her career. They were a good investment, as proven by the respectful look of the guard in his cubicle. He steps aside and shows her a storage room without a door.

She takes a firm position. "This won't do. I need a table. We have papers to fill out and documents to examine. Would you be kind enough to find us a better place?"

It is a little jailhouse, without much activity. With a little effort, he could do her this favor. She looks at him silently, patient, firm. She is complicating his life. There is no rule that obliges him to comply.

He is embarrassed. He thinks a moment or two and then sighs. He does not want to lose face by accommodating too quickly. The time he takes plays in Catherine's favor. He would have said no immediately, so he will inevitably say yes.

"Okay. The classroom is free. I'll open it up for you. You're lucky. It's a calm day."

As if he were turning people away the rest of the time.

This is a method she has learned. Always require better right from the start, piss people off for the principle of it, impose a power struggle, position yourself as dominant, and earn respect. It is also training, because a lawyer should never be afraid to trigger hostilities.

And it works. Pleased, Catherine gives a sharp nod in the guise of a thank you.

She finds herself in a classroom with poor lighting from a high-barred window. Five laminate tables form an irregular central plateau. On the whiteboard, a humorist has inserted the word "blow" in the middle of the sentence, "Get the job done!" Chairs are piled in a wobbly heap. The faded colors of a poster for the movie *Jour de fête* by Jacques Tati, whose upper right corner is sadly drooping, do little to brighten the gloomy room. Instead, they make it worse.

But Catherine has taken on the role of Maître Monsigny, master of the world. She has stainless steel morale. She sets down her bag, takes off her coat, extricates two chairs, tests their stability, and places them on either side of a table. She has plenty of time. Prison staff hurry only when their shift lets out.

She sits down with her back to the window. It is a gray day, but a little bit of light will reach her client.

She deliberately had not checked out the case inquiry file from the court in order to have her mind clear. She wants Myriam to know what she is getting into, so that they can have a freely consented relationship, rather than the arranged marriage that commonly exists between an attorney and a client.

From her bag she retrieves a fine Moleskine notebook, which she has bought especially for this occasion, along with the same expensive fountain pen her boss uses and, to complete her serious look, the printed pages of an old case file.

She hears the barred door at the end of the hallway and approaching footsteps.

"My client," she says to herself, more moved than she imagined she would be, before becoming disenchanted in the seconds that follow.

There is nothing exotic about Myriam Villetreix, née N'Bissi. Confinement has grayed her light skin. She is tall but hunched over. She is a little stocky, she drags her feet, and she is wearing worn-out slippers that make a dull slapping sound. She has on a washed-out sweat suit, and her short hair highlights the very round ball shape of her skull. Her eyes are sad and her handshake evasive. She places a large brown envelope on the table.

Catherine gives her a sign to sit down and asks the guard to close the door.

She expected a colorful, exuberant island bird and finds herself face to face with a featherless fowl. She hears the echo of something another attorney once said during a conversation. "Clients rarely meet our expectations." But now she reassesses and decides that looking like a victim could be an asset for the defense.

"My name is Maître Monsigny. I've worked with Daniel a lot."

"You are, um, very young."

The deception is mutual. Well, that's a good start. Catherine straightens, lifts her chin too high and returns it to the right level.

"I work for a major Parisian law firm that is very well known."

Self-justification is a fatal error. Always. She carries on without any transition, mixing a dry tone with authority and an underlying threat.

"You have the right to request another lawyer. I have come from Paris to meet you and get to know you. There is still time to go back on your decision. I still have not requested the inquiry file. We are both free."

Myriam shakes her head slowly when she hears the ridiculously chosen word "free," which Catherine corrects immediately.

"I mean that after this first contact either of us can decide not to go any further."

Having made her point—that she is not, in fact, free—Myriam Villetreix, née N'Bissi, follows suit and makes her own clarification.

"I'm sorry," she says. "I didn't mean to say that you are too young to handle my case. It's just the image in my head. When you see a trial on TV, the lawyers always have gray hair. You never see anyone who is young, uh, for major cases."

"Everyone starts by starting."

"Not me."

Myriam is not being funny.

"I never started. I mean, I never killed anyone. And you have to know that. Sorry, but it's important. Because..." Her mouth trembles, and her eyes fill with tears. "First, you've got to believe me, otherwise..."

"If I become your lawyer, I will be on your side. Absolutely. It is best that you tell me what happened, in your own words."

Catherine tries to find the right distance. Should she be neutral and kind? She has to do more than that.

She reaches out her hand and touches the inmate's fingers and then dares to cover them completely. The woman's dry, cold hand warms up with the contact. Catherine tries to get the same result with words.

"What if we started at the beginning, with your childhood."

Bad choice. The word childhood triggers a flood of tears. The outpouring catches the lawyer off guard—she had not thought to bring tissues. She still has a lot to learn. She removes a small silk scarf from her bag and holds it out to the crying woman, hoping she won't blow her nose in it. Myriam refuses it with a wave of her hand and is happy to wipe her face with the sleeve of her sweatshirt.

"Sorry. My childhood. My grandmother raised me. In Lambarene. My parents were dead. My grandmother treated me like a princess. She was nice. She spoiled me. She used to say that one day I would become someone. But she died, too. She was a housekeeper for a French couple who were going back home, so they brought me with them to take care of their kids. Until the day I managed to escape."

"Escape?"

"They were watching the TV because of the attack. You know, the planes in the towers. September 11. So I left. They watched me all the time. They treated me bad. And I was afraid they would find me and put me in prison. That's what they said."

Despite her attorney's urging, Myriam refuses to give the name of the family who housed her that first year in France. She is still afraid of them. In addition to her obsession with saying she's sorry, the woman punctuates her sentences with long silences, and her diction is about as loose as her handshake. She is dull and boring, rather than moving. This is a real problem. For a change, both in subject and in atmosphere, Catherine points to the envelope that Myriam has brought.

"What's that?"

Without answering, the prisoner takes out some photos, which she then talks about, one by one.

They are young and laughing. He's wearing a shiny white suit, and she is in a long, flared satin dress, with a veil around her face. The picture is a little blurry and was taken in a studio with a fake Venice background. There is an automatic photo booth picture of Myriam as a child. She is very pretty, with large wide eyes, but she is biting her lip. Then Myriam, older, is holding the hands of two white children, with cactus in the background.

"Those are the family's kids I took care of. There, they were still nice. They were five and nine years old."

Myriam's long hair is tied back in one picture. She looks absent, her eyes staring off to the side a little, her expression fearful. It is hard to guess her age.

"I was thirty-two years old. It was in Africa."

"You were already working for the same family?"

"No. I sold fabric in the market."

She looks younger than she is. There is a picture with Gaston, also taken in a studio. He has sparse light gray hair, a gentle face, no chin, slightly drooping eyes but full lips. He is wearing a checked shirt and cotton pants. He's sitting in a chair. It is easy to recognize the man in Daniel's picture. Myriam is standing next to him and holding his hand. Her long hair is tied with a red ribbon. She is wearing a polka dot dress and high heels.

A selection of photos follows, with her alone, on a carousel, by the ocean, at an outdoor restaurant.

That is the woman Catherine would like to uncover, the pretty, happy woman full of energy, the one Myriam herself seems to have lost. What has whittled her down? What has erased her?

Is it the bowels of the justice system? Or pangs of guilt? Or simply a life that has lost its meaning? At what turn?

When the visit comes to an end, the lawyer can't stand it anymore and is feeling oppressed and nervous. This is more pernicious than the way a prison visit usually makes her feel, and the reason is obvious. "Myriam's heavy, fatalistic passivity spreads like gangrene and will cause us to lose," Catherine thinks.

She resists a strong desire to shake the prisoner until some vital energy reboots her circulation, until curiosity about what the future holds removes the rust from her neurons, brings life to her face, and strengthens her voice.

The picture of her mother intervenes. That smile, that drive, and that energy didn't prevent her death. Had she smiled at her killer with the same trust? It was someone she knew, of course. You don't beat to death just any woman, any stranger. The crime was full of passion.

For so many years, she has managed to rid herself of this insoluble past, and she is irritated to see it come back with such force. That's all she needs. Not only did her mother abandon her, but now she will ruin her life. She had already made her take on the very uncomfortable role of prosecutor.

"I am a lawyer," she repeats to herself. "I defend."

Myriam's voice, submerged by the omnipotent maternal image, takes over again. She is in the process of describing her happy marriage, full of sentimental nonsense.

Sure, in Saint-Jean-les-Bois, you were the only black person in a very small white town. You were married to an old peasant. Life must have been idyllic. I believe you, pet.

Sarcasm is a bad mood trying to be clever, Catherine reminds herself.

She is in a bad mood. That is undeniable. It's her first felony defense, her first client, and she has started off in a bad temper. And her mother keeps running in the subtext.

Something is not right. She tries to focus on what Myriam is saying. She'll have to seem genuine. Even if she's playing a role, she has to be plausible. A win is not guaranteed.

"Okay," Catherine throws out, thinking the contrary. "I'm going to go. Do you confirm that you want me to defend you?"

Myriam agrees half-heartedly. Catherine waits.

"Yes, I agree."

"As you have already written a letter, you have nothing else to do. The next time I see you, I will have read the case file. Don't hold it against me, but I'll have to ask you some questions that are a little, well, mean. Not because that is what I think, but because that is what the prosecution will do. Okay?"

She calls the guard, and as she begins to gather her things, Myriam panics. Is Catherine leaving? Will Catherine come back? Does Catherine believe her? Will Catherine get her out of here?

"Yes," she says mechanically.

She is standing, her papers together, and she looks at Myriam.

"If you didn't do it, who, in your opinion, could have wanted to kill Gaston?"

"Nobody. He was nice to everyone."

"That's a lot of help," Catherine says to herself, watching her client walk slowly behind the guard to the barred door.

So slow.

"Myriam!"

She catches up with her client in a few quick steps.

"Are you taking any medication?"

"Uh, yes."

"What?"

"What the doctor gives me."

"Because you're sick, or what?"

"Because I'm sad and miserable."

"Tell him you have to stop the treatment."

"The doctor?"

Myriam turns away, frightened by the peremptory yes that comes from her lawyer, who suddenly wonders where a woman who is so submissive to authority could have found the determination needed to commit murder.

5

The courthouse is a plain light-colored building that looks, as surprising as it seems, friendly. Everyone, from the guard at the front to the clerk and the investigating *juge d'instruction*, is affable, attentive, and curious but not too inquisitive. Yet they are all foreign to her. She has the same feeling that she had earlier at the jail. A breath of solitude sweeps over Catherine like a small current of ice-cold air, and she starts calculating how long she has to wait for the bus and then the train that will take her back to Paris, back home.

Clearly not so professional, she had not thought of bringing a wheeled suitcase and finds her arms filled with the large inquiry file. She is carefully descending the stairs to the entrance, when she finds herself cut off by a small, sharp-eyed man with a head that looks like a frog.

"Are you Maître Monsigny?"

He looks her over with a critical eye.

"You are quite young."

Old schmuck, she thinks, and even though her arms are starting to weaken, she waits, because he seems to have something to say to her.

"You're from Paris? This is your first felony case? Welcome. Were you forewarned? It's pretty unsophisticated here. Keep things simple. There aren't many of us, and everyone knows everyone else. It's like one big family. When's the trial? In the spring? Well, with a little luck, the witnesses will come, because on days when there's ice on the roads, well... If you need any information, don't hesitate."

"To ask you? That is very kind of you. Thank you, Mr...."

"Roland Perret, presiding judge."

He climbs the stairs quickly, complacently. Shrugging her shoulders, she goes downstairs, impervious to what clearly resembles a hazing. She feels young and strong and invincible.

On the street, a man about the age of thirty is pacing back and forth. He's wearing jeans and a cotton jacket and has short poorly cut hair and a crooked nose. He looks like a decent fellow. He calls out to her with the awkwardness of the timid. "Catherine Monsigny?"

News gets around fast in Guéret.

He introduces himself. "Louis Bernier. I work for the paper *La Montagne*, the crime beat. Would you have time for a short interview?"

She hesitates for half a second before remembering that she needs the media, all of it.

"At a café then. I'm freezing."

He leads her to another square, which is small and attractive, with Italian-style ochre and pink façades.

The town does have some character and an atmosphere that is oddly both spirited and subdued.

They enter a café-restaurant with dark woodwork reminiscent of an English pub. Louis greets the owner like a regular and introduces Catherine, who finds herself out of the familiar and protective anonymity of the big city. She should be able to adjust to it.

She orders a *croque-madame* and a beer. Bernier takes coffee. He explains that the region is calm and safe, that local crime is rare and not very serious, and that the Villetreix case has caused a lot of ink to flow. Nothing like it has ever happened before. Murder, exoticism, and now an up-and-coming lawyer from Paris.

"I won't be able to tell you much. Lawyer-client confidentiality."

"I just have a few general questions and would like a picture."

Catherine thinks quickly. She hasn't put on any makeup, but her suit becomes her. Is this a good idea? She doesn't see how it could harm her. She is not obliged to answer any questions, and she wants people to talk about her, so it's a start.

She explains how she found herself working on the case. Yes, she is new to the region and finds it charming. Yes, the welcome has been warm.

"Do you have any connections with the Creuse?"

"No. Why?"

"An impression."

"This is the first time I've ever been here."

She explains the work she is doing for Rights for All but only says the usual platitudes about the actual case. Her client is, of course, weakened and ravaged. Incarceration is a harsh ordeal.

Louis would, for that matter, like her to pose with the jailhouse in the background.

Catherine goes down the stairs to the tiny bathroom to powder her nose and put on some blush and mascara. Her chignon is holding up, more or less. She glosses her lips, ties on her lucky white silk scarf, which will be her trademark. Criminal court is the important opportunity she has been waiting for to inaugurate it.

She decides not to smile, to have a serious, concerned look on her face, but the looks of passers-by make her feel self-conscious.

"A little smile?"

Bernier isn't finished with her yet.

To thank her, if she is interested, he offers to take her to Saint-Jean-les-Bois so she can get an idea of the setting. And he'll drop her off at La Souterraine. "It will be faster than the bus. And much more pleasant," she says to herself, making a quick calculation of the safety margin she needs to catch the evening train.

The large Peugeot station wagon has a baby seat in the back and small cars scattered on the floor, along with a box of tissues, a stuffed animal, an open bottle of water, and a bunch of newspapers that manage to take up all the seats. Louis makes some room for Catherine, gesturing toward the back with a small shrug, more a sign of resignation than an excuse.

The lawyer succeeds in finding room for her case file and her bag and notes that by keeping her legs together she can manage to avoid crushing anything underfoot.

On the way, he points out the place where the new library will be built and the mosque that is under construction. He is smooth in showing that his town is dynamic and on the move.

Catherine finds him to be clearly very nice but brings him back around to the only topic that really interests her. She would like to know how people feel about Myriam.

"Generally speaking, opinions are split in Saint-Jean, where people had gotten to know Myriam. There are the pro-cousins and the others. The former mayor, who performed Gaston's wedding and arranged Myriam's papers, leans toward an accident. He tries to avoid taking sides, and he did sign the burial release. Otherwise, in the countryside, people don't really like outsiders."

"Not only in the countryside."

"Undoubtedly. Let's just say that an outsider never goes unnoticed."

"And what do you think?"

"I'm a reporter. I don't think."

"Come on, seriously. Just between us."

"I say that poison is a woman's weapon and that when you're not used to it, life in Saint-Jean can be, well, let's just say an accident is unlikely with cyanide. Anyone can get it."

He talks about a colleague who discovered a deserted gold mine where waste from the excavation, particularly some cyanide, was all out in the open, and he concludes, "You also find cyanide in milk-production plants. There have been suicides with it. It's a quick death."

Catherine is spellbound when she sees the first houses in Saint-Jean-les-Bois, with their ancient gardens.

Bernier turns toward a beautiful church. The road bends around a large garden surrounded by a short wall and leads to an immense pond, with a clearing on one side and trees on the other. There is a path to a simple square building. Its wooden shutters are painted olive drab, and smoke is coming from the chimney.

"It's a storybook setting," Catherine says.

"Yes, that too," Bernier says with a smile.

Three modern homes serve as a suburb.

Bernier comes around the village from the back, passing meadows with inquisitive black cows. The car comes to a stop at a small square with irregular cobblestones and a pretty dry-stone well with a walled-up coping.

"They closed it when old Étienne jumped in it."

Catherine looks away.

On a house that stands out on the other side of the narrow lane, a bright pink shutter is hanging off its hinges. The home's rough façade is yellowing with age.

"It's here," Louis says. "The Villetreix family house. The shutters are Myriam's touch."

"But there's nobody in the village."

"Yes, there are people. They are either at home or at work. A lot of them are retired. I'm going to show you a friend's house. He's young and has settled here. He plans to build a completely green house. He's doing everything himself. Do you want to see inside Gaston's house?"

He shows her the large flat stone under which she will find the key.

"How do you know that it's there?"

"Everyone knows."

He lets out a good laugh, looking at her as if she were born yesterday. And then he explains. Yes, everyone knows everyone else. People here may be indiscreet about small things, but when there is a secret to guard, it's inaccessible. And if someone spills the beans and tells what others shouldn't know, everyone will obstinately deny it, even though everyone knows it's true.

"And how do the police, or the rural gendarmes here in the countryside, go about their investigations?"

"Ah, there are informers. Not officially. There are chatterboxes, people who peddle news. A gendarme stops by, has a drink, discusses some news."

"Where is the café?"

"There isn't one in Saint-Jean any longer. Nor are there any shops."

She looks at the abandoned house that wreaks emptiness and absence. Deserted lanes. Silence. A large, gloomy cloud catches up with the sun, covering the sky. The sun disappears in the darkness.

Solitude and melancholy take over again.

She wants to go home. Now. In any case, it's time. She suddenly panics at the idea of missing her train. Why did she put herself in the hands of a stranger, dependent on what he wants to do?

She turns to Bernier and gives him a girl smile while promising herself she'll rent a car the next time.

"I'll wait to visit the house until Myriam says it's okay. It's kind of you to have brought me here. Can you take me to La Souterraine now?"

"La Souterraine? It only takes forty minutes. We can stop by and see Olivier since we're here," he says, getting out of the car without waiting for her to answer. He turns to the right and disappears. Catherine checks the time on her phone.

She is sure she has the time but less sure that she wants to put up with the local eco-warrior, for whom she has no specific questions, and completely sure that she does not want to lose sight of her only way back to the train station. She slams the car door. Doesn't he lock his car? That's his problem. She runs a little, twists her ankle, and turns to the right.

Louis is waiting for her, rolling a cigarette. She tries to act like she hasn't been running and can't recognize herself in this sudden panic attack.

"It's this way."

Just outside the village, he takes a path going nowhere. Well, going to a small patch of woods. A tractor passes in the distance.

"Not afraid," she says to herself, trying to remember if anyone saw her get into the station wagon, if anyone would know whom to suspect if she were never to come back.

The ground is scattered with leaves. Every step makes an enormous racket, but would anyone hear her scream?

Louis keeps looking left and right.

He's checking to make sure nobody is around.

Catherine clutches her bag by the clasp, a weapon to defend herself if she must.

Louis stops, stretches out his neck, and suddenly dashes into the trees.

Catherine tries without much success to say with authority, "It's not that way."

"I'll be right back."

She waits. He is getting a plastic bag out of his pocket, the kind you can use to smother someone in seconds. She calculates that it will take her two minutes to run back to the road if she takes off her pumps. She stays on guard and tries to calm her breathing, keeping a lookout.

Louis bends down to spread apart some leaves. He gently digs and removes a clump of yellow mushrooms that he slips into his bag. He comes back smiling.

"It rained yesterday. This is a good spot, easy to get to."

She puts on a knowing look. She feels ridiculous.

The path continues through the trees and leads to a wood-frame house. Smoke is coming out of the chimney, and music is coming from an open window. It's unexpected: progressive rock by Archive.

Before they even reach the door, it creaks inward, opening to a man, aged thirty or younger. Or older. He has mid-length shaggy hair and the look of a teen. He is wearing baggy jeans and a Clash T-shirt. He has a soot smear on his cheek that looks like a gash. He is not at all surprised.

"Hey, Louis."

The two men shake hands.

"Ms. Monsigny, Myriam's lawyer."

His hand is rough, his skin warm.

"Come in."

"We're not bothering you, I hope?" Catherine asks, discovering a computer screen lit up, with complex equations on it.

"I always have time for a break. That's why I moved back home to the countryside."

Not only does he know who she is, but obviously he is expecting this visit. Catherine turns to Louis, who is deep in contemplation of a small painting that is more authentically naïve than he is.

He has tricked her. She would like to know why but won't do him the favor of asking. To her great surprise, she doesn't have to wait for the answer, which announces a detour that might be more worthwhile than she thought.

"I am happy to see you because, well, I feel a little responsible for this whole story. Not guilty, um, Your Honor. But responsible. A little.

"'Your honor' is an American expression. You don't say that in France."

"My mistake."

Olivier—that's his name—asks if she wants tea and puts water on to boil as he talks. Both his body and his voice are calm. There are children's drawings above his desk, along with the picture of a kid who looks just like him, even with his head upside down, doing a cartwheel.

Of course he's married. You don't come live in a backwoods like this if you're not with someone. The right someone.

She begins to release her absurd anxiety and enjoy the comfort of being in a safe place, feeling warm and sheltered. She listens.

"When I began to build my house, I rented a room from Gaston's old lady. She was a good mother or an abusive mother, depending on your point of view."

Catherine can't help but note that he said, "I."

Louis is warming his back near the fire, even though the house is already warm. Most certainly by habit. He is encouraging his friend.

"Tell her."

"It was September 11, 2001."

"No, from the beginning. Since Camille."

"The whole family tree? I hope you have some time."

Catherine looks from one to the other. Are they teasing her? They smile but without any sarcasm.

"No, not the whole tree. One generation is enough."

"It's funny, isn't it? You say family tree, and it's also a tree that provided the apple to Eve."

"I think we should get back to our sheep here," Louis interrupts, adding for the young woman, "Olivier loves to theorize about everything."

It takes only a second for Catherine to find an unexpected stash of time filled to the brim. Her entry to Olivier's house has stopped the hands on the collective clock, as if this place were enchanted.

The setting is ideal for a story by the fireside, crackling as it lights up the dark room and projects moving shadows.

Olivier has a soft voice that is also full of life. He stands with his legs apart, a mug between his two hands, looking into the flames for inspiration.

Catherine settles against the cushions. She is ready. She has all the time in the world.

6

Men in the Villetreix family have never been lucky. That is their curse, a curse that stems from women. It is not that they choose the wrong women, but that they do not choose them at all. It is the women who set their sights on them. All in good faith. Nobody consciously creates his own sorrow. Hope dictates all of our choices.

This is what happened in the marriage that united Camille and Huguette. It comes late in both of their lives, and the considerable dowry that the wife brings with her plays a leading role. Camille is a gentle man, unfortunately keen on the bottle, which has discouraged more than one woman, including Lady Luck, who sprints by and barely skims his life.

Huguette has a thankless build and a grouchy character and has always been bitter, something her dull life does nothing but amplify right to the end. She inherits a series of estates, houses, land, and leased farms. All that is missing is a husband and, above all, a son. Although she is over thirty, she manages to get both *in extremis*.

She is a woman of discipline, particularly when it applies to others, and she accomplishes the miracle of saving her husband from alcoholism and premature death, certainly to thank him for having done his duty and siring a son. But without his liquor, Camille sinks into a depression. It ends only when he dies, an idiotic death due to a poor calculation—more or less the story of his life—when a tree he has just chopped down falls right on top of him.

This is in 1974. There is no neo-rural return to nature—it hasn't been called that yet—here or anywhere else.

Camille leaves his wife with her assets intact—he never had the good fortune to drink them away—and a thirty-year-old son, also intact, named Gaston.

Gaston does not see Madame Villetreix as the harsh woman everyone fears, but as his mother, the only one he will have, the only one he will ever know. And like all other children, he adjusts to her. He is afraid of her, but that can be like some form of affection, or at least a kind of bond.

Gaston is used to his mother's iron rule and never imagines side-stepping it in any way. He was raised to meet Huguette's expectations and needs, and that is what he does. He is a man of duty who cannot even imagine an alternative.

Madame Villetreix decrees that it is useless to continue going to school when you can do honest manual labor and it is pointless to look for a fiancée when you have a mother to keep the house running and put meals on the table.

Gaston has a good-natured, subdued temperament. The three young women he tries to introduce into their lives never manage to pass the stringent checklist drawn up by his mother, and since the widow Villetreix is in perfect health, Gaston gets used to the idea that his life will continue in the same way between television and reheated coffee and a meal every month with the extended family. The meal is an obligation without any charm, because the cousins— they are close cousins—envy the mother's assets, from which the only pleasure she gets is the satisfaction of owning them.

Then September 11, 2001, happens. Everyone remembers. Everyone is focused on that day's event, on the Twin Towers falling, as if nothing else happened that day.

It is, however, that day that will radically change Gaston Villetreix's life.

He wakes up as usual, at six-thirty, prepares the coffee, and looks toward the stairs, a little uncertain when he does not see his mother appear.

Gaston has never transgressed the monumental taboo of entering his mother's bedroom. He has never gone in there, never snooped around.

When he was eight, he had found a sheep that had killed her newborn lamb by lying down on it. This scene has become an-chored in his mind—the idea that mothers have the right of life and death over their children because they have given them life. This unconscious terror is the foundation of his docility.

Huguette sleeping in, a considerable event in itself, lends uncer-tainty to the morning. He lets the chickens out, moves the cows to another pasture, and jokes with the postman who drops off *La Montagne* every day. Gaston tells him that his mother is still sleeping, which is probably only the second time that this has happened in sixty years. The two men laugh and conclude that at ninety every-one has the right to a little rest.

It is, in this case, eternal rest. Lunch hour passes, then the early afternoon news. The first plane hits the World Trade Center, and only then does Gaston tap lightly on his mother's door. Then he knocks louder. He calls out, taking his courage in both hands, be-cause of Huguette's strong character and lashing tongue. He enters the room.

More precisely, he sticks his head through the doorway. He spots his mother's dentures in a glass of water on the night table. He turns his head to see his mother lying with her head back and her mouth open. It looks suspicious. He approaches and touches her shoulder. She is stiff and cold. More so than usual.

He calls Dr. Blanchard's office. The doctor is making rounds. Gaston doesn't think to call his cell phone. Death is not an emergen-cy. He sits down at the kitchen table and waits.

This death is unexpected. Nothing has prepared him to face life alone. He sincerely thought that his mother would outlive him, which, in his way of thinking, is the natural order of things.

At over sixty he is an orphan, just as if he were a small child. He does not cry. He has not been raised that way.

His mother had always taken care of him. She had been strict but fair. In any case, he had always walked a straight line, since the limits of his mother's discontent were random.

It is difficult to imagine what he is thinking while he waits for the doctor.

The only memories he has of his father are those concocted by his mother. She called her dead husband "Poor Camille," using a tone that did little to hide her contempt. "Some people cut off the branch they are sitting on, but poor Camille stood under the tree he'd just cut down," she said of him.

So her meaning was clear when she said, "Poor Gaston, a spit-ting image of his father."

All this explains why Gaston does not have a very high opinion of himself or his capacity to face life head-on.

One thing is for sure, though. He isn't sad as he sits with his elbows on the oilcloth. A small whiff of freedom has reached his nose, waking up a taste for the wider world that he never suspected even existed.

When Olivier first spends time with him after the funeral, he perceives this difference in the old orphan. He likes Gaston, who is a good person, a mild-mannered man attentive to others. He does not want him to end up at the bottom of the well like Étienne. He needs a woman. It is never too late to set up house. Gaston doesn't like the Internet; he is suspicious of it, which puts an end to the idea of using an online dating site.

But he likes the idea of perhaps finding a mate and proves to be unfailingly persistent. He has just discovered the idea of a future. For the very first time, he thinks that he can take an active role in his own life. He has a plan. And he acts on it.

He goes to the town of Aubusson to buy a gray checked wool jacket and a round-trip train ticket to Limoges.

He doesn't like anything about the matrimonial agency. The woman who greets him wears too much makeup and has a smile that's too big and sugary. He doesn't like what he sees in her eyes. Like all other silent people, he knows how to read what lies behind appearances.

That is not where he will find the solution.

One evening no duller than all the others, he is watching the news on television and sees a man with a beard who looks nice enough. He is talking about an organization that is dedicated to defending undocumented immigrants.

This is the second revelation that will open Gaston to the pleasures of life but also lead to his premature end, because, clearly, there is a price to pay for everything in this world.

He sends a note to Daniel with his picture. It isn't such a bad idea. He has something to exchange for what he wants. A woman for legal status.

Myriam sees Daniel's picture and writes to Saint-Jean-les-Bois. Gaston sends her a train ticket and picks her up at La Souterraine, as proud as if he had invented her. And he's clear about the whole idea: marriage, family, all cards on the table.

He has found a woman and is not going to let her go. No obstacle is too big. She stays.

"Myriam wasn't too hot on the idea," Oliver says. "Oh sorry, I mean finding herself in an isolated village with nothing but white folks around and not the happiest people at that, I've got to tell you. But Gaston went for it and how! They tried each other out the first night, and apparently it worked for both of them. Well enough to seal the deal. And the rest followed."

"You don't think she killed him, then. She didn't have any reason to."

"Truthfully? I have no idea. People are mysterious. I like Myriam. She's brave, and life hadn't given her any slack until she met Gaston. Maybe after she tasted it she wanted more. Or perhaps it was an accident. I ate at their place once. I don't know what she put in those stews, but I almost left my tongue behind. There would have been no way to detect poison in that. Gaston? He was so grateful, he would have eaten shoe leather and swooned over it. Do you want some more tea?"

Catherine looks at Olivier, tilting her head.

"You're making this up! Or you're embellishing. There's no way you could know so much."

"He's a storyteller," Louis says. "That's why I wanted you to meet him. Nobody else is capable of painting a more precise picture of things."

Olivier leans back in his large leather armchair and puts his feet on the coffee table. He almost seems to be purring.

Catherine could fall asleep, cradled by a story without an end. The crackling fire, the pungent smell and the warmth of the tea are all strangely familiar. She feels tears welling. Surprised, she straightens up.

"Oh no! What time is it?"

She sees Louis panic.

"We have to go, right away."

Olivier remains calm. He doesn't have a train to miss.

"Next time I'll tell you about Myriam if you want."

Catherine wants.

Louis says that with his stock of stories, Olivier could open an oral library. Olivier turns sheepish. "I like people. And it's a good thing when some trace remains of people's lives, don't you think?"

Yes, yes, Catherine agrees.

She has no desire to leave, and yet she has to catch her train, which she shows forcefully by getting herself to the door, her raincoat on, bag in hand, all in a few seconds, certainly to convince herself of an urgency she doesn't feel.

7

The room is long and soulless, with prairie-flower wallpaper. There is a queen bed, a single bed, and a folded cot. The bathroom has a folding door; there is a laminate table. It is dark outside, and the atmosphere is dreary.

Catherine's mind is in a whirl. She settles for splashing cold water over her face and running her fingers through her hair to smooth it. In any case, she doesn't have a toiletry bag with her. The suit that was so classy yesterday is wrinkled now. The sky is leaden, and the flickering fluorescent lights seem ready to go out at any moment.

It is six-thirty in the morning, and a contrite Louis is waiting for her in the breakfast room, which is empty but open.

Louis isn't happy just taking her to the bus stop and wants to drop her off at La Souterraine. He is the reason she missed her train. It's the least he can do. He is not even sure that there is a train at this time of day.

She thanks him with such a sour voice that the wary reporter moves his chair back to put some distance between them and ignores her, like a kid.

The night before, he had left her and had gone to join his wife and children for dinner. He did not invite her, which she didn't want anyway, but the fact is, he abandoned her in front of a barely defrosted pizza.

Catherine does not want to put up with his death-row look and simply tells him that morning is not her best time of day—well, at least morning before a cup of coffee, whatever time that may be. Things will be better afterward. She doesn't hold a grudge.

Louis leans forward. If she would give him her e-mail address, he will send her his article before it goes to print.

Without answering, she holds up her two hands. Later, please.

"I CAN'T TALK." She thinks it really hard, hoping that her silence will convey the capital letters.

Louis reaches for his coffee with a look of deep concentration and tries to act relaxed, without much success. He is waiting for clemency, which he guesses is improbable, but a man lives on hope.

His playacting is useless, because Catherine stares at her cup and downs three sandwiches, one after the other, that have been improvised with what is on hand: tasteless ham and thin slices of industrial cheese stuck between two slices of floppy white bread. In the mornings she stuffs herself, like a firearm that needs to be fully loaded to shoot properly.

One thing after another. She is finally awake and goes down her mental checklist.

A text message to the office to let them know she will be there in the early afternoon. A look around her room to make sure she hasn't left behind the panties she didn't want to wear again, a pencil that fell from her bag, a loose paper from the file. Then pay her bill, which, she sighs to herself, will not be reimbursed.

So yes, she doesn't hesitate to allow the reporter to carry her computer bag, and she accepts without appearing too grateful the large plastic bag that he has brought for her to carry the case file in, which seems even heavier and more cumbersome than it did yesterday. Yes, Louis Bernier is nice. At least he's that.

When Louis's car takes the third traffic circle before heading toward Limoges, she is in the process of going through the things she needs to do, starting from the moment she sets foot on the platform in Paris at the Gare d'Austerlitz. Since they left the hotel, she has mechanically been remembering the way to the train station.

Louis has tried ten times to ask permission to disturb her, using a long look and noisy silence. She gives in and turns in his direction. Aware of his passenger's surliness, he uses a careful voice, but she is smiling, she hopes with a trace of kindness.

"Do you think you'll be back soon?"

"As often as I can. Of course, I'll let you know. Now that I've seen things, I think it is best that I rent a car."

She does not immediately register her driver's quick response.

"We can lend you one."

Catherine gives him a questioning look. He has a cousin who has a second car, his ex-wife's car, which he never uses, and all Catherine has to do is cover the insurance for the time she uses the car. Oh, and he has friends with a bed and breakfast in Aubusson. He'll take her to see it. That will be less expensive and nicer for her.

Is this his way of apologizing? Apparently not. It's his nature to find solutions for other people's problems.

"Is everyone like this in the Creuse, or just you?"

"What do you mean?"

"Nice, helpful, finding solutions."

"Yes and no. We are defeatists, pessimists, and scandalmongers. And not very reliable."

Her mistake. They both laugh.

"Speaking of people from the Creuse, do you know the judge on my case? A small guy with a mean look?"

"Perret? Did he give you his welcome message?"

"In a way."

"He loves to make fun of people from the capital. Take it as a sign of his sense of humor."

"I prefer your kindness."

She was sincere, and he takes the compliment without any fuss. Silence absorbs them, comfortably this time.

On the train, Catherine thinks that she has perhaps just made a new kind of friendship, one that is strong and reliable. She wonders if it is not the first of its kind in her life and what that possibly says about who she is.

She immediately chooses to dive into her case files, rather than into an oblivion that is familiar and private. Even for her. Especially for her.

Because Olivier immediately replaces Louis in her thoughts, causing a delicious and troubling feeling of something new.

She doubles her focus on her work to avoid thinking about the neo-rural ecologist and disciple of Scheherazade who manages to fill all the available space despite the lawyer's dedicated attempt to be absorbed by her work.

A familiar voice stops her dead in the middle of the train station.

"Can I drop you off somewhere?"

"What are you doing here?"

Cedric Devers is waiting for her. He has managed to get the time and place of her return to Paris from Sophie, a secretary who is not lacking in cunning. It's that charm, always that charm, she thinks, unreasonably irritated with herself for being an enthusiastic victim of it.

She corrects her initial response, sort of.

"I've got my scooter. Thanks."

"Okay, so I'll invite you to lunch."

She turns to face him and looks him in the eye. "Why?"

"I think you know why, as well as I do."

She's familiar with the chemical reaction that goes through her when she is near Devers. Chemistry and nothing else. All they have to do is tangle their bodies long enough to snuff out the sparks. No risk of fire. And she is not expected at the office for another two hours.

She does not have enough respect for him to conceal her impatience to get on with it. This relationship is inconsequential, she tells herself.

Catherine looks at her watch.

"Do you know a decent hotel in the area?"

He is taken aback but tries not to show it. He is trying to keep the score even with this woman, who is unwittingly blowing on old coals, which he won't speak of for fear of being reduced to ashes. A second time.

"We can go to my place," he suggests. "It's not that far."

He lives in the twelfth arrondissement, not far from the Gare de Lyon, in the direction of Daumesnil. He gives her the address and the door code and takes off in a flash, remembering that a good month ago he vowed to clean up his place.

She probably won't care. But he will.

She knows Paris well. He has done his best to go quickly, but he still finds himself face to face with her in front of the porte cochère, and they go in together.

She is preoccupied with thoughts that clearly have nothing to do with him.

He goes up the stairwell first. She answers the phone automatically. He is reassured to hear that the call relates to work. He is already feeling some dominion over her. A bad habit.

She carefully sets down her computer bag, the plastic bag, her handbag, and her raincoat in the entrance hall. She doesn't want to forget anything when she leaves.

She enters the living room, which is pleasant to look at, despite the dust. Catherine doesn't see the socks that are lying around and humiliating Cedric.

Transformed industrial furniture, a lot of metal, untreated wood, magazines piled on the floor, the remains of last night's cocktail, several glasses, and empty bottles. A large bar separates the living room from the kitchen, where chaos of the first order reigns. A door is partly open to another room, the bed undone and in disarray, clothes abandoned on a kilim that still has bright colors.

Catherine takes it all in, without focusing on the details. She smiles at her former client.

"That way?"

It's a question that requires no response, and she's quick to move toward the bedroom. In the doorway, she stops and turns around. He is still standing in the middle of the room, run aground on a foreign and intimidating land.

"Are you coming?"

She takes off her jacket and shoes.

He prays that she does not get entirely undressed, that she does not do all the work.

In fact, she lies down on the bed and politely waits for him to join her, for him to undo the buttons on her shirt one by one, to explore her skin with the palm of his hand, which slips under her belt, discovering her nudity under her pants.

She smiles at his surprise, sighs with ease, and presses against his chest, undressing him with one hand and coaxing him with the other. A kiss finally gives him permission to fulfill her needs first.

Never before has he felt a woman so violently egotistical in her quest for pleasure. She is irresistible and frustrating at the same time. She does not give him any room or time to approach her, to seduce her, to conquer her. There is something virile in Catherine's ardor that troubles him and throws him off, in every sense of the word.

She doesn't hold back when it comes to expressing her climax, and the man's is pale in comparison.

Different women, different trials.

Monique Lemaire, in the Pigalle bistro, closing hour. There is a lassitude in her look underneath turquoise-colored eyelids. Her mouth appears tired and her lips too red. Her body is heavy, her breasts sag, her hips are stretching the seams of her straight skirt. Half undressed, she has pulpy flesh and reddened thighs. She is passive and obedient. Exciting. He starts to groan when they come, one in the other—he doesn't really know which.

He wishes that he had never met Catherine.

He opens his eyes and feels the empty bed.

She closes the door to the bathroom behind her.

He calls out, "Do you have five minutes?"

She calls back, her mouth full of toothpaste, having borrowed his toothbrush, "No. I'm already way too late." Then she adds in a mischievous tone, as if to make up for what she just said, "It was worth it."

And that bothers him. A lot. In a painful change of roles, he finds himself in the position of the barmaid, ready to take root, to plead for the impossible—perfectly reciprocal desire and feelings. He decides to make an offhand response, the opposite of what he feels. He props himself on his pillows and lights a cigarette.

Catherine comes out of the bathroom, freshly brushed, even prettier, a pink blush on her relaxed face, for which he feels responsible. It allows him to recover a little bit of his male dignity.

"Can I have one?"

She takes the cigarette with childish pleasure and allows herself a pause on the edge of the bed to smoke with her lover.

When she gets up to leave, after a distracted kiss on the cheek, he holds onto her hand, a little too firmly.

"You know what you make me think of?"

She looks at him, falling into the green light, the blinding, dangerous green light. She pulls away, but his other hand is on her back. Catherine's thumping heart warns her of danger.

"A redneck who pushes his plate away when he's done eating."

The moment becomes safe again. She disengages herself gently and straightens her skirt.

"That metaphor is not a nice commentary on your taste."

She turns on her heels, gathers her things, and goes through the door and down the stairs, listening for the sound of an open door, footsteps coming behind her, a furious man pouncing on her to make her pay. God knows for what. Cedric is not a nice guy. She is in a position to know that. The door remains closed, the stairwell silent, and her anxiety slips away by the time she arrives at her scooter. He's got a bit of a paunch, but he's a good lover.

8

Cedric leans against the door to avoid leaving and then goes to the window to watch for her. Catherine glances toward the window, takes out her helmet, puts her things in the top box, climbs on her scooter, starts it, and disappears around the corner.

He must not see her again.

He calls Paul at the agency, and with a hoarse voice announces that he has caught a cold. He's burning up with a fever.

He needs some vacation. That will be the best solution. He'll leave without giving into the temptation. He foresees danger. He's no match for it.

He gets dressed quickly, goes downstairs, takes his car, and leaves Paris. He drives quickly to keep his memories at bay.

As if he hadn't known that he was playing with fire. They are the same. He is the one who has changed.

You go from one rough sketch to another, and then one day, you meet the original. But which one is the original?

He pops in a CD of Massive Attack and ups the sound. A massive attack, a virulent attack. He hums the rhythm of the songs he knows by heart.

How old is he? All of his friends have minivans to hold their families and mortgages on their apartments. Husbands, fathers settled into life, following the path followed by successive generations. They don't drive at breakneck speed listening to teenage music.

He parks in front of the castle in Saint-Germain-en-Laye and walks into the woods, deep into the woods. He hopes that by tiring his body, he will knock out his brain. And then, too late, as if it were today, at that precise instant, time abolished, he hears, "Let me introduce you to the doctor's wife."

He had seen her from a distance, and he saw himself as the hero in Flaubert's novel *Sentimental Education*.

The weather is primeval. The air glistens with life, myriad midges flying in chaos, driven wild by springtime. The swirling river gives a silvery sheen to the slippery rocks on which he and Arthur are maintaining an uncertain balance.

Arthur is fly-fishing. Cedric pretends to want to learn. Another initiation is awaiting him.

He is the first to see the graceful silhouette in a flowery dress, legs uncovered, feet in the icy water. Her hair is tied back carelessly with a large tortoise-shell barrette, showing off a poetic neck, slightly bent over the hand that is skimming the water without ever catching the fleeting current. The more precious the moment, the more precisely you look at it. The senses have intuition. Don't lose any of it, not the tiniest bit, because later you will only be able to relive the feeling by remembering the details. The changing reflections of shadow and light add to the translucence of her skin. There are thin golden rings in her earlobes that the sun isolates with a sharp glint. A straw hat carelessly hangs on a branch. Her knobby little-girl knees are bare. Her skirt is raised to her thighs, which are covered with fine drops of water

She's a nymph who will disappear the second he looks away.

She is absorbed in some daydream that cuts her off from the rest of the world.

Arthur, completely involved in his fishing, flicks his wrist, the long line waving above his head, skillfully missing obstacles in its search for the little creature it will separate from the liquid element when it rises with a small leap before diving back into the eddies.

Suddenly, Cedric sees the line spinning in the direction of the apparition, and he grabs his friend's arm. Arthur yells out a reproach and then, following Cedric's look, discovers the young woman. He instantly smiles, surprised and joyful.

"Cedric, let me introduce you to the doctor's wife."

She does not even start, turning toward them with a face the color of ivory, the outline erased by wisps of hair that have escaped from her barrette. She pushes a rebellious lock of hair behind her ear. Her eyes are the color of the running water, and that is all he sees, the only thing he remembers, that face producing an effect of blinding rapture. He is overcome, his mind goes blank, and he becomes stupid and mute.

There's a smile on her full lips, but her eyes hold a poignant sadness.

"Arthur! You mistook me for a trout."

"You're perfectly safe! As soon as I catch them, I let them go free again."

"Those trout are lucky."

She extends a hand, asking for help as she tries to wade over to them. He hurries toward her, slips, and falls flat in the water.

Arthur, tangled up in his fishing tackle, is laughing so hard, he can't help, and she is the one who wades through the water and extends the helping hand that Cedric could not offer.

She is only slightly older than they are. Married. That is all that he registers. She and Arthur share some small talk. He remains star-struck and just stares at her. Then he can no longer enjoy this bedazzlement, because Arthur insists that they get back to the car as quickly as possible, before he catches his death of cold.

He says those exact words: "catch your death."

Love stories always end badly.

Love is a hoax.

Long afterward, he says to himself that on that day he quite simply began to weave the threads of a fiction.

Perhaps not on that exact day.

Perhaps it began on the day she came looking for him.

It is the following Friday at the market in Felletin. He is reading the paper at an outside table at the Grand Café, waiting for Arthur's mother, who comes by at regular intervals to deposit her purchases at his feet.

"No, don't move, stay there, read your paper."

He does not resist

She is alone again. The young mother, the young married woman who moved to the village two or three years ago appears suddenly in the form of a shadow, this time between him and the sun.

She holds out her hand.

"Are you alone?"

His voice had changed long ago, but he has a hard time getting any sound out, and what does come out is hoarse; he is embarrassed. A little humor. He knows how to be funny when there is nothing at stake.

"I fell in the water, and Arthur ended up with a cold."

"Life is so unfair! Can I sit down?"

He jumps up, nearly tipping his chair over, and goes to get a free chair from a nearby table. She has a barely perceptible accent.

"I feel a little bit responsible. You slipped because you were trying to help me."

"And it's Arthur who's suffering the consequences! Everything's fine."

He can't believe his luck and worries that his friend's mother will come out of nowhere to interrupt this unexpected tête-à-tête. He has thought about her constantly for the past week, discreetly asking his friend about her. Not discreetly enough, though, because his friend has lectured him.

"She is certainly the prettiest woman in the region, but she is married to a public figure who may not be from here, but nevertheless. Here, everyone knows everything. She has no room to maneuver, even if she were to be interested in a pimply kid like you. She's got a baby to take care of and..."

"She's unhappy."

"That's what you think! Don't start making things up. You read too many novels. You don't have to fall in love with a woman just because you can't have her."

Cedric realizes that he has gotten lost on the way. He is surrounded by nothing but trees. He can't hear any cars that would indicate a nearby road. He thought he knew this forest by heart, but it has no landmarks. He left the path, and this is what happens when you let yourself be sucked up by a past that no longer has any reality to it.

The story of his life.

How many times had Arthur accused him of fleeing reality, by which he meant the present, of always being preoccupied with yesterday or tomorrow?

It was his fault. What did he want? To start over again with a clean slate, everything erased and mended. Including himself. Why wouldn't that be possible?

And perhaps one day to talk, to free himself.

"You remember that big curly-haired baby, the poor little orphan? She's a lawyer now. In Paris. She works for Renaud, a friend of my father. Her name is Maître Catherine Monsigny."

Small world.

She could have become a cop to find her mother's killer. After all, she was the only witness.

Apparently, trauma creates memory blocks that remain buried until they rise to the surface. Isolated. Making no sense.

She did not recognize him. That was for sure.

Should he make sure?

That would be so sweet. Life never serves you up the same dish twice. This is like having a second chance. A second chance to throw his life away?

It is damned tempting!

He feels like taking action. Some sort of action to avoid thinking.

In the meantime, he needs to find a way out. There is always a way out. And not necessarily a fatal one.

9

All afternoon, Catherine is a live wire of good humor, which she spreads throughout the law firm's Haussmann-style office building.

She shows her boss the stories in the press she has been reading, which will probably serve no purpose, because it looks like it will be a closed court. He thinks this is unfortunate for the client, who, paradoxically, needs the publicity. She listens to Maître Renaud with a distracted ear. The closed court means no reporters, and no reporters mean an opportunity lost to pitch them the Villetreix case.

"You have a guy who goes through three years of therapy without ever talking about his pedophilia with his shrink. He says, 'I was locked up.' How true. You have a public figure whose political career, social milieu, and family context bind him hand and foot. The day he's arrested, he confesses everything, even what he has not yet been accused of. He has been living in the fear of being discovered. When it happens, he's relieved. Going to jail has played its role, obliging him to face reality."

"Finally freed, but facing an entirely different prison."

"Catherine, are you planning to take my place in court?"

Renaud smiles as he says that, not expecting an answer. He is used to testing his arguments on her. She has good reflexes and serves as a sounding board. She is like a young filly that hesitates between submissive respect and thundering opposition. She could be using him to work out her Electra complex, if she has one. Her mother has been dead for many years, so there was no competition for the father's love. Her father. A booster shot of reality. Renaud is well aware that she is seductive and seduced, of course, but she is not for him. It is useful to make that a mantra. The daughter of a friend of a friend—who could be the daughter he never had. He will never have. The ambiguity of that makes him smile. He sends Catherine away, and to complete the barricade he is building against his urges, he calls his wife to ask her to join him on the Grands Boulevards for the 8 p.m. showing of that romantic comedy she would love to see, and he would not.

He returns to his notes with a clear conscience.

Catherine knows that no comment means he is satisfied with her work, and she sighs with satisfaction. Practically speaking, even though she hates it, she is dependent on his approval. She wants to impress him, to astonish him.

Not on his own cases, though. That would be idiotic.

But with the Villetreix case.

In the twenty minutes she has spent with the boss, the pile of files on her desk has doubled in height. She knocks on Sophie's door, which is unusually closed, and sticks her head in.

"Are they in order of priority?"

"They are all of equally high priority."

"Fantastic. Hey, were you the one who had Cedric Devers on the phone?"

"Yes. Did everything work out? He was very sorry to harass you, but apparently he was worried about some procedural error."

"Nothing less than that!"

"It was nonsense?"

"A pretext. No problem."

And she leaves humming, realizing she is doing it only when she runs into a colleague who tries a benevolent smile out on her. "Ah, you are in love!"

"In fact, not at all! Otherwise I wouldn't be singing."

Joy makes you egotistical. Lucie Bois, aka Maître Raven because of her scratchy voice, has burned her life out taking care of her sick mother. She never goes to court but collects information about all kinds of criminal cases, the media, and case law. She is an encyclopedia and has a prodigious memory. It seems as though love is not written on her road map, and yet she dreams of it, because you have to dream about what you don't know, or else life just shrinks away.

Catherine is radiant, feeling somewhat idiotic and momentarily very happy with her answer. No, love is not her thing, and the day she falls in love, she is sure she'll put on a black mourning dress, she'll take a cold shower, and then she'll take a sedative. But for now, her body is jubilant. Yes, Cedric could do the trick for a while yet, if he didn't take up too much space.

"The next time…" Olivier had expressed a desire to see her again, a certitude that he would.

She shakes her head. The countryside, the feeling, the fire, the solitude—a tiny life. "That's for others," she says to herself.

It is already eight when she stops at the Vietnamese takeout, where she orders shrimp, rice, and fried vegetables with a hot soup. Ten minutes later, she is in her pajamas, covered with body cream, in front of the entire investigation of the Villetreix case, a map of the Creuse unfolded at her left and on her right the dinner that she has heated in the microwave.

At three in the morning, Catherine is halfway through. She is keeping the promise she has made to herself to read the whole thing in order, in detail, with a notepad in hand to write down what she finds interesting in this first reading. She is deep into the autopsy report, but she doesn't understand the terminology. She will ask around.

She stops when her mind makes a connection with the death of Madame Villetreix, the mother. Just as he was with the son, Dr. Blanchard is the one who signed the death certificate with the same diagnosis of cardiac arrest.

The old family doctor made do with a succinct report. He didn't have any more reason to imagine a suspicious death than he did with Gaston.

Gaston was the prime witness. But he is dead. Perhaps he said something to his friend Olivier.

Catherine pretends not to notice that she is collecting excuses to go back and see the neo-rural dude.

What about exhuming the mother for an autopsy?

Her thoughts run wild, imagine that both mother and son were poisoned in the same way. Because Myriam had not even entered Gaston's life at the time, she would be automatically exonerated.

No, not automatically. It's worth digging into.

Her boss's warning comes back to her, and she chases the thought away. If she wants to impress him, she'll have to risk disobeying him.

The September 11 coincidence is interesting. Gaston and Myriam both recovered their freedom on the same day. Perhaps she'll be able to play on that note.

It is difficult to evaluate Gaston's wealth. In the countryside, people guard their assets. Paradoxically, those assets are often more virtual than real. The real price when sold can be less than the estimated price.

What about the gold digger? In six years, the docile son and his diabolical wife had sold one farm to colleagues and a barn to some English people. They sold well. One hundred thousand euros. The couple spent fourteen thousand euros a year more than their usual income that, until then, had been enough to cover day-to-day expenses. There's the rub. The money had been spent, if you will, on absolutely nothing. A trip to the seaside, frivolous decorations for the house, and clothes for the wife.

Yes, the clothes.

Catherine keeps in mind the statements made by the infamous cousins, who filed the charges. Two Villetreix couples. The two brothers, aged sixty-five and sixty-eight, a mason and an electrician, joined forces to build a prosperous business. The women did the accounts and the secretarial work. A good arrangement.

And they were in agreement when they saw the black woman arrive.

"It's crazy to get married at Gaston's age, when you've always been a bachelor. And it's not because she's black. We are not racist. She can't make us believe that she fell in love with an old guy like Gaston. He never had what it takes to please the ladies. Even when he was young. Okay, okay, he was always a joker, and not the last one to dance with the grandmothers, but this wasn't funny. It was ridiculous. At first, Gaston wanted to spend some money, but he took after his mother. The natural side of him came back, and Myriam was not getting what she wanted."

They also explain that they are sure she was a good-for-nothing, a whore even. They had seen it for themselves. One night, in a lit room, they had seen the African woman dressed in a bra, with a cloth wrap around her wriggling hips, made up as if she were going out. And the pharmacist had suggested that the newlywed had gotten a prescription for Viagra. He couldn't keep up with his wife, and she could have gotten him to swallow anything—even cyanide.

Their theory is that Gaston had closed the purse strings and that Myriam didn't like it.

"She didn't get married to live modestly in a plain house, particularly since she did everything. Gaston didn't have a house cleaner. There's nothing to say there; she kept the place spotless. You can tell she was a maid. But that doesn't mean she liked doing it."

Catherine makes a note to see Dr. Blanchard.

And then she remembers Renaud's comment about checking the marriage.

They really did get married in Saint-Jean-les-Bois. It was the mayor who married them. At the time, that was the same Blanchard.

Wedding or no wedding, Gaston had prepared a will giving Myriam everything.

Catherine makes another note. "Check what they used to verify the undocumented immigrant's identity."

There are so many sides to this story, Catherine feels overwhelmed. She knows that it has never been a question of her dealing with the entire case alone and that she can count on Renaud. But she makes it a point of honor to cover as much ground as she can, as best she can. Deep inside, and with no witnesses, she wonders if she will be up to the task. A life is in play, after all, a woman's future.

She throws her Asian dinner leftovers into the garbage. She puts her scattered papers away and closes the file.

Her finger follows the meandering river on the map—what is it called? The Gartempe. What a strange name. She is tired. She would be happy to skip brushing her teeth.

She stands in front of the mirror in the bathroom, pushing the toothbrush right and left, top and bottom, in the back. It was a battle her father fought every morning and night.

10

It's cold when she gets out of the plastic tub in the large bathtub. The bathroom isn't heated well. She exaggerates the chattering of her teeth, because it bangs in her ears and mouth, and she likes the sound. It gives her the shivers, and she continues, even when the big towel, heated on the radiator, wraps around her, and her mother's arms surround her and rub until her skin turns all pink. She cries out for her to stop, stop, that hurts, even when it's not true. It doesn't hurt; it makes her happy.

Her mother says that on the phone. "You make me happy, nothing but happy."

But she's talking to someone else, and the words are branded, sizzling, in her memory. Then they are covered up by many other memories of events that are more or less important.

So why do they reappear tonight?

Catherine shakes her head. Did she invent them?

The words bother her, even in her memory, because they were not meant for the husband or for the child. She is sure of that. Just as she knew when she was that little girl that those were words she should not have heard and should not have understood.

She rinses her mouth and looks in the mirror.

What is happening to her? Until now, she has followed her father's instructions, and not only for brushing her teeth. Don't think about it. Forget. Memory is like a labyrinth. Venture into it, and you risk getting lost.

Could she have memories of her mother? She doesn't know of any, except for the last walk, and now they're coming up everywhere. There's no accent. If she remembered real words, they would have a hint, ever slight, of an accent.

Her fatigue keeps her from sleeping.

She hears her mother's screams as soon as she closes her eyes. Then they are transformed into smothered laughter. It's really strange. Nightmares are often really strange.

She has dropped her cuddly cloth, and she will never get it back. The forest is menacing. She will never cross the clearing. The solution is on the other side, on the other edge. Unattainable.

The telephone rings. It sounds like it is inside her ear, and Catherine has the feeling that she is stuck in a repeating image. That would be the ultimate nightmare. A series of events that repeats itself endlessly, without any beforehand or any afterward. Time stuck, keeping any story from developing.

She checks the time before answering, convinced that it is four in the morning, because she hasn't been able to sleep and has no feeling of rest in her mind or in her sore body.

"Kate? I didn't wake you, did I?"

Immediately she takes it on herself to speak in a clear, distinct voice to spare herself her father's self-flagellation, "My goodness, I woke you, so sorry, really I'm sorry. I'll call back." He feeds the childhood guilt reflex. "No, Dad, you never bother me. You are everything I have, everything I love," she almost responds.

"Not at all, my mouth is full of toothpaste. Wait a second, I'll rinse and be right back."

She rushes into the bathroom, runs a washcloth over her face, drinks from the faucet, takes a deep breath. Her lie reflex makes her smile. Yes, Dad, I brush my teeth every morning and night. She gets back on the phone.

"I was worried when you didn't call me."

"I don't call you every day, Dad."

"No, but this was your first big trip for your job and…"

"In fact, I've been going nonstop since I got back."

"Of course, I understand."

His ritual sentence that means just the opposite. "I do not understand that you do not have two minutes for your father, who will take any crumbs that you deign to throw him."

Catherine remains calm. In any case, she has been reared never to raise her voice. Keep control. Stay calm. Emotional responses should be controlled, lest they overflow, heaving up debris like a tidal wave.

"Listen, it went well. I stayed an extra night, because of a reporter."

She hears him clear his throat. There they are, back in familiar territory.

"It is not what you think, Dad. Your daughter is not a hussy. No, it was a reporter full of useful information and contacts. Adorable. Married. Kids. Not my type. On my honor and conscience."

"Of course. And other than this reporter, you didn't meet anyone?"

"Why do you ask me that?"

"I don't know. Something in your voice maybe."

She's fifteen years old, in lycée. She comes home at seven for-ty-five because in her house, you have to be there for dinner at eight, even though you don't eat until nine.

She spends five minutes on the sidewalk at the corner of her street to calm her heart and let her coloring return, both of which have been disturbed by an hour of frenetic flirting with Thibaut, a good-looking guy in her class. She will get rid of him after she has used him, because he is too romantic, but that is another story. For the moment, her insides are all turned upside down, unexpectedly and deliciously.

She turns the key, enters, and hangs up her coat. Her father is reading the paper in the living room under the single lit lamp. That too is usual, familiar.

She smiles, not too much. "Are we having dinner on time tonight?"

"Who were you with?"

The question, asked naturally, is enough to throw the teenager off. Should she tell him or not? She actually feels like an adulterous wife. Does he know? Could he know? Should she lie or not? Should she stick to the lie, no matter what?

Yes.

"I was working with Alexandra. Like I said I would be. Why?"

"Oh, nothing. I was just wondering. Mrs. Rocard made us stuffed tomatoes."

"Yum."

"Go wash your hands."

What does he want her to wash her hands of? Is she the one who imagines the double entendre, or is he the one who puts it there? The fact is that every time a boy or man crosses her path, her father is on guard. It's as though he has a sixth sense.

Over the years, she has learned to affirm with conviction the exact opposite of what has happened, a practice that is useful in her job.

The problem is, she has never been sure that she has fooled her father.

"I met three clients, a clerk, a train ticket inspector, a presiding judge. Not bad for two days, even for a sex monger like me."

He laughs. She loves it when he laughs. Shared laughter is one thing that bonds them. One of the rare things.

Dr. Monsigny continues to sit by the phone once he hangs up.

He is shaved and dressed. The breakfast dishes are washed and dried. The apartment is spotless. He can't seem to sleep past five in the morning, and the days are long. To fill them, he arranges daily tasks. He reads a lot, but he no longer finds that novels resonate with his life. He feels out of place in those exotic worlds where people feel, live, suffer, fight, and conquer. What's the point?

Now he prefers books about history or economics, which have the advantage of requiring a lot of concentration, a way to escape the real world.

He knows that Catherine has not slept well. He has never been fooled by her white lies. She has her mother's voice, her mother's face, her mother's attitudes, her mother's laugh. He never knows if it is a blessing or a curse. She is the living proof of love that was experienced and shared. And a reminder that it was torn away from him.

Catherine had already developed the habit of working late into the night when she was a student. He would call her in the morning before going to his office and would kick himself when he heard her flat, uncertain voice that betrayed the fatigue of a night that was too short.

He missed her too much after she moved to Paris. He would always miss her. He would always miss them—mother and daughter. He was born under a sign of solitude, with a losing ascendant.

He had been an average doctor. He had accomplished nothing that was vital or essential to justify his time on earth. He wanted to believe that he would join his spouse in another world, where they would be sheltered under the same lotus, in the Chinese tradition. Surely she loved him as much as he loved her.

Would she have married him otherwise? Wasn't she obliged to marry him? She didn't have a choice. Yes, you always have a choice. He had no regrets. He had made her happy.

Well, at least he had offered her the life she had dreamed of.

Sometimes he believes that they played roles. They were like mannequins in a shop window. They offered up an idealized image for others to see. But really, it was genuine.

When the little one was in bed, they would stay up in the living room. Violet would read poetry to him, and he would talk about his patients. He spent all day looking for funny stories, gossip, and anecdotes that could feed their evening conversations and entertain her.

He knew nothing about her previous life when he married her, and his ignorance has eaten away at him. She said that her childhood was a bad melodrama and that she had no love story in Clermont. He didn't press. She was grateful for his discretion, which was only an expression of his fear and insecurity. The trust she had in him was like cement, he reassures himself. She said, "My life began with you and Kate."

If Catherine had gone to school in Bordeaux, he would have taken advantage of her being close by. She was running away from him. Yet he had always been discreet and undemanding.

Did she run away because she found him boring and sad and invasive and dependent? He is surprised by the flash of pure hate that bolts through him. What did she expect of him? Women ask for the impossible, and then they betray you.

He looks at the time. He's going to buy the paper and get coffee at the café on the square. He has an hour filled. Afterward, he'll fix the shower that has been leaking, and it will be time for the news and lunch.

A story from twenty years ago should not interfere with her daughter's life. He has not protected her all these years in vain. He will do anything so that the past remains where it belongs. Forgotten.

He is not bothered by a foreshadowing of something, but instead by the return of a memory. He did everything he could so that nothing...

As quickly as it appears, the breeze of the past dissipates into the flow of the day and not as a result of his willpower.

11

After one of Catherine's clients appears in court in Nanterre, she jumps onto the regional express train. She looks at her watch every five minutes as she sprints to the courthouse. She stops herself just short of running into the imposing person of Maître Renaud. He looks noble, dressed in his impeccable robe, wearing perfectly shined Westons, his fingernails manicured. The only thing he does not try to control is his hair. It's deliberate, as it gives him an impressive leonine look.

Well, a look that impresses Catherine, at least.

It's just like her to arrive like Jerry the mouse in front of this old cat, who gives her a dark look while holding back a smile.

"I was afraid I'd be late!"

"The trial is starting late," Renaud says. "The media is here. In the end, they did not ask for a closed trial. I don't like this case. I don't have a good feeling about this fellow."

So now he has feelings about his clients? The trial lawyer continues talking in his rogue tone, as if it were her fault. "He's perverted. Deep down, he's a pervert."

"Do you mean he's dangerous?" Catherine asks.

"He's a pedophile, and like many of his kind, he pretends to consider that bad, but in his mind, he can't find anything to reproach in his actions."

"Do you mean that if you help free him, he will start over again?"

Renaud shrugs, annoyed, and says, "Evidently."

"And, um, is this a problem for your conscience?"

She can see that she is annoying him—he does nothing to hide it. But she needs to know.

"No, I do my job the best I can. That is why he is paying me, and paying me well. It is the state's job to get him convicted. May the best man win. Listen, think of it like jousting in the Middle

Ages. Two knights in armor throw themselves at each other with a lance in hand. All you have to do is convince yourself that God supports innocence, and then the result of the combat represents an irrefutable judgment. A court does not seek truth. That is perhaps the work of the police. As for us, we fight, more or less cleanly, and the one who wins is the good guy. Let's go."

Sometimes Catherine would like to be a small part of him, to follow him through the twists and turns of his reasoning and his knowledge. In the meantime, she follows him closely, whispering to him that she will be in the first row, there, to which he nods. Catherine is not hoping for more. The reporters will be able to see how close she is to Renaud. She sits down slowly, giving the media a friendly smile.

She hasn't eaten all day and is starting to get hungry. Great. This is hardly the right time.

Around her, she sees Hermès scarves, Loden coats, cashmere sweaters, and strings of pearls that announce the glitterati, the defendant's world before his fall. Today he is alone in the docket reserved for the accused, and despite his well-cut dark blue suit, his pale gray shirt, and his elegant tie, he is excluded. He has crossed the line. He undoubtedly has lost weight during pre-trial detention, and his features are graceless. He seems astonishingly calm, almost serene, and very attentive.

The witness who stands up to give his testimony is sixteen years old. He has a chubby face and is relaxed despite the setting, his straight blond hair falling around his neck. He has the ease of his social upbringing. When he mentions his assailant, he looks over to the accused without any sign of discomfort.

Yes, Mr. Lunz offered to give him private classes so he could get to the top of his class. Yes, he was flattered. Everything was normal at the beginning, and then one day on the sofa, the adult put his arm around his shoulder. He can't remember how they got to that point, but in the end, they were naked, and the teacher was rubbing himself against his stomach. Yes, until they both ejaculated. No, there was no penetration or attempted rape.

His tone is calm, factual. He shows no discomfort at the inquisitive questions asked by the presiding judge.

The defendant does not deny anything. In fact, he acknowledged everything as soon as the cops arrived at his place, and the court has commended him for this. He expresses himself well, but his words are cold, without a shadow of emotion. This is undoubtedly the perversity Maître Renaud mentioned, an inability to consider the other person as anything but an object of his desire.

Catherine has a fleeting thought about Cedric Devers. Could there be something perverse about the relationships she has with men? Is she like Lunz, just a consumer of flesh?

Lunz couldn't resist. Now he has mentioned the word love. The word that is supposed to erase all crimes. "I made love to him." One word too many. Even the judges squirm like schoolgirls. Nobody wants the word love associated with deviance. Catherine, with all of her lack of experience, says to herself that love is the most used hide-all. "I loved him so much I strangled him." "I loved him, and he loved it when I caressed him and fondled him." That's enough to make the judges even more cynical, perched as they are on their raised seats.

It's been two hours already. The plaintiffs' counsels are hard at work. It's never-ending, all the more so because everyone—the two children's attorneys, the attorney representing the school where Lunz did his dirty work, the attorney of a children's defense organization—is saying the same thing.

Catherine listens only more or less attentively, but she never once takes her eyes off Renaud. Sometimes he seems absent, his way of showing that the words being spoken are not important. Then suddenly he straightens up, alert, and walks to the bar, getting ready to speak when the judge asks, "Does the defense have any questions?"

Renaud takes his time, looks at the young people and the judge. Everyone is waiting, and then all he does is wave his hand in denial and say, "No. Thank you, Madame the Judge, no questions." And then he sits down.

But when he finally does ask a question of the school principal, who is evasive, he is unyielding, brutal, and direct, with the look of an inquisitor. Subtly, he shifts the guilt to the authorities in charge, to the head of the school.

Catherine takes advantage of the break to join a group of crime reporters smoking in the courtyard. Catherine asks for a light and introduces herself. She tells them that she did not assist Maître Renaud on this case, but she came to learn and prepare herself for her first major felony case in March.

Any slight interest dissipates when she mentions Guéret. It is too far away and too rural. She continues in a perky tone, telling them about the legitimate marriage between an undocumented African immigrant and a retired farmer. Only one reporter, from the daily

Le Parisien, pretends to be interested. She manages to get his card, then puts on a busy look and leaves.

She says to herself that this is just an appetizer but notes that the card doesn't have the reporter's cell phone number on it. She digs through her bag as she climbs the steps but can't find any chocolate or even an old cookie. It's time for the concluding remarks now, and she is afraid her stomach will start grumbling.

While the courtroom fills up, she catches the eye of the reporter from the *Le Parisien,* then hopes he won't try to pick her up.

The defendant is unpleasant. The only emotion he shows is self-pity. The children have been courageous, yet they have not managed to budge Catherine from her basic belief in the fundamental guilt of the victims. These kids are far from being innocent creatures. They were flattered by the special attention they got from their teacher, and they certainly used their power of seduction to keep their status as teacher's pet.

It's time, and Catherine grows nervous for Renaud, as though he were a venerated star about to go on stage. She worries that he will mess up his lines, make a mistake, or bore the audience.

Renaud stands up and pauses as if to meditate on everything that has just been said. Then he looks up, addresses the court respectfully, and in a powerful voice announces his client's undeniable, established, decisive guilt.

This disconcerting announcement is followed by a defense and a rapid illustration of the defense's role. In view of the general fatigue and knowing that there are other cases to follow, the lawyer affirms that he will be as quick as possible but that, of course, nobody in the room, least of all him, would like to see the sacred and inalienable role of the defense be cut short

He bases his argument on the defendant's crushing solitude, how a deaf and blind family forced him into silence, how a social class preferred cowardly denial to confronting reality and truth, how his superiors shirked their responsibilities. Little by little, as if Renaud were removing the peel from a fruit, he creates an unexpected sympathy for a man, who, in the end, kind of deserves it. And he does not hesitate to mention, harshly, what seems to be a form of parental complicity. Finally, he hands the decision entirely over to the court, committing it to the judges' infinite wisdom, without asking for anything but a fair verdict.

Catherine immediately decides to work on her voice. Hers is too weak. How can you have such a resonant voice without flexible, well-muscled vocal cords?

She rises with everyone else when the judges leave to deliberate. She goes outside, descends the monumental staircase, and takes refuge in the courtyard. All of a sudden, panic grips her. She sees herself confronting a jury of her peers and kicks herself for alerting the media, worried it will be a public fiasco. She lights a cigarette and sees the reporter from *Le Parisien* charge down the stairs. Furthermore, he sees that she actually has a lighter. She feels ridiculous.

He walks in her direction. She puts on a distant look. He has a favor to ask. She relaxes. It is late, and he has to leave. Could she send him the verdict by text?

By all means. She records his number on her phone, congratulating herself for not being all that awkward after all.

She hears a familiar voice calling her. "You're not going to wait for the verdict. It is late, and it's cold out."

"If you don't mind, I would rather wait."

He smiles.

"Okay. I'll take you to Caro's afterward," Renaud says. That is the bistro where he always goes to eat oysters when he gets out of court. It is the first time he has offered to take her, and with the oysters there will be bread and butter, which will fill her up. Life is full of simple solutions.

Renaud walks away with a colleague from the prosecution who has come to congratulate him. To compose herself, she takes out her cell phone and calls Cedric Devers. Two rings and a message, "Cedric Devers. I'm not here. Leave your number, and I'll get back to you as soon as possible."

The message needs to be short. There's time for two sentences, and then a beep. "Catherine Monsigny," she says. "Too bad." She hangs up and bites her lip. How stupid. "Too bad."

Two rings mean he saw her number come up on the screen and decided not to answer. Asshole. She straightens up and lifts her chin. Jerk. She's going to have dinner with someone a whole lot more interesting than he is.

It is ten-thirty at night when the court comes back after deliberating. The judges look tired after a day that has been too long and is not yet over.

Lunz stays in prison. Renaud manages to get his sentence shortened by a year, but the defendant's shock is visible. He has already imagined himself free. Hope. Hope always tricks everyone, even the bastards.

Catherine waits for her boss, who is whispering some comforting words to his client. That is part of the job. The hallway is emptying. The mother of one of the victims, wearing a kilt, a twin set, and a religious medallion, is waiting. Catherine readies herself, wondering how to keep her boss from having to face a scene. He doesn't seem all that bothered. He stops in front of the woman, looking attentive and available. She says in a formal voice that she didn't want to approach him before his final remarks, because it wouldn't have been correct. She preferred to wait. In fact, the two of them know each other. Well, not directly. She went to school with his sister, Isabelle Renaud.

He is kind and courteous, interested in what she has to say. He shows no real surprise. "Oh yes, you went to Passy with her. What is your maiden name? I'll tell her I saw you."

Renaud takes Catherine's arm and walks away with her quickly, whispering, "That's the best one yet."

Catherine remembers the harsh even violent words he has used to denounce the world his client comes from, which used to be his and is still the world his family lives in. He is such a free thinker, she has a hard time imagining him coming from a God-fearing, wealthy Catholic family.

As if he were reading her thoughts, he laughs and says, "Yes, you can politely detest the world you come from. At the beginning, you love it, because you think you know it, and then one day, that is no longer the case. I was a student when a young woman found me to tell me that she was my half-sister. My father had lived a double life for fifteen years."

Renaud goes quiet for a moment, and Catherine does not dare ask anything.

"After fifteen years, he must have started to find that tiring, and he cut things off with his mistress, leaving her to fend for herself," Renaud says. "He was an important judge. People respected him. I hope you like oysters."

12

There is an elegant balance of words and pictures. There is a picture of a man floating above a hill, representing the unsteady economy and upturned values. The image grabs the eye but must not distract readers from the text. In the meeting with the magazine team, they focused mainly on the text-image ratio. They wanted to make a radical change to the layout. At the same time, they were afraid of attempting anything too out of the box.

She called him. He was right not to answer. Danger. He must keep repeating it. "Catherine Monsigny equals danger."

"Too bad." What a strange message. Too bad we will not meet up, that this story will not take place? Or too bad you're not there. I will call back?

She did leave a message. That is a fact. It was ambiguous enough to allow him to decide. It is up to him to call back or not.

He reduces the image on the screen. If he frames it, separating the paragraphs with a heading in color, with a good question or an intriguing lead-in like, "What is money? Where does it go?" No, that doesn't work. He is tired.

Cedric pulls up his English competitors' website. He tries to imagine the layout they are going to propose. They are all the rage, but French readers do not have the same visual habits or the same taste for what works in English. The bid specifies daring. But how far can he go?

He is obsessed with this woman. The woman from before. He does not know her. She consumes his thoughts, because he lost his opportunity to know her. It is dangerous to try to find her again in Catherine, whom he cannot seem to separate from death. He went because, otherwise, the frustration of not having tried would have killed him. Yet this is the vainest quest imaginable.

He thought he had gotten over her. He had every reason to believe that. He paid dearly for the cure, so it had better be effective. No, he would not call her. It seemed so innocent, so pure, and so inevitable.

The café in Felletin on Friday morning. Is the weather nice? Yes, the weather is perfect, of course. While he is still looking for something to say, she asks him, out of the blue, "Do you have an address?"

He has just told her that he is leaving for Paris the next day. She can't hide that it upsets her. "We could write each other. You can tell me what you're doing. I could tell you…"

Arthur's mother arrives, at just the wrong time, and when she sees the young woman exclaims, "What a nice surprise."

She greets her coolly. They are not close. Good.

"I was just saying to our friend that you are sure to meet nice people at the market in Felletin."

Cedric has just entered another world, a clandestine world of concealment. Here they are, bound by a secret even before they have anything to hide. So, they are going to have something to hide. The idea of a married woman with a child is exhilarating.

The two women talk about uninteresting things he doesn't listen to. He is leaving tomorrow and will probably not see her again. When he speaks, his tone is so unnatural, he's afraid he'll be uncovered immediately, "In any case, I can't wait to come back. That is, if anybody wants me around."

He's quite pleased with that sentence, which is really intended for her, if she would want him around. Arthur's mother smiles and says that would be a pleasure.

"Yes, that would be lovely," she says with her charming touch of an accent and her Anglicisms. "Oh, I will give you my address, if you would kindly send me the specifics about the book we were discussing. We are ravenous for news here."

As she talks, she writes down her address in small, precise letters on the receipt from the vegetable stand and then hands it to him.

This piece of crumpled paper will be his talisman for months, until the day he tears it up, just as he buries the letters she sent him in the bottom of a box, all those words that brought her life back in color, along with the one photo of her that he took.

The words were an illusion, heart foolery, a virtual love, a fiction that had so little connection with the real world, it could resist anything, even time.

The first time in the woods, despite the wet leaves, they lie down on a tarp, their cold hands warming up against skin, under cumbersome clothing. There are feverish kisses and *her* words, "Come on me. In my mouth. Between my breasts. Come. Come again." Her panting breath does not stop her illustrating, tempting words. "Do you like that? Do you like that, my love?"

She glides her head under his sweater and sucks on his body, inch by inch, using her lips and her tongue until he can't hold back any longer and penetrates her abruptly, plunging deep inside her, coming too quickly.

Is it because she disappeared that she remains so present, literally there as soon as he remembers her, abolishing time?

The meeting is tomorrow morning. He has to work.

What if Catherine manages to erase the other's ghost? Isn't that also tempting? Her abrupt manner, her declared detachment could chase away the shadow of dependence, with its constant demand for proof and sacrifices. Catherine is independent, strong, self-sufficient.

He was so young. She wanted too much, more than he could have given her.

If he wants to get his work done, he first has to make a decision. He listens to the message again on his phone. This is only the twelfth time. She said so much with so few words, "Too bad." These words are driving him crazy. He enlarges the picture on the screen and tilts it.

It will be all the more disturbing if you have to turn the magazine to find the right way to look at it. Just when you think you've found it, that's when you are no longer there. He touches the callback button and yawns to loosen his throat. It goes to voicemail. What a relief. "Hello. Cedric here. Sorry, am on deadline. It's a rush for tomorrow morning, and I'll be on it all night. Don't hesitate to call. That will give me a break. Uh, great. Maybe we'll talk soon, I hope."

He started off all right, but the end was a mess. Shit. But he did get the right tone, both distant and friendly. He abandons the idea of too much intimacy, just as she has. Is it the situation, this ghostly double from the past that is making him uncomfortable, making him feel like a young man again? What's charming at seventeen is grotesque at forty.

The match has begun, they've played a few balls, and the outcome is uncertain.

Now he's not going to wait for her to call back. Considering the time, it is unlikely she will. Her cell phone is turned off; she must be asleep.

He attacks the books section of the magazine. That's easy. A central article placed off-center on the bottom of the page and smaller illustrated stories with book covers and author photos.

What an ass! Why didn't I just say, "Call me." Everyone says that. It's a polite way of ending a message that doesn't really commit you to anything. Really. "Maybe we'll talk soon, I hope." How stupid. Hopeless. There's no better word. You've got to be more inventive if you want to be a sharp-shooting lady killer.

That is perhaps what he missed the most: their words. She had given him talent. He became a storyteller, a comedian. He became interested in everything that could possibly feed her curiosity. Why could they not keep it at that? Why do we always want more? Why not keep it at that with Catherine? A beautiful fleeting memory is better than a long ordinary reality.

Letters to the editor. No ideas needed here. Great.

He needs a little drink. Just one to raise the troops. An ice-cold bottle is calling out to him.

Women! They are all the same.

The drink warms him, relaxes him. Three glasses later, he finds the solution. He doesn't need anyone, and most of all, not a woman.

Take a married woman, a mother on top of that, with a man who busts ass so that she has everything she needs, who worships her. That's the trouble. With women, if you drop your guard even for a minute, you're dead. Even when you're crazy about them, you have to put them down so they'll stay in line. Like Lemaire, who sued him so she could get her so-called barmaid's dignity back. It's not as if he beat her. He wasn't violent. She's the one who fell flat on her face. A little dignity, please, at least. What did he do with Paul's file? What a mess the desk is. Oh, here it is. Okay, that's done. What else does he have to do?

He types quickly; it's a little cacophonous but not bad, throwing you off without losing you. Very straightforward fonts rather than subtle variations. There you go.

To go home or not to go home, that is the question. He lies down on the couch, his bottle within reach. He will follow her. That is the solution.

He will call her to get some news. He'll talk to her about the magazine project. He's good when he talks about his work. He'll flatter her by asking for her opinion, like it's nothing. He'll ask her how her case is going, and, surprise, he'll be on the train.

Returning to the scene of the crime.

He'll be clear in his head.

Women talk and talk. Too much.

"I don't like my life. I thought I loved him, but I don't love him anymore. Since I met you, I'm ready for everything. We can start again from scratch. And the child? The child will survive. But I'm the one who is slowly dying in my prison, surrounded."

Just the child, without a name. Children never die. They are survivors.

What a mess.

No. The layout is good. It is very good. We'll win the bid if we let Paul do the talking. He's good at that. I'm the creative one, the creator.

Tomorrow, the sun will rise.

He sniggers.

Insha Allah.

Only God knows. And the God I know isn't going to let me in on the secret. What is it? The unforgiving silence of the stars. No. That's not it. Who gives a shit anyway? About anything.

13

In the clarity of a winter that is neither sad nor monotonous, landscapes unfold with an incredible variety from town to town. The houses are beautiful, rustic, without any flourishes, save the sometimes exuberant colors of the shutters. They're well built, made of large, solid stones.

Catherine removes the key from the magnetic support under the back fender of the dark blue VW Golf parked outside the train station. The papers are in the glove compartment, and Louis has made a so-called secondary itinerary for her to discover the region if she wants to waste a little time, which would be time well lost.

She is tired. She has worked really hard to have four days in the Creuse, and as soon as she starts up the car, Paris disappears into the stratosphere, and an incredible sense of freedom overtakes her. It grows on the highway that takes her quickly to the town of Guéret, where she decides to skip out and take the route the reporter has recommended.

The road becomes narrower and hillier. It narrows even more when she turns at the road sign with a horseback rider announcing a riding club.

The instructions say to continue straight on after that, even though the road just keeps twisting. Visibility is so constricted, Catherine must stay in third gear, attentive. She is driving through a forest and feels like she wants to walk.

Her cell phone vibrates. She glances at it. It's Cedric. She does not answer. For the last two weeks they've done nothing but miss each other on the phone. She thinks it's a sign. She firmly believes in synchronicity. Although she has never encountered it, in her opinion it signals true feelings. She believes in everything that she has not experienced.

There is a small abandoned mill on the left, with a guidepost announcing a village named La Lune three kilometers farther on and the salutary signs certifying that she will eventually come to the city of Aubusson.

Two hours later, she reaches it. Yes, this route was clearly longer than she had expected, but she does not regret the drive and doesn't feel tired anymore.

She takes a right and finds the traffic circle. Straight on after that, she veers to the right. She is starting to understand the local code. "Straight on" is a figure of speech, a way of warning against any abrupt deviation. She accelerates and nearly misses the gate on the side of the road just as she leaves the town.

A pretty sign in old paint announces the bed and breakfast. She takes a quick look in the rearview mirror, backs up, and swings into the drive that leads to a square building with large workshop windows facing the yard. She parks next to a white truck.

"I'll be right there," comes a woman's voice out of nowhere, preceding the arrival of the property owner, who welcomes her simply. Her name is Françoise, and she is sorry about the rubber gloves, but she is in the middle of painting. Her husband will be here in a minute, and he'll show her the room.

There he is. A big bearded man with clear eyes who comes rushing up from the back of the yard. He introduces himself. "Jean-Claude."

The sound of a nearby river drowns out the traffic on the road.

The woman returns to her workshop. Catherine follows Jean-Claude to a small one-story house, which will be hers. There are books on the shelves, abandoned magazines, old furniture, fireplaces, and good armchairs. There is a fully equipped kitchen for her to use, along with a comfortable bathroom and a spacious bedroom, painted an old washed-out pink, with red linen drapes and thick rugs.

She can make a fire and work in the small living room, where she finds the issue of *La Montagne* featuring her photo. She has already seen it, and although the photo isn't as flattering as she would like, the copy in her room is a nice touch.

She can't get over having such a great place to stay and paying so much less than she would have at a hotel. Louis worked things out well. She feels safe here, between the country and the city. She settles in and then goes to the nearest supermarket to buy some supplies.

Four days seem like an eternity, but it's really not enough time when you have so much to do. She begins with what is least urgent. She lights a fire. Well, she tries to light a fire.

She hears a knock. Her watchful host asks if she would like him to start a small fire for her. The used matches on the fireplace give away the Parisian's incompetence.

Jean-Claude explains how to add the kindling and light the paper. He is not condescending. Then he leaves.

She calls Louis and doesn't know how to thank him. They make an appointment for the next day at the end of the afternoon.

She takes out her Moleskine notebook, which is already not as brand-new, and starts to review the questions she has to ask Myriam. She nods off, and when she wakes up, it is dark out. She finds a small pot of soup on the stove with a note, "We had too much, if you want some."

She feels rested from her nap and lets herself enjoy this moment of relaxation, quite unusual for her—too bad for her list, too bad for her work.

A gentle knock on the door wakes her up in the morning. She gets up quickly to open the door she double-locked the night before, and Jean-Claude laughs. "We never lock things up here, not the houses and not the cars," he tells her. She feels stupid.

He gives her some fresh bread and worries about having awakened her. She thanks him. She was sleeping so deeply, she could have stayed in bed all day.

While drinking her coffee, she remembers what she dreamed that night. Cedric lying down naked, offering himself up like a woman, with a very handsome young man's body. His words conveyed the opposite message. He couldn't sleep with her. It was over, and that was all.

She feels hurt by the dream, and that makes her laugh. Right, he doesn't want her anymore. For sure, he's addicted. Here's a demonstration. She dials his number and makes a capricious face waiting for his voicemail. "Sorry, I didn't have time to tell you that I was going to the country for a few days. Too bad."

She has made it a playful habit to end her messages with a "too bad" as a reminder that they've had a light relationship—if you can really call it a relationship, because they've only been together once.

Everything in her wants to take it easy, and she has to force herself to review her agenda for the day: grandmother, bosses, marriage, murder.

She taps on the atelier window where Françoise is stripping an old armoire. They wave at each other, and Catherine makes a face of admiration before getting in her car. She starts it up and then stops abruptly at the road, barely missing a truck that comes speeding by. It would be strange to die here without having accomplished anything. She shakes her head to chase away these morbid thoughts.

This time she takes a more direct route and has to slow down after ten kilometers. She's unable to pass a tractor because of the constant flow of cars in the other direction. As she watches for an opportunity to pass the machine, she realizes that she'll have a hard time adjusting to the local pace. She finally overtakes the tractor, accelerates, and brakes just as quickly, causing a furious honking behind her. She waves to excuse herself and parks on the side of the road, getting out of the car and walking over to the sign that caused the untimely and irresistible stop: Lavaveix-les-Mines.

She sees the picture of her mother in front of the sign with the letters "vave le." It just popped into her head. Could this be a coincidence? Maybe. Maybe not.

Or maybe she has slipped into a parallel universe.

She gets back into the car and drives on slowly. The town does not remind her of anything. It's a village, split in half by the highway, depriving it of an identity. A series of stores line the left side of the town, which is longer than it is wide.

Once she drives out of the town, the question jumps out of her: "Who killed that pretty, inoffensive, trusting woman in the picture?" It's followed by another question. "Why?"

She bursts into tears. She is not used to expressing her emotions. She is not emotional. She is factual, pragmatic. Questions with no answers are not good questions. That is all. There is a good reason not to ask them.

She sniffs, grabs a paper towel tucked into the car door, rubs her face, and blows her nose. She feels like she has just run a marathon.

Her senses are perked for the rest of the drive, on the lookout for any sign that would, like a dart, reactivate the information lurking in her memory. There's nothing but a blank. That would be too huge a coincidence. Life does not grab you by the hair and drag you backward. Unless, perhaps, it has old accounts to settle?

14

In Guéret, traffic moves like a drip-feed, slowed by a series of traffic circles, even though there are hardly any cars or pedestrians. The city looks almost deserted.

It is just the opposite on the main square, where it seems that every driver has an urgent appointment. You have to drive around and around until a car leaves and then quickly slip into the freed parking space.

Catherine has three parking places pinched from her before she manages to grab one, and she is upset. She puts on her coat, gathers her things, and locks the car. Then she decides to do what the locals do and unlocks it.

A different guard leads her to the visiting room before she thinks to demand a better space. She tries to concentrate, but her mind is flitting and can't settle anywhere.

Myriam arrives at her nonchalant pace, her complexion gray, a worried look in her eyes that immediately inspires antipathy in her lawyer, who has only one desire—to shake her client violently to wake her up. She controls the instinct and forces herself to find a small bit of temperance, then stands and holds out her hand. Limp handshakes disgust her. A little empathy couldn't hurt, but her client is really not helping her out.

Catherine thinks about imprisonment, solitude, and fear and smiles to chase away these dark thoughts. She recalls her boss's masterful voice, tries to soften hers a little, and says, "I have good news. I'll be staying until Monday, and I'll come back to see you before I catch the train."

It doesn't look like Myriam registers what she has said.

"Did you stop the medication?"

Myriam shakes her head and looks guilty.

"Why not?"

The prisoner does not know why not. They give her pills at night, and she takes them. She is used to obeying orders.

Catherine lets it go momentarily and says, "I'd like to bring your grandmother here for the trial."

"That's impossible," Myriam says from her heart.

"Why?"

"Because she's dead."

"But you're not sure about that. It would be worthwhile investigating."

"She would not have left me so long without any news. And she was old."

"But maybe your employers intercepted her mail or her calls."

"She didn't have a telephone."

"You must have an address or something."

"Uh, not really. Even if she did go back to her village, it's impossible."

"There's nobody I could contact? Some friends maybe?

"That was a long time ago."

Myriam won't make the effort. It's incomprehensible.

The rest is in keeping, right down to her birthdate: unknown. It's the neighbors who know who her parents were and when she was born, approximately. As long as someone knows. Yes, of course, on her passport it was marked January 4, 1968. But that's a guess. And the wedding? The mayor figured it out. After that, he got her papers. She is French. She wants to erase the past and start with a clean slate. Her life began as Mrs. Villetreix from Saint-Jean-les-Bois. And her employers? No, their name is not Lévêque. Yes, that is what the local paper wrote, but they made that up.

Who made that up? The mayor? The reporter? Myriam? She can't remember. The name of the street they lived on? She doesn't know, can't remember. That *would* be useful. Myriam seems indifferent to everything. Hopeless.

Catherine has brought her clothing and magazines. She takes them, thanks her, and then yawns without making any effort to hide it behind a hand.

"Do you want us to take a break?"

"No, no."

Catherine goes over the investigation carried out by the gendarmes. Did Myriam do anything else on the day of the murder—rather, the day Gaston died—after she prepared the chicken? Did she leave the house?

"No," she says. "Not for a second. I stayed to keep an eye on the stew."

"How can you be certain?"

"Because that is what I always did."

Myriam did not seem to realize that if the pot had been left unattended, that would make things better for her.

"Did you eat any chicken?" Catherine asks.

"Yes. It was dinner."

"What had Gaston done that day?"

"The usual. He read the paper," Myriam says, searching her memory.

Catherine tries to be patient. Myriam seems mulish and short-sighted. She doesn't understand why. The medication doesn't explain everything.

Myriam's childhood can be summarized by proximity to warm bodies, sensations more than memories, the rhythm of her mother's steps bouncing the baby's belly against a protective back, where it returns and sticks again like a suction cup. Myriam's body is never imprisoned in cold solitude. It is placed under an arm, crushed against a chest, kneaded by large hands, constantly in contact with warm flesh, feeling a breath, a heart marking the other's tempo, the pulsing of organs, a purring belly, slivers of conversation, laughter. The little girl is never set apart, is always connected to another life.

Until the separation of death. Her father had gone somewhere where he was less needed, leaving her mother and cousins and aunts and old women and passing men. Men, screams, and tears. And sickness.

And death. Celebration too.

The dances, when her mother dresses her up like a princess and looks like a goddess in an immense headdress and a bright blue cloth draped over her like luxurious packaging. It starts with little steps, slight swaying, the time to judge the room, to greet friends, before the warmth of the rum and the beer raises the temperature, accelerates the dancers' rhythm, and highlights the clapping.

She will never be tall and beautiful like her mother, but as a child she poses like her, with her hands on her hips, her chin lifted to scold, to demand, to exist. She taps her bare feet, slap, slap, her shoulders thrown back, her head reaching for the ceiling.

Then one day, her mother is a corpse, a skeleton, a face without cheeks, sunken sad eyes, her skin burned out, all of her burned out.

She doesn't want to touch her daughter anymore or kiss her. She doesn't want to contaminate her.

Cold and solitude begin then. And last forever.

How could this prettily dressed lawyer, just barely out of school, imagine the effect that prison could have on Myriam?

She had hung out on the streets and lived in squats, but the cold solitude of this place separates people, not only from the outside, but from each other, with invisible internal walls.

The inmates in her cell are Arabs, Muslims. They talk among themselves in their language. They only talk about practical, down-to-earth things with Myriam. She is black and a murderer; her soul is black too. She is used to the laughter rolling out in a cascading echo, palms slapping, hugs, loud voices filling the air, the distance, the space, the indifference, the silence, the cold.

It is not a lie to invent a grandmother for difficult times. A grandmother who makes bread, who kneads the dough while Myriam practices stick writing and repeats the words aloud. A grandmother who tells stories about magic serpents that talk and about lovers separated by tribal disputes, stories that never have happy endings but say that life is a story you have to imagine. She repeats them in her head to keep from forgetting what she should be.

Then you remember the black moonless night with no stars. Under the folds of sleep, you can hear fear, hear frightened murmuring and feel it too, at the risk of suffocating, the sour, unpleasant smell of the old lady who hugs too tightly on top of the large, scratchy cloth.

Because she can't see anything, she still hears the crunch of the straw, the dull sound of boots moving around. Through the cloth, a hand flattens over her mouth. Be quiet, despite the explosions all around you. She opens her eyes wide against the cloth and silently panics, tries to stay awake in order not to die.

It is written down. This will be her story. Her parents were killed, shot, their bodies carried off so there could be no ceremony. Her grandmother saved her, took her to her cousins' home, a new family where another mouth to feed did not change much, even if life was hard.

Her grandmother's skin color changed. Its brown was streaked with gray that Myriam follows with her finger to recompose an image that has disappeared.

Of course her grandmother is dead. She wasn't the kind of grandmother who would abandon her granddaughter. That is why she wanted to believe the white people, on whom all hope for a better life depended.

It is well known that black likes color. So she too liked colors and used lots of them in Gaston's house. That is what would have been expected of her, the exiled African lady.

She says to Gaston, "The sun doesn't laugh a lot where you come from, but it will always be welcome in our home." And then she starts painting everything in pink and blue and yellow.

One day, she can't remember when, the initial wonder dies, taking with it the old farmer's amazement at having such a beautiful woman all to himself. He forbids her from touching his mother's room. The African tornado has to content herself with the ground floor.

Myriam resigns herself to this, as she resigns herself to the silence that falls over their conjugal life, as she has always resigned herself, even to the worst. Before springing back.

At the beginning, he laughs with her, tells his stories, listens to hers. Takes her on trips, builds a book of memories of their union with souvenir photos.

She talks a lot, sometimes talking as though she were singing, for the pleasure of the sounds, before the habits come back. Gaston's habits.

She is grateful to him for trying, for having taken the risk with her, and for that, she pampers him, tries to conform as closely as possible to what he is looking for. But it is a marriage of an oyster and a trout.

Perhaps, if there had been a child. Okay, she had lied. Lied about everything, first of all, her age. But that was not really a lie. She feels like an old soul, as the old Chinese woman had said to her in the squat. She'd liked that. An old soul. That is what she is.

When the truth is too ugly, you are not going to tell it. It is better to weave terrible, scary, incredible stories instead of ugly ones. Stories of Africa, war, and betrayal.

What could Miss Monsigny, so proud and sure of herself, know or understand about all this?

Myriam is not stupid. She can hear behind the words. She knows what Catherine expects of her, but today, she could just lie down and die from discouragement and fatigue. She could even end up missing the taciturn, cautious, timorous Gaston.

She answers questions with single syllables. She can barely hear them. She cannot tell the lawyer the truth, because she would come to the wrong conclusions.

That night, she prepares the chicken, and she has nothing but bad thoughts in mind. Maybe that is how the poisoning begins. She says to herself that she is not making the most of life and that life is speeding past her, not waiting for her. She knows from Gaston's confidences at the beginning that he is rich, and she cannot understand his crazy desire to keep everything. Being rich means spending. Otherwise you are just poor.

First she tells herself that if she were a widow, she could do anything she wanted. She could sell everything and leave. Maybe she could even leave for her imaginary country, where you live to be very old when soldiers don't shoot you dead. And she could buy a house for her grandmother, who would not be dead and who would start making bread again and throwing little pieces of dough to her as she would to a small dog. Her grandmother would tell her stories and sing her songs and help her find a man, one of those good-for-nothing smooth talkers. But she would have money now. She could keep a handsome dandy who would boast and lie but would be kind and respectful and loyal. Even if he were only loyal to her money, he would still be loyal.

And when she goes into the living room where Gaston is reading *La Montagne*, into this room where all the accumulated colors now seem ugly and artificial, a bad décor in a bad play, she says in a joyful voice that you can smell the aroma of her chicken all over the house. Then, without even lifting his head from the paper, he suggests that she close the door, so as not to smell up the house.

She is facing the mirror above the fireplace, and she sees herself, old before her time. She looks at his feet in slippers, his shapeless pants and his old sweater. It is also his fault that she is letting herself go, that she is getting stuck.

She stands in front of Gaston and says, "Things are not right, Gaston."

"No, they are not," he says. "If you don't change your ways, things cannot go on."

That is when ice surrounds her heart. Her husband is ready to chase her away, like the hired help.

In the visiting room, she lifts her head and says to Catherine, with a note of profound boredom, "That night, as usual, I joined Gaston in the living room, and we watched the news on television and talked about what we were going to watch afterward. I was tired, but Gaston did not want to go to bed. He was not sleeping well. He preferred to fall asleep in front of the television and come up later.

"Ah," says the lawyer, taking the bait. "He wasn't feeling well?"

"It had been awhile. He would get really, really tired. I told him to go see a doctor, but he said he didn't need one. He wasn't raised to see a doctor every time he felt a little ache or had a little sniffle."

"Did you tell this to the gendarmes?"

"I don't really know, but I do know one thing. They only believed what they wanted to believe. When I said something different, they called me a liar."

"I don't see that in the interrogation."

"I wasn't the one to write that either."

"But one thing is certain, there was cyanide in Gaston's stomach. If you didn't put it there, who did? One of the cousins or both of them? And why?"

"If I'm guilty, they are the ones who inherit, right? And if I'm guilty, who, in fact, is going to pay you? You should work things out with them, don't you think? Seeing as you don't believe me either."

Catherine is not supposed to have doubts, but she can't see herself teaming up with a client whom she not only doesn't like, but also doesn't understand, a client who is resolutely hostile to her and can be aggressive at inopportune moments. She needs to think, to find a parry or a path that will lead her to Myriam. But not now. Not today. Neither of them is in the mood. Catherine stands up, cold, closed, gathers her things and calls the guard.

"See you on Monday," she says.

Myriam does not react. She remains seated, leaning over as if her head or, rather, her thoughts were too heavy for her to carry.

15

Objectively, it is not such a bad case. There was cyanide, stored in a jar in the cousins' barn. Everyone knew it was there or could have known. This includes Myriam, according to the wife of one of the cousins, who has the distinct memory of discovering that the jar had been removed from the barn. She had found it in Myriam's kitchen.

If she had killed her husband, why would Myriam have left such incriminating evidence behind her, when all she had to do was put the jar back in the barn?

The truth is that there is no tangible proof against Myriam at all, a bundle of clues perhaps, but nothing that should get her convicted if the case is handled correctly.

The problem is the African's personality, the human factor, and Catherine wonders if she is capable of dealing with its complexities. Is there a cultural issue, an intrinsic difference that is feeding the misunderstanding? If so, the lawyer has to repair it and remove the nerve. She has already defended Africans, whose nonchalance gives an impression of insolence and casualness that is really more indicative of fatalism.

On a day like today, with her antipathy and passivity, Myriam reeks of guilt.

They have barely three months to work on her character, but for that, they both have to be willing. Right now, she doesn't want to help her. And the way she looks at Catherine is discouraging and even hurtful.

I should not feel hurt, Catherine tells herself. Renaud had often advised her to leave her sensitivity at the door.

"Don't worry. You will find it intact again when you are finished."

She wonders if it's just stage fright and if it is not in her interest to take advantage of this slump to examine her conscience and avoid letting her mind wander to an intimate and inaccessible past that could blur her professional present. The latter must remain her priority.

"Stay focused," she tells herself. She can do that well. She has passed up Lavaveix without even realizing it. She is completely in the present, where, unfortunately, bottomless discouragement has replaced yesterday's euphoria. She continues her recap as it comes, reviewing all of the corroborating statements, including those made by the cousins: "Gaston was happy. He was never suspicious of his wife. He kept repeating, 'I am lucky, and so is she. And when I'm no longer here, she'll get a good deal, and so will the little one.'"

He dreamed of having an heir, which never came in six years of marriage.

Catherine has a hard time imagining this Gaston, whisked away in a whirlwind of dreams after such a controlled life. He had refused to be submerged by the current of his life after his mother's death. He had dared to marry, to have a baby with a black woman.

Gaston deserved to live.

She should not wonder if Myriam is guilty or not. In a way, it is none of her business. She needs to build on everything that works in her client's favor. And that is where Louis comes in.

Once again, she almost misses the turn at the guesthouse. She speeds down the sloped road into the courtyard, slamming the brakes to avoid the white truck, which is parked in the middle.

Jean-Claude sticks his head out the window and says, "You don't give your game away, but you're a real stuntwoman."

"Sorry."

"On top of that, you crashed into our beautiful antique gate!"

"Well, nearly. Don't you ever get angry?"

"I don't hesitate when there is good reason. Otherwise, I don't waste my energy. How are you? Did you have a good day?"

"Uh-huh," she says.

"Do you want to see the craftswoman at work?" he asks and then yells, "Françoise, are you in there?"

"I'm in the back room."

Catherine had already recovered her calm, having avoided the gate despite her uncontrolled skid. Never had she felt so protected as in this place. Sorry, Dad, she thinks to herself, not without pity.

She leaves the case file in the car and goes to wait for Jean-Claude at the bottom of the outside metal staircase. He comes down quickly and carelessly. "For future information, don't do that when it freezes," he says.

"Believe me, I won't risk it again even when it's warm and dry."

"Follow me," he says, "The boss is customizing some cheap wooden furniture."

François hears him and protests, "Cheap! I wouldn't go to so much trouble if it were cheap."

She has painted a large charmless armoire a mousy gray that she is in the process of watering down. It gives the piece new character.

"Tomorrow I'm waxing."

He adds, "And the day after tomorrow, it heads off to a trendy Italian decorator for four times the price we paid for it."

"It looks good. And like a lot of work, no doubt about it!" Catherine says, showing admiration.

"I can tell you're a lawyer."

"Oh, if all my cases were as easy as defending you."

"What are we being accused of again?"

"Fraud."

"Ha-ha! We are not pretending it is anything other than a re-painted armoire. No fake documents, no lies. Just decoration."

They hear the sound of a car approaching. It stops, and a door slams.

"Are you expecting someone?"

"Oh yes, Louis!" Catherine says.

"Business? When you've finished, the two of you should come and have coffee with us upstairs. Have you eaten anything?"

"Yes, in Guéret, and yes, with pleasure, for the coffee."

It's easy to get comfortable with people like them, and that is not the least of their charms, Catherine thinks as she leaves the couple. She returns through the windowed workshop and walks into the courtyard, where the Golf is parked, the door open and the engine and the blinker still on.

"Are the cops on your tail?" Louis asks.

"No, my mind is elsewhere." She gets her things out of the car, precedes her visitor into the house, discovers that the kindling has been stacked in the living room fireplace, and is moved by being so well taken care of.

She takes a moment in the bathroom to refresh her makeup and comes back. She's feeling like herself again, ready to attack head-on, but the indigenous pace first requires that they talk about the weather, comment on the landscapes they've seen, and discuss general news.

She warns Louis that they are expected at the big house for coffee later. It is her way of letting him know that there will be time later to chat, but the Parisian lawyer has to admit to herself that she is not the one in control. She resigns herself to letting go. She talks about how much she admires the landscape, especially the forests, and all the bad things she thinks about Guéret, in particular the traffic. But everyone seems to be so nice. And how was his day?

"Dead calm," he sighs.

She jumps in. As he has some free time, could he get some information for her? Everything from the police investigation is automatically placed in the case file, which is why Catherine hesitates to ask for new statements from people when she doesn't know if they will be favorable to her or not. But if Louis could find some new elements, she could sift through them to determine what might be useful. And the reporter would get first-hand material for his paper.

"Wait a second. Slow down," he says. "The gendarmes have investigated. The work has been done. I don't feel up to hunting, when the game is already in the bag. And furthermore, I'll add politely that I don't need you for that."

"It's just that, well, I have a theory. You see, I'm being straightforward."

Louis gives her a skeptical look, one that nears fundamental doubt about a lawyer having this improbable quality.

"I think Gaston and his mother were both poisoned," she says.

"What? You're kidding," Louis bursts out laughing. "What, is it some serial killer? Now that you mention it, if you're set on creating an event, you might as well go all the way."

Catherine feels she has hit bottom on the credibility scale, which just boosts her combativeness. "I am perfectly serious," she says. "After all, Dr. Blanchard signed both death certificates. And the symptoms were the same."

"One family, one weapon, one killer? At the time, Myriam did not even know that the Creuse existed."

"Exactly my point."

"You're working from the principle that she is innocent."

"No, that not all the leads were explored."

"Do you have any other leads like that one?"

"Not yet."

"I recommend that you come back down to earth, Catherine. You're in Creuse here. We are simple people. You are coming up with a scenario that is way too sophisticated."

"Well, I think that greed sharpens the mind. And in this case, there is money at play! But okay, give and take. I'll give you front-line information on the hearing, and you help me a little to prepare it. Nothing illegal. What's the risk?"

"That it won't reflect well on me."

"Think about it. We'll talk about it later. Shall we go have that coffee?"

"You've got some nerve!" he laughs.

She tries not to think about Renaud's reaction if he were to hear what she has just set in motion. She comforts herself. Only results count. And it is a form of professional duty, having to load the dice to support what you believe.

She changes the subject as she crosses the courtyard. Can he tell her about some hikes she could take? "Near what is it called, Lavaveix-les-Mines? Are there any pretty places around there?"

"I prefer to walk near Ars, which is to the left when you go toward Guéret. There are also some nice places on the way down to, um, I'll show you on a map."

"Great. Thanks," she says, expressing exactly what she is feeling. It is great, thanks to life, and everything is going to be okay. Everything. And she should just drop Lavaveix. Certainly there are dozens of other signs in France with those same corresponding letters.

16

At ten that night, Catherine is lying down, propped against three enormous pillows, her notebook misshapen under her elbow, the case file scattered. She is taking notes and feels her eyelids drooping; she yawns, and the lines dance. She lets go, pushes everything to the floor, turns out the light, hugs the pillow, and pushes her cheek against the softness with satisfaction, freeing her nose to breathe easily.

She thinks about the fire she sat in front of. It was not completely out. Embers could pop out, and a spark could land on the stuffed armchair. The fire would catch on the cloth and swan's down, smoldering at first, then spreading to the rug and the sofa. Even if the heat awakened her, which might not even happen, it would be too late, and she would be reduced to ashes in this wooden house, its sole occupant incinerated.

She lifts her three tons of apathy, turns on the light, and crosses the room in her bare feet. Did she hear gravel crunching?

She stops, perks her ears, and hears a step.

These are sounds you hear in the country, with no murmuring city to mask them.

She crosses the hall and throws a quick glance at the glass door. It is dark outside. How could she have seen a shadow pass by? Ridiculous.

The hearth is glowing red. She was right to get up. She opens the fireguard and spreads out the embers. The air lights the rest of the log. Bad move. She wriggles her frozen toes on the tile floor. Flames return and take over the fire. Cedric has not called her back.

She wraps her feet in the blanket tossed on the sofa and crouches, her eyes absorbed by the changing colors that rise, mix, and disappear.

Very close to her, a voice whispers, "Are you asleep, my little sweet?"

She lifts her eyes, trying desperately to see something. It feels so good. There is a sound like distant fireworks. It's so soothing to melt into the heat that is warming her face, with her feet cozily wrapped under her mother's sweater.

If she starts to drowse, she'll be picked up, taken from the warmth of the kitchen through the cold of the staircase, and then tucked into the cool sheets, surrounded by the hard bars of her bed. And then she'll settle into the solitude of sleep.

"No," she says, without emitting a sound.

She is in her bed. It is too late. She missed the crossing, during which she slept. The silhouette bends over her. The hand she is holding means that her mother is there, watching over her. She squeezes the hand that will not let her go. Ever. Orange lights play over her head, the shadows of small farm animals turning endlessly around and around, and a voice sings a familiar tune, "Hush little baby."

She is not alone. She will never be alone.

I miss you, Mom. Catherine's face is covered in tears. The fire is no longer keeping her warm. It has gone out. The embers continue to glow gently. There is no longer any risk. She adjusts the fireguard, rolls up the edge of the rug to be safe, wraps herself up in the blanket and goes back down the hall, shivering in the draft. There's a light on in the brick house. She is not alone. She can go to sleep.

She drops the blanket to the floor, too tired, crawls back into the warmth of her bed, takes her pillow back, and snuggles into its softness. But sleep escapes her. It's replaced by pointless worry, the worst kind.

Why pointless?

I miss my mother.

Just as she misses the presence of a body, the echo of attention, the return of words, a look that gives her texture.

What is this old sadness that is submerging her, making her vulnerable to everything?

"I am the child left on the jetty washed to the open sea." She can't remember the exact poem. It was in the collection of Rimbaud's poems where she found the one photo of her mother that had escaped the paternal holocaust.

How is it possible to erase a person, to refuse to let a single trace of that person remain? It was a protective wall he tried to build around his little girl. Why did she not have any grandparents?

His father's father had died in an accident. His mother had to send him to boarding school, and it was his spinster great aunt who took him on vacation. He didn't want to talk about that either. It was a hard life. That is all he said about his own absent, sick mother.

She sees a procession of ghosts rise from nowhere, beckoning her. She has built her person without ancestors, without a history, without references. She has convinced herself that this is her strength.

She falls into a pocket of sleep populated with a blur of night mares. She wakes up gasping for breath, as if she has been diving without air. Words emerge from the nocturnal chaos. "Twinkle, twinkle, little star."

It's daytime. Noon. She has scared herself, like a ridiculous city dweller, but she has found a lullaby, the real one—"Twinkle, Twinkle Little Star." It's as if she's reinventing her mother, piece by piece.

Jean-Claude is leaning over the engine of his truck. She opens the door and greets him, breathing deeply. She goes to scrub herself down in a long shower, washes her hair, slathers cream on herself, and settle into the kitchen with a series of geological survey maps her hosts have found for her.

She lets chance guide her through the names of the hamlets. She will certainly find a small inn for a late lunch. She is floating.

She puts on a pair of jeans and rubber boots she has found in the hall closet. She picks up her bag from the living room. The blanket is spread on the sofa. She hesitates for a moment. She has a vague memory of the mohair overlay falling to the floor in her room. The rug she rolled up toward the sofa is unrolled. Françoise and Jean-Claude have been through here.

This troubles her. They never entered while she was there without warning her.

She hesitates about asking them. It would be rude, like a reproach. She was so muddled last night. She should be cautious about the exactness of her memories.

She is in a region where nothing happens, without any events, surrounded by kindness. There is no risk.

When she starts the car, Françoise calls out to her, "Do you have our cell phone number? In case you get lost?"

"I'll follow the hiking paths. They'll be signposted."

"Have a good walk. See you later."

She feels like walking, like exerting her body, which is still bogged down by an uncomfortable feeling. She wants to get into the silence of nature, where she has no recollections. She wants to be reminded of nothing but the indifference of time and what she believes to be inanimate objects, which take the form of trees.

May indifference be with me, she says to herself, without a trace of irony.

She leaves the car on an embankment after a crossroad that she could get back to, thanks to the names she has found on the map.

During the last twenty minutes, she hasn't passed a single car. She'll only have herself to rely on, but paths exist because they go someplace, she reassures herself as she follows the one she has chosen. And in the distance, she sees enough smoking chimneys and bright rooftops to know that people have not entirely deserted the area.

The path is strewn with brilliantly colored leaves, a goldsmith's carpet, all nuances of gold, red, and shiny yellow. She has the feeling that she is slipping on shifting ground.

The path climbs a little, but it is wide and well used. She walks quickly, breathes deeply, and lets the air separate her ribs and loosen her throat. She exercises her voice, "How little skill you show in defending yourself, you, a courtier and a man who must be accustomed to such things."

She repeats herself, louder. Her voice rises. She looks for deeper tones.

She sees a hill topped by a closed building, a white cube like a water tank or a relay. She climbs onto it to get her bearings and discovers a landscape that draws her eye far into the distance, across prairies and hedges, without a single house this time, like a land without people.

The planet began without people and will end without them.

"Why don't you tell me that business of the utmost importance that forced you to come away without letting me know."

The path narrows a little but remains clearly marked.

She spots an opening in the trees and moves away from the path. She takes another path that isn't as worn but heads toward the clearing. A few steps later, her foot becomes entangled in some brambles, and she loses her balance. She just barely saves herself from a fall by grabbing the trunk of a tree. She is hot, and her chest is throbbing idiotically. She calms herself. Like a mirage, the clearing becomes more distant, inaccessible. This strengthens her desire to reach it.

She stops. What's that? An animal? She hears branches cracking and leaves crunching.

She looks through the trees.

There's nothing.

She feels a little disappointed and starts walking again. As she continues, the ground becomes sticky and swampy, and her feet begin to sink in the mud. The idea of returning the way she came is unacceptable. She moves along the outside of the muddy ground and hopes to find a spot that will put her back on dry land.

She swings around. She has the feeling that she is being followed. She tells herself that the fear of losing her way is getting the better of her.

She digs around near a fallen tree and finds a good-sized stick. She tests its strength. It will lead her steps, warning her of obstacles.

Catherine tries to find a point of reference to reassure herself. In the distance there is a darker area with pine trees. If she walks around the pine grove, she should come upon something. Maybe a field. Real distances are infinitely larger than the ones that her naked eye sees. She is hungry and tired. She hasn't even thought to bring a bottle of water. What a twit! One not in the mood to laugh. Why is she so incapable of sticking to a wise decision, like following the marked trails?

She already imagines herself calling Aubusson. What would she say? How would they find her? Her concern rises, and she forbids herself from stopping. "Walk. Walk," she tells herself. She turns around again.

The forest is naturally noisy. But it is also a good place to attack a hiker with little experience!

Nostalgia for the city invades her, for its named and numbered streets, its buses and subways, its passers-by, its cars, its constant points of reference. If she ever gets out of here, she won't do this again.

She will get out of here.

Then she sees a green spot that is so clear, and it guides her. She quickens her pace—not running only because she doesn't want to trip and fall—until she gets out of the woods. The green patch turns into a field, empty, but beyond which she can make out a path and even hear the sound of a tractor in the distance. Civilization is near.

She stops for a moment to enjoy the feeling of deliverance, of regaining safety, before she starts walking again, taking long strides.

She walks around the pine forest, climbs through the barbed wire, beyond which a few cows sluggishly raise their heads to look at her. This is the final obstacle, because on the other side, there is pavement, a road, a real road she manages to reach without getting trampled by the peaceful herd, which reassures her. "Not scared!"

In the distance, there is a crossing with a sign. She takes out her map to check. At the end of this road, there is her intersection, where her car is waiting and after that, a small country inn.

A wall attracts her attention, unexpectedly charming, nearly fully preserved. Shiny green bay trees rise nearby. She breathes in. Something inside her is speaking an unknown language, and when she sees an indistinct path like a large alley partially invaded by a wild jungle open up on her right, she can't resist. She is careful this time, noting the path she has taken, going forward with a feeling of déjà-vu. She shivers with a kind of joyful exaltation.

She advances into the middle of the evergreens and again delves deep into the tangled forest.

17

Something both urgent and mysterious guides Catherine through this confusing labyrinth. She no longer feels worried or tired. She is going where she has to go. She stops in front of a bright yellow bush the color of the sun, shining with a luminous intensity reminiscent of springtime. She feasts her eyes on it before again sensing something that is simply out of synch. The burning bush marks the entrance to another world. Two steps are enough for her to discover the ruins of a mansion.

The details that remain indicate that this home once had a nobility. The structure no longer has a roof, and the walls are crumbling, but there's a small, elegant wrought iron balcony, a stone staircase with a subtle curve to it, and splendid window frames. These ruins are more romantic than worrisome.

She decides that it is Sleeping Beauty's castle and thinks about her mother, because, clearly, everything comes back to her mother.

"It was a dark and stormy night. The wind blew—woosh, woosh. The doctor-prince roamed the streets, sad and alone. He was prepared to wait his entire life to find the woman he would recognize at first sight."

Catherine knows the rest. She laughs, her eyes bright with certitude.

"But he was wrong, because she was waiting for him, invisible and poor, soaked by the rain, sitting on a sad bench, and if there hadn't been a flash of lightning that caused her to cry out in terror, he might not have seen her, protected as he was by his umbrella."

Catherine never tired of this fairy tale her father had invented, certainly to console her for the loss of her mother. Kind princesses die in stories too, struck down by evil witches. If reality resembles stories, if little Catherine were born from a magical, extraordinary encounter, with a father who played the role of providential prince, then her life could be like a fairy tale, full of magical and happy events.

Yes, these ruins remind her of a fairy tale.

The story her father found was not so bad. He did his best, she told herself often. It was not easy for that solitary older and out-of-sync man to raise a little girl. Despite herself, she had inherited his reserve, his taste for secrets and solitude, but also the ghost of an imaginary and vulnerable mother, a victim who contradicted her precious picture of a conquering, self-assured Violet.

There is something happy about this house.

Bracing herself against a still-solid wall, she climbs the staircase that winds toward the inside, which is invaded by a barbaric tree in the middle of a dense thicket of brambles.

She locates the spot where the fireplace used to be and then sees a black stain that is incongruous with the palette of natural colors. Black is not a color. Catherine stands on her toes and loses sight of it. She leans over to try to see behind the tree, where someone is hiding. This time, she is certain there is a person, a man dressed in black who is watching her. A stone gives way under her foot. She feels herself falling but catches herself.

She waves her arms and cries out, "Hey, is someone there?"

Then she goes down the stairs as fast as she can and runs toward the form she glimpsed. Without thinking. If someone is following her, she wants to know why. She takes a few steps to the right, then back to the left and keeps going, looking in front and behind.

She hears a car door shut, an engine, the sound of it driving away.

The intruder is gone. She turns around and no longer sees the ruins, which should be nearby. Is it white or black magic? She hopes she is going the right way as she makes her way back. Finally, she sees the crumbling wall.

The ruins can only be seen close up. Otherwise they blend with the surrounding jungle. She nears it, intrigued by a dark red stain on the staircase.

A single long-stemmed rose, so sumptuous it looks purple.

How did the intruder manage that? Could there have been more than one person?

She looks around, uncomfortable. She doesn't feel anyone else. It has to be someone from here. And it is for her.

Is it Jean-Claude? Olivier? Louis?

She takes the rose and smells it. It is a spineless rose with no smell. Too bad. It is a gift. And it is a rose, so the intention cannot be bad.

She starts walking toward the road, with her rose in hand. She'll come back here.

"I'll be back. I'll be back, my little sweetie pie."

Mommy goes to pee in the grass. Mommy helps her pee in the grass because it's soft, with little blades caressing her bottom. She shows her the weeds that sting and make little red spots all over the skin. To avoid.

Mommy tells stories about Messy Mimi and the three little bears and then sings lullabies with made-up words.

There is only her mother in the world of this childhood, as if it were just the two of them, one for the other.

Catherine stops. "Could I be an adopted child?"

She knows that everyone has had this fantasy at one time or another. Not her. Never.

And yet? There never was a picture of the three of them. She has no memories of the three of them.

Back in the car, she drives by a clean, well-defined pasture, where a small black dog is running around. It must be young, considering the energy its thin body throws into its sprint. Its long ears rise and fall in pace. It is alone. It looks like it has a goal, and yet, all it is doing is running in a circle that brings it back to the same place at the end of each round. Catherine slows and stops, fascinated by what makes no sense. To her. It most certainly makes sense to the dog.

She starts up again, her eye noticing the gas gauge, which is in the red zone. She doesn't know how long it has been there. All of a sudden, everything is a metaphor, which is absurd.

She drives toward a small signposted Roman bridge. The countryside is empty. She is going to run out of gas.

Finally, she sees a tractor, stopped at the side of the road to let her go by. She breaks alongside it. The driver is a large solidly built woman, beautiful, like a heroine in a Western.

"Gas?" the farmer repeats, taken aback and thinking. "The nearest is about twenty kilometers from here, at the entrance to the supermarket. You can't miss it. It is straight ahead."

Catherine holds back a smile, but for once, it is genuine. When she drives into the supermarket parking lot, a young blond man sitting on his car smiles at her. She responds with a nod, again appreciating how nice everyone is.

She fills up the car and drives slowly to the cashier's booth. The cashier takes her credit card, looking distant.

An inn? For lunch? Now? It's two in the afternoon! Perhaps you can find something at the café, which is straight ahead, that way. They could make you a sandwich.

The young woman stops moving behind the window, Catherine's credit card still in her hand. "I dropped my son off at my in-laws, and I forgot to give him his jacket," she says in a hushed voice.

Catherine is taken aback and tries to reassure her. "Everything should be okay. It's not cold. Is there a problem with…"

She wants to talk about her credit card, but the cashier continues. "His cousin told me that his father thinks I'm ugly and stupid. He's ten!"

Catherine is lost and looks for something to say. It's not serious. Children are sometimes provocative. But the woman continues. Catherine has no answers for her and just listens. The woman knows for a fact that her brother-in-law doesn't like her, but it's not good for a kid to repeat that. Catherine cuts her off. She's sorry, but she's in a hurry.

"Of course," the cashier says, busy and mechanical again, right down to the automatic depressing smile that punctuates the necessary formula, "Thank you, and have a nice day."

Catherine accelerates and checks the rearview mirror without thinking. The young blond man has started up behind her. She turns right, onto a small street. He follows.

She tells herself that she is becoming paranoid, that she needs to calm down, when the driver pulls to the left and accelerates to come alongside her, sending her a questioning look and indicating the nearby woods. She shakes her head, accelerates, panicking now. He also accelerates and cuts in front of her. Then he starts to turn around and, furious, gives her the finger through the window and takes off.

She looks at the rose. She always finds some meaning in things that happen, but the information that has been coming her way is both aggressive and contradictory. Unpleasant. She takes the flower, breaks the stem, crushes the petals and throws the whole jumble out the window.

When she finds the main road that goes to Aubusson again, she calms down and wants to go back to thinking about something else, to stop asking questions she cannot answer.

And once again, crossing through the gate has a magical effect that allows her to reconnect with the normal world where there is kindness.

Françoise has prepared an apple pie, if she wants some.

They have invited some theatre friends over for dinner, if she'd like to join them.

She says yes to everything, because it will all be good, and it is all fine, right until the middle of the night, when an insistent look pierces the depths of her sleep. She hesitates on the threshold of waking up, held back by a dream in jeopardy of being lost forever.

Her survival instinct wins out. She is in danger. Someone is in her room.

She opens her eyes to a silhouette sitting in the armchair near the door, immobile, a silent, blurry ghost. She breathes heavily and emits a short, small cry in the dark—a cry of surprise, fear, and disbelief. She looks blindly for the switch and knocks over the light. The crash covers up any other sounds.

She panics, gropes around, recognizes the feel of her cell phone, and presses the button. A reassuring light comes from it. She holds out the device like a flashlight. The chair is empty. The room is empty. The window is closed. The door is open.

Frightened, she recovers the bedside lamp, sets it on the table, and turns it on.

The room is filled with light. There is no darkness, and clearly, there is nobody. She gets up and pauses for a moment at the door to her room, which is open. Didn't she close it? She hits all the light switches as she goes by them. In the empty hallway, she picks up the abandoned walking stick, and the idea of having a weapon renews her courage. She goes from the living room to the bathroom, checks the kitchen and corners, and chases away any shadows.

She is alone in the small house.

Outside, night reigns, and everything sleeps. She turns on the outside light. Nothing moves. The truck and the Golf are where they should be.

She doesn't dare go out to check the yard. She locks the door. Who cares if it is ridiculous.

From behind the white truck, he observes her, exposed in the full light. He can make out her thin body, despite the large wrinkled pajama bottoms and shapeless T-shirt.

She is fragile and vulnerable. She is afraid. He's excited by her fear, which is a new kind of pleasure. He controls her. Immobile, invisible, he can watch her and petrify her with his look or give her the illusion of being safe again, of having invented an intruder, before he bursts in again and then retreats, leaving her disoriented and uncertain.

It always starts like a game. Inconsequential until there are consequences. Serious consequences.

Arthur starts down a rocky path and stops the car. "Let's go cool off before lunch," he says.

"And your parents?"

"I told them I would drive slowly. That gives us some time."

At the end of the path, there is a small sandy creek and a lake that stretches as far as the eye can see, clear and calm. It is hot, and the air is still.

They get undressed and dive into the cool water that is full of icy currents. He floats on his back, drifting slowly under an ideal sky dotted with minuscule cumulus clouds. He wants to take in this endless, wild nature with arms wide open. His heart and his sex throb with expectation: he longs to possess and be possessed by a woman. But how can it possibly happen in this lonely countryside?

Then, like a little ghost, your heart fainting,
You'd tell me to carry you
Your eyes half closed.

He cries out, "Lighter than a cork, I danced with the sturgeons that they call the eternal churners of virgins!"

"Speak for yourself!"

The lake carries him, eyes closed, toward the one who will so ideally meet his expectations. He will transform her into a dream woman.

He is cold. He's had enough.

Hidden behind the truck, he looks at Catherine, who is still exposed in the full light. The night is cold, but he is burning up. He is the master of the world. He is the elusive shadow that enters and leaves, dropping clues, small pebbles, reality jammers.

Is she playing games with him? It's his turn now. The irony of her sentence on his voice mail and her "too bad" feel like ridicule.

He is holding her in the palm of his hand. All he has to do is close his fingers. She feels it. He sees her locking the door. Oh, he won't be able to go back into the house. She is afraid. He feels the brewing anger and feeds it gently so it lasts, smoldering. He controls her. He will decide when the fire blazes.

18

The sky is blue, and the sun is demonstrating its power by saturating the miraculous azure. The birds themselves seem inebriated from so much light and fly all over the place, incapable of setting themselves down and basking in the radiance.

The road is little more than a carpet of tinted leaves whose outlines can no longer be distinguished. Because the pavement under the thick foliage is so hard to discern, concentration is required to stay out of the ditches. The nearly bare trees are the only indicators of bends and straightaways.

On this cold, dry Sunday, the horizon is a brocade, a sumptuous backlit fabric and a meticulous network of inspired embroidery. The golds have an iridescence that ranges from hazelnut to pomegranate. Some of the silvers have an aged patina, while others gleam in the sun. Rusty hues explode into oranges of varying intensity. It all sets off the splendor of the celestial ceiling.

Catherine sees him but doesn't care. Barricaded in her house, she has slept poorly. She has been overwhelmed by frightfully realistic nightmares.

Cops surround a very handsome young man and push him into an elevator. He throws her a mean look that says he'll get her, even from far behind bars, that he is the one who has won, and as he ages right before her eyes, his beauty transforms into a hideous mask, wrinkled with maleficence, his mouth turning into a bloody line.

He's an abstraction of a man, without a face, without any real shape but very real, very present, armed with a thick, solid branch. That is all she really sees as he swoops down on her. She opens her mouth to scream as loud as she can. No sound comes out, and no one comes to rescue her.

A full night of being threatened, attacked, and beaten has left her skin both wrinkled and tight. Her hair is dull, as undone as she herself is.

She turns the rearview mirror and looks at herself, dismayed. She searches through her bag and takes out some mascara and powder. She feels weak, tries to put on some eyeliner. It is too thick and overdone. She looks a hundred years old. The powder settles in her hollow cheeks, marking her face even more. She takes out a tissue to clean it off and ends up spreading it. A disaster.

Discouraged, she leans back in the seat and remembers that she must have some cream in her bag, which she lathers on her face to cover up her poor attempts at camouflage. She pinches her cheeks, attempting a smile that does not make it up to her eyes.

She is seriously tempted to give up.

But she wants to know before tomorrow how Gaston was able to legally marry an undocumented immigrant and if Myriam inadvertently provided any specific information about the family that had reduced her to slavery.

She is not out to seduce anyone. That would be counterproductive.

She has made an agreement with Louis, and she wants to find out Madame Villetreix's symptoms at the time of her death. Then she needs to see how easy it is to access the barn where the cyanide was stocked and how often the cousins and Myriam and Gaston visited one another.

She has told Louis that she will handle Olivier, the neighbor, because they had a good first meeting. There is nothing compromising about that. For her.

When she and Louis spoke on the phone, she was sincere and professional. Her state as she drives toward Saint-Jean-les-Bois is far from that. She is nervous and intimidated, with the additional problem of feeling exceptionally ugly, which gets her worked up even more for being so affected by it. Thorns just keep poking through her skin. Great.

She is tired and still has no idea how to handle Myriam.

Other than that, she remains a rookie lawyer full of promise who judiciously chose a case that is too big for her.

Scowling, closed up, tense, and determined, she parks in front of Saint Jean's church, walks right up to Olivier's house and rings the bell. Fantastic. The doorbell doesn't work. Long live modern ecology! Furious, she bangs on the door.

A disdainful silence responds.

Relief, chagrin, and anger mix in a small cocktail of contradictory emotions that finish the work of making her unstable.

She leaves again, as if she had not come for this one reason, and goes into the village, where she sees a curtain close abruptly in the house on the other side of the street and finds herself ridiculously humiliated. She lifts her chin. She is not going to feel intimidated in that way.

She walks to Gaston's house, finds the key, sticks it in the lock, and the door opens without her having to turn it. She doesn't know what she is looking for, but she is determined to justify coming all this way.

She hesitates on the threshold as she faces the dark room and closes her eyes on a mixture of burned wood, old stone, and wet earth, an odor reminiscent of her childhood. She shivers. But that's as it should be; it is cold.

Her father takes her in his arms and swings her around in the air like a top, and she screams with fear and excitement. Catherine feels around and presses the switch.

She holds back a gasp when all the lights go on, revealing a cacophony of colors, from the gaudy fabric on the walls right down to the stuffed furniture covered with multi-patterned prints. Everywhere, colors jump out, with mosaic mirrors, hot pink lace curtains, and bouquets of plastic flowers in vases that are shaped like huge yellow, red, and pink flowers. The dust that has settled since the house was abandoned weeks ago does nothing to overcome the reign of color.

Nor does it cover up the huge flat screen that dominates the living room with luxurious splendor. The African touches triumph in the kitchen, a long room to the left of the entrance, where shelves are filled with tinplate dishes, flower-covered bowls, and gold-rimmed glasses.

The contrast is striking on the second floor, preserved in maternal juice, where the rooms have austere wooden beds and stiff mattresses covered with flannel bedspreads. The spaces are burdened with solid night tables and heavy armoires.

In the hallway, there's a picture of Gaston's parents, Camille and Huguette, that has escaped the African sirocco, and the bathroom has kept its original uncomfortable stench. The showerhead on the worn claw-foot bathtub droops from a rusty support. The sink's ceramic is yellowed.

It is a strange juxtaposition of two worlds that didn't know how to mix. Could that be the key to the mystery? Catherine wonders.

She wants to leave as quickly as she can. She doesn't know if the sadness that has taken hold of her is related to the recollection—lurking inside her, ready to burst out—of a childhood happiness she couldn't hold onto or to the story this house has to tell, which is gloomy, because life has been absent from it for so long. The dust accentuates the garish look and inexpensive fittings the foreigner tried. The chill weighs down the stagnant air, and even the walls are dreary and cold from not having been lived in or looked at. The silent despondency makes the atmosphere sinister.

In the attic, Catherine glances over the piles of yellow newspapers. There is an old trunk full of moth-eaten clothes, a rickety armchair, straw chairs that have been gnawed on, mouse droppings, spider webs.

The atmosphere is depressed, as is her morale. Not wanting it to sink any lower, she decides not to visit the basement.

A door creaks downstairs. Catherine is sure of it. It isn't the wind. There is no wind. Something or someone is sneaking around.

She quietly descends from the attic. And just as she reaches the second floor, she hears heavy footsteps reverberate above her head. Someone is walking. Catherine stands on guard, her eyes steady, ears perked, sandwiched by threats above and below. A quick movement attracts her eye. A mouse has just followed her out of the attic.

Catherine runs for the first window she can find, where she can push open the shutters and be ready to scream if she is attacked.

She looks for a weapon, sees the poker in the empty hearth, and grabs it, holding it tight. It's comforting.

Now she is certain that someone is climbing the stairs to the second floor. And a commanding female voice calls out, "There's no sense hiding! Show yourself!"

Catherine hesitates, her arm raised in front of the apparition in the doorway. The face is vaguely familiar. A sheep's head. That is the image that comes to her. The intruder is older, over sixty, with a shapeless rectangular body, rubber boots, and an impeccably clean light blue apron with yellow flowers.

"Hey, you're not going to hit me with that. Drop that thing!"

Catherine is brandishing the poker and hasn't even realized it. "Sorry," she says. "I was scared."

"That's normal when you go into someone's home without being invited."

"But nobody was here."

"My point exactly."

"Mrs. Villetreix said it was okay."

"This isn't her house."

"I'm…"

"I know who you are. Now you need to come downstairs."

"Wait, there's someone up there. I heard footsteps."

"It's the dormouse. You disturbed it. That's all. Come on. You can put your mess back where it belongs."

The woman has gray hair pulled tight against her head. Her face is gentle, despite her rough tone.

Catherine sets down the poker and straightens, holding out her hand, "Maître Catherine Monsigny."

The woman does not take her hand. "I told you I know who you are," she says.

"And you are?"

"I am Gaston's cousin's wife. Is that good enough for you?"

With all fantastical impressions vanquished, life could assume its normal course again. Catherine's nature takes charge. This rough, condescending woman does not impress her.

"I ask you to change your tone. I am Myriam Villetreix's lawyer, and she asked me to stop by her home. When I came with Louis Bernier, I was not under the impression that it was the least bit problematic."

"We know Louis. It's not the same. It's your business if you want to defend that guilty woman, but it's not your place to come nosing around like this."

She attempts to save face, but her heart isn't in it.

"You know that Myriam denies everything. The trial serves to bring out the truth."

"I'm telling you. The truth doesn't need no court. I don't want to badmouth the dead, but Gaston was weak. He was kind, but he didn't invent the butter knife either. Myriam was clever. She pretended to be an exotic bird, but she was a hawk. Ask around. She put him on bad terms with everyone. She acted like she was at home here. Our family has been here for generations. We never moved from here. And here she comes and wants to start a revolution."

"You're Josiane, right?"

"What of it?"

"You yourself told the gendarmes that Gaston was happy with her."

"At first. It wasn't planned out for him to have a wife. He couldn't quite get over it. That's normal. But he ended up getting over it, believe me. And if she weren't in prison, mark my words, the house and all the rest would have been spent away, gone just like that!"

The purpose this encounter serves, Catherine tells herself, is to show her a witness at work. A lawyer who is forewarned is worth two. Now it is time to bring this to a close, and that she knows how to do. It's a practical exercise. Change of tone and attitude.

With cool authority, Catherine asks the cousin's wife to leave the premises. She is in Myriam's home until otherwise notified, and if there is one person who has the right to be here, it is clearly the lawyer who represents the legal owner.

The Josiane in question leaves, mumbling under her breath about what the world has come to.

Catherine, feeling saucy after this not-so-glorious victory, sets out to find some souvenir to take to the prisoner, a sign of peace and consideration. She opens the large armoire. Sheets occupy the upper shelves, and Myriam's clothing the two lower shelves. There is a small box filled with colorful bead necklaces. There are some pretty scarves, but she is not sure if they are allowed in prison. Then, between two sweaters, she sees a small rag doll with homemade stitching, certainly the only toy that survived Myriam's epic story. It is black and has bristly hair made of thick yarn and a heart-shaped mouth. It is dressed in a small cotton tank top and a pair of striped pants. The fingers and toes are carefully cut out, and felt sandals are on its feet. This is exactly what she needs.

While she is at it, Catherine opens the dresser drawers.

These are Gaston's. On the bottom there are coarse linen pants with stripes, clothes that have remained neatly folded for a long time. On top are two pairs of blue jeans, a pair of cotton pants, two zipped turtleneck sweaters, somewhat shapeless underwear, and woolen socks. Undergarments do not necessarily reveal a person's sex life.

The closet reveals dresses on hangers, including the polka dotted one in the picture, and a man's suit and white shirts. In the bottom, toward the back, Catherine extricates an old gilt-edged bound missal. From it falls the picture of a boy making his first communion, his damp hair plastered down and parted on the left. He has a serious and regular face and a smooth, confident look. It's a handsome face, Catherine thinks, a face that breathes of a wide-open future. Gaston at the age when everything is still possible.

Catherine wonders at what moment the possibilities merge into a single narrow door, and she puts the book back.

She glances in the nightstand and sees a packet of adult diapers.

Nobody mentioned that Gaston was incontinent.

Shocked, she closes the drawer.

She is impatient to leave.

She locks the door behind her and puts the key back in its usual hiding place.

Melancholy overtakes her, and her brain has started to feel fuzzy. She opens the car door and is ready to get in, when a voice calls out to her. "You could at least say hello!"

She turns with a huge smile meant to cover up her deathly pale look. Pleasure, worry, vexation, relief. Absent or present, Olivier the neighbor has mastered the art of causing explosive chemical reactions.

19

The sun is in the wrong place and saturates the image with light. The church loses its contours; its rustic and robust silhouette sways slightly. In reality, the solid structure is swaying only because she's squinting, Catherine reassures herself in the face of a vacillating world.

Olivier is also steady on his two feet, which are slightly spread apart.

Catherine takes a step toward the shadow of the gate and can make out the details. The eco-freak is carrying a pack of beer under his right arm, a newspaper in his left.

Catherine immediately justifies herself. In fact, she stopped by his place. She wanted to see him, and then, since he was not there, she went to Myriam's house. She stops in the middle of a sentence, goes silent, tilts her head and smiles, hoping it looks self-effacing. "Hello."

He looks at her. Really. This man always seems to have the time. The most beautiful of possessions, Catherine thinks, realizing that she has never thought of time this way before.

"You look a little pale," he says.

This observation, made kindly, is impossible to take the wrong way. He seems to be thinking without taking his eyes off her and says, "Are you in a hurry?"

"Of course not. It's Sunday," she says.

"Then I'm going to take you on a picnic. But first, I don't know if you have looked or not. No, clearly you have not. Come to my place to see something rare and beautiful."

His place is not locked either.

She follows him. They cross through the house one after the other. With a gesture she recognizes, so similar to the one her mother used when she offered her the gift of space, of the universe, he offers her his garden.

It looks like the leaves are falling from the sky, but in truth, they are falling from the branches. The leaves, again and forever the leaves, multicolored, gracious, light confetti, filling space with their continuous falling and staggering regularity.

She looks for a comment other than, "It's beautiful."

"Fall is late this year."

That is more original.

"Ah, exactly. This is not your ordinary autumn. It is the first time that I have seen this. Fall is late. It was very cold last week for two days, and I think that accelerated the death of the leaves that had nothing but a thread to keep them on the branches, and because there is no wind today to carry them away, they just gently slip to the ground. Unless I'm very much mistaken, it's a quantum phenomenon. Come on, let's go."

He gives her a critical look and says, "Look in the basket at the entryway. You'll find some boots your size. Do you like smoked salmon?"

He spontaneously starts taking care of her, generously and firmly. She is not used to this. She loosens up, like a tight knot whose ends have been freed. She breathes, tears rise to her eyes, and she heads quickly to the entryway to keep him from seeing her this way.

Olivier drives a Fiat Panda that looks like it did not stay new for long. Keeping an eye on the road, he asks, "Do you want to tell me what happened?"

"Nothing out of the ordinary. I don't know why I'm so bothered."

Catherine realizes that she is not answering the question. This man's simplicity exposes the smallest curve ball, the slightest affectation. She starts again. Differently.

She tells him about her visit to the house and how Josiane's arrival interrupted it. He does not ask any questions and takes the time to size up the situation. Then he says, "In the countryside, people are often abrupt because they are shy. They see the pretty Parisian with her cashmere sweater and her straight-out-of-a-magazine pants, and they anticipate your presumed arrogance and respond to it in advance. Josiane is not a mean person. She is defending her territory. Isn't that what we all do? The difference is what we consider our territory. What would yours be? Your land, your private domain, your secret hiding place?"

"My childhood," she says despite herself. But he does not push her to say more.

She feels contemplative and savors this new sensation of being still, of allowing herself to be carried along without effort.

"Pretty Parisian." So he finds her pretty.

The car slows down, gently, and he turns off the engine. He nods to the spot where she should look. A fawn bounds, its lightness denying gravity, and then it's gone.

He starts the car again.

While driving, he recounts Gaston and Myriam's wedding. A real country affair. A whiff of folly. A pretty folly.

"I went to see Myriam in prison. It's the Myriam of before-before, I think. The caged bird in a beautiful upscale Parisian apartment, the eternal victim, conned by life, swindled by life's storms. For me, that is not the real Myriam. It's hard to explain, I have to admit, but..."

Gaston is wearing a tie. He is standing very straight, shoulders back, but he is fiddling with his hands and says, "I'm going to get married."

A couple is a couple. There are many improbable couples who, in all likelihood, should fail, but they stay together, solid. Others, who seem to be perfectly matched for all eternity are swept apart by the first gust and separate in acrimony and violence.

Gaston and Myriam. She gives him a virility that he did not know he had. Not only sexually. She makes him the image of what she has always needed: a solid build, roots, loyalty, and courage.

He attempts to resemble the reflection in the mirror she holds out to him. For a period of time.

Two people mistreated by life get themselves back on their feet together.

It is contagious and spreads to all of Saint-Jean, because a beautiful story is a beautiful story. You can't remain grumpy in the face of such glaring evidence. Myriam comes from much farther away than Gaston. To arrive on dry land in Saint-Jean, she has needed phenomenal energy and vitality.

And after all, she is like everyone else. She believes in miracles. The marriage, the papers, the legitimacy, the estate will guarantee happiness. You never know what will bring happiness. You only know if you are happy or not.

But she is afraid. Afraid of a glitch, of the police, of the past. She should be happy, but she is not. She looks for what will satisfy her.

She and Gaston take off to the sea. To Brittany! The face-to-face idleness is a foreseeable disaster.

When Olivier is in Creuse, he has all the time he needs to busy himself with renovating his house. His trips away are short. He doesn't have the means to pay contractors, so he keeps himself busy, very busy. So, one day, knock, knock.

"It's me. I brought you…"

A pie, some fruit juice, potatoes, whatever. And Myriam settles in with nothing to do. She is bored. She wants to chat, and here it is coded, just as it is everywhere else. People talk among themselves, about gossip and news. Myriam is not a member of the tribe. She needs to fit into the shared mold, but she has other ambitions. They are undefined ambitions, without any reality to them. Something else. Olivier seems to be the closest to her. He is more understanding, because he is from here and from elsewhere too.

He parks at the bottom of a hill and laughs, "We're going up there, but you have to deserve it!"

Catherine can't resist asking, "Then you think she's guilty too?"

"I have no idea."

"Is she capable of being guilty?"

"Aren't we all?" he asks. "Now silence, city girl!"

At the bottom of the hill, they come to a small old bridge, an arch of stones that spans a waterway.

Beyond it, there is a patch of jungle into which Catherine follows her guide, trying to adopt the same calm, even pace.

When they get to a rocky patch they must climb, he reaches out a hand behind him. She lets herself grab onto it and discovers the firmness of his grip.

Water flows down the slope they are climbing. Its pitter-patter accompanies them.

They pass a house with shutters closed and a yard surrounded by a small wall. The grass is cut short. There isn't a leaf to be seen, and no trees either. A hedge is pruned into a selection of hourglasses.

They cross a small barrier and come out near a three-foot-high waterfall surrounded by flat rocks, with a picnic table and a stone bench.

"Now, into the water!" Olivier commands.

She follows him, her feet unsteady on the slippery rocks. He leads her with his arm and only lets go when her stability is ensured. Then he advances again in front of her and returns to his role as knight of the brook.

Time stops, despite the movement.

Catherine has the strange sensation that the flow of the water is lifting her from the everyday flow of life. This could last forever. There is nothing but their breathing, mixed with the even lapping of the water and the splashing caused by each of their steps. The tangle of trees and brambles on either side screens them off from the world.

They arrive at their destination. There is no reason to say so, and for that matter, he remains silent. Here, the river has widened into a water basin.

He removes his backpack and takes out an old bedcover that he places on a flat rock. A slightly lower rock serves as a table. He sets out their meal: the large loaf of bread, a package of salmon, a good-sized piece of cheese, two apples, and a bottle that he uncorks first. He pours some white wine into two plastic cups.

He invites her to toast, and they drink, savoring an earthy table wine. Then he starts daydreaming. She doesn't feel excluded, though, and allows herself the pleasure of following the silver fragments of sunshine on the water as they quiver between shadow and light.

He is the one to prepare the sandwiches and says, "In my house, woman is not a synonym for domestic help."

They eat in silence. She devours the food. He keeps filling their cups until the last drop of wine is served and puts the empty bottle back in his bag. Then, with a gesture of triumph, he takes out the final surprise, a thermos of hot coffee.

There is a gentle silence.

He makes a quick movement and suddenly grabs a sliver of silver and shows her a small panicked trout in the palm of his hand. He throws it back into the water, where it swims off, disappearing in the current.

"A future mother, for sure," he says.

"I had just turned four," Catherine hears herself say calmly. "Someone took my mother like you did that trout, but instead of throwing her back into the water, he massacred her."

"Where did that happen?"

"I don't know. Somewhere in the countryside," she says. She smiles very slightly. "That must be why I haven't been able to stop thinking about it since I got here."

He doesn't ask her anything, but for the first time, she tells someone other than herself about April 12, 1988.

As the sun's rays grow reticent, and the shadows begin to win out, the two put away the rest of their meal. Olivier adjusts his backpack, but they do not return along the river.

There is a path on a muddy arc that serves as a beach; it is easy enough for her not to need help, which she finds herself regretting. It brings them directly to the road, and all that is left to do is walk down to the car.

"It is more mysterious going up the other way," is all the explanation he gives.

On the road, he says that in his opinion, she has more in common with Myriam than she thinks.

"Why is that?"

"Someone killed both her parents, but she was, like you, little and scared."

Later on, he talks about the Villetreix family and the cousins. He tells her why he left for Paris and how he decided to come back.

Then he takes her back to her car, without suggesting a stop at his place. When she is in the driver's seat, he leans into the open driver's side window and says, "There are secrets that the dead prefer to take with them."

She feels sad, disappointed, and vexed. She starts the car.

He waves to her. "When are you coming back? To see me, I mean," he says.

She has not put on the heat, and the windshield has started to fog up. He leans into the car once more and writes his cell phone number on the glass.

20

On the platform in the train station, Catherine feels irritated and humiliated, and she's mulling it over. She is furious too, overtaken by an irresistible desire to punish that con artist who wants to have everything without giving anything. She can just get herself another attorney who is willing to defend her for a pittance! She'll see the difference!

Myriam had refused to see her.

There must be some riposte to this kind of situation, a technique to get back on your feet. Renaud said she could ask his advice. Because she is unable to focus on anything else, she presses her boss's cell phone number, praying that he'll answer, which would be a sign that her luck has not run out totally.

"Yes. Hello, it's Catherine Monsigny. I was supposed to see my client on Monday, and she refused to leave her cell," she says, barely able to control her spontaneous, whiny tone.

A calm voice answers, "She needs to think things over. You must have unwittingly put her in a quandary. I find that positive. She is active, in a way, by not being there, waiting, preparing to stand at attention and follow you.

How can you follow someone while standing at attention? Had she surprised Renaud in the arms of a lover? She looks at the time, which is the lunch hour, during which he is away from the office every day. It is strange that he has never tried anything with her.

She shakes her head. She must stop her schoolgirl fantasizing, with the eco-neighbor on one side, the obsessional lover on the other, and the father figure in the middle.

"Excuse me?" Renaud asks, having heard a strange sound at the other end of the line.

"Sorry, no, I was just clearing my throat. From that perspective, okay, um, I was afraid she might not have found me up to the task."

"You must never, ever consider how other people assess your value. And most of all not your client. Do you understand? That is rule No. 1. Animalistic relationships dictate what we do. Others immediately discern doubt, and that is when you lose all credibility. Let her wallow. Keep moving forward, and keep her informed. Go on, trust yourself. I know that you can do it, but you are the one who needs to be convinced of it more than anyone else."

She lets out a little laugh. "Now that is an unbeatable argument."

"When are you coming back?" he asks.

"The train should be here any minute. I will be at the office this afternoon."

"No, you have a court appearance. I'll pass you over to Sophie. She'll explain."

Catherine smiles at the world. Life is back on course. Her boss believes in her. Hiccups cannot be avoided. There will be others. She is jubilant. She's back in the saddle, with work goals in sight, framed, precise objectives. Pavement and pollution, here she comes! Trips to the open skies only get her recounting crazy stories about her mother, the neighbor, her father, not to mention that ridiculous encounter with Josiane. This is not serious work. It is not her.

In the train, she settles comfortably into her seat, opens the fold-down table, takes out her computer, and starts answering her late e-mails.

Her phone announces a text message, and she glances at it. She sees Cedric's number and reads, "Be right there."

She takes a few seconds to wonder how he knows that she is on the train and that she is arriving in Paris and then realizes that his message doesn't mean anything. He's showing off. That's just his style.

She takes out her notebook and jots down that she needs to look into the death of Myriam's parents. There are always wars in Africa, along with massacres and epidemics. That could be a framework for the defense. A child who grows up amid terror and violence, betrayed by the adults she has trusted, would never poison a benefactor when she has finally found asylum.

That argument could prove to be counterproductive, because violence engenders violence. And she is not going to ask Renaud what he thinks every three seconds. She lacks material and information to work with because she does not have access to Myriam. That is the result of her point-blank refusal.

She takes out her cases for the next day. In misdemeanors, she has two drug dealers, aged nineteen and twenty. Repeat offenders. They're not living in the real world. They picture themselves heroes in a video game and would dumbly put their heads on the chopping block.

This is what she mumbles to herself, but she loves them. She's going to have fun. These are her favorite clients, most certainly because they've been on a one-way street since they were born and because, after all, pot smokers shouldn't be buying or smoking. If you put these guys in prison today, you are preparing them to be real criminals later.

She fantasizes that one day she'll focus her court arguments on the underlying causes, something about the state of a mixed-up society. She is certain that it would do a lot of good for the entire judicial system—the ones applying the laws imposed on them by the government. It is hard to believe in those imposing the laws. How is it possible to take politics out of the judicial system? Democracy resembles tightrope walking: unstable, uncertain, demanding relentless vigilance. She shakes her head, half laughing, half mocking. When she gets on this kind of horse, it's because she wants to move forward. That's a good sign.

Olivier is a nice guy, but he lives on another planet where she would get bored quickly.

She dives into the Bouscard case, a case she has gotten from Renaud. A splendid Moroccan woman sold all of the jewelry belonging to her ex-husband, an antique dealer at the Louvre who disappeared in the desert the same week the stones disappeared. A perfect crime. Catherine likes it when women strike back and belie the notion that men kill more often. Equality in every area!

This is the kind of work she loves, tracking down the flaws in a case. It requires attention and concentration, leaving no room for anything else, exactly the type of exercise she needs. Renaud will be happy if she finds some procedural technicality.

And she finds it! The Moroccan woman will get out. She was presented to the investigating juge d'instruction twenty hours and fifteen minutes after being taken into custody, when the legal limit is exactly twenty hours. The cops are going to eat their hats.

Of course, Cedric is not at the train station. She is almost sorry about that. He would have been a perfect way to end this imperfect weekend, which was really four days of worry, weakness, and indecision. She cannot recognize herself in that person.

She looks at the time. Her suitcase is very heavy, and she drops it at left luggage. She heads to the courthouse. She argues for an acquittal, which she gets. The client, a repeat offender, is happy too. "See you soon for a new series of adventures," she says to herself as he walks off.

A Tunisian pickpocket recounts that when he got out of prison, he made a notch in the wall to mark his place. He expected to return there one day or another. She should tell that story to her dealers.

When she finally gets home, dragging her suitcase up, step by step, incapable of carrying it, she discovers a deep red rose on her doormat, like a threat, she thinks.

The staircase is empty. The time switch turns off while she is emptying her bag in search of her keys. The light goes back on without her doing anything, and yet there is no sound in the stairwell.

She digs around, a little more nervous. Her keychain is there, she feels it under her fingertips. It's stuck on something, on Myriam's doll. She jerks the keychain loose and manages to insert the key in the door, turn it, push her suitcase inside, throw her bag on the floor, close the door quickly, and turn the lock.

Ridiculous.

An attacker would have had more than enough time to strike.

Safe, she can think more clearly. She says to herself that if it is the same person—and it must be the same person—who left the rose here and there, that person is trying to worry her, not attack her. He is sending her a message. But why?

Could it be linked to Myriam's story? A rose?

The telephone purrs. It's Cedric. Unexpected relief. She answers.

"Are you back?"

"Just right this instant."

"Can I invite you to dinner?"

Catherine says nothing.

"Come on. I'm sure you worked all weekend and on the train, and your fridge is empty."

"Cedric?"

"Yes?"

"That rose, was it from you?"

"Uh, a rose. Shit, a rose would make you happy? Damn it, who is it that offered you a rose instead of me?"

She laughs. She accepts the invitation. He is funny and charming. She tells him the story of the Moroccan woman, about Myriam, about the Creuse. And because she has no desire to be alone, and she is feeling good with him, and it wouldn't cost her anything, after all, she suggests that he come over. She hesitates to warn him that there is a potential danger.

If some weirdo has a fixation on her, he could attack Cedric.

But no, everything works out smoothly, and desire takes up all the space.

While she abandons herself to her lover's skillful hands, passive this time, she feels opposing forces of repulsion and attraction. The other day she used him, and it could have been anyone. Here, it is strange. She holds it against him that he is so eager, when she would like it to be more surprising. There is disgust in the desire she feels. She wants him to really take her and already holds it against him for daring to subjugate her. She is not used to having twisted relationships. She wants to hurt him and digs her nails into his hips and holds him at a distance so that he will force her. And he plays along, if it is a game, or rather, he takes possession and ups the ante until it explodes, expelling the miasma and the pus, the dirtiness, which is followed by an enormous feeling of relief, the calm after the storm when the sky spreads its benevolent clarity.

Something has changed between their bodies. She is not in control, as she was the first time.

Cedric closes his eyes, and the features on his face lock up instantly in a mysterious mask.

She examines him, draws the lines along his nose, around his eyes and lips, which come back to life one after another, and he smiles, opens his eyes, and looks at her with tenderness and even recognition. A metamorphosis.

He holds her against him and says, "You drive me crazy."

She takes that as a compliment.

She knows that she cannot ask him to leave. They have a precedent now, and he would take it the wrong way. She resigns herself to making room for herself against his back, wrapping her arms around him. The bed is too narrow, anyway.

She is exhausted and falls asleep easily. She is already asleep. She is blinded by a green light as penetrating as an infinitely repeated musical sequence. She hears him get out of bed without really getting out of bed. It must be nighttime. She sleeps.

He is discreet and silent. When she wakes up, he is no longer there. He has left a short note on the stove. "Don't hold it against me. I sleep better alone." Just as she does.

21

Blond hair in half undone ringlets frame the smooth oval face, with its small, capricious mouth, its calm and attentive look. The woman, seated on the right, is wearing a long gown, held against her breast, its red orange reflecting the pale light. Blue silk or satin fabric lined in yellow falls in large folds from her shoulders to the ground, marking the separation of her thighs, forming an ample, sure base. Her bust is very straight, leaning slightly forward, indicating an alertness that is still reserved. Her left hand, with curved fingers and forward-facing palm, is a mixture of openness and rejection.

The woman's chair is set out on the terrace of a house, with only a wall and an opening to a dark interior visible.

An angel with the pure look of a child is kneeling on a bed of greenery outside, raising its right hand in blessing.

Dr. Monsigny comes alongside Catherine and follows her eyes, pretending to examine the painting and then moving on to the next. They are in the Uffizi Gallery in Florence. This short trip, just the two of them, is a father's gift to his daughter.

The Baroque idea of choosing rail travel proves to be conducive to this change of scenery. The poorly ventilated train, with its thousand stops, noise, discomfort, and overheating, imposes an old-fashioned charm and opens up a perfectly unexpected digression that perhaps Catherine has needed.

Florence looks like a stage set: the old worm-eaten hotel with its high bourgeois windows, the Visconti-style living room, somewhat decrepit nonetheless, which makes it less intimidating, the small eateries they choose by intuition, the dark, mysterious streets with luxurious store façades, the language that is both familiar and foreign. This is as unreal as the relationship between the father and his daughter. They come and go like Henry James characters, wandering and strolling while the demons get restless and massacre their lives.

Her father has planned an intimate weekend together where they take part in a shared pleasure of art and discovery, their conversation tirelessly fed by their walks and their observations. Yet she remains quiet about the one real topic that counts, the basis of their relationship, the secret that now obsesses her.

Instead of gamboling in the field, she is a dog digging at the ground where the body is buried.

And because her father does not ask her a single question that would take them out of this Florentine fiction in which they are acting, she holds it against him for being as cowardly as she is.

They hide behind a foreign language, behind their status as tourists, behind a willed good mood; they force themselves to be funny.

Dr. Monsigny has an atrocious accent and strives to explain that Catherine is his *figlia*, because they are easily taken for a couple, despite the age difference. Catherine suggests that he just accept it. It is because she is *chiari* blond, and he is *rossiccio* brown, and his insistent denials make him all the more suspicious. In the end, it is rather flattering. For him.

He pretends to laugh, which rings false even more than his Italian accent.

She puts on a mask of joyful surprise but is counting the days—only five of them. Until the day of the museum. Their third.

There is a light sprinkling of tourists. The only group is Japanese, and they remain stuck together around sculptures that do not interest the Monsignys, who feel like masters of the place.

The painting Catherine is falling into is da Vinci's *Annunciation*, and it is most certainly the Madonna's resemblance to her mother that makes her stop at it. She becomes aware of the time she's spending in front of the painting only when her father joins her, for the third time.

"She looks like you. Is that what fascinates you?"

"No, I wasn't thinking that. Do I look like her?"

She examines the face, with its resigned look and drooping eyelids. She tries to imagine a laughing Mary, and, indeed, she does see the face of her mother from the photo.

She feels her father's discomfort as he stands motionless behind her, looking over her shoulder, and it seems to her, all of a sudden, that they have come to Florence just to see this painting, that it is the key to their trip.

"I find it mysterious," she says. "A mixture of acceptance and refusal, of resignation. It is strange. Would it bother you if we left? I don't want to see anything else after this."

He never refuses anything she asks, in any case. Because this constant consent to her desires and caprices irritates her, she tries to take his arm, proposing that they go to a café.

She thinks about it all the way through the gallery until they find the sidewalk and the small street that leads to the covered market. She puts her hand under her father's arm. They walk at the same regular pace.

She tells herself that she cannot let the opportunity slip by. It would be too stupid, too foolish to be afraid of transgressing who knows what taboo.

"How did she tell you that she was expecting me?" she asks.

She continues walking, and her father's sudden stop pulls her abruptly backward. She stumbles. He seems so lost that she jokes to cover up her discomfort, "I'm pretty sure it wasn't an angel!"

He is taken aback, at a loss for words, incapable of dissimulating his confusion.

This trip to Florence was meant to protect them from the past, from the tension he has felt rising in Catherine since she took on this inopportune trial. The change of scenery, the discovery, the exoticism were meant to shelter them, to provide them with a setting, with subjects to extract them from reality. And all it took was one painting to throw them back into the quicksand of a past that is more dead than alive.

His thoughts race, and he decides to improvise a happy, light story, the opposite of the reality, whose images he is always blurring as they bump around in his memory: the noisy little café, her look that was both steadfast and trembling, her hoarse voice, so low that he had to perk his ears to hear, and his shock, his anger, and, finally, his promise, which he had kept to this day. He will always keep it. He begins by playing for time in order to calm his panic.

"Sorry, darling. I didn't understand until you mentioned the angel. You went from the *Annunciation* to, uh, us. I get it, the Madonna looks like you. It is you, and it's your mother at the same time, of course. She never saw it. I mean the painting. Let me remember. I'll tell you as we walk."

He waits until they have found a quiet table on a covered terrace, until they have ordered a *vino bianco,* and until the waiter has served them. Then he gives his daughter his improvised story. At first, he looks her right in the eye, a prime characteristic announcing a lie, one Catherine has not yet learned to recognize.

They were newlyweds, married for only two months, and they had put off their honeymoon, which was still beyond their means. It was supposed to be a trip to Florence, for that matter. The doctor was noting down an appointment on his schedule, when he saw three full days crossed off. He asked his young wife, and she gave him a mysterious look. It was a surprise she had prepared for him. She wanted him all to herself for three full days.

The first day, she took him to a do-it-yourself store and had him buy paint, wood, an armoire, and fabric.

The second day, she helped him empty the room next to theirs.

On the third day, she prepared a candlelight dinner, put on a long pleated tunic that she tied with a ribbon under her breast, and held out the positive pregnancy test.

"You hadn't figured it out?"

"No, actually."

"Hum. That is a nice story. And you never made it to Florence?"

"Never. I had a clientele to take care of, and then you were a baby and after that, well."

There they are, in the forbidden zone. Catherine doesn't test her luck; she has gotten her bone. She lets it go, saying she wants something to eat. It is time to find today's restaurant.

She tries not to think about him taking her on the trip that he had planned for his wife. She doesn't know how to interpret this decision. She clearly doesn't understand anything about her father's behavior. Why deprive her of inoffensive memories whose gentleness would have lessened the brutality of what was to follow? Had she been wrong to play the forgetting game? Had she been wrong wanting to know today? She would like life to choose for her.

The weight of their silences covers up the words, and each day of their trip seems more endless. She wants to scream at her father's too attentive, clumsy presence, him trying so hard to make her happy. Scream to break the silence, for which she is responsible.

She had counted on the only vacation she would have until March to relax, to leave behind Myriam, the Creuse, life, love, the past, the present and the future, all corks that pop back to the surface with a force proportional to the depth at which they have been pushed under.

It is all making her crazy.

The fifth day would have seemed infinitely longer, had it not been their last. She cheers herself up with the idea that giving time to her father buys her some freedom in the future. He won't be able to complain that she is neglecting him.

She promises to find a present for him in Florence. She gives it to him when they arrive in Paris, before he runs off to take his train home. She knows that it is a mean gift. Yet it seems inevitable. She had to give it to him. He is free to get rid of it.

Her gift to him is a finely framed reproduction of da Vinci's *Annunciation*.

Monsigny suspects as much when he sees the rectangular package and tests its weight. He is unable to open it until he gets home in the solitude of his room in Gaillac, where he will not have to hide the expression of bitterness and sorrow that makes him look like an old man in the throes of death.

22

The syncopated rhythm of a rap singer replaces the drumming. Instead of loincloths, there is the uniform of the moment—designer jeans, body-hugging dresses, vertiginously high heels, and sneakers. It is a group ritual reminiscent of traditional ceremonies, gathering forty or so friends in a basement rented for the occasion. A video projection shows a succession of the same faces and the same bodies on the dance floor, where the members of the tribe raise their arms, wave their hips, and hammer out all together, "Suck my dick." An overexcited group gets thrown out and disperses. People hold onto each other's waists and shoulders, hug briefly, periodically mimic copulation, laugh hard, and dance a frenetic salsa with wet hair sticking to their foreheads, shrill lipstick smearing the corners of their lips. Catherine is completely carried away by the choreographic trance, endlessly throwing herself forward with wild abandon and then leaning back in a dislocation of arms and legs. She would love to be able to dissolve all her thoughts, to lessen the unwanted flashes that are burdening her.

She doesn't recognize herself in the seasoned partier who doesn't have a taste for the party anymore. A glass wall separates her from the others, from her friends and acquaintances. She makes the gestures and says the expected words, but she is elsewhere. It's the same at work day after day. She feels like she is in a Carpenter film, where an alien invades a human body, keeping its appearance and controlling its actions.

She is "acted upon." Her alien comes from the past, but she has not identified it.

She says to herself, repeats to herself that her father has the key, that she has to question him, but what a joke. She has not been able to act on it since their tête-à-tête in Florence. What can she hope for from a distance?

They never talk, never do that thing called talking. The silence is a cover, and underneath it things swarm, simmer, cry out perhaps, underlining the emptiness of the formal politeness above, with its conventional feelings.

A pressure cooker would be a more accurate image. The burning steam escapes only through the safety valve, which swivels, whistling indistinctly. She'll have to burst the thing open, directly attack her father's weak spot, and she is not ready to face the consequences of a second paternal breakdown. That is the truth. She is a coward.

She throws her hips forward and hunches over, her arms bent.

A hand grabs her waist and stops her back-and-forth movement.

Stephanie screams into her ear, "It's great, isn't it?"

Catherine agrees, falsely joyful. She feels the half-moon smile that has been hanging on her face since she arrived. It must be a little crooked now.

Stephanie rolls her eyes, put her hands to her mouth like a loudspeaker, and articulates, "Is anyone there?"

Catherine shakes her head with an intense, knowing look, which seems appropriate for any situation.

This time, Stephanie takes her hand and drags her through the crowd that closes behind them, each step leading to a string of expected pecks on the cheek, slaps on the back, winks, and bursts of laughter.

Catherine thinks calmly that she is in the process of going crazy. It is not normal to feel so foreign in a world that is so familiar.

Stephanie pushes her into the room next door that is serving as a bar, buffet room, and cloakroom and coils herself around a boy who spits out half his beer, the amber-colored liquid flowing down his chin. He turns around and kisses his attacker smack on the lips while she licks up the foam with the tip of her tongue. She spins around, shining, and says to Catherine, with a large sweep of her arm, "This is Fabien."

"Hello, Fabien."

The man in Stephanie's life seems nice and decidedly ordinary, which his uncertain teenager looks won't camouflage for long.

"You are, um, Catherine! My respects!" he says, kissing her hand. She is going to stink of beer. Love is a disaster. What does Stephanie see in this big, ordinary, limp dude?

"Come on," the female lovebird says, "Let's go for a smoke."

And the two women go up the narrow staircase to the metal door that opens onto a courtyard, where a gigantic ashtray overflows with cigarette butts.

"So? See?"

Catherine tones down her smile. "Uh, yes."

"And...?"

Oh dear.

"He looks great," Catherine says.

"Wait, he's the best. He went to Harvard. He adores me."

"It looks that way."

Catherine feels a vibration against her ribs. She takes her cell phone out of the small bag she has slung over her shoulder. What do you know? She feels herself blush.

"Excuse me."

"Your features are blurring, brave Amazon," Stephanie says. "It's a man? Are you going to tell me about him?" She twirls around when she realizes she won't be getting an answer right away and goes back inside.

Catherine hits "answer" and says, "Dad?"

"Am I bothering you? Where are you?"

"Oh, at a party, but it's funny, I was just thinking about you."

"That's nice. I wanted to call you before your admirers attack. Happy New Year, my dear, and all the best for the trial! Speaking of which, if you agree, I'd like to come."

"When?"

"Well, in March, to Guéret, of course. I don't want to make you nervous."

"Listen, we'll talk about it later, but right now my mind is elsewhere. You've taken me a little bit by surprise. It must be the New Year's effect, wanting to start things off well. Listen, I wanted to say we can't go on like this."

She has said it too loudly. She has almost screamed it, and she retreats to a corner of the courtyard, against the wall, her head leaning into her cell phone. She now speaks softly without taking any precautions and says it all. She needs to know. She wants to know more about her mother, about her death. She wants to understand why he let it go unresolved. She wants to know every detail of the investigation, where it took place.

He stammers. Why, why now? What good does it do, except to open old wounds, hers above all, and everything he wanted to save her from, everything he always protected her from.

"Why didn't I die with her?"

She's thinking fast now. It's true, she was a potential witness, even at her age. She was there, after all. Perhaps she even saw more than people think.

There is a long silence, and then she hears her father's sad, tired voice. "This has been my greatest fear. That is also what I was protecting you from. If he didn't see you, if he didn't know that you were there, if he discovered it one day, I didn't want him to be able to find you."

"But the newspapers…"

"The newspapers talked about it. That's why we left and went far away. It was important that nobody be able to identify you. Catherine, something happened. You have to tell me what it is. Why now?"

The metal door opens behind her, the music and ruckus rush out. Someone calls her, the karaoke is starting.

She cries out that she is coming.

"I don't know, Dad. I feel like a prisoner. You have to free me."

The metaphor tells him what she is feeling. The words she wants to speak come to her, syllable after syllable, but she cannot say them: "I died that day."

Instead, she says, "No murder happens by chance."

More silence.

"These are terrible questions you are asking. They are complicated. Serious. Don't you think that it's this case that is getting under your skin? Defending felons was not a good choice. You still have time to…"

"On the contrary. On the contrary. Dad! I don't have anyone else to turn to."

Someone calls after her again.

"Go back to your party. I'm not avoiding anything. We'll talk. Even if I don't believe it will help, we'll talk again. I promise you. Don't think about it anymore. Have fun. Believe me, there is no prison worse than memory. We'll talk about it again. I love you very much. I'm here for you. Kisses, my pet. Happy New Year!"

She hates it when he calls her his pet.

She looks at her lifeless telephone and turns it off. There is a bottle of vodka at the top of the stairs. She drinks a mouthful from the bottle.

She is going to blow them away in karaoke.

She takes off her heels to go down the stairs, uncovers a strap of her red bra, which she lets fall over her shoulder, and undoes her hair, allowing a lock to fall over an eye.

She makes a thundering entrance, "Rita Hayworth! 'Put the blame on Mame.'" She extends an arm and calls out, "Felix, Claude, Philippe. You're the chorus."

Whistles and cheers.

She leans on her boys' hands, and they push her up to the small podium. It's a number they've perfected during their years at school, a number that is all the more expected, because everyone knows it.

She turns her back to the crowd, wriggles her body. The music starts, and she turns around, her hair falling in front of her face. She whisks it away with a swing of the head. A smile.

She sings.

A flash of emerald green.

The cherished inaccessible cuddly cloth. The belt that is holding her in her seat. Her arm is short, too short, the worn cloth too far.

A shadow covers her up. It is huge, masking the sky and the sun. She lifts up her head. A flash of emerald green. That was it. Nothing else, no other detail, just a presence, nothing worrisome at all. She had no reason to be scared and never had any. She moans a little and lowers her head toward the cloth, saying, "Reuteuteu."

It's incredible. She had forgotten. She called her cuddly cloth Reuteuteu.

And the large shape standing against the sky bends over, picks up the cloth, and raises it to where she can reach it. She grabs it and holds onto it, sucking it with all her strength, all her energy. The enormous distorted hand a few centimeters from her face causes her to blink. A hand of fire, with red fingertips, crippled, the hand of the devil.

He has left her, leaving the fear rising in stifled sobs. She is alone, abandoned at the edge of the woods. Who else could it be but the killer who knowingly spared her?

Why this absurd, pathetic gesture? This miserable attempt to make up for what he had done? So that she doesn't attract attention with her screams? So that she remembers that caresses follow beatings?

She sings. She thinks that kindness can camouflage a ferocious animal and that limitless love exposes you to inevitable abandonment.

She sees the familiar faces. In the first row, singing along, are Fabien and Stephanie. Everyone joins in the refrain. But in her head, she's singing something else. "Put the blame on men."

She bows to the audience. There is thundering applause. She waves her arm to her chorus boys. They pick her up and set her down in the middle of the crowd.

Stephanie and Fabien take her place for an "I've Got You" duo.

"Without me," Catherine says, and she blends into the crowd.

They barely have time to start the refrain, when the overheated crowd starts pounding out the countdown.

Happy New Year!

Catherine kisses and lets herself be kissed.

She finds a bottle of water and empties half of it.

And attacks again with warm Champagne.

She'll go dance. She's bored. She drinks until she's sick. Until she can't take any more.

Her legs are weak. "Not scared."

She finds her coat, locates her scooter, puts on her helmet, and starts right up.

It's going to be okay. She's invincible.

She speeds off, without her lights on, without the blinker, hears a car arrive behind her at full speed, has the reflex to pull off against a parked utility vehicle. The car whizzes by, barely missing her, and disappears. She puts a foot down on the ground, totally sober now, sober enough to know she is in no state to drive.

She is calm, parks her scooter on the sidewalk, chains it up, calls a taxi, and waits. For a long time.

In the taxi, she starts to shake all over.

At home, she goes to bed fully dressed. She's shivering. She looks for a blanket and then her winter coat and curls up with herself.

She waits for sleep to deliver her from the year that is starting with an endless procession of shadows.

23

The ring wakes her up. By reflex, she looks at her telephone. It is three. She came home at three in the morning. It is three in the afternoon.

Catherine has cramps all over. She throws off the heavy pile—coat, blanket, comforter—and pulls herself out, sits up, feels like throwing up, and waits for the room to stabilize.

The ringing persists, like a police siren.

She calls out that she is coming, her voice as wobbly as the rest of her.

She stops in front of the door, her hand on the handle. She had sworn that she would install a peephole.

"Who is it?"

"It's me."

She opens up immediately. There stands a tall figure, impeccably dressed in a straight-cut overcoat, with a cashmere scarf knotted around his neck, a small travel bag, and a clean-shaven serious face. Her father already looks worried. She thinks he has always been almost handsome, but his regular features, his strong, straight nose, and his large bare forehead lack the divine artist's touch that brings them to life. It is as if the painter gave up on the sketch that had gotten off to a good start but did not entirely satisfy him. This is the first time she thinks this, which startles and silences her.

He interprets the quiet in his own way and says, "I should have warned you."

She then sees herself in her father's eyes, and she becomes immediately aware of a feeling of guilt.

"No, no. Sorry. You know, it was a New Year's Eve party."

And when he wants to embrace her, she moves aside because she feels dirty and stinky. He freezes up, wounded, and in two minutes flat, the whole story of their relationship has played out.

She has to overcome the nausea, a cotton-filled painful head, and the weight of yesterday's tears to dig up her usual reflexes. Then she smiles. What a relief. She did it. She poorly imitates an ironic laugh and says, "The night was short, unlike the party. Come in. Get settled. I'm going to take a shower. And, my darling Daddy, you will make me coffee as you do so well. Very black and very strong. okay?"

He comes in, muttering that he should have called first. It's January 1, to boot. An idiotic feeling of panic has taken hold of him, as if there were some emergency, and he can't lose a minute. It's one of those anxieties that hijack reason. He knows his way around. She takes her time. He prepares breakfast.

When she turns off the shower, she hears the front door. She comes flying out of the bathroom, wrapped in her towel, and sees that he has left his bag and his scarf.

He will be back.

She grabs a pair of jeans and a sweater, her weekend clothes.

She closes herself in the bathroom. She cleans off the last traces of makeup that made her look like a sad clown. She dries her hair. She lathers on cream. She drinks from the faucet. She is as thirsty as sun-scorched land.

Her mind is empty.

It's her daddy. He has come to her rescue. He is kind. He will help her out of this strange maze that has appeared all around her. Then again, maybe this maze has really been there all this time.

It smells like coffee and toast.

Dr. Monsigny has always known how to listen. That was his talent as a physician, but words come to him with difficulty.

Catherine thinks that she is the exact opposite but holds back and chews slowly on her hot, crispy baguette.

He has bought a full load of groceries. Grapefruit juice, eggs, fruit. He must have gone to the Sri Lankan grocer, the only one open on holidays.

He refuses her help, cleans up, does the dishes, and puts things away. The kitchenette has never been so tidy.

She is dying for a cigarette but restrains herself and sits on the sofa, folding her feet under her. He pulls up a chair in front of her. Gray corduroy pants with a crisp crease, a checked shirt, and a charcoal-colored English cardigan. American moccasins, the same ones he has worn as far back as she can remember.

She does not need to activate her memory function to return to her position as a child in front of an adult.

"What's making you laugh?"

"No, nothing. I feel like I'm twelve years old."

"I can reassure you right away. You're not twelve. And I've thought of you as an adult for a long time now," he says. "Catherine, I am going to ask you a question, and I want an honest answer." He is calm and serious, searching.

"Did you meet someone?"

"Uh, yes, well, no."

"Which is it?"

"I mean yes, I met someone, but it's just someone, not someone! Okay? Why are you asking me that?"

He stands up and starts pacing, which is what he always does when he is too nervous to think clearly.

"You never asked me anything. Never raised the slightest question. You were doing well. You are doing well. You got good grades in school. You are successful at work," he says, listing the elements that have always reassured him. His child, now grown up, might have been a bit rebellious at one point, but she never seemed to have any significant problems.

"And then, all of a sudden, you want us to talk. We spent five days, just the two of us, during which you said nothing. So I'm thinking that if you want to know more about your mother, it is because you are starting your life as a women and perhaps even as a mother and that…"

He is postulating this as if it were a reasonable theory, which both moves her and irritates her.

"Not at all!" she responds instinctively.

"Say what you will, but don't forget that I know you better than anyone else, because my love for you is absolute. I had time to think last night and on the train. I'm going to tell you what I was unable to tell you when you were a teenager. There is only one question I can't answer: who killed your mother. When I met her, I was starting to become a hardened bachelor. I was alone. Atrociously alone. I worked at the hospital in Clermont. My life followed a routine. I dreamed about another life elsewhere, taking off with Doctors of the World or something like that. I wanted to do something else with my life."

On a dark evening at the end of summer, the moon is nothing but a small medallion in the sky; there are no stars. It is the kind of night that does not help you see things clearly. A solitary sad man is wandering the streets and hears a sound—surprising in this deserted town. It is the sound of crying. The person he approaches is the source.

He sees a young woman under the sad glow of a streetlamp, as alone as he is. She is leaning her head on her arm, which is folded on the back of the bench, and her back convulses irregularly. He does not want to scare her. He coughs first. She lifts her eyes. The yellow light pales in comparison with the radiance of her face. The man is taken. She incarnates vulnerability. She is unhappy and lost. He, the shy one, feels like he is putting on a new suit that is tailored just for him. He does not hesitate; everything seems simple and obvious to him.

"Come, let me buy you a drink," he says, holding out his hand. She takes his hand to stand up and quickly pulls it away and puts it in her pocket before starting to walk alongside him, small and frail, until they reach the lit sign of an unknown bar.

The entire evening he relives that fleeting sensation of their skin touching.

He is attentive and patient, getting her to talk. He has always known how to do that, how to listen. She ends up telling him everything. About her relationship with a married man whom she has regularly tried to leave but cannot resist. She knows that she is ruining her life, but she does not have the strength to give up that relationship. She teaches English. He is the father of one of her students.

The man is touched by the young woman's naiveté and the trust she shows him. Destiny has sent her to him just when he has wanted to transform his life. She is the change he has been waiting for, his future raison d'être.

It takes some time. He is patient, understanding. They see each other. She has had a falling out with her family in England, but she talks to him about her childhood in the countryside.

He takes on her dream of living in a small town far from the rest of the world, near nature, peaceful, without any destructive passion. Just a gentle way of life and tranquility.

He feels that gentleness and tranquility.

That first night, as he pays the bartender, he looks at himself in the mirror lined with glasses and bottles and sees a handsome man, virile and attractive. He is another man.

He marries her. She is already pregnant.

Together they go through the classifieds. They make their calculations. There is a lack of doctors in the Creuse.

Catherine interrupts her father, "The Creuse?"

"Yes, the Creuse. That is what scared me. I thought that you had met someone there and that the whole story was starting up again."

Catherine shakes her head. She does not understand.

"I lived in paradise for four years."

This simple sentence explains her familiarity with the places there and the surge of memories that followed. It is as if nothing ever happens by chance, except the strange coincidence of having gone back in time, blindly, without knowing or wanting to, toward her mother.

24

His young dozing wife extends her face, warm like a croissant just out of the oven, for a good-bye kiss. She puckers her lips like a child before settling deeper into her pillow. He tiptoes down the steps to avoid disturbing her further.

Violet emerges from the steamy bathroom, Catherine's plump body wrapped in a large towel, her hair, golden down, standing up like the feathers on a fledgling.

"Look what I found in the woods today!"

"Oh, the pretty little boy."

The little girl giggles, shaking her head.

"In any case, you did the right thing bringing her back to the house. She is very cute. What is her name? Grumpy?"

"Noooo," Catherine cries out.

"Kate," her mother says, "Pretty girl Kate."

She sticks the small, round wiggly body in his arms as she goes to find pajamas in the dresser. He tries to be tender, something he feels intensely but still has trouble conveying with his touch.

He envies the little girl's trusting abandon, her way of snuggling against him, her head on his shoulder, how she grabs his hair, rolling it around her finger to examine it closely, then letting it go and pressing her cheek against her father's, forcefully, passionately, and then smothering him with hugs.

He hates that he feels relieved when he hands their daughter back to her mother; she is so much more at ease. He thinks that is the purpose of maternity, of nine months of being one with a child, enough time to overcome all forms of shyness.

He looks at them—his wife, his daughter, the perfect representation of happiness.

He says to himself that he is lucky. He is happy that he has the prettiest woman on earth and that she has chosen to leave everything behind her to build her happiness with him, in a relationship of total trusting dependence.

He says to himself that they do not need anyone else. Theirs is a small, self-sufficient unit.

Why does life give you the rarest, most exquisite dishes to taste, just to whisk them away from you?

On April 12, 1988, it looks like it is going to rain all afternoon. The sky is nothing but a compact black block that is advancing like the front lines of an army. And then the enormous block breaks apart, leaving thick clouds in its place.

The doctor does his rounds in the afternoon, as he does every other day. More specifically, he is with one of his oldest and favorite patients, Melanie Rondeix. He changes a bandage, makes sure the wound is healing properly, and gives her the day's news. Roland's cow took off once again, and, as usual, stopped in the middle of the road as soon as the first car came by, creating an absurd traffic jam on a road where so few people ever travel. And Michelon's daughter tried to run away but was found at the train station, waiting for a train to Paris. She didn't have a ticket or any money. She wants to be an actress in the capital, all because her friends nicknamed her Marilyn, undoubtedly just to tease her, because the only part of her that looks like Marilyn Monroe is her fake blond hair.

Then he gently reminds Melanie that it is past three, and he still has people to see. He will be home so late, and if his wife asks him for a divorce, he will hold Melanie responsible.

And they laugh. He knows that she will fall back asleep immediately, as she was dozing when he arrived. At ninety-five, Melanie is a small uncertain flame that the slightest sigh of destiny could put out.

Dr. Monsigny is driving when his pager goes off. The gendarmes are waiting for him near Pierre Levée. His wife has had an accident.

"And Catherine?" he cries out, expecting the worst.

"Your daughter is fine."

But the worst is far worse than he imagined. The worst is that his wife has been slaughtered, his ever-so-young wife, the vine that connected him to life by sharing his existence as a rural doctor, living in a tiny hamlet with hardly any inhabitants, and all of them aging. He said that one day, when Catherine was older, he would settle his family in a large, light-filled happy city, like Toulouse.

But there won't be any afterward for Violet, who has been beaten to death with a fierceness that speaks of insanity. Or passion, which makes him the prime suspect.

He identifies the corpse, from her dress, from her ring, and mostly from her hair. He leaves his body while he answers the questions, drinks a glass of water that he throws up immediately, and tries to pull himself together before joining his little daughter, who was given to a secretary who works at the city hall.

Catherine didn't see anything, which is the only good news of the day. The stroller was facing the woods, not the clearing.

Xavier Courtois, who found the body, explains what happened. He was looking for mushrooms, using his walking stick to rummage around the pine trees, when he heard a child crying. It was about two-thirty. He had gone out right after lunch.

He followed the whimpering and saw Catherine, her little hand desperately reaching out to her favorite cuddly cloth, which she couldn't reach. He gave it to her. She shoved it in her mouth and started sucking on it, her index finger rubbing the edge of her nose in an incessant movement that seemed to calm her. He glanced around, calling out.

He was visiting friends and didn't know anyone in the area. It was only when he neared the clearing that he saw the long dark stain that had been the flowered dress Violet was wearing.

He called his hosts, who called the gendarmes, and he waited next to the stroller, talking and talking to the little girl, telling stories to distract her.

"And that is that," Monsigny concludes. "I didn't keep in touch with anyone. It wasn't easy, but I managed to change our name to my mother's maiden name. I wanted to protect you from everything, to build an insurmountable wall around you."

Catherine thinks about the feeling she had on the dance floor. She wants to tell him that the wall is there and that it cuts her off from the world more than it protects her.

She asks, "Did he have green eyes?"

Her father starts, "Who?"

"Xavier Courtois."

"No. Well, I don't remember. Why?"

"No reason."

Because he has kept silent for so long, the anxious father, the inconsolable widower, the uncertain educator does not know how to stop. Each of his solo breakaway monologues ends with a "there's no use coming back to all this," which he then contradicts immediately.

There is what is said, and what Catherine hears. Her mother was like her but more so—more beautiful, more charming, more everything, all apparently frozen in inaccessible perfection in death.

Her father had not wanted to know anything about that first unhappy provincial love affair, the one before him. It was a painful subject, and he respected his wife's silence.

As for the place where they lived in the Creuse, he says he has forgotten the name, affirms that knowing serves no purpose, and ends up throwing out that their house was destroyed. Yes, after the murder. It was a fire caused by a spark from the fireplace.

She is dumbfounded. That's not nothing. When? After they left for Bordeaux? Or before?

The day before.

Their stuff had already been moved. They had spent the night at the neighbors' house. The fire hadn't been detected until the early morning. That just strengthened his decision to break all links with the past.

"What were the neighbors' name?" Catherine asks.

"They are dead. They were elderly."

"But your patients? You must have had friends. There must be people who knew me and who knew Mom."

"Four years is not very long. I couldn't tell you."

She tries to convince him. He has to understand that now there is no going back. She knows too much, even though it is not enough.

She insists, "Did she have a lover?"

"No."

"How can you be so sure? And that man, the married man? He couldn't have come back to claim her again?"

"She would have told me."

Catherine thinks about all the things she has not told her father since she was a child, about all the things she will not tell him. She doesn't know what it is like to be married. Neither does she know much about the intimacy he supposes. But she does know a little about people, and one thing is sure: her father is not a man of intimacy. And if Catherine has always protected herself from his anxious affection, why would her mother have been any different?

From the start, he puts himself in the position of a judge, as I do, she thinks.

A thousand new theories come to mind, and she says, "Did you talk about it to the gendarmes? It's a lead."

"No, I didn't want to dirty her memory."

"But Dad..."

The paternal stubbornness puts up an impassable wall. She can't understand. He chose to let the crime go unpunished for the sake of keeping an ordinary little secret hidden.

"What could I have told them?"

"You had some elements. He was the father of one of her students."

"And risk destroying some family's life? I always tried to be aware of the consequences of my actions. And you see, I was right not to tell you anything, seeing how you get carried away, letting your imagination go wild."

"Now there is a welcome expression," Catherine says to herself.

He does not want to give in. Neither does she.

"At least tell me our name. Or my mother's maiden name. Give me something."

"What good will it do?"

"It will be something to start looking with, to work my way back."

"Nineteen years later?"

He returns to the litany of his old arguments. Hadn't she lived just fine up until now without knowing? She would waste her time and her energy, when she has a life to build, a career to boost. Chance led her to Creuse, but that is just happenstance. What about going for a bite to eat, perhaps a movie?

She reflexively closes up. He thinks he can distract her so easily from her preoccupations! She hates him for always deciding, like some old Zeus encrusted with certitudes about what the rest of the world can and cannot do, should and should not do, what is good and what is bad!

She explains that she has work to do. The coming weeks are going to be full, and she needs to take advantage of every day off to work on her court case.

He understands. As always, he understands. Better, he offers to help her. Because he's here, she should take advantage of him. He is here for her. He must have some useful skill.

She immediately sees how she can kill two birds with one stone. Keep him busy to be rid of him, and have him unravel the autopsy report she totally does not understand.

The parent–child relationship is not that complicated. All you have to do is distribute the roles fairly and reverse them when needed. Once again, all you have to do is put on an act.

25

Catherine is on her bed, with her papers in organized disorder around her. She has given her computer to her father so he can do his research.

The apartment is tiny, and all Catherine has to do is turn her head to see him at the kitchen counter taking notes in his tiny, tortured handwriting. When he feels his daughter looking at him, he lifts his eyes and smiles.

It's sweet and comfortable.

He gets a role in his daughter's life; he is happy to feel useful. It takes only a day closed up in her apartment for his color to come back and life to return to his eyes. It would be ideal if he could stay at this distance, but Catherine knows that the first chance he gets, he'll latch onto her like a shellfish that only comes off if it's broken. Does everyone else move forward by trying not to get caught up in the knots of their own contradictions?

"Do you want some tea, darling?"

"Yes, thank you."

"I also have some almond cookies."

"Mm. Great."

She dives back into her papers, but her mind is sailing out in the open seas, where one idea, *the* idea, is floating within reach.

She could put up with her father for two or three days. In his favor, he has an endless capacity for listening. He knows how to create trust, and his facial features, under perfect control, are totally nonthreatening. He could play the same role in Paris that Louis plays in Creuse.

And who knows, maybe living together and working closely could encourage him to talk, to continue talking, to remember some names, some contacts, to tell her about a thousand meaningless things that, little by little, would bring her mother back to life.

And because this solution is convenient for her, she sees no reason to oppose it, except for the limitations of him living with her and the momentary loss of freedom, "momentary" being a key word.

She goes back to the notes she took with Olivier and Louis. She is still looking for clues, any leads that will help her find the slave-driving couple. But there is nothing, no street name, no family name that has come out in conversation. She could always base her arguments on the nightmarish and degrading conditions of confine ment. They made her life with Gaston so reassuring, it would have been absurd to endanger it. But direct testimony from the couple or from one of the children, subpoenaed by the court, would carry more weight.

All she knows is that they lived in the sixteenth arrondissement of Paris, which is too much and too little information. She would need a private detective to find a bourgeois family that brought back a young black woman from Gabon to live with them as domestic help, and she doesn't have the means to employ one, nor is she allowed to.

That evening, at a Moroccan restaurant, Catherine feels exhausted from an agitated night, her emotions, the work, the revelations, and the decisions to be made. She gives into the comfortable feeling of being taken care of and paid for. She orders couscous and a pastilla, with every intention of ending the meal with honey pastries and mint tea.

The heavy wine goes to her head. She enjoys talking about the case with unusual freedom, sure that the person she is talking to looks upon her kindly. Father and daughter whisper to each other, their heads leaning in, like co-conspirators.

Catherine, freewheeling, tests out the theory that Gaston committed suicide after killing his mother.

"Overtaken by remorse six years later? And in rural areas, people tend to hang themselves."

"There are cases of cyanide poisoning. I checked. You'll see. It was the big thing among spies, wasn't it? And that Nazi woman, Goebbels' wife, didn't she kill her whole family that way?"

"You are going to come off as sweet but a nutcase if you use examples like that."

She pictures poor Gaston as OSS 117 in hiding and has to admit he's right.

The doctor becomes serious again. He has no theory about Madame Villetreix's death, because he does not have the medical report. But it is true that cyanide poisoning has the same symptoms as a heart attack if the body is not examined quickly.

"In any case, I'm not going to ask that the old lady be exhumed. That initiative would have to come from somewhere else, and I don't know where. But suicide works. Gaston feels he's not good enough for his new situation. He misses his mother. He's afraid he's got cancer."

Her father's amused look sends her the message that she is going on and on.

"You're right. I'm imagining things. My mistake. Sorry, Dad, I'm wasting your time."

"No, I'm thrilled. I haven't been bored for a single second. This is a change for me."

He says it without complaining, without bitterness. It is delicious to see him with bright eyes and an energetic voice, to feel that he is happy to be there, simply happy to be alive. Without thinking, Catherine tells him about her idea of his staying on to help her.

When you allow yourself to relax and consider new possibilities—if only for a moment—reality comes galloping back. The ordinary Monsigny reappears as if he had never been gone. Won't he be a burden? The apartment is small. He would love to, of course, but he should take a hotel room.

Catherine forces herself to be enthusiastic, exaggerating her smile until it digs painfully deep into her cheeks. No, it would be fun, really. They could camp out. And because she is tempted to say, "You're right, let's call it off," she ends up saying, "Come on, Dad, say yes. Be nice."

Her cell phone throbs. Cedric. Back from the dead. What funny timing.

"Yes, I got your text message, thanks, and the same to you, a dream year! I'm talking quietly because I'm in a restaurant. With a man, yes, in my neighborhood. It was great! Oh, yes, that reminds me about my scooter. I have to go get it. Listen, I'm not going to recount my life over the phone. Come join us. You can have tea with us! Yes, if I'm suggesting that you come. See you right away."

Cedric is at the door of Catherine's building, and the restaurant is nearby. What's she doing? Flirting? Setting up some rivalry? Trying to make him feel jealous? Or playing some other game? She had handed him a bunch of lame excuses to avoid spending New Year's Eve with him. She pretended that she hated such contrived celebrations. The beginning of a new year didn't matter all that much to her. She said she was going to a party organized by her friends, which she didn't want to take him to because it wasn't the right context for an introduction.

And now, apparently, it is the right context. She wants to introduce him to her everyday fiancé, the one who got her on New Year's Eve too. Just to drive the point home?

He is at the door of the restaurant with its multi-colored lanterns. He opens the door. A heavy drape separates the entrance from the dining room.

Catherine gives her father an amused look and says, "You are going to meet someone who is not *someone,* but is, kind of. You see, spending a little time with me is worth it."

"Does your someone have a name?"

"I know how to withhold information too." The words escape from her mouth, but he laughs, and she thinks again that part of the protective shell could fall away and that it is worth trying. She asks, "So?"

Cedric recognizes Catherine's voice, opens the curtain gently, and sees her sitting at a small table on the right, looking directly at her companion, a gray-haired man whose silhouette, with its back three quarters to him, seems vaguely familiar. Cedric pauses, overcome by an anxiety he can't explain.

"On principle, I agree, but I'm afraid that you will regret it. I'm sure you are already wondering if you made the right decision."

"Dad!"

"I do know you a little bit!"

"And me too, I know you! So? Stop playing smart, my dear darling Dad, and we'll save some time here."

Cedric lets go of the curtain and flees.

The husband of the doctor's wife, as he called the intruder in their dream story, where real-life names were not legal tender. Catherine with her father? Is this a trap?

He pulls out his cell phone as he walks away and sends a text message.

He never should have chosen her as his lawyer. It was crazy. He has to give her up. It is crazy to pursue this impossible dream. But he can't. He doesn't have the strength. One day he is going to convince himself that he is responsible for the events that take place in his life in order to control the tide.

Does he need the truth to come out, whatever the consequences?

No. Brutal, unexpected death, when it cuts off one life also interrupts others, which are cleanly amputated, left without any follow-up, no conclusion, eternally connected to nothing. Did she have a foreboding about the brevity of her passage, she who always said that life was unfair?

Would their love have remained impossible? Would they have met up later? It is dangerous to bet on the impossible, to rewrite a story that cannot take place. These questions have kept him from living his life. Now Catherine has shown up, like a miraculous opportunity to continue an unfinished story. If he can conquer her and possess her absolutely, he will be free. Finally. How many ways are there to possess someone absolutely?

He would happily go see that waitress whose name he can't even remember, who was born a slave, ready for anything. But he prefers resistance, as Catherine resists him, and because a victory is only worth the risk you take, it will be her and no one else.

His phone rings. It's her. No, it's Paul. He answers.

Okay. He'll stop by and pick him up before their meeting tomorrow morning.

Life goes on.

They need this contract. No matter what it costs. There too.

When Catherine invited Cedric to join them, she was looking forward to the introduction. But when she receives his text message excusing himself because something came up at the last minute, she is both terribly disappointed and relieved. Life is often a balance of contradictions.

Her father is more relieved than disappointed. He had feared a breach in the intimacy their evening together.

Catherine has no appetite for dessert and is feeling full. The conversation breaks off after they agree to prolong her father's stay for a few days, and they return to the apartment with weary steps.

They open up the sofa coach, setting up the camping arrangements for the days to come, and Catherine goes to bed, determined to take things as they come.

The book of Rimbaud's poems is on her night table. She opens it and looks at her mother and her forty-carat smile. Violet. She hesitates, closing the book, holding it tight against her heart, and goes to stand in front of her father, who is coming out of the bathroom in shorts and a T-shirt. He takes a step back in a way that Catherine finds touching. He had always been a prude.

"Actually, I have a picture of Mom," she says.

She had not expected his reaction. His face falls apart, but he hastily puts it back together. "That's not possible. Do you have it here?"

She lowers her head toward the book, which opens to the right page. Her father holds out his hand.

"You'll recognize her," she says. "I think you were the one who took it. But I don't want to…"

She wants to tell him to sit down. She is vaguely worried about his emotional response, but he has already grabbed the book and grasped the picture. She understands instantly that he has never seen it before, that he is not the one who took it, and that bright smile was meant for someone else.

She is mortified and pretends to believe him when he says he recognizes the picture. It's the one he had forgotten. Yes, of course, now he remembers, they had gone for a walk.

And so the first day of the year ends with many variations of the same lie.

26

A man sleeps amid the regular vibrations and noise of passing trains, but no one pays any attention to the mass of blankets surrounded by bloated plastic bags, from which emerge used shoes on one side and a filthy hat on the other. Farther along, a young couple with a dog, which is just as gaunt as they are, drink at a faucet, empty food containers at their feet.

Dr. Monsigny has been in the subway for all of two stops since he got on at the Place d'Italie and is wondering how anyone can survive in this urban hell.

In the subway car, a red-faced guitarist with bags under his eyes sings Bob Dylan in poor English to the indifferent crowd. "Once upon a time you dressed so fine…"

A teenager, her cell phone plastered to her ear, has a conversation with a girlfriend. She speaks loudly so she's heard and raises her voice even more when someone cries out, "The door!" The doors open with a roar. A large woman with a cart obstinately stands in the middle of the passageway, staring at the wall, where ads leap out with huge, happy faces that have teeth that are too white, bodies that are too thin, and colors that are more vivid than life itself. A traveler protests and pushes her to reach the exit.

Everyone is dressed for a funeral in this dark and gray underground place. Young people carry backpacks that at the slightest jolt bang into other passengers. Everyone adjusts. Apparently everyone adjusts to everything, to letting go, the indifference and the solitude.

Lethargy reigns.

The guitarist leaves the car with meager earnings and moves on to the next car.

A junkie follows him. In a whiny monotone, he apologizes to everyone for interrupting, but he does not have a job or a home, and

if you don't have coin or a meal voucher, would you please offer a
smile?

Good luck.

The next one is just out of prison and asks for help not to go back in.

Monsigny gets off the subway. There is no hurry. The open air
of the street seems like heaven. The Seine seems reminiscent of the
open sea.

He turns onto the side streets once he's past the Gare de Lyon
and comes upon a small square that is entirely Chinese, where shops
sell electronics, cell phones, computers, and repairs at incredibly low
prices.

When he reaches the Rue du Faubourg Saint Denis, he's in India
or Pakistan. Crowded shop windows gleam with gold-trimmed saris
in oranges, ochers, and pistachio green. The foreign grocery stores
are colorless, though, filled with boxes that have no writing, where
the customers know what they are looking for and where to find it.

He continues along the overhead subway line and comes upon
a noisy, multi-hued market somewhere between Sub-Saharan and
Northern Africa. He stops at the Barbès-Rochechouart intersection.
He is exhausted. In his right hand, he is holding a map of Paris open
to the eighteenth district, and in his left hand, he has the paper on
which his daughter has written in large assertive letters the association's address and directions to get there from the subway stop.

Daniel has been warned about his visit. The novice investigator
decides to start at the source, a building that is cracked as if it has
just experienced an earthquake. The door opens by itself on the first
push, but Monsigny knocks anyway to announce his arrival.

A nasally voice calls out at the same time that a bugle goes off,
"Come in! You must be Catherine's father. Pleased to meet you! Do
you want some coffee? Sorry."

A big bearded man in jeans, sneakers, and a sweatshirt interrupts
the bugling by answering the phone. Rolled-up banners and piles
of leaflets fill the room. Even in this relative calm, in these deserted
offices, crowding and disorder reign in the same offhanded way
they prevail in the subway.

"In front of the squat on Rue de Montreuil. Be there at eight. I've
told Morin. He'll send a team. I'm sleeping there, and if there's a
raid, I'll let you know, and you can relay."

Naively, Monsigny has not imagined this kind of life for his
daughter. For him, a lawyer's world means court robes, formal
courtrooms, a rich clientele, and a world of the elegant bourgeoisie.

Daniel serves the coffee in paper cups. The electric coffee maker is plugged in nonstop, and the coffee, a warmish slightly fatty liquid, tastes dull.

Daniel does him in with his kind, slightly patronizing tone. "Is this the first time you've been to Paris?"

"Do I look so provincial?"

"No, no. It's not that. It's just…"

But Catherine's father imagines himself through the eyes of this young energetic activist and sees a man from another era with an antiquated elegance, spared the social realities and hardships of life. As if you could depend on appearances.

"You are busy. I don't want to waste your time. I think Catherine explained."

"How is she? We don't see much of her these days."

"She's working a lot, and there's this case."

"I'm going to need her. We must respond forcefully to the occupations. I don't know what it's like where you live, but the number of empty buildings in Paris is absolutely scandalous."

"That's not really her specialty."

"It's going to be violent. We are likely to be carted away without a hearing. That will be her area.

Violence, his daughter's area. That's logical.

"She's effective. It's the first time we have someone of her caliber. We won't keep her long. I really like Catherine, but she's here more to serve herself than to serve others."

Monsigny is careful to cover up his sense of satisfaction. He repeats that he does not want to bother Daniel anymore, as he looks busy.

"I prepared it all for you. Here."

He's an efficient fellow. That is a welcome surprise.

The picture was taken during a small party. Daniel is holding a young cappuccino-colored woman by the shoulders. She is more charming than she is pretty and has a lot of hair held together with a ribbon. Her face is wide, and her nose is a little dented, but her eyes are big and shiny, and her wide, bursting, impish smile recalls childhood.

"You can cut me out so you just have her. I don't have any ego issues."

"Is that Myriam? She looks like a good person. Catherine has described her as rather glum and burned out. Of course, she is in prison.

"She's a chameleon. Sometimes, she is the perfect victim, humble, unsure of herself, a little bit two-faced even, and then... Well, take her marriage. I didn't believe in it for a minute, but she did everything it took, rose to the situation, and held on for years. I know that there were experiments in the past with African women sent to repopulated rural areas, but can you imagine the culture shock? In every sense of the word."

Daniel has added a card for the "cousin's" hair salon to the file, but he does not think that she will be able to add anything. Myriam's reticence about discussing her past is nothing new. This is more or less the rule, he explains like a professional. The association always tries to convince the victims to press charges so the bastards lose their sense of impunity, and the undocumented immigrants feel like they have some rights. But fear of retaliation is stronger. When you are powerless, it is dangerous to attack those who have power.

"And then there is the 'I'm here, I survived, and it's pointless to return to the past' approach to life."

"That is a wise attitude, as well."

"Yes, but that's why nothing changes. In any case, there's no need to despair. It all takes time."

Daniel has no other information about the neighborhood where Myriam used to live. She didn't go out often, did not know the people working in the shops, did not mention any specific landmark or even a metro station.

"In any case, that's what she says. She has to know more than that. You have to convince her to talk, convince her it is useful. She has a good survival instinct."

"For the moment, she is even refusing to speak to Catherine. It is total silence."

"She is afraid," Daniel says, as if it were obvious. Monsigny hears "afraid" echoing "silence," and he feels a hole opening in his chest. Two Siamese words, one following the other and vice versa. Silence is the hallmark of fear.

Then Daniel speaks, the words disappear, and Monsigny's blood flows normally again. "How would you like for all three of us to have dinner together while you are in Paris?" Daniel asks. What about Ethiopian cuisine? There's a restaurant I wanted to take Catherine to. That could be fun, don't you think?"

"I'll talk to her about it," Monsigny says, thinking, "If it's Ethiopian, it's not for me." He stands up, thanks Daniel, and gets ready to leave.

He thinks about the someone from yesterday, about the Daniel of today, and who else is there?

His intuition has been wrong. If there are several, then there are none.

When he gets out on the sidewalk he blinks, surprised by an unexpected appearance of the sun. He sighs. If he can't relieve his daughter, maybe he'll be able to impress her. Or at least get her out of this world, where she does not fit. She doesn't have the weapons to confront the darkness of the world and its injustice.

Blind and cold destiny is leading him to the edge of a cliff. Still he pretends that all is normal, because life must go on.

27

No explanation needed. They are two cops, dressed in the same jeans, sneakers, and jackets, except that the young one, about thirty, has shaved his head to try to cover up his expanding bald spot. The older one, about fifty, keeps squeezing his colleague's knee and giving him encouraging looks. They are witnesses in one of Catherine's cases, and their statements are a text they have memorized. She can imagine them agreeing on a story, like children who think they are clever, and giving their instructions to the subway inspector who started the mess. "So the dude is over there. You are here, and we arrive from over here. He pushes you, and we intervene, because you called us."

Since the beginning of the trial, Catherine's client has been pulling on her sleeve as if it were a church bell. It's a colleague in court for insulting an officer during a ticket inspection on the subway. She was flattered that he called her to defend him. It was a sign that her reputation was growing. But she was surprised by the knowing looks she got when she announced the news. Now she understands. Nobody else wants to defend the lost causes of this congenitally high-strung man.

He is as agitated as a tick. He constantly talks drivel and is seriously antagonizing the presiding judge, who has already chastised him twice. Catherine has sent him warning looks five times. He won't let go of her sleeve. She leans toward him. He has set down his case file on the bench next to him. It is bigger than hers. He pulls out pictures taken at the République subway station by surveillance cameras.

Catherine turns toward the man, who talks all the time, whether anyone is listening or not—he's a caricature of the profession—and she looks at the picture. There is urgency in his voice. "You can tell by looking at the picture that they couldn't see anything from where they were. Look, look at me. I had already gone by. They caught me and busted up my phone. I had a briefcase in my right hand and my phone in the left."

Catherine whispers to him in exasperation. "Roland, if you continue, I'll have you cuffed."

The judge intervenes, "You may not be at all interested in the witnesses' statements, but at least have enough respect to be quiet."

"Sorry, *Madame la Présidente*."

Roland is furious and turns his back to the bar. He leans against the bench to pout.

Catherine makes a sign for him to sit straight and show some respect.

Okay, the three have told their story. The same story, word for word. They are really too stupid. And pleased with themselves.

Their lawyer, who specializes in defending the police, does not even look bothered. He's used to it. He does what he can. It's a good, regular income.

Everyone comes together in front of the presiding judge to examine the video surveillance footage. It has been chosen carefully, but it still materially contradicts the witnesses.

Privately, Catherine understands the cops. She can see Roland looking down on them, not even imagining that he should interrupt his telephone call to show his ticket.

Yet they didn't have to cuff him and take him to the station. The media are focused on police abuse these days. There is so much, people feel intimidated. This is a key argument.

Roland calls out vehemently to the judge, and Catherine tries to cover it up with humor, saying, "He's not used to this, *Madame la Présidente*."

Then she turns her back to the court, stands directly in front of Roland and very clearly articulates in a whisper, "Shut up, Roland. Let me do my job, or I'll leave you to defend yourself."

He lowers his head sheepishly and seems to have understood this time.

It is a tiring trial.

Which they win hands down! Which is news that will get around their small world. In the end, it was worthwhile taking care of this pain in the neck.

She goes to put her robe away in the cloakroom and checks to see if she has time to eat something in the cafeteria. A daily special and coffee. The table of regulars is full but will soon empty. People eat really fast, take a few digs at someone, and spread rumors of nominations and transfers.

Catherine learns fast. She knows the value of details. The presiding judge sets the tone. The more you know about the judge, the better you can hone your final arguments, the central focus of the trial. She slips out the name of Judge Perret, whom she met in Guéret.

All those who know him agree: he is persnickety but fair.

Since returning to Paris, she has written to Myriam, as if nothing has happened, to suggest an appointment. If she doesn't get an answer, she'll consult Renaud, but it is hard to work without communicating with your client.

Her phone vibrates. It's Daniel.

"I didn't picture your dad like that."

"Oh, so you saw him? What did you think he was like?"

"I don't know. More modern. Rounder. You must look like your mother, right?"

"Apparently."

"Won't you introduce us?"

"She's dead. Don't worry. It was a long time ago. So, tell me, did you have a specific reason for calling me?"

Daniel backpedals like a maniac. Finds an excuse. Myriam. Of course. The token undocumented immigrant.

"Your father talked to me about your problems. You'll have to go against your nature, Catherine, and be empathetic and agreeable."

"You mean rather than disagreeable?"

"I know you are suspicious of touchy-feely compassion, but that's what it takes with a girl like that. Life has always been a bitch to her. She ended up on the wrong side of the law without doing anything wrong. I don't know if she is guilty, but I don't think she's a killer. You'd have to check the stats, but undocumented immigrants commit misdemeanors, steal, and deal because they are not really given any other choice, but they don't kill. They come here to live free and better lives."

Catherine thinks that he could be a witness if he didn't go on about legitimate causes for committing misdemeanors, which would not be appreciated. He doesn't look like a pretentious Parisian show-off. He is a nice guy who's convincing. And he would do it. He would do it for her.

She gulps down her coffee, heads toward the exit, remembers that she has three case files to get, and turns back. She'll go by the office, and then she'll be off to Nanterre, no more delays.

If she could stop by the Versailles courthouse while she's at it.

Oh, Versailles! Its staircases! It's a good thing she planned a long lunch.

Just as she is leaving the office, her boss calls her in.

"Have you worked things out with your client?"

"I hope so. I sent her a birthday card proposing a date for an appointment. No answer yet, but I'm confident. I was wondering…"

She throws herself in headfirst. The mother's death, the possible exhuming of her body… She falls apart slowly under Renaud's look of dismay.

"You don't need me to comment on that, I believe. I want you in my office in two weeks with a summary of the case and your arguments. No wild imaginings, no novels. The facts and your plan of action. What you'd call a pitch."

She leaves, walking as quietly as possible, which is ridiculous but instinctive.

She is chatting in the attorney's room in the Bobigny courthouse when her telephone rings. She doesn't recognize the number.

The voice is soft and controlled, but she recognizes Myriam, "Thank you for your card. It was nice of you to think of it."

"Myriam, we are not allowed to… Where are you calling from?"

"Don't worry. Someone lent me a cell phone. Nobody will know. I wanted to say I'm sorry and thank you and let you know I'm okay to see you on February 8."

Catherine mumbles a quick okay and hangs up, looking at her cell phone as if it were going to blow up in her hands. She tries to think about the possible consequences of her client's initiative. Myriam must have borrowed an illicit phone. All she can do is hope that no one finds it, that no one notices the call.

A colleague comes up to her and starts telling her the story of a gang bang case she is handling. Catherine escapes and doesn't stop to breathe again until the evening, when she climbs up the stairwell, yawning carelessly. She's had enough. She's totally worn out. She's wet, too, from her head, through her shoulders and down her back and legs. It has rained. She wouldn't be surprised if she has caught a cold. Cedric has not called back, and she smells cooked leeks in the stairwell.

The closer she gets to the door, the stronger the smell. Soup! Could her dear dad have made her some soup?

She opens the door. It's going to smell all night, but who cares. Then she stops, stupefied, and stifles a laugh, because, clearly, it is her fault.

The elegant Dr. Monsigny has rolled up his pants to his knees and is soaking his feet in a pot of steaming water. He raises a questioning eyebrow, and with his most caricatured schoolteacher voice he says, "You don't even have a large bowl!"

"I know. I'm useless! Did you walk that much?"

"I walked everywhere! I don't understand anything about the buses, and the subway depresses me. Did you know that you have a great little market here on Wednesdays?"

"That is the first I've heard of it."

"How do you nourish yourself, my girl?"

"Mostly with sushi."

Well, tonight she's going to get a homemade meal of soup and steamed fish with chilled Chablis and a report from her investigator.

The "cousin," Tania, was fun. She remembers Myriam really well. Because of September 11. There's nothing like a traumatic event to fix something firmly in one's memory.

Catherine doesn't react, as if this sentence did not echo their own situation. She takes the time to sit down, because her father loves to go into the details. He starts his story with a sigh of ease, Epsom salt being the supreme relief for sore feet.

It's a calm day at the hair salon. Tania is sitting on a swivel chair and talking slowly and calmly, swaying right and then left. She is very pretty, with big eyes and a wide mouth that pronounces every syllable of every word. She has a network of tiny braids that form regular geometric shapes on her very round skull. She is wearing huge hoop earrings and a black leather mini-skirt. She remembers how Myriam, a real old trout, talked about her grandmother and her princess childhood and her mean employers and how bad they treated her and how worried she was that they would find her. She was terrorized by any mention of the police. Tania remembers a detail: Myriam came to France with a valid passport, which her employer-torturers had hidden. And she had asked the hairdresser if it cost a lot to get fake papers.

That is when Tania sent her to see David. She doesn't like to be involved in shady affairs.

Monsigny asks the question that comes to him spontaneously, intuitively. "I have the feeling, well, the impression that you didn't like her so much."

"I wouldn't have wanted to do her hair!" Tania says, breaking out in laughter to soften this spontaneous exclamation. She loves her job, loves playing with people's hair, finding the style that complements the person.

"But I also understand. My life was easy, and when you haven't had to face hardship and pain, you become, well, selfish is not the right word. But I had the feeling that she was looking around here, at my salon, my jewelry, and envying them. It was as if she were casually sizing me up. But I know, that's normal. In her place, I would probably be the same."

Catherine sighs and says, "Well, that's one witness I won't bring to Guéret."

"I'm telling you what she told me, which is not enough to judge your client's guilt."

"I have to think about it."

"I hope you will approve of my initiative," he says, pointing to his bag, where she finds little posters with a picture of Myriam. They ask for information from anyone who knows her.

Tomorrow he will post them in shops at various places in the sixteenth arrondissement. He is certain that will bring some results.

After dinner he puts on his formal, serious daddy voice that brooks no reply and sends her to bed, adding with a falsely accusatory voice that he will take care of the dishes because he loves doing that. Sometimes he is touching, Catherine thinks, pulling the comforter up to her nose. She grabs her phone and writes a text message to Cedric. "You have until Friday to meet my dad! Too bad."

28

The restaurant is uncluttered, with nothing but large black and white photos to provide a foreign feeling, with their vast desert landscapes and strange villages. The stiffness of the benches, which masses of cushions help to soften, reminds Daniel of Dr. Monsigny, who is rigid yet affable.

The activist is pleased to share Catherine's father's last evening in Paris, a favor he takes as a good sign, without reading too much into it, except that Catherine wants Daniel to come into her family's private circle.

While the two men try to outdo each other in niceties, Catherine thinks of Cedric. She wonders why she has this urge to introduce him to her father, when she sees no advantage in making their liaison official, if that is what you want to call it. She thinks in passing that the word liaison itself is strange. Is she trying to prove to her father or to herself that the umbilical cord connects her elsewhere?

Cedric may be sulking or just lying low, but in any case his absence is benefiting Daniel, who is not skimping on his efforts to seduce her. Poor Daniel could bend over backward and still not get around Dr. Monsigny, who is convinced that no man is worthy of his precious daughter. In the meantime, the protector of the undocumented is again taking the burden of her father off her by listening to him recount his mission impossible, which has been a failure. In this era of paranoia, where everyone thinks that he is systematically and automatically being watched, all you need to do to be invisible is be destitute. The poor do not have cell phones or credit cards or subway passes, and they are untraceable.

She watches her father talk and fidget like a chatterbox, a metamorphosis that stems from his great solitude. Despite himself, he is enjoying the company of others again. He mimes a druggist who ran her finger over Myriam's picture as if she were trying to remove

the color before saying delicately that people of color were rare
among her clientele. Even the babysitters. It was more fashionable
to have Scandinavian girls in this neighborhood.

Monsigny makes faces, encouraged by Daniel's flattering laugh.
The young man tries to seduce the daughter by pleasing the father.
Catherine sees her father more clearly and is beginning to forgive
him his former awkwardness. He didn't have any references. He had
to shoulder the role of father without any instructions and add to
that the role of mother, against nature. So the child she was slipped
into the role of the model little girl he had invented.

Claude Monsigny, model father of Catherine Monsigny, model
little girl.

He comes to get her at an afternoon birthday party. There are
just moms. He is the only man. The women are skilled at discussing
insignificant things that signify a bond, a kind of sharing, being part
of the community. He thanks them, ill at ease.

She, in turn, is ill at ease, the mirror effect, and says, "Thank
you and good-bye," as needed, with a stiff smile.

"Don't I get a kiss?" asks Justine's mom, an affectionate, demon-
strative woman who often opens her arms, takes her in, squeezes her,
hugs her, and covers her with kisses. Catherine is uncomfortable, as
if her father were tacitly accused of something. She is dying to let
herself be hugged but closes up in solidarity.

On the sidewalk her father takes her hand in his, but there is no
heat circulating under his skin, which is soft. He takes it to guide
her, not for any pleasure of being near her. She suddenly becomes
very cold, a symptom of withdrawal, because she refused the warm
maternal hug from Justine's mom. She starts to cry.

Her dad becomes alarmed. "Did something go wrong? Were
they nasty to you?"

"I miss Mommy," she sputters.

He lets go of her hand. Not to be mean. He is hurt, offended,
and, above all, he does not know what to do, because spontaneity
is not one of his usual tools. He places his hand on the crying little
girl's head and says that he is sorry. She feels guilty and chokes back
her huge grief.

It is not his fault. It is just that way. She does not know him better
today than any other day. Who was he with his wife? She has no
representation at all of what a couple is. Is that why she is so abrupt
with men?

When she has those rare flashes of her early childhood, she hears her mother's voice, her laughter, smells her smell, but she has no recollections of her father. Nothing, as if he weren't ever there.

Could he have adopted her and wiped out all traces of it?

But her mother existed. The picture is proof of it. She is proof of it. She possesses the features and the energy and confidence of the woman in the picture. She does not recognize herself in her father or in what her father recounts of her mother.

She gets out of the bath, dripping. He wraps her in a large towel, rubs her back. He always stays at a distance. He is uncomfortable with the child's body.

An inhibited man? A man in love.

She never again says that she misses her mother, and she saves her grief for the silent solitude of the night.

Daniel has just spoken to her. What did he say? Something about dessert. The two men are looking at her. She has seriously been elsewhere.

She puts on a surprised look and says, "Ethiopian desserts?"

"Hey, if we're bothering you, we can go sit at the bar."

"Sorry, but I was thinking about a case I have to defend tomorrow."

"We are here and now."

"It is my fault. Catherine has already heard all the details of the story."

"Dad, I am old enough to take full responsibility for my own rudeness." She takes a deep breath and feels her stomach tighten. That horrible tone. Her father's tone. Oh yes, she can sometimes see herself in him.

"I wanted to talk to you about that, Claude," Daniel says. "Your daughter has really bad manners. I acknowledge that the raw material was not the top choice, but really."

Tight smiles around the table. It is not funny, but his intentions were good.

"And I have something to tell you about Myriam. I remembered a couple in the association who put her up for several weeks. I wrote down their phone number."

Her father, the king of encouragement as an educational principle, adds, "That's good. It could be interesting. More interesting than my vain searches."

"They were not at all vain, Dad."

A small repair that he accepts as an excuse. He pats her hand with a good smile and gets up. He is going to pay. He knows how to do that well. She will be his accomplice.

She turns to Daniel. If only once he would forget his basic principle that he is there to help others, not judge them, that he should leave his subjectivity at the door. It's important. She wants to know if he, like Tania, has any reservations about Myriam.

The seemingly banal question catches him by surprise. It takes his breath away for an instant. She holds his eye, "What?"

"When you're in trouble, you do what you have to do. You manipulate people. We shouldn't judge that."

"Daniel. What? What happened with Myriam?"

He fidgets, as if he were facing an inquisitor. She won't let go. He knows it and gives in. "I slept with her."

"You had a relationship?"

"No, not a relationship. I don't know, two, maybe three times."

"Did she live with you?"

"No, I didn't want that."

"You didn't do it at the office, did you?"

"Once. Listen, I don't have to tell you all this," Daniel says, getting up to leave. "It's none of your business."

"Yes, it is my business. It is also her lawyer's business. Is this a regular practice of yours?"

Dr. Monsigny returns with a satisfied smile and says, "Shall we go?"

"Give me five minutes. Can you wait outside? Sit down, Daniel, please."

Daniel keeps standing. He is dismayed. He is the one who was supposed to pay; it was his idea.

"Daniel, sit down."

Monsigny sees that the atmosphere has changed and disappears. Sometimes his allegiance proves useful.

Catherine is not his friend anymore. She is working. Daniel has already seen this side of her, sharp as steel when needed, attacking cops or witnesses, but never him, never in this disconcerting tone that makes him shy away. That's the way it is.

"It never happened before, and it hasn't happened since."

"Are you saying that she raped you?"

"If you say it like that, no, she did not rape me. You're trying to be clever. She seduced me in the true meaning of the word."

"Tell me about it."

It is a depressing night at the office. Everyone has left after a series of endless meetings, all of them futile, that turned into power struggles dressed up as ideological disagreements between fervent supporters of militancy and the more commonplace activists, like him, who were trying to temper those in such a hurry to achieve their ends.

He does not want to go home. He is feeling pessimistic about his prolonged bachelorhood, his inability to build anything, and his work, which he has been using as a distraction from the gnawing fear that life is speeding past him while he's stuck.

The office is dreary. He smokes a cigarette, opens the window, and leans his elbows on the sill. He can smell the sweetness of spring in the air, even in this hemmed-in street. A small crescent moon is hanging over the rooftops. He hears the hum of the city where others are busy loving, enjoying, and he sees a shape on the sidewalk below that he recognizes. He calls out, "Myriam? Is that you? What are you doing there? Come on up."

She is a chameleon. She is wearing sandals and a dress that's knotted at the waist. Her eyes are lined in black. She is wearing golden earrings. He is happy to see her. Perfect timing.

He tells her as much.

He announces some good news. He may have found her a job. Nothing much, but it would help out a friend. She'd have to go pick up some children at school for ten days and get them a snack. Something she's familiar with. It is in the neighborhood.

Afterward he interprets the face she makes, the expression of disappointment. She wants and deserves more than that, won't be satisfied with less. But this impression dissipates as soon as it arises.

Myriam's arrival absorbs all the air in the small office. It is thick and suffocating.

She does not take her eyes off him. She undoes the knot at her waist. Her dress falls opens and hangs around her hips. Her belly is round and shining, her thighs muscular, her breasts small, the nipples pricked to the side. He does not know if she is beautiful, but here is a woman offering her body to him, tempting him to bury his solitude and anxiety. She talks dirty in his ear throughout, and it lasts. She knows how to hold back, to rekindle him. She moans and cries out, grabs onto him, laughs. He feels like he has never experienced a woman so alive.

Afterward she goes to pee, comes back, puts her dress back on, knots it up, and says, "When you call me, I'll come."

"Did you call her back?"

"Three times," Daniel says in a weary voice.

"Why not more?"

"She wanted to get married."

"Ah ha. I see. Did she say it like that?"

"Like that," he says, opening his hands and shaking his head. "We agreed to put an end to it there."

And I sent a birthday card to that whore, Catherine thinks, being entirely unreasonable. Then she sighs, because she has just lost a good witness.

29

Catherine awakes in a panic. She didn't hear the alarm. She's late. This never happens. It's a disaster. Her legs already half out of bed, she grabs her phone. The numbers read 8:42. The additional information has trouble getting heard in the commotion of her turmoil. Then she realizes: it's Saturday; it's the weekend; she can and must relax, a little.

Is there anything sweeter than a scrap of time, a gift from above? She snuggles deeper into the pillows, her hands sheltered under the pulled-up comforter. Nice and warm, she closes her eyes. A little softness, a little padding against the roughness of the world.

Speaking of which.

She half-heartedly picks up her phone and checks her e-mail. Look at that. Cedric, back from the dead. He will wait.

Stephanie reminds her about her gym lunch date. Good.

Viagra, delete. Huge cocks, delete. Petition to defend freedom, delete.

Olivier Huguenot… That would be… Oliver. Click, open… It is.

She puts her hand on the screen and closes her eyes. Now, now, there's no reason to get all worked up. She slowly returns to the screen.

> Louis told me you'd be coming in two weeks. I am starting to clean the house, mostly the windows. I'm hanging out the red rug that smells of mothballs, but I'll wait to get a manicure until the day before you come to dinner. Okay? Tell me when, and then I will be my calm self again. Say no, and you will have to live with the eternal regret of having known so little about me. O.

You know, dear O, sweet man, how adorable you are?

But because it is better not to show how she's feeling, she will not answer right away.

She will answer right away. He is not plotting, and neither will she on the pretext of being sophisticated and in control, of roleplaying and games.

Which brings her back to her dad. Catherine had perceived the underlying tension that had been a discreet but constant companion during his stay, disappearing the second he left to catch his train home.

She closes her eyes. Spontaneously, he had recreated the couple they had been. It is not entirely his fault.

She had pulled out the scalpel without any scruples on the day she understood that it was vital for her to tear herself away from him as quickly as possible. She should have kept it at hand.

She is seventeen years old and has a brand new lover. Her first. And she likes it. She has chosen him, having picked him out in the first year of her studies. The time has come. He is a teacher. A new teacher. The only one who is a little hip. Married. She has been feeling him look at her since the beginning of the year. She feels his pleasure when she talks and firmly defends her pet subject of the moment: living your life according to a clock or a calendar leads to a loss of individual freedom. It robs you of liberty, marking the beginning of oppression. The teacher laughs. Without any measure of time, how would they meet up in class every day?

"We would meet when the shadow of the tower reaches the foot of the chestnut tree, because we want to and for the pleasure of it."

There, the words came out. Second step, she buys two tickets for a Bruce Springsteen concert and asks him to join her.

Third step, she delicately removes his scruples, one after the other, like the spines of a sea urchin, reassuring him that it is an affair guaranteed to be without repercussions.

She cannot tell him that she chose him because he is married. Nor can she tell him that she is convinced that he regularly commits adultery.

The campaign is tough, but it is worth it, and they burn the candle at both ends without exhausting it.

He has a friend who lends him his apartment. They meet up afternoons, and one night they have it until morning. They make the most of it. She gets home at four. Tiptoes in. Nothing moves.

The confrontation comes at noon.

The doctor, bags under his eyes, doesn't dare to look at her. He prepares scrambled eggs for Sunday brunch. He asks if she has used contraception.

"Yes, of course. Who do you take me for?"

He turns around, his face livid. "Well, you must understand that you have a choice to make."

She wonders if he intends to give her a list of contraceptives to choose from.

"It's him or me."

She breaks out laughing. She can't help it. It's a mean laugh; she can hear it. It is exaggerated and shrill. She tries to soften the brutality and says, "I don't think you really expect that of me. But if I were forced to make a choice, as you put it, my decision, of course, would be him!"

And spontaneously he spits out a curse, "You are a monster."

Sudden zoom out. The word instantly separates her infinitely from the dried-up rigid old man, who is nothing but a tiny indifferent shape. The bond is broken. Then she breaks up with her lover.

Neither the father nor the lover understand what has happened.

She starts working like crazy. She wants to have a very good year of preparatory studies and then flee to Paris to study law.

She decrees it. If her father wants to cut her off, she'll find a job. She's not afraid of anything, and all the less afraid because she has finally determined, without a shadow of a doubt, what she wants to do with her life. She didn't know then, nor does she today, that her determination is her greatest strength and her greatest weakness. Her conviction rarely imposes itself, but when it does, it bears no obstacle.

Her father is the first victim. His daughter's determination subjugates him. He bows down to it without protesting. He sets up his defense strategy in the form of a deep and solid trench meant to last: guilt.

That's fair enough.

Her lover is despondent and waits for her at the corner of the street to cry and beg her. She detects a masochistic pleasure, that he is reveling in the scene. She observes his reaction like an intrigued entomologist, horribly objective. Eliciting so little reaction, he tires of the effort, proving her right. She walks away with an implacable distrust of emotional demonstrations.

Yes, you can recognize deep pain by its silence.

She opens her eyes and checks her schedule. She had planned on a day trip to Guéret, but she could stay on through the weekend. She types a quick answer to Olivier. She's offhanded. She is not trying to charm him. She suggests February 8, Friday night, after her jail visit. It will be solace in one way or another.

Life has its system of road signs. All you have to do is follow the arrows.

That's taken care of. Now to Cedric. Missing in action. What has become of him?

An e-mail apology. Damn. Has something changed in him? He has something to celebrate that will amply justify his recent silence. Would she let herself be invited to Paris's top Chinese restaurant? He seems to have noticed that she favors all things Asian. Saturday night? If, by some miracle, she is free?

She is. Perfect timing. It will be a rest after working the abs.

Stephanie is looking a little pale. She is wearing one of those unbelievable outfits that only she knows how to wear, even to the gym, signed super sexy. A low-cut, cleavage-showing red leotard and striped tights on a lethargic, stooped body. Her hair is at half-mast, her eyes are sunken, her lips tight. She throws herself into each exercise carelessly. She is going to suffocate.

When they get out of the shower, Catherine asks her what she is punishing herself for. Did the meeting between Fabien and her parents go poorly?

"Don't even mention it," she says, a sign that at lunch they will talk about nothing else. Or rather, Stephanie will talk about nothing but that. She needs someone to listen, not comment.

Marco, who owns the place where they like to eat, loves them. He can judge their moods by what they order. The huge portion of greasy fries followed by chocolate mousse with whipped cream looks like despair and a failed love story. Marco pampers his two customers more than ever.

Catherine whispers that he would be the perfect solution for Stephanie, with his soft paunch, his shiny skull, and his gray moustache, not to mention his steady job, of course.

They drink three quarters of a bottle of Sancerre, which helps Stephanie wallow in humor rather than complain.

Calmer, she goes home to go to bed, and Catherine heads off to prepare for the wars to come, the battle of the Creuse first of all and her presentation to Renaud as the follow-up.

She opens the chapter, "The Defendant's Personality." An orphan robbed of her parents by war, then torn away from her beloved grandmother, falling under the yoke of people who exploit and terrorize her when they are supposed to protect her.

She chews on her pen. Something bothers her in Daniel's story, and now she knows what it is. She calls him and asks if Myriam seduced him like a professional, and because he doesn't understand, she adds, "Like a slut."

This simple question throws him into an absurd confusion. Could excessive prudishness be a male characteristic?

"Daniel, I don't want to pry into your personal life. I am just asking if she had the know-how of, well, a mercenary. You must be able to feel it, can't you?"

"The truth is, I asked myself that very question."

"Ah ha."

"It doesn't prove anything."

"Of course not."

"I'm not much of a regular…"

"I understand."

He changes the subject and informs Catherine that, in fact, the day the activists she is representing go to court, a whole bunch of friends will meet in front of the courthouse.

"Oh no, not another demonstration!"

"It's good for you, isn't it?"

"Daniel, let's be clear about this. It is not good for my clients. It is good for your own publicity. The court doesn't respond positively to activists who use pressure tactics."

He will not take her arguments into account, in any case, so there is no sense in wasting her energy. The road stops here. Been there, done that. This will be her last contribution to the association. She concludes with, "In any case, Myriam was not a frightened virgin."

Daniel lets out a half sheepish, half boastful mumble, which is a confirmation.

There's no file on Myriam, or else the police investigation would have uncovered it. Either she is lying about everything, or she worked the streets, for want of anything better, after leaving her jailers.

Catherine has no intention of broaching the subject head-on with her, though, considering that she has to re-establish an atmosphere of trust.

She makes a mental note: "possibly ask Renaud."

She finishes reading the expert's report. He evaluates Myriam's intelligence as average. Nothing particular noted. No sign of trauma. He would probably say that the grandmother did a good job. Myriam does not have high self-esteem.

That will do. There is no reason to bring in an outside expert as a witness. The facts pose a more delicate problem. Death by poisoning is indisputable. Even if Myriam's guilt is nothing more than conjecture, the prosecution will certainly bring up her delay in calling for help. She says she woke up and found him dead. In front of the television that was still on. Yet he suffered before his heart gave out, which must have made some noise. On the other hand, she was asleep. And their bedroom was some distance from the living room.

At the very least, Catherine can argue that Myriam should be given the benefit of the doubt.

There really isn't anything but circumstantial evidence.

The theory of an accident wouldn't hold up, but Catherine does not want to rule out suicide just yet. The truth is, she is dying to argue Myriam's innocence, because she is dreaming of winning, and that would be a much flashier victory.

She decides that she really deserves a nice bubble bath, in which she almost falls asleep. It relaxes her before she prepares to see Cedric, who is going to get the whole works, she decides, with an uplift bra, a skillfully unbuttoned cardigan and a narrow straight skirt, fishnet stockings, and ankle boots.

And lipstick.

She looks at herself in front of the mirror, thinks about Myriam, and wonders who the slut is.

30

Catherine feels like an adventurer, with her skirt up around her hips, straddling the motorcycle behind Cedric. She hadn't thought about the motorcycle issue, but without any hesitation or fuss, she hoisted up the tight cylinder, which, fortunately, is made of stretch fabric. As a result, he's the one who throws embarrassed looks around and seems to be reassured when the tiny street behind the Gare de Lyon, where the newly opened restaurant is located, is perfectly deserted.

Were it not for the small altar garnished with flowers and gifts to a good-natured Buddha, it would look like a contemporary American restaurant. There are few tables. Theirs is reserved and isolated. A red rose lies on Catherine's plate. Is this to make up for the one he did not put on her landing or to confirm that he is the one who put it there? But then, did he also leave the one she found in the crumbling mansion? Cedric's decidedly very green eyes are shining, but he does not answer her silent questions. He has changed, she says to herself. He is relaxed and happy.

"I'll explain later. Tell me about you. Where have you been? How are you? But first, can I see my ring?"

She stares at him with a foolish look on her face. Ring, what ring?

"You decide to introduce me to your father without first asking for my hand! You should do things in the proper order. So where is my engagement ring?"

She blushes. He puts on the face of a wounded man holding onto his dignity.

"Very well, let's forget it then. But the next time you ask me to marry you, it will be on your knee with your hand on your heart. And I cannot guarantee what answer you'll get."

She laughs louder than the joke deserves. More roleplaying. Right on target, Cedric. Subtle.

They don't have to order, as he has prepared the menu ahead of time, and with simple curiosity in his voice, he starts asking questions that quickly sound like an interrogation. "How old is your father? What does he do? Seventy? Retired?"

Yes, she is the daughter of an old man, but her mother was very young, which balances things out. Dead, when she was a kid. She doesn't want to talk about it. Her father was a doctor, retired now. No, he never remarried.

And his family?

He would love to introduce her to his parents. They live in the burbs. His father works in construction. His mother is a housewife. He's an only child. He'll introduce her if she's not afraid of slumming.

She's offended. If only he could see the clients she has to defend! They laugh. Like most other members of the middle class, she sincerely believes that she is socially mobile. But in France, there is no social mobility. People stay within the boundaries of their respective classes, each with its own rites and codes.

She tells him that he has hidden his working-class garb so well, it's indiscernible, then cuts him off to get back to square one, saying, "Come on! Tell me what is making you so happy!"

No more pretenses and no more banderillas either. Cedric does not have to be asked twice to announce that in the face of rugged competition and huge stakes, his agency has landed the job that they have worked on for weeks. He mentioned it to her. Did she remember? He tells her about how they presented their layout proposal to top management at the daily, the battery of questions they had to answer, how he had to react without being prepared. And then he tells her about the second meeting, where they put together new proposals based on the first project. In the end, they beat out the English! It is the revenge of Trafalgar, France's flouted honor finally intact again, Joan of Arc avenged!

"You should see the front page. I can show you the draft layout with all the graphics and the lead photo in a month."

He scribbles on the paper tablecloth so she can see the size of the headlines and how the headings and the content are posted like a movie trailer. For that matter, some of the online content will be video. Everyone totally believes in the idea. This is his first free night. They have been working night and day, spending hours in the newsroom, watching how it works close up. It is exciting. A paper is a living creature, right to the last minute. A news event is like a cell that transforms the entire organism.

Catherine tries to leaf backward through the photo album of her memory: Cedric, the handsome arrogant guy, the lost dude who picks up a waitress and carelessly knocks her over, the ladies' man, the lover, the one so sure of himself and the one so unsure, and now the passionate one, talkative, enthusiastic, younger. She thinks that she likes him like that, from this perspective and, nonetheless...

He stops talking, looks at her, his face still lit up, happy, but something in his look remains dark, impenetrable. She feels devoured when he stares at her like that. Uncomfortable, she breaks the silence. "I love your eyes."

"Oh no. Not my green eyes. Not you too," he says, with a look of mock despair.

"I had nothing to do with them," he says. "They jumped a generation and come from my maternal grandfather from Kiev, with a hint from my father, who inherited a light-colored halo from his mother, which makes her my paternal grandmother, who is still alive, poor thing, hanging onto life, but in such a state!"

The dishes follow each other, at the same pace as his animated words: small mouthfuls of dim sum, black mushrooms, delicately flavored soups, unusual salads.

Little by little, it is as if they are finally getting to know each other, starting from square one again, after erasing the previous episodes. The shadows of the past dissipate in this fresh light, this entertaining and comfortable exchange.

Catherine talks about her work, about her concerns, about her ridiculous excitement the first time she left her court robe in the attorneys' cloakroom, how she watches the nonchalance of lawyers she admires in order to copy their casualness, how she is getting her bearings little by little. She explains what is at stake in a felony trial, the uncertainty when you face a jury of regular people, rather than the professional jurors found in less serious trials and whom you more or less understand.

He toasts the justice system that has allowed them to meet, the Chinese food that is bringing them together, a future full of promise for each of their careers, an eternal homecoming, to green eyes, to their irresistible charm, and to the question of the evening, "Your place or mine?"

"Mine."

But first, he takes her to the banks of the Seine, parks his motorcycle, and leads her on a lover's walk to the Square du Vert Galant, where they pretend not to see the homeless crouching with their dogs, their hands extended over an improvised fire. The couple hug and kiss in front of the river in the intense artificial light of a *Bateau Mouche* sightseeing boat with excited tourists capturing this picture right out of Hollywood on their digital cameras.

Catherine smiles and says, "Have you seen *Charade?*"

And she tells him about Audrey Hepburn falling in love with Cary Grant, not knowing if he is going to kill her or marry her. There is a scene on a riverboat that is the most wonderful cliché of Paris. She will show him the DVD.

She hears herself making plans. That's a change for her. He likes it.

Cedric has transformed into a prince charming. If he is playing this role so well to seduce her, then part of him must be like that. If he is going to so much trouble, then he deserves a response, and she says softly that she feels good with him, and he whispers that he does too and that they would feel even better in a big bed, freed from their rags, off to look for...

He takes on a strange Dutch accent and a rugged voice. "Off to look for the naked man." And he explains he's being simian. He'll explain another time.

It's as though they have their entire lives to reveal themselves and discover each other.

In bed, it's a confrontation. A joust somewhere between play and combat. It is troubling, exciting, disturbing. Catherine tells herself that, unlike sanitized sex, this contradictory mixture of abandonment and refusal has a real honesty. She refrains from hurting him when she kisses him, even though she is harsh, provoking him. She almost holds it against him for building up such reckless desire for her. She wants to frustrate him, to torture him, to dominate him, and then he gets the upper hand and subdues her.

In this moment, time and ordinary life have no hold on them.

In the morning, she is overflowing with energy. Her body is a perfectly oiled machine, her face, which she looks at quickly in the bathroom, is round and pink like a child's. She is thrilled to see her refrigerator still full of paternal provisions. She shouts out the choices in a clear voice to the man who is still buried under the warm sheets, "Scrambled eggs? Ham? Coffee? Tangerines?"

He answers that he's Cedric, then strings together onomatopoeias full of "mmmm" and gentle "ohs" and "ahs." She makes fun of him, while noting, amazed, that they slept—a little bit, but well—together. They slept. They rested one against the other without getting in each other's way, and she can't get over it, does not want to get over it. She prepares and dresses a table as she has never done before. In the middle stands the symbolic rose.

He joins her, in boxers and a T-shirt. This handsome body of the mature man who pulled her out of her little-girl preciousness is all hers. She likes how he is at ease in accepting the start of a paunch, his soft thighs. She loves his way of grabbing her as she goes by, pulling her against him, of kissing her lips, of taking possession of her hand to caress it. He has the authority of his virility, but she has the resources of a warrior. They are equals.

She tells him about the dream she had when she found herself captured by a ray of green light that kept her from moving, which went out all of a sudden, leaving her in the cold.

He would be happy to be her ray of green light and tells her the legend.

Later, much later, when they accept everyday time again, and their work obligations catch up to them, when they agree to separate to meet again for a late dinner, when they get dressed, playing that they are undressing each other, stealing a sock, a T-shirt to delay the moment of separation, when that moment arrives, when he verifies that he has his keys, his gloves and hints that he's missing a kiss, she says, "Hey, about the rose. You said, later. It's later."

"Yes, later than this later."

She does not really pay attention to this quick response that is a pure and simple refusal. Or perhaps she only hears it and needs to get rid of any hint of doubt that would ruin the perfection of their brand new encounter. She says, "No, now. No secrets. You said, 'later,' not 'later than later.' Come on, please. It's going to bother me."

And he takes the leap to tell the truth. Later, she will try to remember that he could have lied.

"It was me."

She doesn't understand until he spells it out episode by episode.

"The rose on the landing was me."

"And in the Creuse also, in the abandoned house?"

"Yes, it was me. I followed you. I wanted to surprise you, and I didn't dare."

"Oh, that is not enough. I need to know more."

He tries to explain the strange pleasure of seeing without being seen, of melting into the shadows, of following her like a prey.

She feels cold and smooth, like a stone in a freezing stream. It comes out in her voice.

"Of scaring me too? Was it you in the night? Why?"

"No reason. Just like that. It was stupid. It was before."

"But..."

"No. Don't hold it against me. Forgive me."

"There is something else. I can feel it."

He laughs. What is she imagining? Of course not.

He is lying. Everything is fake. The laugh. The words. The covered-up discomfort.

"So, like we said? I'll see you later? Do you forgive me?"

She says yes, distracted.

She wants him to leave.

He feels it. He leaves.

The empty bed, the deserted apartment, the silence, the abandonment, the discomfort that grows, twist up her insides, out of proportion, excessively, grotesquely. On the verge of tears, she opens all the windows, changes the sheets, does the dishes, takes out her case files, and sits down at the table.

31

It's 2:06 p.m. Another hour to wait.

The file is in front of Catherine. It is clear-cut. She knows what she has to say by heart, but having her notes nearby is reassuring. She checks the order of the pages. An accident can happen at any time. And Maître Renaud is giving her an hour, an enormous amount of time, four hundred euros at his friends' rate, and for her it is free. It is priceless and therefore exorbitant. Or at least precious.

The essence of her arguments can be summed up in a few lines. Then she will answer questions and ask her own. Select, key questions. He does not like the superfluous. He does not like waste. It is grotesque that her hands are damp and her throat dry. Fluids have this way of spreading to the strangest places, perfect, objective, and precise witnesses of discomfort and uncertainty.

What will it be like when she does this in a real live court!

Her nightmare last night. She is naked, of course, in a gigantic courtroom. The jury, the judges, the prosecution are so far away, she cannot distinguish their faces. There is a heavy, crushing silence. Who is she defending? What is the case about? She has no idea, but she is expected to speak. It is the defense's time to speak. It is the voice of God coming down from heaven. "Disappear." The anxiety wakes her up.

She gets up. She knows what she has to do: get on her scooter, drive to Guéret, see Myriam, ask her two questions, and get back in time for her appointment with Renaud.

Cedric's voice on the telephone. "Is it because I followed you?"

"No, I told you, I got too far behind. I have to catch up, and I'll only have one appointment with Renaud. I have to be prepared."

"It's because I followed you. You would have preferred that I lied?"

"No. Listen, I'm not in the mood for this. Let's not talk about it anymore. I'll call you back."

She wants so much to talk about it that she can't think of any-thing else. Why not tell him? "Yes, I feel betrayed. I don't know who you are. I can no longer believe in any of the roles you play, because there are too many of them."

Inhuman screaming. The sound of regular, relentless blows. Silence. The huge figure in front of her when she lifts her eyes. The green ray of light. The old piece of cloth. The panicked sucking.

Invented memories, recomposed recollections, her father says.

She dragged one name out of him. His trembling finger looking on the map.

His plea. "Do not go there. Do not go back to the past. You can't reach it."

"Mom's killer lives somewhere, free with a secret that impacts us. And you don't even care?"

There is suffering in her father's face. "How can you say that? It's monstrous."

Monstrous?

And what if he were right? What if it were none of her business?

Had her ignorance kept her from living her life, from being, from working, from loving?

From loving, yes. But that is not necessarily because of the secret. Perhaps she is simply lacking that capacity.

At the age of eight, her girlfriends and she compared plans. "I will have two children, a boy and a girl, Clovis and Lila," one friend said. "Me, I'll have three boys, Pierre, Paul, and Jacques," another responded. And little Catherine: "I won't have any children, I will buy a red convertible, and I'll drive along a cliff road. It will be beautiful, and I will be free.

These might not have been her exact words, but that was her plan. Her girlfriends looked at her with undisguised pity. "And you won't have a husband?" Fearful stupefaction. No, no husband.

Not normal.

2:07.

That can't be. Her telephone is lying. She glances at the clock in the entryway, which she can see from her office. No, time is taking its time. She is no longer in sync with everyone else's time.

Myriam is even grayer, more listless, more vacant, and her cour-age wavers. Catherine shouldn't have come. She takes out the little posters her father has made, and Myriam rebels. "You don't have the right. You should have asked me."

At least that wakes her up.

"At least tell me if these people really exist."

With a challenging look, she spits out, "No one will know what they did. First the father, then the son. I don't want anyone to know."

"Okay, I'll remove them. But, Myriam, that is exactly how I want you when you appear in court, alive and willful. Promise me you will stop taking the pills tonight. Too bad if you can't sleep. Okay?"

"Okay."

She takes it in. All of a sudden she is fierce, unrecognizable.

Then, without stopping, Catherine asks, "Did you kill Gaston?"

"No."

An immediate answer.

"I'll see you on February 8."

And the whole way back, she feels exalted, wild like the wind, a movie star. As long as Renaud never finds out. It is everything he detests. But she needed it. She needs it. She had to make clear what was at stake, to note the importance of the relationship, to engage her client to engage with her. And Myriam understood. She is sure of that.

2:09.

When the clock is so mocking, it is best to be indifferent, something like, "I've got all the time in the world. I'm going to call my friend."

Stephanie whispers that she is in a meeting, can't talk, hangs up. Why does she answer the phone then?

Should she go for coffee?

What if she falls on the way and breaks her leg? What if she is hit by a car? "Don't take the risk," she tells herself.

She's nuts. "You have to calm down."

Some perspective now. It's a working meeting, work in progress. She does not have to focus on results. That is not what he expects of her.

Her desk phone rings. "Are you coming? I'm waiting for you."

She looks at her cell phone and sees that it's three. Time has sprinted ahead after languishing miserably.

Some mysteries cannot be vanquished.

She knocks on the door. She enters.

He smiles. She sits and opens her file on her knees. The papers start to slip out of the file. She grabs them, closes the file, and places it on the chair next to her.

She notes that he has blank paper in front of him and an un-capped pen. Something rises in her, setting her arteries ablaze. Desire, momentum, excitement. She's off. She talks.

What she presents is the reasonable version, the base from which to improvise. After she sees how her boss reacts, she'll propose her crazier ideas.

The entire prosecution is based on circumstantial evidence, suspicion, and rumors. The defendant, who dreamed of nothing more than being accepted and integrated, who hoped to make a solitary and sad man happy, is rejected. She is the foreigner. Her very difference is the basis for the prosecution witnesses' statements, which are, in truth, inconsistent.

What was so reprehensible about her taking advantage of her husband's assets with his full consent?

Only one thing is certain: Gaston Villetreix ingested cyanide. How? Nobody can say. The poison was there in the open barn for anyone to take.

Ah yes, the jar was found in the Villetreix kitchen, and the chicken was, in fact, spicy.

All the witnesses say that Myriam Villetreix made spicy dishes. That night, like all the others.

So what are the theories?

There is a noisy dormouse that lives under the Villetreix roof. They talked about it a lot. Couldn't Gaston have gone to get the cyanide, which was there for anyone to take, because he wanted to get rid of the animal?

It would have been prepared with an egg, which the dormouse loved, so it is logical that he put the poison in the kitchen. And that he neglected to tell his wife about it.

Catherine is soaring and mentions the possibility of suicide, the slight depression that Gaston seemed to suffer, which worried Myriam.

She ends with the motive, on the vain search for a motive. Money? Her husband refused her nothing. Myriam Villetreix had finally found security, a family, a place to belong, everything that life had refused her and that she dreamed about. Would she then destroy this paradise that she had finally built?

Two solitary people had found each other to become one, an unusual one perhaps, not conventional most certainly, but it was a bond that both had consented to and only death could undo.

"And then I ask for acquittal, if only for the benefit of the doubt. There you go, the main lines of my arguments. I don't have the specifics on the witnesses I intend to call, but this is the direction I'll take with my questions."

She feels good, freed up the more she speaks, the more she feels she is right. Without the slightest doubt.

Renaud lets a moment of silence go by.

He attacks gently. He would have preferred that she not argue in front of him. He had wanted her to simply lay out how she was organizing her arguments.

Too bad.

He begins by telling her that she needs to choose. Either she pleads innocence, knowing that it's double or nothing. Or she pleads doubt and argues in that direction. But she cannot do both. "You have to draw a clear line for the jurors to follow," he tells her. "Most of all, you must not confuse them."

"In any case, you can never be certain what will happen in court. You have to remember that the case file is not taken into consideration. The only thing that counts is what is said there. Witnesses are unpredictable. The prosecutor is more predictable, but he will not forewarn you about his own arguments.

"It is good to think of different options so you are not caught by surprise. But once you choose which direction to take, the minute you start pleading your defense, you don't slalom. You go straight downhill.

"In this case, the defendant's personality will have a huge impact. You have to know what you can expect from her, but do not hope for a miracle. Do not try to turn her into someone other than the person the jury will see."

In this regard, Catherine mentions Daniel's confession. And what if Myriam is lying? What if she is not this poor courageous victim, but a professional, a manipulating prostitute?

"That is a potentially damaging piece of information. You are talking about the defendant's personality. Imagine that it comes out, say, from a witness. Is there any trace of this information in the file?"

"Uh, no."

"I have to tell you something, Catherine. We must be careful about our own prejudices, particularly those that could resonate with the jurors. Popular clichés have black women, African women, being crazy about their bodies, being nymphomaniacs and liars. The speed at which you drew conclusions from an event that could be interpreted very differently is revealing. For your client's good, do not even go there. Except to refute it if ever the subject is raised in court. But make sure you are honest with yourself. Another thing, only risk the suicide theory if you have some specific support from witnesses. Otherwise, forget it."

"So should I plead innocence or reasonable doubt?"

"That is your job. I will not decide for you. I also wanted to say that when you are selecting the jurors, it is a bonus if you can give those you accept the impression that they have been specially chosen."

"That would mean that I will have to challenge the juror choices in a way that is a little…"

"Unpleasant, yes. You have a natural tendency to dramatize. You lay it on, so to speak. That is not a criticism. Don't worry. It's an asset. The *Cour d'Assises* is a good place for that, but you need to be constantly aware—during the questioning, during your final arguments, and even when you listen—that you have real people in front of you, whose faces you see, whose ages and professions you know. Talk to them. Remember that. And don't worry. It will go well. Did you work things out with your client?"

How he is looking at her! She puts on an evasive look. Let's hope he doesn't suspect anything.

"I think so. I'll be going back next week. For that matter, I'd like to stay three days."

Renaud just raises an eyebrow.

"Yes, that will allow me to get a feel for things, for the atmosphere. You know, it's another planet there."

"It is not so different. Catherine, no investigating, right? You are not getting carried away, are you?"

"No, no. Thank you, Maître."

"And congratulations on the Bouscard case. Good discovery, the twenty-hour rule! Did your father enjoy his stay?"

"Yes, thank you."

She returns to her messy office, relieved, very relieved and wonders how it is that he knows everything that is going on. She had not told him that her father was visiting. Sophie? Of course, Sophie. Sophie sees and hears everything.

Okay, that's not all. She looks at the pile of rulings to file. Damn. She'll never be finished by seven-thirty, and she really wanted to see the Jim Carrey movie.

Duty first.

Her phone vibrates. Business is picking up again. It's Stephanie, and now is not the right time. But then she remembers that she is the one who called her friend, who is just responding. She is not going to admit to her that she was just looking for something to fill the time. She answers and improvises. "Do you want to go to the eight o'clock movie? The Jim Carrey?"

"Is it okay if I come with Fabien?"

Catherine says nothing.

There are silences that are easy to interpret. Stephanie gets it right and says, "Oh listen, I'll tell you all about it. No, you couldn't even imagine everything he invented to get me back, and the truth is, I'm crazy about him and that's that."

That's that, Catherine thinks. It's her life, not mine. Never.

32

At the top of the stairs after the underground passage, a wall rises on the platform, where letters stand out in a color that is as faded as the prosperity of years long gone. They read: La Souterraine.

The Golf is in its spot in the parking lot, as is the key. Every landmark—the fishing store, the empty outdoor café tables, the sleepy Grand Hôtel, the house for sale, the furniture shop, the road lined with large, middle-income homes with open yards, the traffic circle, the gas station—is a sign of welcome, renewing the current passing between the person arriving and the region. The sky is uniformly gray, the rain regular, the countryside curled up on itself, time slowed. The feeling is comfortable.

Last week, when she had done that quick round trip, her eyes had never left the road. This Friday, Catherine feels an invisible bond that attaches her to this place. Is it because she now knows that this is one part of her childhood?

The strange coincidence that brings her back here is not one. Her past is reaching out to her, reminding her that it exists, that it is here for her, that it is part of her life. This is not chance that has brought her back here. Rather, she is following the signs that point the way at regular intervals. In life, you are at liberty to follow the signs or disregard them.

The young smiling woman in the picture, so alive and mute, is haunting Catherine's sleep more and more often. Sometimes her lips mouth inaudible sounds. Sometimes her face streams with tears, but she continues to smile forever. She is the age her daughter is now. She could be a friend, a sister. She incarnates all the promises that life will never keep. She has no resentment, sharing her joy and her trust. And her sadness.

Catherine now keeps the photo and its cardboard frame with her. She has slipped it into a zip-top bag and put it in her purse, like a talisman.

On this day, though, finding out more about the young dead woman is not a priority. She has pressing tasks to tend to and problems to resolve. It has been twenty years since that picture was taken. A few months won't make any difference.

This stubborn land will end up accepting her if she keeps returning to it, even for short periods, and then she will come back again and actively search for traces of her mother when she was alive and try to solve the mystery of her death.

Even if there is no real tombstone, her father did deign to tell her where he had scattered her mother's ashes. At Devil's Wash.

Catherine will go there and pay her respects.

Later.

She passes the Saint Vaury exit, where there is a psychiatric hospital. She knows she is halfway there.

The Cedric issue was resolved with a single sentence sent by e-mail, a more ceremonial than anecdotal text message, "I don't want to see you anymore."

Send.

Her computer alerted her to a return message, and when the name Devers popped up in her inbox, her heart started beating hard. She noted her agitation, and she realized she was anxious to see his answer, that an e-mail, even one announcing a breakup, continued to weave their bond. Danger. She deleted the response without reading it, just as she deleted all the following e-mails from him. She does not read his text messages, does not answer his calls. She imposes this necessary violence on herself.

Sometimes she misses him so much, she is dying to call him. "Come, now, right away. I am waiting for you." Her attraction to him is equal to the danger. She met Cedric as a result of violent circumstances. She has to flee him. He is a liar and underhanded and perverse. Too bad for the interlude of grace, too bad for that vertiginous pleasure.

Too bad. Their former slogan is now their epitaph.

Love is not her priority, nor her concern, and the reason she is allowing herself a break to have dinner with Olivier is because he is part of the case she is working on. Myriam is the priority. Nothing else.

She takes a deep breath. There. It's clear. Her discipline and her new resolutions are her safeguards. She has regained control of the little boat that the contrary winds were knocking around.

And she is rewarded with her client's transformation as soon as she arrives at the jail. Her face seems softer, her color that of a husked chestnut, shiny and smooth, her eyes bright and lively, and she is smiling when she enters the room Catherine has gotten for them.

She has the shy smile of a worried child.

She seems reassured by the hand that Catherine holds out to her, which she shakes firmly, proudly announcing that she has followed her advice and refused the medication they brought with her meal. She speaks clearly, and her energy is palpable. She again expresses her determination to fight.

"Great!" Catherine says.

"Yes, I was so scared you wouldn't come back, that I had let you down. You are all that I have."

"Not exactly. There are people in Saint-Jean who like you. I should be seeing Olivier later, and he speaks kindly of you."

"Oh him, he's nice with everyone. But even he wasn't able to do anything."

"You know that as soon as the process got underway, there was not much he could do."

"Do you call it a process when things are not going right with your husband?"

"No, I mean the legal proceedings that are the reason you are here. What do you mean? Things weren't going well with Gaston?"

"First explain the proceedings, from the start, because the truth is, I don't always understand exactly what's happening. The doctor came. I called him. I have nothing to hide. He said it was his heart. He never said anything about poison. Everything was normal at the burial."

It is perhaps just as well that they start over from the beginning. Catherine explains that Gaston's heart stopped. Yes, when you die the heart stops, but in this case, his heart gave out on him, and that is what killed him. There had not been an autopsy because the doctor had not noted anything suspicious or strange.

"The suspicions arose later, after people started talking about it. They were not happy because you were going to sell and go away, and the estate is important to the family. The cousins thought you were in a hurry to bury Gaston. They remembered that the dead man had never had a weak heart and that he was in good health. They remembered the day that Gaston said you had threatened him with witchcraft."

Myriam's jaw drops. Then she breaks out in loud spontaneous laughter and says, "That was a joke. I told him he'd married a negress and that I could use black magic to turn him into a penguin if he wasn't nice to me. Sometimes he said he would take several wives like in Africa, and I threatened to cast a spell on him. We were joking."

"And then they discovered that the cyanide wasn't in the barn, but in your kitchen."

"It wasn't me."

"Yes, but they got a lawyer who put together a case, and the judge opened an investigation. You are the one who benefits from his death, and since there was a risk, in the judge's opinion, that you would run, he chose to put you in jail."

"And just for that they can leave me in prison my whole life?"

"I am here so that your stay there is as short as possible."

"Go ahead. Ask me all the question you want."

Catherine begins by taking out a box of chocolates hidden at the bottom of her bag and uses this moment to follow Daniel's advice. She tells Myriam that she believes in her, admires her courage and tenacity in rebuilding her life, her certainty that she had made Gaston happy.

Then she explains the options: innocence or reasonable doubt. Myriam does not hesitate and chooses innocence. Because that is the truth.

Catherine believes her but advises that she listen to both arguments before deciding.

First, she goes back to the family that mistreated her. One last time, their testimonies could help them. Is Myriam sure that she doesn't want to give their names?"

They are people who know important people. They are capable of hurting her. She is afraid. She is wary of them because she knows them.

"But we will not be able to prove that your story about mistreatment is true."

The defendant just shrugs, and Catherine rejects on principle the doubt that she has just felt.

She decides to move forward, even though her destination is unclear. She raises the question of the wedding. You need papers to get married. The police investigation did not bring into question the legitimacy of the wedding, but the subject could come up in the trial.

Myriam keeps her obstinate look and says, "I had papers. It is not a problem."

"Were they fake?"

"No."

"You were undocumented. What did you do?"

"I didn't have the papers to be in France. But I know who I am."

"I thought your employers kept your passport."

"I fixed things with an employee at the embassy."

"How?"

"Gaston gave me money. But you can't tell anyone."

"But is Myriam N'Bissi your real name?"

"Yes, that's me."

Catherine doesn't like victims. Here she is with a client who talks back and is aggressive, perfectly capable of having plotted a murder, confirmation that there is no such thing as a perfect client.

The road becomes smoother when she talks about Gaston's life. Myriam speaks with emotion. Was it genuine? She tells the details with precision, as if it were yesterday.

A man in gray pants and a beige cotton jacket is there on the platform at the top of the stairs. He is carrying a sign with his name, Gaston, written on it. He looks younger than he did in the picture. She has also sent him a picture. Myriam smiles at him, and he blinks twice, as though he is surprised. She thinks that maybe he has never seen a black woman before. She is wearing a new pair of pants and a jacket that Daniel has given her, all too happy to be rid of her.

She lifts her eyes and looks at Catherine. "Daniel didn't say anything, did he?"

Catherine gives her a surprised, questioning look. "Tell me," she says. "What is it? You know that I am bound by client-attorney privilege."

"Oh my, it's not a secret!" Myriam says with a mischievous look, not at all embarrassed. "I could tell that he was attracted to me. And I thought, why not? He's nice, French. I must not have been the first, considering his job. Then I asked him to marry me, and he said 'Oh, no, no, no.'"

She does a great imitation of Daniel, panicked like a rabbit running back into its hole. Catherine smiles, hesitates, and then says, "You mean you..."

"Yes. Daniel is cute."

The lawyer wonders what her client's sex life must have been like, considering her strange life, but Myriam keeps talking about Gaston.

So it is the first time at the train station, and she is careful. She is dressed like a super normal, super ordinary French woman. Perhaps he was expecting something more exotic. She is afraid that he is disappointed.

Silence settles in the small utility vehicle he's driving, so she carries on the conversation all by herself. She puts on an exaggerated African accent to tell stories about imaginary friends, "Oh, if you marry a white dude, he'll wash you out, girl, like bleach. You need to see the witch doctor first."

She tells him about witch doctors, how they're all business. First they help you out once or twice, all friendly, and then, when something good happens to you, they say it's because of them, and then people find out. You trust them, send your friends, and then they start making money. They buy a nice house, and everyone says they must be good witch doctors if they are so successful.

She is relieved when he starts to laugh. He talks about the superstitions where he comes from. And that is the first little connection. The second is that where she comes from and where he comes from, everyone knows who you are, who your parents are, and so you don't ever wonder about your identity.

She hesitates, but she has promised herself that there would be no lies between them, and it is easier while he is driving and not looking at her. She warns him that she has already been with other men. Two of them.

"Me too," he answers.

"Two men?"

"No, two women."

She is joking. He realizes it. By the time they get to Saint-Jean, they know how to laugh together, and that helps her get over the shock she feels when she sees the little town with its houses all closed up and nobody in the street.

"Sorry," Catherine interrupts. "I have to ask a few questions that could…"

"No, I told you, you can ask me anything."

"You said that you had been with two men. When?"

"The first was back at home. The first ones. Because of the war, but we shouldn't talk about that."

She won't say any more. Catherine reminds her that she needs to know as much as possible, even if she doesn't use the information, because it is worse to have a witness reveal an unexpected secret.

"Don't worry. In any case, sex is not important. If you need to do it, you do it. Otherwise, you go without. It will be okay."

Myriam pats her arm, mimicking a comforting gesture, totally reversing the roles. Myriam is smart. She knows where she wants to go, better than her lawyer. She anticipates the questions, decides what will come into play or not. Yes, she has the composure of a mind-reading witch.

Catherine shakes her head. Renaud was right. She is carrying around a whole load of stereotypes.

33

The traffic is calm. Catherine is in no hurry. The cold cuts through her. The trees are bare, absorbing the light rain that is starting to fall, as though they are impatient to be dressed in green again. She is going to slightly twist her principles, justifying it in advance because it will help her overcome a problem that isn't one.

Two locals are chatting as they lean on their carts under the awning in front of the supermarket. They stop talking to follow the newcomer with their eyes, showing no curiosity, emotion, or discomfort. They are just looking at her.

A worker in overalls, with a baguette under his arm, hastens to his double-parked car.

Catherine locks her car, takes a few steps, and then goes back and unlocks it. It's a habit to learn. To unlearn.

Catherine adjusts the photo in its cardboard frame, using her hand to protect the picture from the rain. Catherine finds the right distance from the "Lavaveix-les-Mines" sign and dispels her final doubts. The sign's letters coincide with those in the picture.

To really make sure, she checks other details, the house that can be seen behind and to the right. Catherine moves left without thinking and finds herself in the middle of the road, causing a surprised driver to honk and swerve at the same time. Catherine is just as surprised and jumps to the side of the road. The picture falls, dropping out of the frame, and is immediately blistered by the rain.

Catherine tries feverishly to put it back in place and feels punished. Stupid Pandora. Is it a sign that she shouldn't go or that she should?

She slips the picture under her raincoat, gets back in the car, and turns the heat all the way up. The dampness has penetrated her bones. She shivers and lightly touches the picture laid out on the passenger seat.

It will dry. It will be easy to put it back in the frame.

Her father did not take the picture. He did not recognize the photo. Why did he lie?

Why lie about an innocent picture?

It is not that innocent. That smile full of passion is for the person behind the lens.

But then what do I know? Catherine immediately questions her authority when it comes to lovers. Perhaps it was a girlfriend. Or the self-portrait of a narcissistic beauty.

She is beautiful! Why would such a beautiful woman bury herself here with a man who is not very much fun to be around?

Maybe she needs to stop seeing secrets and mysteries everywhere. You meet a man, you fall in love, you follow him. It's that simple.

The rain is now combined with a fog, dropped in layers that conceal the road. She can't see anything with her lights on high beam. She needs to keep switching from low to high and back again. It's as harrowing as a horror movie, and the landscape at dusk makes the atmosphere even more unsettling.

Catherine locks her doors as she drives on. She feels ridiculous, but there's no one there to know.

She drives slowly. It's as though night has fallen all of a sudden. Her anxiety rises each time a car comes up on her. She is afraid that she will pull over too far and find herself stuck in a ditch. So she slows nearly to a stop to allow the more skilled local drivers to pass her.

"I'm such a chump," she says to herself and wonders where that word comes from.

That is the question she asks Olivier when she finally crosses his threshold and immediately forgets the infinite time it has taken to arrive safe and sound. She's here. It is warm, and it smells of lentils. Several lights are on, blocking out the night.

And Olivier has an answer. It is not the last time he'll have a prompt solution for an incongruous problem.

So she gets the explanation even before a hello. "A chump is a short, thick lump of wood that has come to mean a blockhead, which, I assure you, you are not."

"Sometimes I wonder!"

"It's like a combination of chunk and stump."

"Thanks. I stump for my clients, but some days—take my word for it—they stump me. Now give me something to drink before I founder in despair."

"Red, white, or bubbles?"

"Red, thanks."

It's crazy. The charm is working again, even better without the rough edges of novelty. Olivier is as familiar to her as his region.

She had to stop herself fifteen times from asking Myriam about the nice neighbor's wife, what she's like, what she does. That would have been so unprofessional and so revealing, if only to herself.

And here she is, barely sitting down when she hears herself ask, "Are you separated from your wife?"

"Can't you tell?"

"And I'm prying."

"You can always ask."

"Why did you separate?"

"That is not the right way to ask the question. But I am going to answer anyway."

"You should have been a judge. Or a grade-school teacher!"

"Oh no, not at all. The simple answer is that we got married young, and then we grew apart, because we didn't pay attention. But I could just as well respond that we separated so that I could meet you and have dinner with you tonight in my ecologically correct home."

Olivier feels a hollow in his stomach, a little pocket where his sweet wife still nests. Always wearing jeans and a T-shirt. Her tomboy body and her long, straight, nearly blond hair. A practicing Catholic. Not prudish but seriously committed. In love, as well. Pure. A rare specimen. Elise, his chosen one.

So pure and so rare that the question of choice does not even come up. They'll have a child once they get the apartment, a second one when family finances allow it. There is no visible tension, no apparent disagreement, a tacit, inescapable duty—happiness. At any price. The happiness you read about in magazines. An image, a pretty showcase. Elise wants to stop working but does not say so. Olivier starts a computer business that loses money and takes all his time. On Saturday night, they play cards with couples just like them.

Elise begins to sink into a depression masked as chronic fatigue. She dotes on their son, Gaspard, while giving Oliver no more than a dribble. Oliver finds that he has fewer and fewer reasons to go home.

Finally, she is courageous, transgressing all her taboos, and takes a lover, a brutal act of pure provocation.

Olivier's world cracks and caves in. They divorce. Now she is married to another man, a nice, reassuring man who is good for her.

"Maybe the questions should have been: why were you drawn together?" Oliver says. The reality is that we were certainly meant to share the same path for seven years and to give birth to a boy, whom we are raising as best we can and who exasperates and fulfills me at the same time."

By tacit agreement, Catherine and Olivier avoid any further risky mention of a real past and instead launch into an intense and futile argument over destiny and free will. Catherine feels terribly intelligent before she starts getting a little bored, something she doesn't want to admit to herself. Sometimes Olivier is pedantic and sententious. He dwells on abstract concepts and tries to win points in a rather unimaginative way. She knows it and at the same time forbids herself from knowing it, because that would project her into an unappealing future when what she wants is to dream. A little bit more.

Fortunately the discussion comes to an end. They have a shared domestic tasks: tasting the lentils, adjusting the seasoning, setting the table at the last minute, and, finally, eating in front of the fireplace with their plates on their knees.

Over a period of a few minutes, Olivier's voice, in the process of recounting some episodic story or another, fades and disappears into a silence that is far from comfortable.

Catherine fights against sleep because she wants to listen. It is hot under her mother's sweater, and the silence is full of anger. She wants to hear what will happen when she is in bed. If they forget her, if she becomes light as a feather, as invisible as a chair or a rug, then she will know why she is crying. It is not just a tantrum, as they keep repeating. She cries out of fear. You shouldn't throw tantrums, Kate. That's not a good thing.

"Are you falling asleep?"

"No, sorry, was I asleep?"

"You were somewhere else, but it's my fault. Do you want to go?"

"Oh, no!" she says and then corrects herself, confused, "No. We haven't even talked about Myriam."

"Do you want to sleep here?"

Oh dear.

"I mean, there's a thick fog out there tonight. You could get lost, and I have a guest room."

Oh dear. Not the slightest ambiguity.

Why is she so disappointed when he behaves the way she wants him to? She's feeling uncertain—she, the one who always knows what she wants. Why doesn't she know anymore?

Even the wall she built between Cedric and herself is more a hastily improvised defense than a clear expression of her will.

Just thinking about driving back under the rain tires her, so she says yes, that is a good idea. She is tired.

The room is perfect, small like the cabin of a boat, with a two-person bed, a dresser, and mushroom-colored walls.

He brings her a large shirt and a hot water bottle, which she wraps herself around in order to fall into a universe without decisions, without determination, as if life were a movie in which she was both an actress and a spectator. The experience is restful and, ironically, harrowing.

Olivier is in his car. Elise is sitting next to him. He turns to Catherine, whom he is about to leave by the side road, and throws her a magnanimous kiss while he takes his wife by the shoulder. He has made his choice. The light is harsh. It is cold. Elise turns around then. Catherine recognizes her mother, who is wearing that bright smile from the picture. The car speeds away, faster and faster. Catherine is alone. Other cars pass. Nobody sees her. Nobody hears her.

A ray of sunlight warms her neck. It filters through the closed shutters. There is a bathrobe on the bed. She puts it on and goes downstairs, her face wrinkled with sleep and marked by the pillow. The smell of coffee guides her.

Olivier is working at his computer. He asks if she has slept well without taking his eyes off the screen.

She says yes. You always say yes in the countryside, because you are supposed to sleep well. And she knows that. And really, she did sleep well. It is eleven.

"You didn't have an appointment, I hope. I almost woke you up."

An enormous feeling of guilt invades Catherine. Her hosts must have been worried.

Olivier has let them know.

He is too perfect, and she wants to ask him what right he has to take charge of everything and to do it so well, and why nothing seems to annoy him. She understands Elise, who certainly wanted to break down this nonchalance. Catherine remembers that she is not at her best in the mornings.

She remembers that she was at her best in the morning with Cedric. Sorrow.

"Oh thank you," she says.

And of course, as he is perfect, Olivier lets her drink her coffee, toast her bread, and dip her bread and butter in the dark liquid without leaving his work.

Afterward, she asks him if he would like to testify at the trial so that the jurors can picture Myriam as she was. Then another question escapes before she can catch herself. "She never came on to you did she?"

"Myriam! No. That's not her style. Or maybe you think I'm the town stud."

She moves on quickly, "And the cousins. What kind of relationship did they have with her?"

Yes, he is a good witness. He describes very vividly and simply the unbelieving stupefaction that meets Gaston's announcement about the arrival of a potential fiancée.

Not-so-subtle jokes and mocking comments follow until they accept the inevitable, not with resignation, but rather with an actual collective agreement.

Myriam does everything she can to be admitted into this microsociety. She is humble, asks advice about everything, from the best and least expensive brand of laundry detergent to the right soil for growing parsley and coriander. She helps out wherever she can—a little ironing here, a bouquet of wildflowers there. Olivier is the only one to refuse any help from her.

Catherine smiles. "In your house, woman is not synonymous with domestic help."

A hard-earned state of grace in the small town and an easy and willful conjugal honeymoon last for nearly two years. The first nettles appear when the couple goes on vacation. Everyone is shocked. Why go elsewhere when you live in the countryside? Vacations are for city folks. And the cost. Gaston might have assets, but he has worked for them, and they're meant to last, not be wasted.

And no matter what Myriam does, she is different. She sings when she does the dishes. She ties up her skirt to mop the floor. She walks around barefoot. Little by little, her joyfulness begins to erode. She becomes bogged down in the humdrum routine that Gaston has returned to, finding the easy pace that suits him. She guesses the commentaries, the gossip behind her back. It is not mean-spirited. It is a way to be interested in life as it goes by, and Myriam is still a new flavor.

That is when she begins to visit Olivier every day. She's looking for friendship with someone who isn't talking about her or judging her. Everyone has to invent a way of living with others. There is no user's manual.

Evidently, after Gaston's death, the talk and the speculation just intensified.

"His heart attack shocked everyone," Oliver says. "And Myriam, feeling like she was being suspected, was clumsy. She didn't talk to anyone, turned away so she wouldn't have to face the cousins, distrusted the mailman and the baker when they did their rounds. And she managed to antagonize the estate lawyer, as well. That didn't help. But that doesn't help you either. I mean, what I've just told you."

Oh but yes, it will, later. It is what she will do with it that counts, the questions she will ask. She will be well informed so she won't have to improvise. She closes her notebook, full of notes. When she leaves, she is dreading that Olivier will ask to see her again. She is disappointed when he doesn't say anything and sighs when she turns on the car. Their relational mode is in place, and it's pathetic. Unless it's just her.

34

Yes, pathetic, Catherine thinks again, taking her bags out of the trunk of the Golf. She had said she would arrive yesterday, and she gets here today, with a casualness that her refined, attentive hosts do not deserve.

Jean-Claude sticks his head out an open window on the first floor of the brick house, asks if she needs help, and laughs when Catherine starts apologizing. Françoise appears behind her husband, looking happy to see her.

They are all of forty or so years old, not old enough to be her parents, yet she feels prepared to adopt them as ideal parents who, far from questioning, doubting, and criticizing, accept her with generosity, kindness, tolerance, and even affection, although she does not understand where any of that comes from.

She immediately tempers her enthusiasm with a cynical reminder that they certainly act this way with all their guests. It is good for their business. She's a member of an anonymous crowd, nothing but an ordinary customer.

Ordinary is not a qualifier she usually uses to describe herself. Clearly some screw has come loose.

Jean-Claude knocks on the door that is already open. He is bringing her some potatoes, zucchini, and lettuce from their garden. And then he brings out the eggs. "Real ones!" he says before offering to help Catherine, who is perplexed by the cardboard frame that refuses to go back into place.

It is best to take it all apart, flatten out the cardboard, strengthen the whole thing, and then put it back together again. If she wants...

She wants, is grateful, would like it if he could also put her life back together with his knotty craftsman's hands that maneuver so delicately.

"Wow, a picture taken with a traditional camera. You can tell the difference. The work of a professional. Look, there is still a stamp from the shop on the back."

No, she had not seen that. It is slightly wiped out, but you can still see the letters "ri" and then "ga" and a final "d" at the end. She thinks: a maternal puzzle. Another one to put together.

"Does that mean anything to you?"

He does not understand the question.

"Could that be the name of a shop in the region, one that develops pictures?"

"The picture's from here?"

She explains her theory that the picture was taken in Lavaveix. Perhaps it was developed there.

He asks her about the picture because the woman looks so much like her, and she explains in a neutral voice that the resemblance is understandable because it is her mother, and this is the only picture of her that she has. So she would be really grateful if Jean-Claude could repair it.

"Let me take care of it."

Letting others take care of things is all that she wants right now.

He removes the frame, concentrating on the small pieces that he is putting back together. He doesn't ask any questions, only suggests that she ask the regional encyclopedia, Louis, who goes from one place to another, gleaning all kinds of information, registering events, the small events that make up life and people of every rank. Perhaps he would have an idea.

While he is working, Catherine tries to organize her schedule, but the distractions of her life interfere until she feels as disjointed as her mother's picture.

She prepares coffee. They chat. Jean-Claude goes to look for a little glue, scissors, and cardboard. His workshop is a junk shop full of solutions.

"Françoise makes fun of me. I keep everything. All the same, it is useful."

While mending, he recounts that he was a photographer in another life. He lived near Paris, in La Courneuve. He worked in one of those shops that developed film before everything became digital. Although he wished he had the genius of Robert Doisneau and Edouard Boubat, he never managed to make a living with it. Photography is still one of his hobbies, though.

Catherine knows nothing about photography. He will show her. He has all the books, he concludes with a sweet and sour irony.

"How old was your mother in the picture?"

"I don't know. Twenty something."

She does not know exactly. It is the only age she knows her mother at. She is such an ephemeral creature, born fully grown without any origins, no past, and dead, living just long enough to leave a three-dimension reminder, Catherine, who is responsible for saving her from nothingness.

She becomes angry. It's not normal. It's not fair that her father knows so little, as if he married a Myriam, an undocumented immigrant with no identity, the difference being that Gaston proved to be much more curious about his young Gabonese woman than Dr. Monsigny was about his young English woman.

What is this family without ancestors, without a history?

She, who felt free because she didn't have roots or bonds now feels stifled by their absence, by the absent one.

She is grateful for Jean-Claude's discretion. She would not know how to answer ordinary questions, those you ask people you don't know, those she has always avoided.

He talks about his life. He tells her that they ended up here by chance ten years ago. He and Françoise had thought about selling antiques abroad to save up money to go elsewhere, and then the place enchanted them. "It's a place where everyone knows everybody else."

"Where everyone knows everything about everyone else."

"That's not so bad either, you know. Because we follow closely what the others are doing, we see people at work, with their passions, their sorrows, and their difficulties, at all ages. I think we understand more than city folks who see everything in rough outlines from a distance. We look at the details, as you do in a photograph. The details tell the essential story."

The Amazon, who dashes through the city on her scooter, free and solitary, protected by her anonymity, hears proximity and thinks promiscuity.

"That is because you are young. Are you going to talk to Louis while you're here? Okay, I'm taking the frame and putting in under a press to dry."

And then he leaves.

She doesn't know what to do. She doesn't want to work or read or make a call. She falls into a small slump, a little hole of solitude where she is paralyzed. Like an echo of Jean-Claude's words.

She puts water on to boil. She takes out her work. She arranges her files, places them on the desk, and pulls out her Moleskine notebook. She was somebody else when she bought it.

How long has it been since she checked her cell phone? She rushes to find it. The battery is dead. She adjusts the charger. Six calls, three text messages, five e-mails.

She grabs onto this lifeline thrown out to her by her previous life.

The office. Sophie has left her the latest news from the front. A certain Brigitte Raymond for drugs, complicity. Her lover had hidden them at her place. Catherine will find the rest of her appointments for the week in her e-mail. Stephanie has seen Catherine's dream purse. It's a little expensive, but it will soon be on sale. Her father is worried because she hasn't called. Is she angry with him? Cedric doesn't understand her message. Is she angry with him?

The way both her father and Cedric say the same thing amuses her.

And then Evelyne, whom she can't place right away. A colleague. The message goes on and on in the voice of chronic depression that Catherine finally remembers. She would like to hand over a case, well, mostly a client, small-time fraud, numerous times, a swindler, a Rom who is very, very attractive. Well, she made a mistake, and she has to stop. She sounds like a junkie, and then, all of a sudden, Catherine catches on. It's well known. Evelyne is always taking on lost causes, and when she does, she falls in love. She has the nurse syndrome and should start by healing herself. Maybe. Catherine likes Roms and their sense of honor, their Old France or rather Old Romania attitude. And finally Stephanie, in tears. Can you call back? Fabien is a prick! You have to wonder if her friend's ideal negative model is not the real reason they are friends. In any case, she is in no mood to be a crutch. Who will be her crutch?

The three text messages are from Cedric. She hits delete without reading them.

She repents, but it's too late. They have disappeared.

The e-mails are just work, work, work and then Olivier. Her heart skips a beat for nothing. She will read it later.

And Cedric Devers. No way.

She lets her phone charge. And she does the same, lying down to charge her batteries. She falls asleep.

Knock, knock.

Drops of water fall on her head and resonate. She is in an elevator, stuck between floors, emptiness above and below her. Panic.

Knock, knock.

She emerges, gasping for breath.

It's Louis. Oh dear, what time is it? She's a mess. Yes, by the look on Louis's face—and what he says—she must have been in the middle of a nap.

"Did I get the time wrong? Sorry."

"No, no, it's me. Come in."

And there, a peck on the cheek.

She doesn't give much explanation. No explanation for this invasion of sleep after an eleven-hour night. Coffee. More.

He sits at the kitchen table and makes small talk while she busies herself. He spots the picture, and he falls silent, ready to say something else, she would swear to it, but he shuts up and turns over the picture, as if to disguise a lack of composure.

Then he says with what sounds like relief to have something to comment on, "What do you know! That comes from Trilabaud. How we used to tease him about his name. The poor guy!"

"Do you know him?"

"Oh yes, Old Trilabaud is alive and well. He's been retired for a long time now. This is crazy."

Catherine hears, in his way of saying crazy, that the coincidence is huge. Much greater than the presence of a local photographer's stamp on an old picture. She stands in front of the reporter, waiting for his explanation.

"The resemblance," he says. "It's crazy how much the girl in the picture looks like you."

"It's not that crazy. She's my mother."

"Oh, that's it!"

You don't make the connection because a mother is necessarily older than her child, Catherine thinks.

"Yes, she's very young. I mean, she died very young, so she is very young in the picture. But there is something else, Louis. What is it? Do you know this picture?"

"No, but... The face, well, your face..."

He feels uncomfortable, has to justify himself ahead of time for what he's going to say. But what? He is certain he had never met Catherine before that first day in Guéret, but she looked familiar. He had a vague impression he had seen her before.

Deep in contemplation of the picture, he says, "It's a face you never forget. The same applies to the story, but I didn't make the connection immediately. I did some research because I was curious and annoyed that I couldn't remember. And it's kind of my pet subject. I was pretty sure it was some local news story. We don't have much news here, as I said, and this one left its mark. At the time, I wasn't here, I was at boarding school in Clermont."

Catherine can't order her thoughts enough to find questions to ask. There are so many. She wants him to get to the point.

Louis tramples the same thought over and over again. He is sorry. He didn't think. It must be very painful.

"No, tell me. What is it? Go on. Spit it out. Why are you hesitating?"

"Since you told me you didn't know Creuse, I really thought it was a coincidence," he says with a surreptitious glance at his briefcase.

"Do you have something for me? About my mother's murder?"

An Olympian calm comes over Catherine, and she distances herself from both herself and her confusion. She pours some coffee. She needs to reassure Louis. He needs time. She must not go to fast or use force. Her professional reflexes come back to her.

But so do his, as a result.

He prefers to start with Myriam, if she is okay with that, so they don't mix everything up.

She agrees, even though her curiosity is boiling over.

For Myriam there is good news and bad news.

She chooses the bad news first.

35

At the age of eighty-eight, Elianc is still active. This Sunday after-noon, she is raking leaves and putting them in bags. She works slow-ly, but her past vivacity expresses itself in precise, alert movements.

Eliane is bothered by the fact that Gaston died before his time. His heart going out is one thing, but poisoning...

Louis is patient. He lets her come around to her story and creates junctions, clearing the road with phrases like, "It is rather strange, isn't it?" and "After the gendarmes came..."

"What do the gendarmes know? If only they were serious, but you remember the pilot. I saw that parachute fall!"

"But Eliane, they looked for it!"

And there they are off on an old story about a mysterious pilot ejected from a mysterious plane, who dropped in the middle of the woods and was the focus of conversation some five years ago. After a few days of vain searching, the gendarmes ended up blaming Eliane's long-winded report on age and boredom or some hair-brained idea. And Eliane found out. At that instant, the gendarmes took a harder plunge in the old lady's esteem than the pilot's fall to earth. Their stubborn witness wouldn't budge an inch from her story and was more headstrong than a woodpecker at work.

Nobody ever goes into the Villetreix cousins' barn. The door sticks. You have to give it a hard pull, and it makes a terrible noise unless you lift it up slightly so that it doesn't scrape the floor.

Eliane is in her armchair near the window, reading the paper. She must have fallen asleep, because the creaking wakes her up.

Myriam is wearing overalls, a strange thing for a woman to wear, after all, and pushes the door carefully. There is a glass jar at her feet. She is wearing gardening gloves, which is strange too. You can tell she is not at ease. But it is possible that she has gone to borrow something without telling anyone. Everyone knows that

France and Africa get along only halfway. And poor Gaston is stuck in the middle.

Eliane knows that the Villetreix cousins kept cyanide back in the day, but she hasn't thought about it again. It's when she learns that Gaston was killed with cyanide that she remembers the glass jar in the barn. She tells Louis about it, because they talk, but the gendarmes can just figure it out for themselves, because, in any case, they don't believe her.

And Louis concludes, "When the gendarmes asked her, she said she didn't know anything. I don't think she'll go back on that. But if she were to say she knows something, she would be quite a witness for the prosecution."

"It's true, I would have preferred it if she had seen Gaston come out of the barn, but, in any case, with the previous airplane story, I would have no difficulty discrediting her testimony."

Louis is not naïve, but this brutality shocks him. Deep down, he hopes that Eliane will not have to testify. The lawyer has already moved on.

"And the good news?"

She'll judge that for herself.

Louis leaves Eliane and drives about ten kilometers. He parks on the side of the road and slips under the fence that lines the field, his eyes on the cows that are grazing peacefully. He is wary of cows, because of an accident he had when he was a child.

Two of the cows lift their heads, vaguely intrigued. In the time it takes them to register a presence and decide whether to go see it up close, indolence overcomes curiosity, and they lower their heads again. He arrives safe and sound, passes a stagnant pond surrounded by a few twisted beech trees, and climbs a small hill. From there you can see a house with an unusual wooden veranda at the top of a wide undulation that overlooks a small valley where a reach joins two lakes. A small patch of woods starts on the left. A young donkey watches his mother gambol in the grass that leads to the house. A few yards away, a potbellied but well-built man is cleaning a shack.

It is acceptable in the countryside not to warn people that you are going to visit, but you always announce when you are approaching.

"Dr. Blanchard! It's Louis Bernier. I came to see what your little paradise looks like."

His timing is perfect. The shack is clean, and Blanchard, happy to see him, offers him a beer on the deck.

The two men go to the house, and Louis sits down facing the superb Corot-like romantic landscape, while Blanchard goes to get the beers. This peaceful island at the back of the village is invisible, unexpected, and, indeed, reminiscent of paradise.

They have known each other for a long time, which compensates for not knowing each other well. The recently widowed Blanchard is pleased that Louis has come to visit, and he is ready to spend time with him.

The reporter talks about the time when, for lack of a specialist, the local doctor did autopsies on farm tables, until, finally, Blanchard himself mentions the death of Madame Villetreix, the mother, and the coincidence of her having the same symptoms as Gaston, which he interpreted as a congenital weakness. He didn't say anything to the police, because they didn't ask.

Everyone knows that Blanchard is a good, devoted doctor, always ready to go see his patients, so nobody is going to make any trouble for him because he didn't imagine a murder in a place where there are none for the most part, except the appliance salesman done in by a farmer in debt, which people still talk about thirty years later as if it were yesterday.

Myriam had told him that her husband complained about pain, that he was tired, but Gaston said no, it was nothing. Gaston did not know how to complain. He had not been raised that way.

The doctor had signed the death certificate without further delay.

Poor Myriam, all worked up, couldn't stop crying and kicked herself for having slept while her husband died. Blanchard comforted her as best he could. It wouldn't have changed anything, he told her. But she kept saying that it was so sad to die alone.

The case still torments the doctor, because he fears that he lacked judgment. Mention of the wedding brings color back to his face. It was the first interracial marriage in the village. At the time, everyone was proud. That poor girl had only known misfortune. She brought him papers from the embassy that were in an incomprehensible language. He asked her for a translation and made do with that. Her papers didn't appear to be current, but they would be once she was married. Enjoying a normal life was not too much to ask. As far at this is concerned, he has no doubt that he made the right decision.

It is a local tradition to protect the innocent who are hunted down. Like all those Jewish children who were taken in during the war. It is a good tradition.

And when Myriam got her French citizenship, they had a little ceremony at the city hall to welcome her and thank her for having chosen France and Gaston. Blanchard laughs. Any occasion to have a drink is worth it. The town hall was full.

"He sounds like a nice man," Catherine says. "Thank you. That is big help to me. Will you be able to do anything with all these stories?"

"I think so. Perhaps later, when I'm retired. I'd like to preserve something of these people's lives. Can you imagine, in three hundred or four hundred years, when people want to put the past back together, they will think that our lives were like some boring show on television. But I won't take your time with that. My wife always tells me that I'm the only person interested in banality."

"There is nothing very banal in that."

"Nothing is ever banal."

She takes advantage of the word. "Come on, Louis, be brave. I don't know anything about my mother's death, only that she was murdered. I find myself here, completely by chance, and I've had enough of groping around in the dark. So help me if you can, even a little."

Since he still seems to hesitate, she tells him that she has been wrong not to look into it earlier, but it was her father's fault, because he wanted to protect her, and he, too, was wrong, and... She leans toward the reporter, joining her hands despite herself in a gesture of prayer, her look a petition to him alone.

Louis begins with the names. His research in the local archives has revealed that the beautiful victim's name was Mertens, not Monsigny.

She repeats it to herself. "Mertens, Catherine Mertens."

That is the name that must be on her birth certificate. Her father had always taken care of the paperwork, but he could not have eliminated all traces of her identity. Had he ever intended to reveal her original name?

She remembers.

She leaves for Paris alone the day after she turns sixteen. She will live in a home run by nuns in the fifteenth arrondissement.

Her father pretends to be his usual self. But he is not. He keeps bumping into things. He loses his glasses. The noodle gratin burns and is inedible. They go to a restaurant. Catherine can't wait for tomorrow to arrive. She is incapable of taking on her father's sadness. She has no sympathy for him. He is a burden. That's it. She thinks that she is right to leave. If she had been able to go farther away, abroad, she would have, but she wants to study criminal trial law in Paris. The umbilical cord will never be long enough to cover that distance.

That is what she thought.

She listens, distracted, while he talks to her about a file he has prepared and always keeps in the right-hand desk drawer. If anything were to happen to him, she'll find everything there. Bank papers, things to do. He is taking care of the details in his methodological fashion. He explains that everything has its own envelope.

At the time, she only hears one thing, that he is making her feel guilty, implying that he is going to die. Now she understands that this is the way he has always been—ordered, organized, anticipating problems and taking care of them in advance.

She also thinks that perhaps the file contains explanations and details, such as their real identity.

Details.

The devil is in the details.

One thing is sure. At this stage, she will not wait for her father to die before going to see.

Only one picture of the dead woman had appeared in the papers, but that face stuck in teenage Louis's memory, not only because she was young and pretty, but also because he had seen a seriousness in her look, like a foreshadowing of her tragic destiny.

"My wife always says that I have too much imagination to be a journalist."

"Do you have the picture?"

"I have all the articles. Photocopies of them."

Louis looks at the leather briefcase with its worn handle and flap that closes with a small latch that slips into a ring. He leans toward it, presses the latch, and pulls, lifting the flap. Jean-Claude knocks and comes in.

Catherine is relieved.

Catherine will not have to discover her story in front of witnesses.

She throws a questioning look at Louis. It's a little early for her to have a cocktail, but perhaps not for Louis. She smiles to reassure him that it's okay, that he has done the right thing, that she is ready, so ready that she can wait patiently.

She prefers tea. It's just the right time. What a good idea. She and Louis are finished. Perfect timing.

She calmly asks, "Can you leave the papers with me?"

Louis takes out a cardboard file and hands it to her in a gesture of solemn transmission.

She says, "Thank you. Very much."

She puts the file in her room and comes back out again.

She would like to stop time, but Louis stands up. She follows him, and their movement already transports her to later, getting her closer to the moment when she will return to her room, alone.

36

Catherine, Captain Courageous, holds up, pretending to be interested in the banal conversation, while inside contradictory feelings of resentment, suspicion, and betrayed love keep jibing, swaying in the story, foreshadowing a shipwreck. She endures, looking peaceful until she reaches the door of her small house, from which she watches Louis climb into his car. He has suggested that he go question Trilabaud, which will probably lead nowhere, as his memory is probably faded, but it would be nice to hear news about the old photographer.

Catherine nods. He could add a little more or a little less to the flood of information, and it would change nothing in her capsizing worldview.

Louis starts the car, turns around, lowers his window, and says, "Do you have any idea when the picture was taken?"

She thinks quickly. Her mother is wearing a wedding ring. She is not pregnant. She died April 12, 1988.

"Between 1985 and 1987, I'd say. Spring or summer, if you go by the dress."

"No promises, but you never know."

No, you never know.

The articles are arranged in chronological order and cover the period of one month.

The first is illustrated with a picture of the crime scene. The gendarmerie cars are most visible. The inside page has a small map, the name of the location, Pierre Levée, the closest village, Meynard, and two crosses, one marking where the corpse lay and the other the child in the stroller. Her.

There is a picture of the hiker, Xavier Courtois, and his story. As in a fairy tale, he was guided by incongruous crying and found a clean well-dressed little girl whose face was disfigured by tears and fear.

Everything blurs. Catherine puts her hand against her chest to still her heart, which is threatening to break through her skin. She does not, cannot, fight the feelings of incomprehension, shock, panic, the screams, the wails of fear and pain that are endlessly bouncing around her saturated mind. She could not have invented them. The beastly stridency. She was not sleeping. Perhaps she did not see her mother's agony, but she experienced it.

It takes all the strength she has to become invisible, to stop breathing. Disappear to avoid being annihilated in turn. She shoves her little hands between the stroller's canvas and her back. Don't touch the little string of multicolored balls. She closes her eyes so she can't be seen. She lowers her head, rounds her back, which hurts from the tension. She pushes away the screams, muffles them in a padded cocoon. Her legs are tingling. She must resist. The bubble ends up full, entirely sealed. It would take nothing to pop it, and then there is just that, nothing. Everything stops. Life stops. There is the absolute silence of solitude. No appeal, no escape. Totally alone, abandoned, and so little.

She is cold, so cold she starts trembling convulsively. She looks for a sweater, a scarf; she muffles up.

Today, that secure, invisible bubble is still her haven of peace, the safe place that nobody else has the right to enter. It shuts her off from the world forever.

Much later she reads. Beaten to death. Her skull cracked from being smashed against a tree. Staggering violence.

There are no witnesses. There is a careful investigation, tenacious gendarmes. The child's presence adds to the horror.

One theory follows another. The woman, feeling impending danger, hid the stroller behind a tree and moved closer to the murderer to shield the child.

A chance encounter. A vagabond who fled. He had time to get away, because the hiker, alerted by the child' crying, didn't find the body until three hours after the murder.

The investigator affirms that this case will never be closed until…
Until nothing.
The investigation stagnates.
The husband is cleared, thanks to the patient he saw at the time of the crime.

The murdered woman is a victim above all suspicion, devoted to her family, a full-time mom who had adopted the region. She loved nature and solitude. She was reserved; it was her English nature.

There is nothing but generalities. A sketch of a woman nobody knew because she had never let anyone enter her private sphere, with the exception of her daughter and her husband.

One of the articles about the crime includes the statement of a neighbor who watched the little girl when the mother would go off to take long solitary walks. Otherwise, she always had her daughter in a baby sling and later in the stroller when she went to do errands.

It was an ordinary family.

Until the murder.

Catherine has everything. The places, the people. She sees clearly that the gendarmes were serious about the investigation and put their hearts into it. She will not try to find the man or the neighbor or the baker or the gendarmes, because it is too late. It is clear that all this information is coming too late and will change nothing. Even if she had access to the murderer's name, it would not compensate for her mother's absence.

The shroud around the murder of Violet Mertens will never be lifted, and Catherine will continue to live with the maternal mystery, with the enigma of her death. Yes, perhaps her father is right. Knowing more changes nothing. She is no further ahead today than she was yesterday. Why should she have expected anything else?

What remains are pins and needles inside. She was there, the only witness. Something inside her knows, has a little key.

But why?

Her father is right. It is too old, too far away. She has built who she is on a foundation of absence and abandon. Why take the risk of destroying this bedrock that serves as her identity?

There is a picture of her father, with a blanket over his shoulders. His face looks like stone, closed, frightening at the start of a long nightmare after the collapse of happiness that was still being constructed.

You build your house brick by brick, and even before the roof is on, a catastrophe transforms it into a pile of stones, without you ever knowing who destroyed your universe one day or why.

She begins to understand what a huge task it was for her father to take his daughter under his wing, to give her a brand-new foundation so that she, at least, could have something other than quicksand underfoot, so that she would never know that reality could devour dreams in mere minutes.

She acknowledges her debt.

He did his best with what he had.

She promises herself that she will love him or at least stop being so spare in her demonstrations of affection, even if they are feigned. But she is not the one who kept him from living. That he did himself. She will not bear responsibility for it.

She examines a picture of her mother that the paper printed.

It is another face, unknown. The black and white of the photo throws it back to an ancient era. The young woman herself is outside space and time. She is looking down, to the left, but her veiled eyes are not focused on anything. Her eyebrows are very arched, thick, giving her face definition. Her nose is small and a little turned up. She has very long ears. The corners of her mouth are drooped in a frown, and the rest of her face is slack. The only trace of life is a rebellious lock of hair pushed behind her ear. There is a little tuft stuck on the side of her forehead, showing the impatience of the hand that pushed the bothersome hair aside. She is wearing a dark blouse with a white collar.

She is certainly beautiful. Like an image. Already dead.

Catherine will continue to hold the other picture dear, the one in which she prefers to see herself, the one that shows a drive and confidence destroyed by something she will never know.

Her mother's defeat will never be hers.

She puts the articles away, looks at the map that localizes the scene of the crime, puts on a hat, then a coat, grabs her car keys, sits in the driver's seat, and does not start the car.

She listens closely to a voice inside. Why go to the place of her death, a visit that will only stir the ashes to rouse a faint ember of bogus emotion?

She had decided to stop here, so she should stick to it.

She leans back, her spine relaxes, and her neck loosens a little. She is exhausted.

She will leave the dead to bury the dead and return to her life, the only one worth living, taking care of Myriam's future, upon which her own depends.

She returns to the house. She crouches in front of the fireplace. She stacks the kindling, places a firelighter in the center, cheating like a city dweller. She lights the flame and feeds the hesitating fire with short, judiciously touching branches. Then she places two logs next to each other, leaving room for air to circulate. More than a little proud of herself, she settles into the armchair, the teapot at arm's reach, a pack of cookies on her knees. The heat is perfect. She has provisions for the entire evening. She feels like she has miraculously escaped a terrible accident.

She hears the ring announcing her father and answers the phone with a new gentleness and without, for a second, wondering about the coincidence.

Yes, she is well. Her voice? She is tired and half asleep, not to mention she has a cookie in her mouth. In fact, she was thinking about him. She would be happy if he came to see her in court. In any case, she'll have stage fright. A little more, a little less...

No. Nothing new.

And really he shouldn't worry. She has decided to go forward without being saddled with before, to leave the past behind her.

She adds, "Behind us."

She is moved to hear his voice relax and earnestly begs herself to never again revive paternal anxieties and insecurities.

"You know, Dad, you should cultivate nonchalance. That would go well with your English gentleman look."

He clears his throat. "It's funny you should say that. Your mother thought I looked English."

Life seems simple. For Catherine, it is a good sign that he can mention her mother naturally, like a presence in their lives.

Louis has no idea the gift he has given her. He has freed her.

It may even foreshadow an emergence from that bubble, which she has finally acknowledged as a protective shell. Perhaps she had to return to its place of origin in order to abandon it definitively. Something in the ordinary ease of life in the countryside will help her, perhaps allowing her to grow the roots she has lacked.

She says good-bye to her father, promising to call him as soon as she gets back to Paris.

With a determined click, she opens Cedric's e-mail and is surprised to find him funny and persistent, rather than complaining and defensive.

Why avoid passion and its risks? Cedric acted like a shy, clumsy, impulsive lover without imagining the consequences. He told her everything, and she slammed the door in his face. She misses him. Life is short. Risks, passion, or, at least, lovers' games are part of it. If they stop, then you die. "Not scared."

She writes three lines in the form of a summons. The day, the time, the address, and then she signs off: "Too good." She immediately gets a happy response, "Better weather ahead. Yes. You're good."

It's the heady smell of dead flesh that forces a dog to dig and dig until it finds the source. But Catherine does not imagine for a minute that the source of her decision is in Louis's file.

37

Catherine races through the month of February. Preparing for the *Cour d'Assises* is like breathing fresh air. The rest feels like holding her breath underwater. Cedric brings life to her days and nights because he shakes her up more than he reassures her. He is unpredictable, changing, making routines and habits impossible. They never again mention his shadowing of her or the roses. His attraction also lies in his shadows and secrets. Catherine acknowledges that and tries to be consistent. He accepts her moods and absences, does not expect her to be otherwise. She likes that he never lets go. She wants to do the same and accepts him as he is, one day at a time.

"Catherine, do you have the pictures?"

"Yes, sir."

She has been able to look at them only once and refers to them by number only. They were found on the Internet, the most unsafe place in the world, where everyone thinks they can hide their secrets by posting them publicly. The trial begins.

The twelve-year-old victim was raped regularly, subjected to her father's inventive fantasies in front of a camera, and the images were sold to a wide audience. The mother disowned her daughter, accusing her of wanting to destroy the family, of being responsible, a tease, guilty of seducing her own father. The child knows that she will no longer have a family or support, that she is becoming an outlaw in her own community, but she also understands that this is the only way she can survive. Catherine has taken her under her wing, remaining with her constantly, protecting her as best she can, surprised to identify with her.

Renaud is particularly harsh with the witnesses and underhanded with the defendant, with whom he first establishes trust based on a supposed shared notion of virility and its inherent urges, and then he crucifies him, leaving him distraught, hesitant and humiliated.

He looks into his young client's eyes; sometimes he squeezes her hand. He describes her as a heroine and allows her to become one, offering her a beautiful image of herself to grab hold of.

Catherine knows that he will not let her go after the verdict. That is why he is a good lawyer. He is consistent. He does not restrict his commitment to the courtroom. Here, he has the upper hand, but he wants her to triumph. This is vital for the child.

Catherine listens, learns.

Counsel for the defense bases his arguments on the defendant's cultural origins, where fathers have every right over their children. He points out his client's marital troubles, blames the wife, who is so much a mother, she refuses him. This is delicate, treacherous terrain, where his client will end up sinking.

Catherine would have mentioned the economic and social misery that caused him to lose touch with what was good and what was bad. She would have argued that since his incarceration, he has started to become aware of his wrongs.

She finds it easy to project herself as the defense lawyer and can even imagine herself one day facing Renaud in a singular combat where her possible victory would announce her emancipation.

The one called a victim has been able to transform her status into a lethal weapon. The defendant's last words are that he is sorry. But he is so unconvincing, everyone—including his attorney—realizes that the final nail has been pounded into the incestuous father's coffin.

Catherine brings the little girl outside the courtroom while the jury deliberates.

The child is frighteningly thin in her dark turtleneck and wide pants. She tries to deny her body at all costs. She never cries, is fierce and determined. Hate has saved her. A cold, harsh hate. If the police had not resolved the case, had not gotten her out of there, and if the justice system had not supported her, one day she would have taken justice into her own hands and found herself on the defendant's bench. Catherine is sure of that.

He is sentenced to fifteen years without parole.

The mother spits at her daughter, who does not even turn to look, fully focused on the defendant, who, standing, hears the sentence and does not understand until his lawyer explains the consequences to him.

At that instant, what Catherine reads on their client's face is not the triumph of vengeance but deep sadness and pain. Everything is always more complicated than it seems.

Catherine sighs.

Tonight, she is sleeping at Cedric's place, and she hopes with all her heart that he will be gentle and comforting, as he sometimes knows how to be.

In fact, it is yet another facet of himself that he unexpectedly presents. He seems uncertain, destabilized. As a result, instead of telling him about the complex contradictions the day's ruling have raised in her, she worries about him, asks him questions. A setback at work? Family problems? Bad news?

He says no, no and tells her not to worry.

It is troubling to discover a weak spot that silences this man, who usually finds words easily. She notes it as an additional touch on the portrait of this versatile lover, who, when faced with a thought that he finds wounding, is capable of upping and leaving her in the middle of a restaurant and disappearing for two weeks, while allowing himself, under the cover of humor, to throw out scornful and bitter answers that leave her defeated, on the edge of tears. She tells herself that maybe the ballet is all the more beautiful when you don't know which foot to dance on.

Tonight, his behavior seems to be the expression of a malaise that is just waiting to be healed. By her, of course.

So even though he is fifteen years older than she, Catherine feels stronger and better armed.

To put a quick end to the questions, Cedric takes over the kitchen and cooks risotto, leaving her on the sofa with the day's newspapers and the TV remote close by. She is not in the mood to listen to the mumblings of the world. She curls up against the pillows, her legs folded under her, and she lets herself daydream, enjoying a well-earned rest.

She thinks about her secret weapon and can't help but smile with a kind of unconscious meanness. She has slept with Olivier. She didn't resist. Because he is the opposite of Cedric: stable and certain and always constant in his unchangeable mood.

The ritual has taken shape on its own, innocently. When she visits Myriam, she sees Olivier, stops by to drink tea or have dinner, depending on their schedules. Sometimes they do not even talk but listen to music or go for a walk. Sometimes she asks for his advice, uses him to interpret an unknown language, and in exchange, she tells him the latest Parisian gossip.

One day, she arrives at his place irritated at everything, including his imperturbable kindness and the old-fashioned friendly way he welcomes her. Why does he never show even the slightest inclination to seduce her? Why does he never make the minimum effort to find out if, by chance, she would be interested?

When he gives her a welcome peck on the cheek, she prolongs their hug a little. Using the pretext of helping him, she brushes against him, then says she's sorry. She feels him feigning and frightened at the same time, which multiplies her irritation.

She ends up patting the sofa next to her with an inviting look that leaves no room for doubt.

She chuckles at the memory. He springs from his armchair to join her. Incredibly self-conscious, he grabs her hand and shakes it wildly. Her own desire wanes instantaneously when she discovers that he has been waiting for the opportunity without ever daring to take the lead. She helps him as she can, putting her head on his shoulder, re-establishing—or rather establishing—him in his male role, and feels it unfair to deny herself this pleasure, because he proves to worry about it more than most lovers she has known.

She takes advantage just one time. If Cedric finds out, he will kill her.

All evening, behind their everyday talk, she wonders what could have destabilized him so blatantly and ends up asking him if he did something really stupid that begs forgiveness.

He barks back, "Why do you say that?"

"Because you look so aggrieved, as if you feel bad about something. But if you say it's nothing, then okay."

"It's nothing, nothing at all."

She gives up. Other than that, they are having a nice evening, savoring a magnificent mushroom risotto, watching an irresistible Cukor DVD, and their lovemaking is different. He takes her, literally, penetrates her without any precaution, and Catherine discovers a delicious, irresistible pleasure in giving in without any games or resistance.

He is lying on his back, his eyes staring at the ceiling, deep in impenetrable thought. She snuggles against him with the delicious fantasy of being some gangster's chick. When he turns toward her, leaning on his elbow, she turns her back to him so he'll flatten himself against her and hold her, which he does immediately. There is never any misunderstanding between their bodies.

She does not see that he was prepared to talk. At no moment does she understand that he is trying to tell her something terrible and that at each aborted attempt he feels relieved at having just escaped.

And then he puts it off definitively, cowardly, until later. He will talk to Catherine another time. There is no emergency. He is afraid to lose her, afraid of her reaction, whose consequences could be serious. His fear is divided into multiple fears. It's a monster that grows another head every time he wants to confess the truth. But if he continues to keep the secret that lies between them, it will grow and invade everything, ruining everything.

Not knowing which of the two evils is worse, he doesn't decide.

38

Clocks tell the time of day. But they're not always an accurate measure of time, which can expand and contract, seemingly at will.

Cedric has warned her that he is leaving early. He leaves. Even though she is awake, Catherine turns over, grumbling to let him know that she does not want to be disturbed. She stays buried under the comforter, her eyes closed. She will stay there the time it takes to make sure that he does not come back, having forgotten his eyeglasses, telephone, or keys. False starts are one of his specialties.

She gets up and imagines his place as her place, later. Their place. Pretending. Playing house.

As the coffee brews, she carefully makes the bed, opens the windows, and washes and puts away the glasses that are lying around.

She takes over the living room rather than the kitchen, sitting deep in an armchair, with her feet on the coffee table. She would straighten out the sofa to delineate the space more clearly and put the armchairs at an angle, breaking the symmetry.

They would have to repaint the room a more daring color and move Cedric's desk against the bedroom wall. He'll enjoy more light that way. She moves to the swivel chair and turns around once, grazing the end of the table with her finger, only touching the edge because the top is littered with drawing books. She picks one up and looks through it. Sometimes he sketches moments, and Catherine likes his style, while other times he elaborates more, and she likes it less. An enormous picture book about what lies underneath Paris, which they looked at together the other day, is also on the table.

She places it under the desk to make space. She does have work to do.

She pushes the book against the wall with her feet. It bumps into something. She bends over and finds a metallic cookie box decorated with an insipid drawing of a horse-drawn carriage, a dashing officer, and a dull blonde in a long dress.

A secret candy stash?

She opens it, amused.

It holds letters in envelopes addressed to Cedric Devers.

She feels a twinge.

These have to be love letters, preciously guarded, which means that the story is not over yet. But the envelopes are yellowed, and the writing is faded. And the temptation is too strong.

Catherine spreads them out with her hand, takes one, and then sets it down again.

She sees the corner of a photograph and can't resist. She takes it out from under the letters, and the truth is, she is not even surprised. It is as if she has expected this. As if it had been written since the beginning.

It is exactly the same picture of her mother standing in front of the Lavaveix sign.

She hears a sickly refrain in her head: "I knew it, I knew it, I knew it." She is sleeping with her mother's lover. The shining, love-filled smile is for Cedric. The shadow of doubt does not appear at all, that shadow she has let hang between them, the source of her constant swing from repulsion to attraction.

She feels that much more tarnished, dirty, abused, because she knows she is an accomplice. It is like incest, the worst kind, with a dead woman.

She went for it, happily. Went back for it when he had turned away. The responsibility is equally shared. What perverse pleasure he must have felt, seeing the mother's expressions in her daughter, causing the same sensual reactions in the after-lover as in the before-lover.

She leaves the box open on the desk, goes to dress quickly, washes up without even brushing her hair, and gathers her things, making sure she doesn't forget anything. Leave no possible bond, even a temporary one.

She returns to the table. On her telephone screen she sees a text message from Cedric: "You are the sunshine of my life, a ray of honey in my heart, I miss you already."

Did he write these same words to Violet?

She deletes the text message. "Yes, delete. Thank you."

She looks at the box and takes an envelope, removes the piece of paper, and discovers slanted, regular writing, elegant with clean horizontal strokes instead of loops. There is no signature. The date reads, "September 14, 1986."

The letter begins, "My you."

No. She can't. She refolds the paper, puts it back in the envelope, sees three others that are still sealed at the bottom of the box, and takes them immediately.

She will leave a bitter note. He will never get over it. She scribbles in hateful writing, "Never come near me again, you bastard. You're a swine. Loser."

She scratches it out.

"Perverted, lying hypocrite. I feel dirty having known you. Forget me."

No. Silence is the best response.

The open box will say more than enough.

Sophie watches her rush in, raising an eyebrow, "Weren't you going to take the morning off?"

"I changed my mind. But I can leave again if my presence bothers you."

Sophie looks back down at her appointment book, and Catherine slams the door in her storage-room office.

She has no reason to go to the courthouse. She has no reason for anything.

She takes out Myriam's file and gives up on it quickly.

She decides to go see Oscar at La Santé Prison. She hasn't seen him in a long time. He has good reason to complain and be unhappy. It will do him some good, she says, thinking more about herself.

He had joined up with a gang of down-and-outs for a heist that could never have been carried out successfully, and he did all that just to please Mina, a half-whore who painted him a picture of settling down in a good house and a good life. The heist went wrong, Oscar got ten years, and Mina was quick to dump him.

"Much worse than me," Catherine says to herself, without conviction.

The harassment begins that afternoon, at three. Calls and text messages. She doesn't answer. She doesn't read them.

She has made a decision and knows that nothing will ever make her forgive this betrayal.

She busies herself at work, when all she is doing is thinking about what happened. She convinces herself that he chose her on purpose, that he has been tracking her all these years. She calculates the dates. He was really young, still in lycée, and Violet was already in the Creuse, already married and a mother.

But maybe he was the lover from before the marriage. Violet was a born liar.

Poor Dad believed her from beginning to end.

She sniggers. What a perfect missed opportunity, because he *is* the person who is best placed to tell her about her mother, in detail please. But to tell the truth, she doesn't want to know anything else about the woman. Talk about a victim! Here is her theory, with more than enough proof to support it: Violet is no poor little bird who fell on a mean predator. On top of that, she is a rival. Thank you very much. A rival to her own daughter!

Catherine rages that Cedric must have found her very dull in comparison, so available, so free and loyal.

The idea paralyzes her at an intersection. She is stopped at a red light, which turns green while she remains still. The honking pulls her out of her stupefaction. She pushes her bike onto the sidewalk, steadies it on the kickstand, and, feeling her legs literally collapse under her, she sits on the ground, taking her head in her hands.

An old lady's voice pulls her out of her numbness. "Did you have an accident? Are you okay?"

She gets up to prove that, yes, she is okay. No, no accident, not that kind of accident, and she goes to plop down at the nearest café, where she orders the recommended treatment for shock, a Cognac. She has never drunk one before, but it works and gives her a boost.

The question is throbbing in thundering capital letters in her head: "WHAT IF CEDRIC MURDERED MY MOTHER?"

That would explain why he wanted to find her again, her, the only witness. It was a risk, but more absurd things than that have happened. Perhaps deep down, he even wanted to be recognized, accused, and have the burden of his guilt lifted.

She looks at the time.

Yes, that changes everything, because with a possible solution, it is worth going back in time. And if she could confound Cedric, her victory would be two-fold and her liberation total.

She turns back and goes to his place. She can't see his motorcycle anywhere. She starts by listening to the messages he has left. He'll probably be late tonight. What would she say to a candlelight dinner? Then she reads the text message that follows, "Say yes. Come on, say yes."

He hasn't gone home.

She goes up to his place, opens the door. Everything is where she left it.

She mixes up the envelopes in their initial disorder, closes the box, puts the big book back on the table, and pushes the box against the wall. She looks around carefully, making sure she is leaving no sign of her discovery.

She hears the key in the door and turns around, standing still.

Cedric does not seem surprised to see her.

Is this a trap? Did he follow her?

Did he come home after she left and see the open box on the table?

Catherine has all her antennae up, trying to capture the atmosphere, to decipher anything potentially left unsaid, trying to keep her face looking as normal as possible, too normal to be natural. She manages a relaxed look, inexpressive but with a smile all the same.

"Did you stay here all day?"

"No, I came back. I forgot my charger."

"Stay. I'm finished. It's a good surprise.

"Oh, I would love to, but..."

She never talks like that.

"I promised Renaud I would finish a case file, and I have to run to the office to talk to him about it. I'll be working on it for the better part of the night."

"I could come to your place. I'll make you dinner while you work."

"Thanks, but I'll work at the office. I've got to go now, really."

He keeps his eyes on her, skeptical. It's his turn to try to read what is hidden. Did he glance at his desk, under his desk? It's crazy that he has left such a compromising clue in plain sight, as if he wanted her to find it.

Catherine forces herself to think about something else. It's possible that he could sense what she's stuck on. He grabs her by the wrist, a little harshly. She thinks he knows. He's going to do her in, right here, now.

He pulls her to him and noisily sniffs her neck, as if to fill up on her smell or devour her neck.

"That's too bad. It was good. I like it when you are here. Did you get my text messages?"

"Yes, thanks."

She is useless when it comes to forcing normal conversation. Nobody is ever good at it. Well, at least she isn't.

"I didn't even have time to answer you. It was nice."

"I am nice."

"That's true. Will you let me go now?"

"I'm hesitating."

"If I lose my job, you will have to support me, and you know my taste for luxury."

"Ouch. An unbeatable argument."

He lets her go. She blows him a kiss from a distance.

She takes off.

She has the feeling that she has just escaped an immense danger, which is absurd. If he had wanted to do her in, he would have done so a long time ago.

She holds the dynamite and wonders how to ignite it without blowing herself up. Who could she talk to? Stephanie is a real gossip and capable of all possible stupidities. She is not the person to take advice from.

Sophie? No. It is best not to mix work and personal life, particularly this personal life.

The same with Renaud. He should not get the idea that she could go off at any moment because of an old trauma, that she has some serious pathology that makes her unreliable.

Her father? He would react head-on. She might be totally confused right now, but she finds herself suddenly in possession of a secret that could open Pandora's box. If she really does have her mother's murderer in sight, she will find a way to punish him, whatever the risk.

And her father would never let her expose herself.

Louis? A reporter? That would be crazy.

That leaves Olivier.

Or nobody.

Is it possible to be so wrong about somebody?

39

"A murderer can have a dual state of mind that allows him to commit his crime without knowing that he has done so. The action remains isolated and is not transformed into a memory. The same phenomenon can occur when traumatic events are too painful to face. An amnesiac murderer can repeat his actions because his unconscious mind remembers his impunity. A murderer can incorporate the memory by understanding the action and acknowledging responsibility. Even a direct mention of the murder can trigger his memory. The triggered memory then returns with such intense acuity that it can lead to a mental collapse, the murderer being incapable of bearing the weight of responsibility for what he has done."

Catherine leafs through her books on criminal analysis. She has underlined passages that interest her or might be helpful in her work.

"Collected eyewitness accounts demonstrate that a large part of our memory is invented, either from stories, through reconstitution, or from pure imagination."

"Conjugal violence is rarely a single isolated occurrence. The destructive urge to do away with one's spouse, to reduce her to nothing but also to dominate her almost always has its roots in a man's childhood, although each case is individual. The man is as genuine in his fury while he is hitting as he is when he is repenting, apologizing, and promising to never do it again. He is all the more convincing because he is convinced of it himself. But he will always start over again. For some men, the pattern also has something to do with the partners he chooses or who choose him. There is a meeting of two neuroses, of two pathologies. One cannot make absolute generalizations, but violent men, those who hit with fury and repent with tears and pleadings are often chameleons, a pleasure to be around, ladies' men, attentive and then cold, harsh, and disdainful. Their alternating relational modes sometimes change without any warning. They are narcissistic and have trouble seeing other people as human beings."

Catherine recognizes an exact portrait of Cedric, particularly in this last sentence. Amnesia is not possible, because he would not have kept Violet's letters or her picture if he had erased the memory of his act.

The Monique Lemaire case, far from being a hiccup, clearly establishes who he is.

Catherine has revisited her impulsive judgment from top to bottom.

Violet has a moment of weakness. She is bored in the countryside. Her husband is so busy. She has a little girl who takes all her time, and she can't resist an attractive, passionate young man when he shows up. It is easy to imagine the young Cedric stalking this charming Madame Bovary.

But he is a kid, and she loves her family. She would never deprive her daughter of a father and a stable environment. She is honest and upright, and rather than writing a letter, which she thinks would be cowardly, she sets a time to explain that they shouldn't see each other anymore. She needs to break up with him, definitively. She has chosen her husband. She is sorry, but there is no going back. She asks him to forgive her for leading him to believe in a story without a future.

Cedric refuses to admit it. He loves her. She loves him too. Love is all that counts. He will take her as she is, with her child too. He has said so. He promised her.

Violet, at all of twenty something, preaches reason. He is young. He doesn't even have a job. It's unreasonable. She would just be a burden. When the time comes, he will meet a woman he can build his life with. And you can't build something solid on a foundation of destruction. Life is a series of choices. And renunciations. Happiness does not necessarily come from the immediate gratification of your desires, but from self-abnegation in the name of higher values.

Catherine is certain, despite the emotion she feels when she imagines this touching scene, that she is attributing improbable words to Violet, who loved poetry, not woolly psychological treatises or advice from women's magazines.

Yet she continues her reconstitution.

Cedric sides with immediate gratification. And while Violet glances over at the stroller where little Catherine is sleeping, he grabs his mistress by the shoulders so she will look at him. It is the first time that Violet has brought her daughter to one of their meetings.

His words are closer and closer together. He shakes her so his ideas will sink deep inside the fragile young woman, who, despite the increasing rage, continues to reason, to explain and ends up saying that she is going to leave, because he refuses to listen to what she has to say, that she is sorry it is ending this way.

Perhaps she cries a little bit. She feels more sadness than fear when she turns her back to him, triggering an outburst. He holds her by the shoulder, slaps her, then punches her, leaving her groggy. She fights back, tries to escape. He catches her again, his excitement increasing, and he hits and he hits until there is nothing left of her beauty, her smile, her liveliness, nothing but a contorted body, silent and repugnant.

His hands and arms hurt. He is exhausted, but he must walk away quickly, making sure he doesn't leave any evidence behind. The child's crying rises in the silence.

He hesitates. That could attract attention and raise the alarm too early, too quickly. All of his rage has dissipated.

When he turns his back on the scene of the crime, it disappears from his memory. He wouldn't hurt a fly, much less a child.

From a distance, he understands the situation. The little girl is reaching out to a light-colored spot, a doll or a toy that has fallen to the ground. He approaches and picks up what is, in fact, a piece of white cloth and places it in the hands of the little girl, who raises her eyes to him.

Freeze frame. The killer's green eyes. The child's trusting look.

The final vestige of his misdeed remains in his memory, that instant when he thinks that she will never forget his face, that she is the Nemesis who one day could condemn him.

Had he taken out his violence on other women before Monique Lemaire? There is nothing in his record, but women are stupid.

"As I was," Catherine says.

Today the situation is clear. Cedric made sure that she would not recognize him, and he wanted to possess her in the way he failed to possess her mother. He is crazy, clinically crazy.

The train enters the La Souterraine station, perhaps for her last time. It is the final stretch before the trial, which starts in two days.

Her father will come, but Catherine has asked him to stay at a hotel, because she won't be available to see him until after the trial. She wants to remain completely focused.

Cedric is not suspicious. He has no reason to be suspicious. She argued that she didn't want to see him because she needed to concentrate on the trial. He did not insist, being respectful, a chameleon.

She does not really feel that she is in danger, even if sometimes she checks to make sure she is not being followed and looks up when she climbs a stairwell to make sure no one is waiting on the landing. Feeling ridiculous, she even writes a letter to open in case she dies a violent death. In it she directly accuses Cedric Devers.

After the trial, she will decide on a plan. After the trial.

Jean-Claude and Françoise have prepared a dinner for her to reheat. They don't want to hear her thanks, and they leave her to her preparations. She had explained to them the obsessive concentration such a trial requires. She doesn't have to tell them twice.

She does lock the door of the little house before going to bed and sleeps right through the night. She wakes up feeling impatient, which she imagines to be what an actor feels with the approach of opening night.

She chooses the clothes that she will advise Myriam to wear, which will not make her too invisible but won't make her stand out too much either. She selects a slightly flared caramel-colored skirt with a beige sweater and a pair of gray pants with a white blouse. Myriam will choose.

Myriam chooses the pants and a sweater of her own, which is bright yellow. She won't change her mind. This is what she is like, who she is.

Catherine accepts her choice without a fight, because Myriam has the right attitude.

Both the lawyer and her client have the same impatience. The team is sound. They have become familiar with each other during their periodic appointments, and Catherine is certain she has unraveled what her client leaves unsaid.

Both see the end of the tunnel, and even if the end of Myriam's leads to another tunnel of imprisonment, at least it will be defined and its term pronounced. Anything is preferable to uncertainty.

Final advice is given. "Be yourself. Be natural, direct. Everyone can sense when you conceal something, and that will automatically work against you. Nobody is expecting you to be the soul of innocence. That does not exist. Do not hesitate to take your time before answering questions. The jurors have the right to hand questions to the presiding judge, so don't get paranoid if you see papers circulating over the table. It's normal. Remember, too, that the jurors only know what is said during the trial and not what is in the case file. So do not refer to it."

Myriam smiles with the patience of an angel, without reminding her lawyer that she has already told her all this many times. She hopes that this novice will be more sure of herself during the trial. Catherine Monsigny believes she is sending out vibrations of assurance that contradict the weakness she feels when she looks for a paper that is already where it should be, her hesitation about what she has already said or not, her little nervous laugh when she confuses one word for another.

She is incredibly naïve for a lawyer. This is an asset for Myriam. She will not impress the jurors, who might even want to help out the clumsy beginner.

Myriam has always thought that life is a throw of the dice. All you have to do is not miss the right moment and not tremble when it is time to act. This trial has almost swallowed her up because she had not been expecting it. She has come some distance since then, and she has prepared for it.

The first court-appointed attorney did not give a good impression, and the pseudo-tenor from Limoges was the exact opposite of what she was looking for. She wanted a woman, preferably a young woman who had a major personal stake in the trial.

As it turned out, Catherine's commitment to the association was not really based on activism, which, in the end, was a very good thing, because an activist bent could irritate the jury.

No, clearly Myriam thinks that everything is working out. Looking frightened, she asks a few more questions, and her attorney recovers her calm by reassuring her client.

Catherine promises to come back tomorrow, the day before the trial, so that the wait does not seem endless and wear on her client.

Myriam thanks her. She also would like to see her attorney one more time before the trial, although not for the same reasons.

The guard comes to get the prisoner.

She casually hands him the clothing Catherine has brought, something her attorney notes without remembering the telephone her client procured in detention. Her mind is too busy elsewhere, and she is too certain that she understands Myriam to question what she knows about her.

That is unfortunate, because she would have understood that Mrs. Villetreix, formerly N'Bissi, like so many before her, multiplies the masks and knows how to turn a situation around in the twinkling of an eye.

While the guard advances down the hallway toward the gate, Myriam turns around and goes back to Catherine. "Remember what I told you," she says in a low voice full of feeling. "I am innocent. Don't forget it. Innocent."

40

Dr. Monsigny is driving along the highway, his eyes on the road and his ears on the radio, so his mind does not wander to the countryside he has not yet reached.

After Limoges, as he nears the town of Aubusson, his mind begins to broadcast memories, against his will. The familiar landscape makes the past audible. A clear light defines shapes and unifies the subtly changing countryside, recalling the broken promise of happiness. In a few minutes rediscovered surroundings kindle the lurking pain, confirming that healing is impossible. He will never know if there really was another man, if he had made it all up, if everything happened because of his limitless insecurity.

He would like to focus on Catherine, the reason he is coming, the reason he wanted to erase all traces of the past until they disappeared entirely from his own memory. He would have certainly been there too if the trial had been elsewhere, but here, where the irony of destiny has brought both of them back, he must be present, vigilant and attentive to his own terror. How improbable. This is the devil's spite.

In reality, he is not deceiving himself. He has been expecting that one day Catherine would call him to account for her past, perhaps the day she had her own child, whom she would try to fit into a background, into a family line.

Like a coward, he hoped that he would be dead before having to say that life was not a fairy tale and that Catherine was not born from a magical encounter between Cinderella and the prince.

All those times she had asked him about their meeting, he had been forced to make up details, which he believed in the end.

It was a dark and stormy night.

The little girl imitates her father, who groans and wails, spreading his arms to show the rain covering the entire town.

The doctor prince has for a long time refused all the good catches he has been offered because he does not like any of those young women, the charming, brilliant, and pretty students and nurses. They have left him indifferent. He has been waiting, ready to wait all the time needed and even longer, sure that one woman and only one has been destined for him and that he will recognize her at first sight.

"He was wrong," Catherine exclaims, bursting out in laughter.

"He was wrong."

He has pulled up his hood and is hiding under an umbrella that obstructs his view. He is walking quickly and doesn't see the miserable woman hunched on the bench, poorly sheltered by the branches of a large oak tree. Fortunately, destiny is on the watch, and a bright flash of lightning illuminates the scene with a crack that sounds like the sky splitting in two, never to be whole again. It is very impressive.

The young woman cries out, and the umbrella inverts in the wind, or perhaps it is the other way around. The doctor prince turns his back to the wind to fix his umbrella, and that is when he sees her.

A little bit of paradise in the midst of a storm.

He has no regrets.

He himself survived childhood with fiction. The stories he told himself, the adventures, rescues, improbable encounters, the recognition, the nobility, the glory. These are the dreams that push you forward, even when they are totally unrealistic, most of all when they are totally unrealistic.

He is convinced that Catherine's strength, her courage, and her success come in part from the myth of her origin. She has always felt supported because she was born in a fairy tale, her cradle duly surrounded by protective fairies.

The advantage of the stage fright eating away at him because he is returning to the footsteps of his past is that he compares what he feels to what his daughter is going to feel before the trial, which reduces his own apprehension.

That is also something he has always tried to hide from her: his insomnia the night before her exams, his anxiety while he was waiting for her grades. He has made it a point of honor to never show any impatience. He would wait for her to tell him what she received on her exams. And he refrained from calling her the night she moved to Paris. He let her make the call.

Yes, the laid-back father, so anxiety-filled in reality.

Catherine has reserved a room in her name. The hotel was not there in his day. He cannot help but note that it must be really convenient for adulterous wives and husbands. "Stop that too," he says to himself. "Stop thinking about unfaithful couples."

Catherine has reproached him tacitly for never starting a new life, but he is convinced that she would have reprimanded him so much more had he done that.

She looks at him from the French window. Does she have the right to bring down the foundations of her recomposed past a second time?

He is sitting in a garden chair, enjoying a bit of sun, a book open on his knees, his eyes closed, his head leaning back, completely immobile. She sees him dead, wonders if she will miss him, hates herself for even thinking that, and calls out to him to break the spell of this moment stopped in time.

He blinks, disoriented, older, slower, she thinks ruthlessly.

Do we slow down when we age to delay the hour of our death?

She kisses him with a rush of emotion that tries to mask her discomfort at such vile thoughts, and he accepts it as he emerges from his daydream. It's further proof that he is right to hide his anxiety from her.

The two find a balance in the same concealment, and happy, they leave together for a restaurant at the top of the main street on a traffic circle. They are sitting down, and she notices that her father has started to chew his nails again. She looks away, pretending that she hasn't seen anything.

She announces that she does not want to talk about work and then talks about nothing else.

He listens, as if that were his only job on earth. For that matter, he seems to never have anything to say. He is so filled with the stories of other people, there is no room for his own.

Catherine tries self-promotion. She congratulates herself for pepping up her client, for preparing her well, transforming a washed-up dishtowel into a starched cloth.

Renaud has approved the outline of her argument. She will combine the benefit of the doubt—that is, the total absence of real evidence against her client—with her personal conviction that Myriam is innocent.

"You should have heard her! All she has to do is say it again with the same certainty in front of the jury, and it will resonate in them, I'm sure."

"It's crazy, nevertheless, to be in the *Cour d'Assises* with such a weak case."

"Money is money. Who did the crime benefit? Yes, she was in the best position to poison Gaston. But that's just it. I am counting a lot on the evaluation of the defendant. Myriam is very intelligent. I didn't realize it right away. As intelligent as she is, she would have taken the precautions necessary to kill without attracting any suspicion."

"According to what you told me, she did not love her husband."

"Gaston? Yes she did, in her own way."

"Well, that's not what I call love."

Her father would have trouble testifying about true love if she told him that his wife, Violet, a newlywed, had engaged in an affair and that she had been killed by her secret lover, who also loved her passionately.

She feels a streak of meanness so vicious that she is left speechless for a moment. It is as though she holds her father responsible for her mother's death, which is so terribly unfair. She comes back to Myriam and explains patiently, which is her way of making amends for a thought that, fortunately, he will never hear.

"She is grateful for everything Gaston did for her. She would have been happy to share everything with him but was not going to deprive herself just because he wasn't there any longer. Hardship makes people realistic. I ended up liking the woman. She has enviable energy, courage, and a way of taking her life into her own hands, despite the obstacles."

"You have to like a defendant to defend her well."

"Perhaps at my level, but Renaud can commit himself fully and effectively, even when he doesn't like a client. Hey, are you sure you're not going to be bored all alone? It was nice of you to come so early, but…"

"I'm used to being alone, and I enjoy feeling like I'm near you."

"Then if you are okay with the situation," she says, giving him a small smile and a loud kiss as she excuses herself and abandons him at the door of the restaurant. He can feel and understand her passion. He does not dwell on the admiration that she has always had for her boss, one that is well deserved, that she could have had for her father. Enough, it is his role to watch from the shadows, without any gratification other than the results.

Catherine calls Olivier to see if he has received his subpoena. Old Eliane has not been listed as a witness. Catherine will take care of the cousins, the plaintiffs. The psychiatric expert she is bringing in from Paris will establish her client's sound mind, intelligence, and resilience. She has even overcome the traumas of her childhood and pardoned the guilty. That would be a two-edged sword, were there any proof of Myriam's guilt, in which case she would be irrevocably responsible, but her expert draws a portrait of anything but a potential criminal. Her questions will lead to this conclusion.

Even Daniel will, in the end, make the trip. He has been on television several times, has a little bit of a reputation, and is someone you like. Since his confession, he has been terrified that the prosecution will raise questions about his sexual relationship with Myriam, which would have a long-term negative effect on what he considers, against all logic, a career.

Catherine has convinced him that there is no risk of the subject coming up during questioning.

She intends to present the improbable meeting of Gaston and Myriam like a fairy tale. Everyone loves fairy tales; everyone wants to believe in them. The poor undocumented exile, without money, without a future, crosses paths with an old farmer in the guise of a prince, more modern, enterprising and brave than many a city-dweller. She is the heroine of a story that is the stuff of dreams.

Even if it means she has to set aside Daniel's original cynicism. She is still not sure if she will read the personal ad parody but has not excluded the possibility to better highlight the simplicity and the sincere beauty of this improbable marriage. As soon as she has gone over the various elements in her head, she starts worrying that she is naïvely basing her approach on the notion of storytelling, the pet theme of the day.

No, of course not. She loves stories, as everyone else does.

It is her last meeting with Myriam before court. The time for doubts and latent defects is long past. Catherine relaxes her face into a smile and strengthens the look in her eyes. As soon as Myriam joins her, she stands, holds out her hand, and says a simple, plain hello.

Does Myriam have any questions, concerns, hesitations?

The required questions bring an automatic "no."

Much to her lawyer's dismay, Myriam announces that she intends to lie about a detail. Catherine's heart tightens at the idea that Myriam is going to reveal something that will make her an accomplice on the day before the trial. It's about the papers, Myriam continues, without leaving any space for an interruption. She prefers to say she recovered them at the home of the people she was working for before she fled, because if she relates how Gaston bought them for her, it will be like he bought her, and it could cause problems for the people at the embassy. Myriam has thought about it all night. The truth will only complicate everything.

It is, indeed, not of primary importance, all the more so because nobody can disprove a statement for which only Myriam has the key.

After feeling the wind of the canon ball, Catherine settles her nerves and reminds her client that she has no intention of speaking for her. Her role is to ask questions, and it is Myriam's role to decide what she is going to say and why. Is there anything else?

No, it is as Catherine just said. She will answer the questions, and because she trusts her attorney to ask them well, there shouldn't be any problem.

When they are getting ready to separate, Myriam launches into a short prepared speech. Even before she knows the verdict she wants to express her gratitude to Catherine. At the beginning, she was suspicious and worried. She was not very nice, but her lawyer knew how to reassure her, and she is convinced now that she couldn't have a better lawyer. She is proud to be Catherine's first major case and confident that this will bring them both luck.

Catherine thanks her, pretending to be optimistic too. In reality, her optimism has been completely undone. While her nerves take over again, she steadies her voice and reaffirms her confidence in Myriam and in the case.

As she goes to her car, she can't help but hear disturbing voices in her head, the voices of those who see Myriam as a manipulator who knows exactly where she is going.

41

The courtroom walls have light-colored wood paneling. At the back of the room, behind the presiding judge and his assistant judges, there are two large windows topped with stained glass. The place itself is not that imposing, but the ritual will make it sacred.

The area for the media, which is directly in front of Catherine, is empty, only for the moment, she hopes.

Potential jurors fill the room. They have just seen a short film that explains the felony court procedure.

The attorney looks at her list of names, birthdates, and professions. She unconsciously checks under her court robe to make sure she has knotted her white good-luck scarf.

Standing at her lectern, with Myriam to her left, she is feeling surprisingly calm. Her private life might be chaotic, to say the least, but her sense of being a professional in the place where she's meant to be makes her feel balanced and strong.

Myriam has been right to wear her yellow sweater. It affirms the innocence of someone who has nothing to fear, nothing to hide.

When the cousins, the plaintiffs, arrive, she greets them with a nod. They do not answer and continue to ignore her, although they are sitting on the bench a few yards away.

Their attorney, who is very young, has a cowlick. He moves around a lot, shuffling his papers and whispering to his clients.

Louis comes in and takes his place in the reporters' area. He nods to her discreetly as he passes.

She sees two housewives on the list of potential jurors, whom she thinks she will challenge, but she doesn't anticipate any problems with the others. She trusts her instincts. Each juror is called and rises, passing in front of her. The first one has a belligerent attitude that betrays an unwillingness to see any opinions other than his own, and she challenges him. She remembers the lesson she has learned from Renaud and spits out her "Challenge!" like an accusation. The man is surprised, humiliated, and those who are waiting, still seated, are suddenly worried. They are being tested, and they are unsure of themselves.

Myriam stands up straight during the jury selection, her arms resting on the podium in front of her. She follows the proceedings with interest, without ever looking too long at any of the jurors.

Catherine has explained each party's role. Myriam's is to be natural, without trying to seduce or show any aggressiveness. "Be serious and attentive. No smiling, no laughing." She is the widow of a man she loved.

When the court returns, there are all of four spectators in the room, including Dr. Monsigny, who is sitting in the back row trying to be invisible. Other than giving a small smile of encouragement, he avoids looking at his daughter as best he can.

The presiding judge summarizes the case, the diagnosis of cardiac arrest, and the death certificate through to the discovery of the poison, the symptoms of cyanide poisoning and those experienced by Mr. Villetreix, the decision to exhume the body, and the autopsy results. He then starts questioning Myriam.

First, Myriam's background is discussed. Her birth in Gabon and her parents' death, which remain a little unclear when it comes to dates and circumstances.

Myriam explains that she was little and that her grandmother had tried to protect her by telling her as little as possible.

"If you say so," the judge murmurs.

Her arrival in France with the proper papers, working for a family that was never found again, the poor treatment she was subjected to, her escape. As foreseen, this is the area that the presiding judge questions most vigorously.

How is it that there is no record of the defendant's entry to France? Her employers had filled out the papers for her. Perhaps they gave a fake name.

Catherine does not flinch but wonders how she is going to justify the marriage papers.

The presiding judge continues. Why did the defendant make up names for her abusive employers at first, and why was she now refusing to establish their identity? Was she trying to protect them?

Myriam affirms that she was afraid for her grandmother and then for herself. Now it's the past, and she doesn't even hold it against them. Anyway, she started a new life.

The judge persists. Myriam had proven that she could lie, invent things, so why should they believe the rest of her statements?

With a polite display of dignity, Myriam says that she was scared. "When you are scared, you protect yourself with lies." Now she is no longer afraid.

Why?

"My husband took the fear away. I could trust him. I never had any doubt about that. Those people no longer have any place in my life."

Catherine examines the faces of the jurors. Yes, this moment is having an impact. She jots down the words "fear" and "lies."

It is interesting that Myriam has never used these words with her. With them, this weak link in her story has become a strong point. Catherine just hopes that her client can remain this good until the end.

She is still good when it comes to explaining her desire to escape an uncertain and worrying life by getting married. No, she did not imagine that it would be a marriage of love. She suggests that love is a luxury enjoyed by those who do not have survival issues. What she saw first was Gaston's kindness. He never made her feel different.

Different?

Because of her color. When she moved in, she could see how the children and even the adults looked at her. But never Gaston. He was even proud of her, and she wanted to prove him right.

"So in a way it was a perfect marriage," the judge says with a touch of sarcasm.

Myriam lowers her head and remains silent.

When she lifts her head again, she quickly wipes away two tears and says, "It was for me."

The cousins roll their eyes with cynicism, but the moment really is moving.

The courtroom has just a smattering of people. The media bench is filled solely with members of the local press. The e-mails she sent to her national press contacts have remained unanswered. A regional television team recorded a few images at the beginning of the hearing. They are probably at the café now.

At this point, Catherine doesn't care. The stakes are greater than she is. She is on board and feels a disproportionate amount of confidence.

When the judge mentions the age difference, Myriam responds that she did not feel all that much younger than her husband. Her misfortunes had matured her beyond her years, and he had been relatively sheltered all his life. His mother had always pampered him. He had never had any money problems, and he was well accepted in his town. He had a good sense of imagination and humor, which helped her when she was in a dark mood.

Ah, dark moods.

Yes, she sometimes had images of the past and thoughts of her grandmother.

Yes, she had tried to find her again, but things are different there. It is hard to know what has become of people when you return to the back of beyond, to the middle of nowhere.

A life that leaves little mark, the judge insists.

A clandestine life, Myriam concludes.

In her way, she always has the last word.

Catherine sees that this irritates the judge.

As soon as possible, she will say something about it to her client. In the meantime, she does not ask any additional questions. She will come back to them later; she does not want to risk ruining the favorable effects of this first examination.

The judge moves on the psychiatric experts. The first one, even with the mike turned on, talks to the side, is inaudible, and uses incomprehensible jargon. That's fine. He has nothing to say.

The second one, Catherine's expert, denies that there is any fabrication. The defendant has a precise sense of reality. When she doesn't want to open up, she doesn't say anything. She lied to the association because the idea of returning to the place where she came from was more than she could handle, but she knew she was lying. That was what she needed to do to survive. She had to start from zero again in order to progress. It was not technically repression but a deliberate attempt to escape her status as victim.

He speaks clearly and directly into the mike and uses simple, understandable terms.

The jurors release the tension caused by the first shrink's indistinct testimony.

During the coroner's deposition, Catherine conspicuously takes her client's hand to comfort her.

Then she attacks, consulting her notes, repeatedly questioning how the poison could have been administered or swallowed. Its effects, its symptoms, its taste.

Imperceptibly spreading doubt about medical certainty.

The day passes quickly. She calls Renaud from the attorneys' room during the first break to tell him how it's going. He warns her about being too confident. Anything could happen in court. It is impossible to tell how jurors are reacting to the arguments. She should remain on guard.

Behind his roughness, she feels his support and trust.

In the end, she gives Myriam the same message. Do not be too self-assured, respect the judge's authority.

She understands in a second. She is clearly a good client.

Her father remains invisible. He does not leave the courtroom during the breaks.

When Dr. Blanchard testifies, he has to face a series of questions about errors in judgment.

Catherine comes to his rescue, giving him the opportunity to say that Gaston's symptoms could very well have been those of a simple cardiac arrest, considering how long after the death he examined the body. And as the family doctor, he had warned Gaston about his tobacco habit and had reminded him about his mother's medical history.

For the first time, Catherine carefully approaches the issue of Madame Villetreix's death, permitting the jurors to put two and two together.

The good doctor leaves the courtroom humiliated and does not return.

The day ends with the cousins' testimony. One after another they explain the same thing and talk about their attachment to Gaston, who was a good and naïve man whose death should not go unexplained. They play on the classic themes of family bonds, long-time affection and loyalty to those who have passed away.

Catherine enjoys turning them over on the griddle.

Without Myriam, they are the undisputed heirs to Gaston's estate. And Gaston had made it clear that he wanted his wife to enjoy a life without worries after having experienced such hardship, as they themselves have said.

In response, they claim that they were very open-minded. They emphasize how warmly the foreigner was welcomed. The inheritance had nothing to do with it.

But little by little, from harmless question to insidious question, they reveal their discomfort with her different ways. Yes, to a certain extent Gaston appreciated the changes Myriam brought to his life, but in the end he often complained about them.

"Did he ever say he regretted his marriage?"

"Not directly, but he implied it. I think he was afraid the entire family fortune was going to go up in smoke."

"He was afraid, or you were afraid?"

The day ends with Myriam's testimony. In a hesitant voice, she retraces her arrival in Saint Jean, explaining how she wanted to be loved by the whole family and needed to belong to a community, because she had never had one.

Not a word against the cousins.

Not one.

Respectfully—and perhaps laying it on a bit too thick—she says she understands their uncertainty. She also wants to know what really happened. Of course she is afraid of going to prison. But it's not just that. It hurts that she is suspected of having poisoned the man who was always good to her. It is true that Gaston had become gloomier during the last few months before his death. She had been worried about his health, as Dr. Blanchard said. She had talked to him about it. People had told her how Etienne threw himself down the well and died, and she was happy that the well had been closed up.

"You imagined that he could commit suicide?'

"Oh no, not that!" she said perfectly spontaneously, exactly as if she had, in fact, imagined that but could not bring herself to admit it.

Catherine quickly chases away the strange impression that her client is playing a role. She observes the jurors.

The only things they know about Myriam are what they have picked up from her live performance. They are attentive, serious, and during the final testimony, six of them are taking notes.

At the end of the day, Catherine is exhausted.

42

Dr. Monsigny wonders when his daughter's separation from him and her emergence as an adult really began. He realizes now that it was a slow progression that he did not perceive as it advanced. But it certainly started well before he was presented with the fait accompli of her decision: "I'm going to study law in Paris."

Looking at her now, he sees a woman who is still so young, so little, so frail but also so self-assured and commanding in her black robe. He has no trouble making out the blurred vestiges of childhood in her large round cheeks, like those of a Russian doll, and her bottom lip, which she would thrust out in a pout whenever he refused her something. He instantly regretted every refusal, because he wanted to spoil her constantly. But he was determined to give her a good upbringing and a good education.

Anything to avoid making the same mistake, of getting too attached to one person, of depending on that person for his life, particularly when she would inevitably take off one day.

A day that came too soon. Because of him.

He knows all to well that in order to keep someone, you have to let go. And his reflex was to close his hand around his treasure and half smother it.

He has learned his lesson. He hopes that he has learned it well. That she feels free, always, so that she will remain imprisoned, always.

Daniel testifies. He is intimidated.

It is hard not to feel blamed in a place where judgment is passed.

When the court enters, and Monsigny stands up with everyone else, he is overcome by an absurd panic, as if a finger will be pointed at him, and he will be called upon to answer for his past before the jurors, the court, and the public.

He can understand Daniel's concern about testifying, but the result is good, as he was certainly prepared well by Catherine. He recounts how Myriam was vulnerable when she came to the association's office and how she was also brave. He sheepishly confirms having teased her a bit, but his intention was not mean. When you are constantly facing the hardship of uncertain lives, you need humor as an outlet. It is true that at first he had a hard time believing in Gaston and Myriam's story, but what followed proved him wrong.

Yes, Myriam N'Bissi stayed for a few days in the home of a couple of activists.

Normally, the association helps the undocumented with their applications and administrative procedures. With Myriam it was easier because she spoke French well and knew how to read and write it without any trouble. When the plaintiffs' attorney questions him about his matchmaking role, he gives a simple, calm answer. He says he is not in favor of paper marriages because he has seen their consequences, which, in his opinion, are disastrous. For that matter, Myriam never asked him for that kind of service. She dreamed about getting married, yes, like a schoolgirl who saw marriage as the solution to all her problems and a way to be happy.

"Was she ready for anything?"

"A lot of young women dream about marriage as a cure-all. But not at any price. Myriam was like that."

He explains that after the wedding he did not hear from her. That's the way things work. The association exists to help people overcome specific problems. You don't see the doctor when you are in good health.

It is charming to see Catherine try to have a cold and distant tone when she questions a witness she knows so well.

When the wife of the couple who housed Myriam testifies next, Monsigny appreciates his daughter's finesse. She didn't want her client's witnesses to be just men.

She is a fifty-year-old activist with graying hair down to her shoulders. She is wearing a tunic and wide pants. There's something about a uniform, regardless of its style, Monsigny thinks.

Sailing through her testimony, she recounts Myriam's need to help people, to reciprocate acts of kindness as much as she could. The undocumented immigrant almost did too much. She had to stop her from cleaning the house, doing the dishes, etc. She was discreet too; she said little about herself.

When Olivier Huguenot testifies, Dr. Monsigny squirms despite himself.

Catherine's reaction is very different from the ease she felt with Daniel. Something in the way she pulls her shoulders back and blushes gives him the impression that she is susceptible to this man's charm.

Monsigny isn't hearing anything anymore, and his eyes fix on his daughter. He has known this would happen one day, and he has prepared for it as best he could, but she has already become so distant from him, the bond is very tenuous. A man staying with Catherine instead of moving on is all it would take to break the thread.

If Monsigny were more certain of the evidence and of the nature of their relationship, he would have been less worried. The truth is, he will never rest. Certain secrets make you vulnerable.

He relaxes little by little. Catherine is attracted to this local man but nothing more. He is not the man who was supposed to meet them at the restaurant. He felt the difference in his daughter's voice, heard the provocation, the challenge, the uncertainty. But it was so mixed up in the threads of his own anxiety that perhaps he read more into it than there really was. Apparently, that man had disappeared from her life. She never talked about him again. He would be here otherwise, here to support her.

The doctor would have really preferred celebrating Catherine's birthday somewhere other than this symbolically charged region.

Not just symbolically charged. Since his arrival, Monsigny has had the impression that witnesses could pop up at any time. But no, twenty years, that is an eternity. Unfortunately, sleep knows how to abolish the distance that separates you from the furthest lands, as witnessed by his first night in the Creuse, from which he emerged gasping for breath and running to open a window for air.

In that horrible dream, Catherine was a child and a woman at the same time and was pointing a finger at him, screaming, "It's you. It's not you."

He does not always know how to differentiate between real images and those from his over-active imagination, which sometimes causes him to doubt what he perceives.

Perhaps he should have started the long process of analysis, which had been recommended, to come to terms with what happened. But he would never risk allowing someone to undo the crude armor he had built over time. Without it, he would have died of pain, and every taste of life would have been poison.

Olivier Huguenot has left the courtroom, and the plaintiffs' attorney is in the middle of his closing arguments.

Catherine shakes her head and takes a few notes.

To conclude, the man with a cowlick addresses Myriam directly.

"Thanks to your marriage, you became the mistress..."

There is overall suspense, during which Monsigny is drawn out of his dark thoughts and fully participates: a revelation? So late in the trial? He watches his daughter intently, watches her send her client a questioning look, but Myriam answers with a gesture of total incomprehension.

"...of your life. And from there you thought you could reign over the life of others. Yes, you were pursuing a dream, a dream without limits, and this court, in hearing the plaintiffs, these two wounded cousins, will impose the full penalty required by law and common decency."

Monsigny looks at the time. It would be terrible if Catherine made her closing arguments at the end of the day, when everyone was showing signs of fatigue.

The public prosecutor is speaking. He recaps the case clearly, succinctly summarizing all the testimony. His arguments do, indeed, lean toward *intime conviction*. He is convinced that Myriam Villetreix is guilty. It is true that there is no direct evidence, no material proof, but based on a precise body of indirect evidence, which he reviews piece by piece—no other suspect had the means and the motive to accomplish the murder—she is guilty. "If Myriam did, indeed, kill her husband, as everything leads us to believe, then the crime is particularly abject."

Catherine looks at Myriam and slips her a short note. She smiles with confidence.

She plays her part for the jurors.

The judge, considering the time, decides that the defense's closing arguments will take place the next morning.

Catherine will make her closing statement on her birthday. That will be hard, but what follows seems to be even more terrible for the doctor: their celebration meal right in the heart of land-mined territory. He grasps at what Catherine has said, that she is joining him in his desire to move forward without the burden of what has happened.

Catherine is undoubtedly trying to lessen the importance of the past, to say that they need to distance themselves from it. Above all, Catherine does not lie. She is too whole, too absolute. Like her mother.

A pizza, television, and a valium. Just one more day to get through.

In the morning he reserves a table in a restaurant that has recently opened in the middle of the countryside, recommended by the hotel director. It is new, without references, without shadows.

It is raining, but it could be pleasant to have lunch in front of a good fire and then return to Paris. He will drive her back and will stay for two days. He has the feeling she will need comforting. She cannot win this case. In another city maybe, but not here. Or perhaps he wants her to lose and have no one else to turn to. It's his way of countering his fear of the day she will no longer need him.

Catherine is already there when he enters the courtroom. She looks out of kilter. Did stage fright keep her from sleeping? Those are not signs of sleep deprivation, but rather of torment. He knows her well. She avoids looking at Myriam. She concentrates on her notes.

She rises and begins. She commences by referring to the public prosecutor.

"Yes, that would be an abject crime, the most abject of crimes, the type of act that one must not attribute to someone lightly. Yet here we have a case where everyone has done his job honestly, seriously and in good faith."

Whatever her worries, Catherine's voice is firm, and she is off on a long statement.

She returns to the cousins' legitimate and touching regard for the gendarmes' professionalism. Yet after such detailed work, what remains? Presumptions.

Presumptions the attorney now reviews one by one to reduce them to improbability.

A village where everyone has access to everyone else's house, because none of the doors are locked. Where everyone has access to that terrible poison and knows its effects but about which nobody thinks when Gaston dies. Because no one can imagine someone killing this man, who was finally making a life for himself. This good man, who was pleased to finally bring happiness to a woman overwhelmed by life.

She goes over Myriam's history and explains that once a widow, she wanted to leave this place where her happiness had become her misfortune. She is a wanderer, and because she had always been refused a calm, sedentary life, it was logical that she would want to leave.

Yes, this woman had overcome obstacles. She had learned French by reading the schoolbooks of the children she was caring for. She had constantly given back, as best she could, for the help she had been given.

And Catherine finishes by telling the jurors that she also has an *intime conviction*. Hers has developed over the period of months during which she has seen her client, heard her tell her story, and explain. Yes, her client is innocent, which is why she asks for a pure and simple acquittal for lack of proof and convincing evidence. The testimony on the prosecution side has made the hypothesis of murder absurd and crazy.

Myriam speaks last to thank everyone for defending her honor.

The court withdraws.

Myriam mouths an emotional thank you in Catherine's direction. She simply nods and assembles her papers, looking busy.

Yes, something happened.

There will be a good two- or three-hour wait for the verdict. Monsigny hesitates. He didn't expect this. The rookie lawyer should be radiant and self-assured, but she looks like she has bitten into a lemon.

He decides to sit in the corridor and wait until she gives him some sort of discernible sign. He gets up when she approaches, kisses her, and congratulates her. Whatever the result, that was a fine statement. She deserves her gift.

She looks completely surprised. Oh, yes, it's her birthday.

"What's happening, Catherine?" he asks.

She drags him away, quickly walking through the hall, stopping just to listen to Louis, who congratulates her as well. She thanks him with a weak smile.

The policeman at the entrance calls out, "Maître Monsigny?"

The blood drains from her face, and she turns around. He has a note for her.

It is Daniel, who is sorry he had to leave right away.

She crumples the paper and shoves it into her pocket.

Outside, far from indiscreet ears, she says to her father, "What is happening? I just defended someone who lied from the beginning. I have just bailed out a woman I firmly suspect is a criminal and who has manipulated me throughout the whole process. That's what's wrong."

Monsigny tries to tell her that in any case, she has done her job, as she was supposed to, and she has nothing to blame herself for. She is not the one to decide on the verdict.

"In any case, if she is acquitted and the public prosecutor appeals, I will not defend her a second time. And I will tell her why."

"Why? What happened?"

"I have to call Renaud."

And she walks away under a downfall of rain, leaving him orphaned in a world that is clearly upside down.

43

Cedric controls himself to avoid speeding through the rain as it streaks across the landscape and his racing thoughts. His regrets keep multiplying as he approaches his destination.

He has thought of nothing but Catherine and her case for the past three days. He is dying to have some news and is feeling great remorse for not having excised the lie.

It is too late for that now.

He had prepared the metal box and was waiting for the right moment one evening or perhaps just when she arrived, as she crossed the threshold, to confess everything.

He had been afraid. He had kept silent.

Just as he did not tell the gendarmes after Violet's murder, for fear of the consequences. There is no reason to close his eyes to it. He was afraid for himself. He knew it then, he knows it today, and he will always know it.

He should have told Catherine everything right away, before getting caught up in the game of seduction. He had been afraid. For the same wrong reasons. He should never have set out to meet Catherine. It was deviant, unhealthy. He could have at least gone through with what he had intended. Because he had saved the letters, because he had pulled out the box and prepared the words he would say. That box, unopened all those years, which he saved nevertheless—thinking about getting rid of it a hundred times and always changing his mind.

Was this his way of repenting?

He should have shown Catherine the letters so she could read them, so she could discover the story, directly, without any intermediary. Instead, he worried about ruining everything and kept putting it off to a later time. A later that looked like never. The proof that he put an end to the affair—he did, not her. He had to convince Catherine that he had nothing to do with her mother's death.

When he really had everything to do with her mother's murder. The rest is indefensible.

Catherine takes shelter in the car and empties her bag onto the seat until the little rag doll falls out. The surprise she wanted to give Myriam on the last day of the trial, right before the verdict, like a good luck charm, a pledge of their complicity, the toy stuffed into her luggage at the last minute, when she remembered having taken it from the house. The toy was a fantastic idea, perfectly out of place, that ended up speaking to her.

Apparently, the day she returned from Creuse and panicked at the sight of that strange rose on her doormat, she tore out some stitching on the doll as she pulled on the key ring.

Before going to court in the morning, Catherine wants to wrap the doll in a box with paper and a pretty ribbon to make it look like a gift. She turns over the little dolly to fold it. The rainbow-colored cloth on its head comes undone, and the flax stuffing begins to spill out. As she pushes it back in, Catherine spots the tip of a clear yellow card, takes it out, and discovers an old French identity card with a photo, never renewed but undeniable. Myriam Malevat was born just outside Paris in Saint-Denis, five years earlier than she has claimed.

It is one piece of information too many, which comes too late.

Her final statement is scheduled to begin in forty minutes. The card, which was issued by the Paris Government Administrative Office, bears a picture of Myriam as a teenager. It indicates an address in the twentieth arrondissement of Paris. She puts the folded card back inside the doll's head and stuffs the toy into the bottom of her handbag.

The past can take on all kinds of interpretations. All types of hypotheses can be imagined. Perhaps Myriam is a murderer, or perhaps she is not. All that work to convince herself of her innocence should not be reduced to nothing. She sorts through her personal conviction and everything that contradicts it. She winds up keeping only her desire to win, to be good, to successfully accomplish an enterprise that has been several months in the making, to carry it through to the end. This is what actors do, despite grief and illness.

She discovers that her job can consist of pure representation, that, in the end, it is about getting people to believe in an illusion, like a charlatan at a fair.

Now she is counting on her boss to know what to do. She is not even sure that the marriage is valid. Do you marry a person or an identity? Why did Myriam dive into this unlikely adventure? Catherine imagines a lot of explanations, including that old absurd dream of starting again from scratch, with the idea of beginning a new life. Except that it worked. That's the crazy part. It worked.

In the car, she focuses so that she can present the situation as clearly as possible to her boss. She calls.

When Renaud hears her flat tone, he asks very calmly if the trial has gone poorly. Her closing argument?

Her statement has been as good as it could be, given the circumstances.

For once, Renaud doesn't know what to say.

He will call her back.

She curls herself up in the seat and closes her eyes.

Cedric has read them only once, two hours ago, but Violet's last letters are carved in his memory.

First he takes the box, determined to make a decision, once and for all. Either he would get rid of it, or he would give it all to Catherine.

He removes the metal cover.

He immediately notices that neither the picture nor the un-opened letters are where they should be. He remembers Catherine's surprised look when he came home. He took it at face value, not trying to interpret it. Just as he didn't interpret her evasiveness and silences afterward.

He decides that Catherine's refusal to see him before the trial was legitimate, that she needed to focus on her case, as he focused on his layout. He even told himself that they were alike in this way.

Using the same stupid reasoning, he has justified staying away from Guéret. She wanted to lead this battle alone. That is something he can understand.

When in truth, so close to her first felony trial, she discovered that she had been betrayed, manipulated. And she chose to shut up without giving him the slightest possibility of explaining himself.

But Catherine is more the type to look for confrontation. Why has she backed away?

Because she wanted to focus on her priorities, her upcoming trial. He opens the two envelopes.

My love, I beg you not to abandon me. I asked too much of you. I was wrong. I miss you. I feel like I'm going to die. You are what keeps me alive, you and my daughter. I don't want her to grow up in the shadow of my sorrow. I want to leave my husband. Not for you. For me. But stay in my life, please. I don't ask anything of you, just to love you from a distance, not to be a burden. It will be fine as long as you send me little signs that you are there and that you care. I understand that you have a life to build, that you're too young to burden yourself with a family as young as you are, but at least leave the future open. Talk to me. V.

My dear darling,
Silence is the worst punishment. I do not deserve that. I know that you will be coming back for the next vacation. Let us see each other one more time. I will be reasonable.

He shoves the two letters into his pocket, closes the box, and throws it into a bag with a toothbrush and a pair of socks. He is not thinking. He is in emergency mode. He has waited too long all of his life. He takes his car and fills the tank.

He'll wait the time it takes, after the verdict, after the celebrations. He will not take his eyes off her, and as soon as he sees her alone, he will ask her to read, just read, and afterward, they will talk. She will understand. She has to understand.

Catherine is in no hurry to know the verdict. Even if she wins, the victory will be bitter.

She should have told her father to keep quiet.

But who would he talk to anyway?

She sees herself disbarred.

What she has done is perhaps outside the law.

First Cedric, then Myriam, her birthday, lying at every level, a muddy past. Nothing makes sense anymore.

Renaud calls back with instructions. Wait for the verdict. Whatever it is, tell Myriam that you will send her a bill, and then give her back her doll without a word of explanation. Forget about it. Wash your hands of it.

Myriam is simply a case, a client like any other an attorney takes on at a given moment in time. Perhaps Myriam has experienced things even more terrible than the story she invented. Perhaps not.

The case is over.

What is important is that nothing connects Catherine to the information. She hasn't talked to anyone about it, right?

Nobody.

A half-lie. To her father, but that is like mentioning it to herself. Or to nobody.

She stays in her car. She hides when she sees someone approaching.

She absolutely must turn this day into something positive. Make it something bright and open. Something that will give her faith in the future. There must be a way.

Remember that there are no coincidences. Her birthday, her first appearance in criminal court, her return to the place where her mother died, her father's presence, her conviction that she has found the killer or rather that he has found her.

And at that moment she knows what to do.

The rain turns the day into night. Every time the windshield wiper goes back and forth, Cedric sees a new piece of the puzzle fall into place. The past is projected onto the windshield of his memory. There is nothing he can do about it, and he lets himself go to it. At the beginning of their short affair, during the times of exaltation and simultaneity, he and Violet agreed on a code to reach each other in case of emergency. Two rings. Hang up. Call back.

On April 16, 1988, the weather is beautiful. He has planned to go fishing with Arthur, who hasn't lost hope in getting him to like his hobby.

The phone rings twice in the entryway and then goes quiet.

When it rings again, Arthur answers and hangs up because nobody was responding to his questions.

Cedric says he has to mail a letter, goes to the public phone booth in town, and calls his cumbersome lover before she calls back and exposes him, because he is afraid there will be a scandal with too many obligations, because the truth is he no longer loves her.

She answers immediately. She talks in a quick and hushed voice. Her husband will be coming back soon. He will be seeing patients all afternoon. Had Cedric read her letters? No? She'll wait for him at two. She'll be with her daughter. He doesn't have to worry. There won't be a scene, she swears. Two in the afternoon in the Pierre Levée clearing.

He tells himself that it is time to bring this to an end and that he has to go. He half-heartedly says yes. He hears the sound of a door on the other end of the line. She hangs up.

He is still hoping that she will not come, that something will keep her.

His love at first sight, so wonderful that he didn't evaluate the consequences, has changed into an irritating wound. It is Violet's fault. She expects too much from him. She has nothing but demands and suspicions. She makes scenes and cries, asking for forgiveness.

It's too much for him.

He is in a lousy mood and prepares himself for a tearful scene with a hysterical woman, with whom he should never have started anything. He thinks this is the last chore, and after that he'll be free.

He has no inkling that he will never be free of this affair, that it will eat away at him, that it will keep him from having any lasting relationship, as if he did not deserve what everyone else has the right to enjoy.

He takes a blow when he meets the little girl in flesh and blood. She has big, searching gray eyes. She is rubbing her nose with a dirty white cloth that terminates in her mouth, shoved in by the thumb she is sucking.

A little animal who leaves him indifferent. He wonders what he is doing there.

To keep his composure, he squats at her level. She blinks, squints, and then closes her eyes because of the sun.

"Let her alone. She's almost asleep. It's her nap time."

He looks at the young woman and sees a mother, another world. He would like to be so far away. He has nothing to say. She is quiet too. It is strange.

They take a few hesitant steps. Not so long ago, they clutched each other, their flesh like two magnets of the same intensity. The distance is much greater than the few centimeters that separate them.

He does not try to hide his sullen mood.

He looks at her when she stops, which obliges him to stop too.

"I'm sorry."

Her sadness and renunciation are heartrending.

"I brought you here for nothing. You can leave."

He is certain that her last words are, "You'll never hear from me again."

Did he hesitate for only a quarter of a second?

He walks away, so relieved that he feels like singing.

That is the truth.

He finds the forest path that leads to the road, hears someone coming from the other direction, and hides. Because no one could know their secret. Tell no one, have no witnesses, beware of everything, especially in this little society, which is avid for other people's transgressions.

The man who goes by looks older and gloomy, ordinary, well dressed, with brown hair brushed back. A middle-class man out for a walk, lost in his own thoughts. No threat at all.

44

Later, Catherine would have no recollection of the hours between her decision and the moment when she left the court after the verdict.

Myriam, crying with joy, takes the doll without showing the slightest sign of concern. Catherine announces that she has to leave and will not celebrate with her. Afterward she thinks that it would have been unfair to abandon Myriam if she was innocent.

Her father is waiting in the hall with a worried look on his face, for a change.

She says nothing until she reaches the sidewalk. "Let's take your car. Where is it?"

He gestures toward the parking lot and takes his daughter's elbow to guide her to the rented Twingo, and Cedric sinks into his seat, following them with his eyes. He has aged, his hair is gray, his back is hunched, but it is clearly the man whose path he crossed twenty years ago, right after he left Violet. Forever.

The man has the courtesy to open the door and let Catherine settle into the passenger seat. He walks around to his side of the car, gets behind the wheel, and starts the engine.

Cedric sees him three-quarters from the back and recognizes, without any surprise, the man he glimpsed in the Moroccan restaurant, Catherine's father, the husband of the doctor's wife.

The man who was walking toward the Pierre Levée clearing, toward the wife who was in love with another man is Catherine's father.

An old feeling of shame strikes Cedric like lightning.

How did he react to Violet's abominable death? He was terror-stricken. On the outside he shared the horror expressed by everyone else. He fled like a coward and waited with deep anxiety to be summoned by the police, to be a suspect, until he was finally reassured that there would be no summons, no suspicion and that life would continue like the sea that closes up after a shipwreck, swallowing it up and allowing other boats to continue their crossings.

He did not follow the case. He didn't want to know. He did not ask himself who could be guilty, did not for a second imagine that he could have seen the murderer in the person of that well-dressed man who was deep in thought. In his own way he had killed Violet himself.

Was it repressed guilt that pushed him to meet Catherine?

What did it matter, after all? He had carried an enormous debt that he still did not know how to pay.

He would find a way. He would improvise.

He is sure of only one thing: this time he will not let it go.

Cedric lets a little old man in an electric car go ahead of him, then a utility vehicle, before taking off behind the Twingo.

From the second her father starts the car, with her sitting next to him, each word and event are engraved precisely and indelibly in her mind. Time stands still, in parentheses that can be recalled on demand, a present that is eternally present, never past.

Dr. Monsigny says, "A sad victory, my little darling. But a victory, nonetheless. It is all the more remarkable because you had to keep up appearances despite your doubts, and you did that admirably."

"I want to see the place where you spread mother's ashes. Now."

He brakes, triggering furious honking from an alarmed old man in an electric car who has slammed on the brakes and stopped just a few inches from the fender.

"Catherine! You said yourself that you did not want to return to the…"

"Everything takes me back there. I need her, after what happened, on my birthday, I need her. I need to visit the last spot that holds some memory of her. Most of all I need to talk to you, and I can only do that in the place where she lies at rest."

He looks at her for a long time.

The old man passes them, trying to destroy them with a dark look of reproach. The father and the girl are impervious to everything that is not them.

Catherine's face seems to have gotten smaller. It is pale and furrowed in thought.

There can be no discussion when faced with such torment. You do not even say that you can't remember the exact place. You say, "Yes, Devil's Wash." You say that it will be easy to find the place where Violet loved the rocks, the multiple waterfalls, the dark mystery, and the crystalline cheerfulness.

Catherine says, "Of course."

There is a smile in her voice.

He is surprised.

"It is raining. It was also raining when you met. You have to be the only person I know who thinks to take an umbrella on a nice summer day just in case it rains."

"Except that it was autumn."

"That's funny, I always thought it was summer."

He could have bitten his tongue until he bled to death if it were possible, but Catherine does not seem to catch on, so he continues quickly. "She dreamed about bringing you there when you were old enough to climb the rocks safely. You're right, it is good to go there."

"Is it far?"

"About forty minutes."

She yawns carelessly and relaxes into the seat, which causes her to feel the fatigue. Letting go of the accumulated tension takes her strength away.

She will talk to him. He will know what to do, as Renaud knew what to do.

She says to herself that she is still way too young for these kinds of adult affairs. She has time to grow up.

She slips into a half sleep, lulled by the back and forth of the windshield wipers.

She opens her eyes when the car stops. They are in an empty parking lot, near a small closed-up house that can be reached by a small bridge spanning a narrow torrent.

Maybe he can still get her to change her mind.

"It's dismal in this weather. Are you sure you want to climb up there in this rain?"

"Yes, I have to go. But I understand that you, well, tell me where it is, and you can wait for me in the car."

How can he remember the exact spot? He doesn't want to let her down, but most of all, by being accommodating, he hopes that she will not start reasoning, that she will continue to feel nostalgic and won't begin calculating dates. He points out a path that goes abruptly down and then up, winding around enormous flat rocks that look like prehistoric animals. He says that it is a spot not far from there, overlooking the river, where he spread her ashes.

"But you wanted to talk to me?"

"Afterward. First I'll talk to mother," she says without any irony.

What could she have to say to her? What counsel does she hope to get from a dead woman? He forces her to put on a Kway, which he has in the trunk.

"My careful little daddy. It's yellow. You'll see me from a distance."

Wasn't there a little bit of a teasing tone in her exclamation?

But no, Catherine is direct, stark in her inability to conceal.

He perks his ears. Is that the sound of an engine? But he only hears the wind blowing, intensifying in this strange procession.

Monsigny is nervous, worried. What he wouldn't give for tomorrow to be here already, to be gone from this place.

No car appears. He has dreamed it. Unconsciously, he is chewing his nails, pulling on the skin with his teeth. Small drops of blood appear on his fingers.

Catherine's shape shrinks but is nevertheless visible in the yellow nylon, with her white good-luck scarf floating from her neck.

A strange good-luck charm.

That is exactly what Catherine thinks when the silk whips her face. Perhaps she will throw it into the river so that it can join her mother in another place that mocks luck and happiness.

Her mind is a sieve. She tries to remember what is bothering her and laughs softly. What isn't bothering her?

The rain doesn't bother her, nor the cold. Quite the contrary. They are waking her up, reminding her that she is alive and that there is always a way out. The effort it takes to climb strengthens her, expels the bad excretions. When she gets to the top, she is not even winded.

Those are some falls! Not much of a wash, but a serious cliff.

The forest sighs and soothes.

She finds a solid flat rock near the edge and sits on it.

She murmurs, "Send me a sign so I know if I should look for the truth, your truth. Cedric…"

She perks her ears, looks, and is petrified when she hears a murmur in response, "Catherine. Catherine, you have to listen to me."

It is not a woman's voice. It is even a familiar voice, but it should not be heard here. That is worse than blasphemy.

She stands up and turns around. Cedric, a ghost among the trees, is standing still, one arm in front of him, his palm raised, like someone taming a rebellious animal. He speaks softly, as if he is afraid to be heard, "Forgive me."

For an instant she wonders if there are two of them, a Parisian Cedric and a Creuse Cedric relaying each other. It's like black magic. The "forgive me" resonates inside her, shaking her up.

"It's my mother who should forgive you."

"I was going to tell you everything, I swear, but I didn't have the courage."

"Right! Don't take me for an idiot."

"Is that your father with you?"

"Yes, he's nearby. Don't come any closer, or I'll call him."

"You're not afraid of me!"

Oh yes, she's afraid. She screams as loud as she can. "Dad!"

He can't hear her. He is too far away.

Cedric seems taken aback. Alarmed. Shocked. He moves, blocking the path she came on, but she could run away through the forest on the left, the way he came. Fear isn't taking her feet out from under her but rather giving her wings.

She runs down the hill as fast as she can, intensifying the roar of the wind that surges among the branches, the noise of the waterfall she is approaching, the blood throbbing in her temples. Then, all of a sudden, she feels like nothing is threatening her, like nobody is following her.

She turns around. No shape is coming after her. There is no sound of running. She hesitates and retraces her steps, slowly, having trouble advancing up the sharp rise, and then she stops. The water does not stop flowing, and the wind keeps howling, but the scene nevertheless unfolds in an unreal silence. On the top of the outcrop, on the flat rock, two shapes are locked in a nearly immobile hand-to-hand fight.

It's her father. He has heard her. He has come to her rescue. She is saved. But Cedric is young and strong. The doctor will never be able to match him.

The sun joins in, emerging from the clouds, dazzling her. Shielding her eyes with her hand, she approaches, little by little, making out Cedric's beige gabardine and her father's gray raincoat.

In this strange silence, the two men are neutralizing each other, as if they don't dare to throw a punch. Or can't. They are even holding their breath. They are grasping each other by the collar, both bodies twisted with tension and the effort to dominate the other.

Cedric hooks a foot a behind Monsigny's leg. The doctor loses his balance and falls to the ground.

Catherine looks around for a weapon and sees a thick, sharp rock.

Cedric raises a fist to knock out the man on the ground. In one movement, Catherine grabs the rock and rushes toward the two men, who are totally absorbed in each other.

She is holding the rock, ready to strike. Cedric lifts his head and loosens his grip. Catherine brings the rock down as hard as she can. Blood spurts from Cedric's head, and he collapses on his side, immobile, half lying on his opponent, who squirms weakly.

Catherine sways, then catches her balance. Her father has opened his eyes, and he is breathing. He slowly shakes his head, as if he can't quite believe that he can still move his legs. He pushes Cedric off him and starts to sit up, while Catherine leans over to help. Her white scarf flutters to the ground.

Her father is a little groggy. A stream of blood is flowing down his forehead.

"It's him," she says.

"Yes, I recognized him," he says. "Her lover. Yours as well."

She tries to say no. Her legs tremble, and she squats down so she won't fall.

"That was your surprise. The two of you trapped me."

She can't recognize her father's face. It expresses nothing. It is cold, implacable, determined. He is another man, stubborn, with sharp features.

He leans over to pick up the white scarf with his left hand. She follows his movement. She sees his hand on the white, with the gold wedding ring, a thick ring. And mostly she sees the nails chewed to the quick, with frayed, bloody skin, and she recognizes the devil's hand.

This was the hand, the very huge hand that on that day picked up the white cloth.

"You were there. You were there that day."

He, in turn, leans toward her, the scarf pulled tight between his hands. He is going to put it around her neck to keep her warm, because he is her ally, her protector, her father.

"You are just like her," he says in a disbelieving voice that also contains anger. "In that, too, you are like her."

That makes no sense. The taut scarf is as strangely threatening as the voice, which doesn't make sense. Catherine backs away, still crouching. If she rises, he will grab her.

But he's her dad. She has nothing to fear from her dad. That should be her ultimate certainty, except then the final piece of the puzzle falls into place. Her birthday is in March. They met in autumn.

"It was you, Father. You are not my father."

He is reliving his nightmare, but now nothing will wake him up. He should not have come back. He should not have kept quiet. He should not have... His gaping eyes no longer clearly see the features on Catherine's face, which mix with her mother's. This time he will perhaps redeem himself and save her. He sees over his daughter's shoulder what she does not suspect, that she has her back to emptiness. He holds out an open hand while she edges back yet a few more inches to put some distance between them. Her heels veer over the edge. She teeters and feels the abyss sucking at her. It is too late to pull herself out.

The killer grabs her shoulder and pulls her forward toward solid ground. She wants to escape from him, and with an abrupt movement, she disengages her shoulder from her father's grasp. His last footing leaves him unbalanced, and he is the one who falls, head first, landing on the rocks. He crashes into the bottom of the wash, where, without a pause, the water dances, joyfully indifferent.

45

Catherine doesn't know it yet, but the parentheses are closed. She is taking her first steps in a new memory that begins by sorting out the future memories on which to build, those to keep like strong tendrils, and those to erase because they contradict the person you have decided to be.

The facts remain, despite memory, detached one from the other, a few seconds slowed down to a stop.

More than an image, it is the sensation of the fall of the one she will always call her father that has made her look below at the contorted cadaver, stuck in an artificial pose, on which the lighter white scarf has landed, a symbol of solitude, the solitude of death, a shroud for the dislocated body.

She puts her hand in front of her mouth to hold back the screams, the shock, the stupefaction.

Cedric is seriously messed up. His hair is sticky with blood and rain, but he is alive. There is no cell phone coverage. Catherine does not dare turn the injured one over. She takes off her Kway and covers him. Two envelopes fall to the ground, near his hip. She recognizes the slanted writing that the rain is starting to wash away. She tucks the envelopes into her skirt pocket. She acts like a robot, the continuous spurts of adrenaline drowning out her sensory system.

She climbs down to the road, her eyes on the cell phone screen, until she finds a signal and calls Louis's number, so he can send help to Devil's Wash.

Then she climbs back up. She puts her hand on Cedric's so that the life circulates between them and doesn't stop. She talks to him, as you would talk to a loved one in a coma.

The time is long and short. Long when it comes to maintaining life with words, a presence, concentration, short as soon as help arrives.

Among the swarming people and the agitation, she is afraid that the thread of life she has maintained between Cedric and herself will break and be left in the hands of outsiders who have no idea what has played out here on the cliff.

Louis is there, thank God. He covers her with a blanket while she looks on helpless at the stretcher taking the wounded man away, and he hands her a flask. She drinks two swallows of a harsh liquid that causes her to cough and cry at the same time.

Dr. Monsigny broke his neck. He died immediately, people reassure her. Apparently one should count life's blessings, even if they are derisory.

Louis waits for her, ready to drive her to the bed and breakfast. She wants to go to the hospital where Cedric is being cared for. She cannot think of doing anything else as long as she is not sure he will survive.

Louis offers to stay with her. He will take her when she is ready. She says no, that could be a long time. She will be fine there, in the waiting room. Louis insists, despite her protests. She reads the worry in his eyes, and she does not have anything to reassure him with.

He calls Jean-Claude and Françoise and tells them what happened.

To distract her, he tells her that the cousins have filed an appeal. He says that her appearance in court has been noticed. Two national radio stations have mentioned the case.

He says that he is sorry about her father, that he stirred things up by giving her those old articles, things that should have remained buried.

She tries to explain that the forces that led to today's events were much more powerful than any newspaper stories or any one person.

They end up being sent away from the hospital, with the promise that she will be able to see Cedric the next day.

Her hosts take care of her as if she were sick, unable to swallow anything except a small pill that she accepts with gratitude, and that does, indeed, put her in a sleep of forgetting.

She remembers the days that follow as a tour of good-byes.

She cannot imagine ever coming back. The healing must be definitive.

Myriam is free, waiting for the appeal.

Catherine does not sidestep her. She makes an appointment with her and suggests that she tell the truth, the whole truth. She gives her the names of three colleagues who can explain the consequences of identity theft.

Myriam claims her innocence. She did not kill anyone, and if she changed her identity, it is because she was in danger.

Catherine doesn't want to know anything about it.

Myriam insists on Catherine's commitment. She listened to Catherine's arguments in court. Now, like her attorney, she is leaning toward the theory that Gaston committed suicide.

Which is convenient for her, of course.

Catherine doesn't lean toward any theory. She leaves. She just concludes with a sentence that Myriam will not consider. "You cannot live with a false identity. You will get caught one day or another by the person you really are."

In Saint-Jean, the cousins' wives throw dark looks at Catherine, which is fair enough, and she gets the feeling that her visit to Olivier, out in the open, makes him uneasy. She now has a finer perception of what is taking place under the surface and is not sure that it is a gift. That is perhaps the key to adulthood, and once you go through the door, it closes behind you, never letting you go back.

In any case, the moment of grace is past. Olivier is as charming and nice as ever, a little cowardly too, she discovers. A little limp, a little bit of a dodger.

Testifying in favor of the defendant was a nearly heroic act for someone who has chosen a calm life. It is an act that perhaps he regrets, without admitting it, because his own life continues in this small community whose rules one must respect. She can understand. But she also understands that it is a screenplay in which she has no role.

She receives permission to bury her father here, in a small village cemetery that Louis has told her about.

No cremation, no romantic ceremony. Let the dead bury the dead. She will never return to his grave.

His not being her biological father changes nothing in her eyes. He was her father. He did his best.

She owes him for who she is today.

It is not for her to forgive the dispossessed lover who preferred keeping a dead wife forever to losing her alive. She wants to believe that love has other faces and that when her turn arrives, she will be loved better.

She will not try to find her biological father. What good would that serve? She was born of a liaison with a man who did not want to change his life. Why would she hold him to account for it today?

He undoubtedly does not even know that she exists, and he is nothing to her.

There has been enough damage.

For a few days, she continues to live with her charming hosts, who surround her without imposing. She has the sense that she's mending the frayed strands of her life, some of which she will finally start weaving into cloth with a pattern and colors of her own choosing.

She is careful and delicate when she cuts the strand that binds her to Cedric, a necessary break if she wants to clear that path that leads to her mother.

Cedric cries at each of her visits. His remorse and guilt struggle to be heard, after having been silenced for so long. She listens, acknowledges, shares. The two of them lighten each other's load, although they will have to live with what happened.

Each going a separate way.

She listens to his story. She reads her mother's letters.

Aloud. In front of Cedric.

They build theories. That Claude Monsigny surprised his wife during her final conversation with her lover.

That he decided to catch them in the act.

That his old patient, with her waning memory and the lengthy sleep of the old provided him with a fake alibi without even knowing it.

That he had not intended to kill her, that he was not himself.

That perhaps he even managed to erase the memory of the murder that would have kept him from being a father to his daughter.

Catherine is convinced that she superposed three hands into a single memory: Cedric's, her father's, and Courtois's, each trying to comfort the child.

She keeps the final secret to herself, one that she will never share: he married a woman who was already pregnant by another man.

After all these visits, after the long period of convalescence, a fork in the road is waiting for them. Neither one wants to follow the same road. They do not need words to share that certitude. This moment of separation is perhaps the moment in which they are the closest. Which is what allows each of them to be registered as part of the other's life, like an essential stage through which one does not go twice.

Cedric finally escapes from the past. Catherine accepts hers.

They will never see each other again.

46

The weather is uncertain, arbitrarily fluctuating between cold and hot. The same goes for the intermittent sun that plays with light and ends up gambling on shadows.

The train station's glass roof transmits and exaggerates the sky's moods. In the train, where the fluorescent light wins out, there is no question. It is artificially warm and fine.

Catherine enters the first-class car, checking the seat numbers.

The first seats are occupied by a young man, well, a man her age and all his stuff. She would like to cure herself of this notion that she is older than the rest of the world. At twenty-six and a half.

He looks up from his book. He has a nice look about him, a round face with strong cheekbones and brown eyes.

Her seat is right in front of his, a window seat.

She takes off her cashmere coat, turns it inside out and folds it carefully. It is still brand new.

She smooths her pinafore dress, which shows her legs, and settles in with her notebook, her case file, and her cell phone. She immediately starts to work.

She feels the comfortable presence behind her, which adds to the pleasure of the trip, without paying attention to it.

The conductor arrives with a couple that would like to be seated together. The inspector asks the young man if he would agree to move up a row.

Catherine follows the conversation from a distance.

Move up a row. That would mean sit next to her. She lifts her head.

The young man asks if the spot is free, if she wouldn't mind.

She doesn't mind. The couple thanks them effusively. The inspector has the satisfied look of someone who has accomplished his duty, and this short moment announces a harmonious world that soothes hearts.

Catherine shares a smile with her new neighbor, who dives back into his book as she dives into her papers. Their closeness changes nothing in the gentleness of his presence, light and kind.

Then she doesn't think anything more of it.

She finishes the outline of her statement. She still has two e-mails to write.

A loud, honest laugh breaks out next to her. It is not directed at anyone but is the spontaneous reaction of a captivated reader who does not even seem aware that he has made any noise.

Catherine cannot remember any book that has amused her to the point of laughing out load, except for Glen Baxter's collections. She wonders if her neighbor knows of them and if he would find them funny.

She is intrigued and glances at the mysterious book without managing to make out the title.

The neighbor is not laughing anymore. He is knitting his eyebrows in concentration. He has expressive features. He has a flat face with a large nose and a wide mouth. He is not handsome but impressive, with a lot of character. He could be a Tartar. Catherine is imagining an image from a storybook, because she has never seen a Tartar in her life.

The modern-day Genghis Khan closes the book, and she looks away to avoid being caught in the act.

He gets up, unfolding his tall body. He is huge and a little hunched. He has long arms and solid hands.

Resigned that he is moving, she waits for him to gather his coat and bag.

No, he disappears to the toilets.

Shoot. He took his book.

When he returns, she can't hold it in any longer and excuses herself. What is that book that made him laugh out loud?

It's a novel she has never heard of. She looks attentive. She's no great reader. He obviously is. He will think she is an uncultured idiot.

He says that a friend gave it to him for the trip, that it is not really a novel, but a different perspective on life. It's hard to explain.

He closes the book and turns toward her. The conversation begins.

And does not end.

Thank you for reading *The Paris Lawyer.*

We invite you to share your thoughts and reactions on Goodreads and your favorite social media and retail platforms.

We appreciate your support.

Acknowledgements

Thank you Creuse, which has always taken in and protected the outsider that I am, and thank you to all those who helped me to get lost there, Nanée Chevrier, still and always, Isabelle Bize, Daniel Taboury, Jean-Marie Chevrier, Patrick Aïta, Philippe Bequia.

Thank you Claire Doubliez, Jean-Alain Michel and Annie Astier for having initiated me into the justice system and Sylvain Tesson and François Raffinot for having helped me research the measure of time. Thanks to Samba, Banta, Apollinaire and Mamoutou for their stories.

And Sandrine Treiner, Marie Descourtieux and Sandrine Dumas, for their support, their attentive criticism and their unwavering affection, mine is none less.

ABOUT THE AUTHOR

Author, screenwriter, and actress Sylvie Granotier loves to weave plots that send shivers up your spine. She was born in Algeria and grew up in Paris and Morocco. She studied literature and theater in Paris, then set off traveling—the United States, Brazil, Afghanistan, and elsewhere, ending with a tour of Europe. She wound up in Paris again, an actress, with a job and some recognition. But she is a writer at heart and started her publishing career translating Grace Paley's short story collection *Enormous Changes at the Last Minute* into French. Fourteen novels and many short stories later, Sylvie Granotier is a major crime fiction author in France. She has met with continued success and is translated into German, Italian, Russian, and Greek. *The Paris Lawyer* is her first novel to be translated into English. This legal procedural that doubles as a psychological thriller is full of plot twists that bring us into the heart of French countryside, La Creuse, a place full of nineteenth-century landscapes and dark secrets. Sylvie splits her time between Paris and the Creuse.

ABOUT THE TRANSLATOR

Anne Trager has lived in France for more than twenty-six years, working in translation, publishing, and communications. In 2011, she woke up one morning and said, "I just can't stand it anymore. There are way too many good books being written in France not reaching a broader audience." That's when she founded Le French Book to translate some of those books into English. The company's motto is "If we love it, we translate it," and Anne loves crime fiction.

About Le French Book

Le French Book is a New York–based digital-first publisher specialized in great reads from France. It was founded in December 2011 because, as founder Anne Trager says, "I couldn't stand it anymore. There are just too many good books not reaching a broader audience. There is a very vibrant, creative culture in France, and the recent explosion in e-reader ownership provides a perfect medium to introduce readers to some of these fantastic French authors."

www.lefrenchbook.com

MORE BOOKS

from Le French Book

www.lefrenchbook.com

The 7th Woman by Frédérique Molay

An edge of your-seat mystery set in Paris, where beautiful sounding names surround ugly crimes that have Chief of Police Nico Sirsky and his team on tenterhooks.

www.the7thwoman.com

The Winemaker Detective Series by Jean-Pierre Alaux and Noël Balen

A total Epicurean immersion in French countryside and gourmet attitude with two expert winemakers turned amateur sleuths gumshoeing around wine country.

www.thewinemakerdetective.com

The Greenland Breach by Bernard Besson

The Arctic ice caps are breaking up. Europe and the East Coast of the United States brace for a tidal wave. A team of freelance spies face a merciless war for control of discoveries that will change the future of humanity.

www.thegreenlandbreach.com

The Bleiberg Project by David Khara

Are Hitler's atrocities really over? Find out in this adrenaline-pumping ride to save the world from a conspiracy straight out of the darkest hours of history.

www.thebleibergproject.com

CPSIA information can be obtained at www.ICGtesting.com
Printed in the USA
BVOW04s1438260514

354488BV00003B/4/P

9 781939 474018